W9-APR-866

# "WE'RE GOING TO TALK," HE TOLD HER.

But what he did next didn't feel like talking.

He climbed onto the bed and on top of her.

He hesitated briefly, then bent to place a kiss at the corner of her mouth. "We'll talk, but not now," he whispered against her lips.

Not now. Not ever. It didn't matter. She was on fire.

Janice pursed her mouth for his kiss, and found herself drowning in sensations with just the touch of his lips. He caught her head and held her still while his mouth explored hers. She ought to be fighting him, protesting, but she could not control her own desire.

"Tell me when, Janice. I don't want to leave you crying this time."

The whisper against her ear startled her. She had been so caught up in the sensations of her body that she had left her mind behind. Daringly, she touched the muscular ridge of his chest. She felt the tension in him, knew the willpower that held him back, and knew she couldn't fight him.

"When, Peter," she whispered, and felt the crush of his arms in reply.

# PAPER MOON

## *Patricia Rice*

A TOPAZ BOOK

TOPAZ
Published by the Penguin Group
Penguin Books USA Inc., 375 Hudson Street,
New York, New York 10014, U.S.A.
Penguin Books Ltd, 27 Wrights Lane,
London W8 5TZ, England
Penguin Books Australia Ltd, Ringwood,
Victoria, Australia
Penguin Books Canada Ltd, 10 Alcorn Avenue,
Toronto, Ontario, Canada M4V 3B2
Penguin Books (N.Z.) Ltd, 182–190 Wairau Road,
Auckland 10, New Zealand

Penguin Books Ltd, Registered Offices:
Harmondsworth, Middlesex, England

First published by Topaz, an imprint of Dutton Signet,
a division of Penguin Books USA Inc.

First Printing, March, 1996
10  9  8  7  6  5  4  3  2  1

Topaz is a trademark of Dutton Signet, a division of Penguin Books USA Inc.

Printed in the United States of America

# One

Townsend emptied the pouch of gravel across the papers on which his partner had been diligently working. "It's there," he announced with quiet satisfaction.

Mulloney spread the dust and gravel into a smooth layer, picking up a small nugget and holding it to the sun. A flicker of something lit up the green of his eyes before he carefully laid the nugget back on the table. His wide-brimmed hat kept his face in shadow, but even if he had not been wearing it, his expression would have been indeterminable.

"We'd better be certain the vein runs deep. Mountains don't come cheap." Despite the rough appearance of his leather vest and faded denims, Mulloney spoke with a cultured accent that betrayed his Eastern origins.

"Get your shovel. I think I've just found a surface layer. The good stuff will be deeper."

The two men hoisted their tools and their packs and strode off into the rocks and evergreens, leaving behind their tent and supplies. The men were of equal height, but Townsend was the elder and carried a thicker weight around his middle. A bristly brown mustache hid half his face and a Mexican sombrero hid most of the rest. He looked almost disreputable compared to the Easterner with his clean-shaven, square jaw and immaculate Stetson. A closer look, however, revealed a clear, steady gaze beneath Townsend's sombrero. The green light of Mulloney's eyes was that of a man on the edge of hell.

* * *

The next morning, Mulloney packed his saddlebags while Townsend set about moving camp.

"I can dig enough to buy the whole damned mountain in three months," Townsend protested as he collapsed the tent.

"You go down there and try to pay the loan off with gold, and the old man will change his mind. He'll know damned well where we got it. Right now he just thinks I'm a greenhorn with too much money and a bee in my bonnet about raising mustangs. Let's just keep him thinking that. You know what happens when word gets out about gold. There's enough money left to buy whatever you need until I get back. Just don't use the gold for anything."

Townsend nodded impatiently. "I don't know where you're going to find the kind of cash he's asking for this place. You'd better have a money tree back there somewhere. I figure he's making a living off what people pay him just to hold the damned mountain for three months. Then when they can't come up with the balance, he runs them off and sells it to the next one in line. It's a pretty good con."

"I can't imagine anyone stupider than us trying to buy a mountain. We might even talk him down when the time comes. You just mine that gold while I find the money. Once we pay off the loan, there won't be a damned thing he can do when we start hauling out gold. I think I can find investors willing to risk that kind of easy return."

"It's likely to be a deep mine. We'll need timbers and labor and machinery to get at the mother lode," Townsend warned.

This time, it was Mulloney who nodded impatiently. "We'll buy them with what you're going to dig out while I'm gone. I know this end of the business, Townsend. Are you sure you're going to be all right out here alone?"

Townsend made a rude noise. "Better off by myself than with some Greedy Gus who'll stab me in the back first chance he gets. We've been through enough, Mulloney. We've got the right idea this time. Just us and nobody else. Just don't forget I'm out here while you're playing up to the girls."

Mulloney managed a wry grin that almost transformed his hardened features into that of a live being rather than a grim statue. "There isn't a woman alive who's going to make me forget that gold. If I'm lucky, I'll be back before you've got the first batch processed."

He rode off, the tail of his expensive bay stallion swaying to and fro as it traversed the rocky downward path. The morning sun was just beginning to rise over the thin line of trees ahead.

Mulloney didn't whistle as he rode. He kept a repeating rifle within easy reach on his saddle and the latest Colt model revolver on his hip while his eyes searched every speck of the trail ahead. In the five years he had been living this life, he'd come to know more dirty tricks and vicious scoundrels than a man had any right to know. He'd learned to survive the hard way, but he'd learned.

He didn't think too hard on the years wasted tracking gold with thousands of other hungry men. He'd been in California, Colorado, and India, contemplated following the hordes to South Africa, but in the end he'd taken what miserable gleanings he'd found and come home. Not home, precisely. He'd never go there again. But he'd come back to the states and the mountains where he'd first started. He was an older, wiser man now, but his ambition hadn't changed. He intended to be wealthy, and he would do it with his own hands, on his own terms.

This time, he meant to succeed. The fire in his belly burned strong as he guided his stallion down the mountainside. The gold was there, and no one else knew about it but Townsend. He'd met Townsend in India, saved his life once, dragged him back here while he still burned with the fever. The man would lay his life down for him, but it wasn't Townsend's life he wanted, it was his knowledge. Townsend was the engineer Mulloney was not. Mulloney was the financier that Townsend was not. Between them, they would not only find the gold, but sell it

without being cheated or murdered in their beds as so
many had been in the past. They trusted only each other.

Mulloney settled himself more comfortably in the saddle as the horse started across a level valley. As a city
boy, he found this method of transportation convenient
but uncomfortable. He'd learned to manage mountain po-
nies, mules, and even elephants, but sometimes he had
difficulty forgetting the proud bays and elegant carriages
he'd once known. At the time, he hadn't realized how
spoiled he had been. Now he knew better.

He wasn't bitter about leaving all that behind. It was a
choice he had made on his own. He had wanted to rid
himself of the feeling of corrosion that taking his father's
money gave him. He'd never felt dirtier in his life than
when he had stood in his parents' bedroom, wearing a
silk shirt and expensive frock coat, listening to the news
that he had an older brother he had never known, a
brother who had been thrown away because of his defor-
mity. His skin still crawled when he thought about it. The
discovery of his father's cruel deception had led to other
discoveries, each one more ruthless than the next. He'd
spent his early years living like a leech off the blood of
the helpless.

So he didn't think about it any longer. He didn't think
about the wealth he had left behind, the wealth he had
known only by default and at the expense of his own kin.
He didn't think of the people whose lives had been
crushed because of his father's greed. He didn't think
about the family he'd left behind. His brothers were in a
position to straighten out what was left of the wreckage
of their lives. They didn't need him. After twenty-five
years of living a lie, he'd had to get out. It was the only
way to save his soul.

Only, somewhere along the way, Mulloney thought he
must have misplaced it. Perhaps he'd never had one.
There were any number of people who could attest to
that. Instead of finding his soul, he'd found a goal. He
was going to be rich again, but he would earn it with his

own hands and mind. And right now, the goal sparkled on the horizon, just out of reach.

If he knew how to whistle, he would as he urged his horse through a rock-strewn streambed. Two days ride ahead, at the foot of the range, waited a little cabin he'd built when he'd thought what he needed was a home. The cabin hadn't held him for very long, but he liked to think of it as home when he was out here with only the sky for a roof. He'd left a warm and willing senorita there last time he'd been through. She'd promised to wait. He wondered if she had. It had been six months since he'd shared her favors. He was more than ready to enjoy them again.

As the first day rolled into the second, Mulloney began to contemplate the woman with more burning intent. She had a body like no other he had ever known, full breasts and wide hips and a tiny waist, all of which she used to advantage. Her voice was low and sweet, and she said all the things he wanted to hear when they were together. He wasn't enamored of Mexican cooking, but he could learn to like it under the right conditions. Lying in her arms seemed right enough.

He hadn't been interested in settling down before because he hadn't reached his goal, but now that it was in sight, he needed to find new horizons. He'd spent twenty-five years of his life surrounded by family, and he'd been happy to escape their limitations. But five years of life among strangers was taking its toll. He could admit that he missed coming home to familiar voices. He'd like to have a decent roof over his head again. The thought of having a loving wife and the smell of baking bread meeting him at the door had been little more than a daydream these last years. The possibility lurked tantalizingly within reach now.

He'd lived a pampered life before and it hadn't made him happy, but he wasn't that much happier living the life he led now. He was a free man for a change, but freedom meant little when he had little to show for it. Maybe once he had the mountain in his name and gold in his pockets, he could ask his little señorita to marry him. They could build a house in that valley back there. They could build a whole damned town if they wanted. Once he and Townsend owned the mountain, they could hire laborers to dig the gold. Then all he'd have to do is go into his office every day, work the business end of the operation, and figure out where to invest the profits. He could go home every night to a decent meal and a clean bed and a wife who would welcome him with open arms. He could be content living like that.

He would admit to needing a woman in his life. His mother was weak and helpless, and he'd spent the better part of his life protecting her, but he missed her soft reassurances, their quiet talks, the little things she did to make his life comfortable. He could find solace in the arms of willing women easy enough, his handsome face was good for that much, but that wasn't the same thing. He wanted a woman of his own, one whose bed was reserved just for him. He had that much of his father in him. He liked owning things. He was a possessive man.

Women were still too few and far between out here. He'd not spent much time looking for one, but he'd seen what was available. His little señorita was the best of the lot. He would stop by the cabin, ask her to marry him, and when he came back with the money to buy the mountain, they'd tie the knot. He could move her up the mountain with him.

The idea grew even more pleasing the closer he came to her bed. Peter could almost taste her lips against his. He liked the anticipation of coming home to a woman's arms.

The sun was setting behind him when the first smoke from the cabin chimney came in sight. He owned this land, but the summers were too dry for farming, and he wasn't a rancher. Grass rippled in the healthy green from early spring rains. He'd sold his horses before he'd left the last time. Catalina couldn't take care of them herself. Peter missed hearing their whinnies as he rode up, but his thoughts were on the woman tending the fire inside.

He tried to envision Cat's thick dark hair wrapped in a

braid around her head, the sway of her hips beneath a long full skirt as she bent over the fire, but the image was slightly hazy as he dismounted. It didn't matter. Once he got inside, she would be in his arms, all round and warm and soft. He hadn't eaten all day, but the hunger he felt now wasn't for food. He'd have her in the bed before he thought about food. He needed a woman right now. He needed her desperately.

The fire was burning low when he entered, and the lamp wasn't lit. A pot of something simmered over the embers, and Peter remembered he had meant to buy her a stove. He would do that as soon as he got to town. His funds were nearly nonexistent after putting the down payment on the mountain and leaving some for Townsend, but he could get by without money. Catalina ought to have the best. He would dress her in silk once they owned the mountain.

She must be in the bedroom. The door was closed, but he could hear sounds of movement. Perhaps she had seen him coming and was putting on clean sheets. That thought made him randier than hell. He hadn't seen clean sheets in six months, since he'd been here last.

He ought to take time to bathe, but he couldn't. She'd have to take him as he was right now. He'd do things properly later, when he proposed. He should have done that long ago, but a wife hadn't been one of those things he had considered back then. He was considering it now.

The last rays of the setting sun filtered through the bedroom window when Peter threw open the door. The rosy haze befuddled his eyes a moment as he stood there in the doorway, expecting Catalina to turn and throw herself at him. A movement from the bed brought his gaze into better focus.

Catalina was there, buck naked against those sheets he'd just been imagining. And so was the rancher he'd called neighbor, equally naked and on top of her.

The man turned his head and looked over his shoulder, paling with recognition. His gaze dropped in terror at the sight of Peter's hand going to his holster.

With only a grating smile, Mulloney dropped his grip on the gun and politely tugged at his hat. "Good to see you again, Roger, Catalina. Just stopped by to tell you I'm heading for Texas and won't be through here anytime soon. If you hear of any buyers for the land, drop a line to my box in town."

He turned on the heel of his worn but expensive boots and walked away.

# Two

Janice Harrison carefully typed the final two words, frowned as the platen smeared the ink slightly, and, deciding it wasn't worth retyping, jerked the paper out of the machine. She had diligently taught herself to type with some competence, but she wasn't impressed with the machine itself. Good handwriting still looked neater.

Laying the letter on Jason's desk, she tidied up her own work space, put on her spectacles, found her straw hat, pinned up her skirt, and set out for home.

The ranch hands working in the paddock yelled and waved as she skillfully maneuvered the tall, spindly front wheel of her tricycle through the gate and out onto the road, hat ribbons flying. Handling the awkward machine on the rutted road was too difficult for her to waste a hand waving back, but they didn't mind. She was the one who wrote out their paychecks at the end of every month.

She had wanted a bicycle ever since reading about one back during the centennial, but of course she had been too poor then to afford one. That had been back in Ohio when she had only been an overworked, underpaid factory worker with younger siblings to feed. She'd come a long way since then with the help of a few good friends. They'd helped her order the bicycle too, only they decreed a tricycle was safer. Since then, she'd decided the two tiny wheels in back were definitely a stabilizing factor on these roads.

Jason had thought it hilarious when she first rode up on her new machine, and it probably had been a sight with her skirts flying up and her hat flying off and the fool wheel tilting this way and that. But he'd had the road smoothed out since then, and she'd learned to pin her skirts up out of the wheels, and practice had made the ride much better. Without the tricycle, she would have had to ride a horse or give up this extra income altogether.

She couldn't afford to give up a single penny. With a worried frown, Janice sent the cycle flying down the open road toward town. Betsy had been looking pale again this morning. She would stop at the drugstore and see if they had any new nostrums that might work. Modern science was wonderful, but so far it hadn't extended very far into medicine. And so far the medicine it had produced was more expensive than effective.

Perhaps she ought to take Betsy back to the doctor in Houston again. He'd worried about consumption and recommended a new tonic that had actually eased one of Betsy's worse attacks. That was before she had heeded her friend Daniel's warning and learned the tonic consisted of chloroform and opium. It had taken Betsy a long time to recover from her need for that medicine. Maybe doctors didn't know best.

Betsy had been doing so well, Janice had hoped that whatever was wrong was getting better with age. Betsy was ten now, and she no longer had attacks that left her blue and weak for days. Maybe if they were just patient, everything would work out in time. And maybe the sun would rise in the west too.

Janice cycled wearily into town. Now that school was out for the summer and her teaching duties had been temporarily lifted, she ought to have more time for Betsy. She could write copy for the newspaper at home, or Betsy could come into the newspaper office when she worked on the copyediting. Mr. Averill didn't mind. He was grateful for all the help he could get now that his twins had grown up and moved away. Maybe they could even teach Betsy to do some of the work around the office, if it didn't involve too much physical labor.

Tomorrow was Betsy's birthday. Ten years ago Janice

hadn't thought of Betsy's birth as a time for rejoicing, but for every year the child had lived since then, it had become a matter of triumph. That first year had been hideous. They'd had to move to Cutlerville, Ohio, where Janice's father could find work in the factory. Her mother had died that year, probably of heartbreak at leaving behind her neat cottage for the leaky hovel they'd had to take. Her sister Audrey had only been thirteen and virtually useless in helping with their younger brother, Douglas, and the infant. And then Betsy had caught that fever that had almost killed her.

Janice shuddered and counted her blessings. She remembered the misery of that year for a purpose, as a lesson in what she would never suffer through again. It had taken her ten long years and a lot of miles to get where she was now, but they had a roof over their heads that didn't leak, friends to look out for them, and she had enough skills to work twenty-four hours a day if she so desired. Unfortunately, as a woman, she was woefully underpaid for all of them.

She still seethed under the knowledge that the man teaching school in the next county was being paid three times what she was paid, and he had fewer students. Jason Harding was no longer on the school board, but when she had complained, he had given her the same answer the board had given her: a woman wasn't as good as a man. That was the same attitude they'd had back in that slave factory in Ohio that she'd escaped from. She had almost walked out on him right then and there, but she had needed the extra money she was paid acting as her secretary.

Thank goodness she was too tired and too busy to stay angry for long. Leaving her cycle at the end of the boardwalk and polishing the dust off her gloves, Janice returned her skirts to the ground and walked toward the dry goods store. Betsy had been clamoring for an art set just like Melissa Harding's. Melissa's father could afford a hundred art sets and would gladly have bought one for Betsy, but Janice had taught the town a long time ago that she didn't take charity. She knew how to take care of herself.

The salesclerk behind the counter greeted her cheerfully. Ellen Fairweather had been Janice's student just last year. Over the past winter, Ellen had managed to fall in love with one of Jason's ranch hands, get pregnant, and get married—in some sort of natural order. Janice felt just the slightest twinge of jealousy as Ellen rested her hands complacently on her enormous belly.

"I've got the set all boxed and wrapped, Miss Harrison. Your sister doesn't suspect a thing. She was in here just yesterday kind of looking at it real sadlike. It's a good thing I waited until now to wrap it."

Janice tucked a few straying hairs more securely into her tightly knotted hair and pulled her hat primly over them. She dusted off her twill skirt with her gloved hands, then removed her gloves to count the change from the purse in her pocket. "You're going to be a good mama, Ellen. When's Bobby going to finish that house so you can sit down and get off your feet?"

Ellen's smile flitted from sight for a minute, then reappeared bravely. "He's working on it, Miss Harrison. I'm feeling just fine. I wouldn't know what to do with myself if I sat down. I'm just proud that Mr. Holt lets me keep working."

Mr. Holt only let her keep working because Janice had pressured Jason into telling him he had to. The fact that Jason now owned the bank that had belonged to his late wife made him a voice of reason to Holt. The fact that Bobby Fairweather was turning into a shiftless no-account drunk had made the decision imperative. Janice found it extremely unfortunate that men were not only the root of all evil, but the root of all power too.

"Well, you know anytime you need some help, you can call on me and Betsy. We haven't got any men tying us down." Janice laid the money on the counter, her smile disguising how much she meant the words.

Ellen laughed. "Ain't that the truth of it? Why, Bobby would have a stroke if I tried to ride that cycle of yours.

Sometimes I think you're the smartest woman in town not to have a man around."

"Well, I imagine I'd have a stroke if you tried to ride that tricycle looking like you do right now," Janice answered mildly, pulling her gloves back on. "You just take care of that baby, and I'll send Betsy in here tomorrow to thank you when she gets her gift."

She was becoming very good at hiding her feelings, Janice decided as she strode briskly back to the street. She was all of twenty-five years old and hid a guilty secret that the entire town would be scandalized to know, but all anyone saw when they looked at her was an old maid of indeterminate age who judiciously took care of her youngest sister. They knew she had family back in Ohio. They knew she was a friend of the Hardings' step-sister, Evie Monteigne, and that was how she had got her first job here. But that was all anyone knew. And they were partly wrong about that.

She stopped at the drugstore to inquire about new medicines for Betsy's chronic condition, spent the last of her few coins on a bottle that the pharmacist said was guaranteed to restore weakened hearts, and rolled her tricycle home.

Janice hid the gift first, then stripped off her gloves and the light cape she wore over her gown. Her one indulgence these days was in clothes. After all those years of scraping by in secondhand rags, she had bought a sewing machine on credit with her first decent paycheck.

Jealousy wasn't a pretty emotion, but it had been a driving force in her determination to have decent clothes for herself and her family. All those years working in a garment factory making clothes for other people while her sister, Audrey, worked in a rich man's department store selling them to people who treated her like dirt had eaten an acid hole through her insides.

So now she earned those clothes her own way. That meant scrimping and saving and working every hour she wasn't asleep, but she was doing it. And now that Audrey was about to be married, and Daniel Mulloney was training her brother, Douglas, to run a newspaper, Janice didn't have to worry so much about sending her family back in Ohio part of her wages. She and Betsy would be able to indulge themselves much more frequently.

They were living the all-American dream, raising themselves from rags through education and industrious labor—with a good helping hand from knowing the right people. Janice cut some slices off the ham hanging in the pantry and threw them in the skillet. She wasn't an optimistic fool. She knew she could be scrubbing floors right now if it weren't for friends like Daniel back in Ohio who had helped her escape the clutches of the Mulloney family monopoly. She also knew her family could have lived much more comfortably if it hadn't been for the rest of the wretched greedy Mulloneys who had believed in slave labor long after the war ended. If she had time to hate, she would hate those Mulloneys for what they'd made her and her family suffer all those years.

While the ham cooked, Janice started on the biscuits. At twenty-five, she knew more about life and people than most did at forty. There were those who probably thought she looked forty, if truth be told. She deliberately encouraged that idea with her choice of hairstyle and glasses. She certainly wouldn't get away with as much as she did in this town if they thought she was still a young woman. Even Jason Harding thought she was older. Now that his wife had been dead this past year or more, he'd been looking in her direction, and she wasn't discouraging him any, even if he probably pushed forty-five or better by now. She had decided a long time ago that she would marry any man who could give her the comforts she had so long been denied. He could be eighty, and she'd marry him. The security of money meant a great deal more than looks or age.

Emotion played little part in her life, so love wasn't a factor to be considered. Janice had learned to use her petty jealousies and resentments as a productive force, but she didn't expect to feel anything beyond that except her love for Betsy, and even that was tainted by the circumstances of Betsy's birth. Emotions were irrelevant to surviving. She'd learned to cope, and she could cope much better if she had a wealthy husband.

A wealthy, *indulgent* husband, Janice amended a moment later as she heard the sound of a carriage pulling up outside. She heard the shouts and cries of children saying farewell and the patter of Carmen Harding's expensive leather shoes on the porch. Jason's wife hadn't given him any children. It was Jason's younger brother, Kyle, and his wife, Carmen, who were providing the heirs to the Harding ranch. And Carmen had everything she could ever possibly want just for looking at it longingly.

Still, Carmen remained as serene and unspoiled as she had been as a child. Betsy threw open the front door while Carmen Harding remained outside, making a polite knock. "Janice? Are you home?" she called in her soft accents.

"Come in, Carmen. You must be exhausted after looking after this crew all day. How's your uncle? Did the children listen to his lessons?" Janice wiped her hands on her apron and moved forward to hug Betsy and greet her guest.

Carmen smiled. "Betsy listened and learned. Mine climbed trees in the orchard. Uncle James didn't mind."

"Your uncle has to be the sweetest man I've ever known. I don't know how he has the patience to try to teach these wild Indians about art. All Betsy does is talk about him when she comes home from his lessons." Of course, neither woman mentioned the fact that Betsy didn't have the strength to climb trees, so the lessons were all she could do while they visited.

"Uncle James is a character. I'll grant him that." Carmen's smile hesitated slightly as she glanced to an eager Betsy who jumped up and down as if anxious to say something. Carmen drew a deep breath and plunged in before the little girl could die of excitement. "As a matter of fact, he's wanting to go visit Evie and Tyler this summer. You know how bad things are at the ranch, so Kyle can't leave, but Tyler's sending a private rail car so the rest of us can go. The children want Betsy to go with them. She wouldn't be any trouble at all, and Uncle James would be delighted to have her to teach more often. He says she's quite talented. Please consider it, Janice."

Janice went still. She didn't dare look Betsy in the face. The child was ten years old and no bigger than Carmen's six-year-old. The fair white skin for which Janice had received so many compliments was pale and shadowed on Betsy. Betsy's hair was a finer gold than Janice's, but it had been cropped short during a fever last winter. The tiny tendrils surrounding her peaked face now made her look an ethereal fairy from some Shakespearean play. How could she let a child like that out of her sight for more than a few hours at a time?

"You're welcome to come with us, Janice," Carmen murmured. "Jason can live without you for a few months. But she'll be just fine if you need to stay."

Janice wasn't at all certain how to take those words. Was Carmen telling her to stay away from Jason? Or was she being just as honest and straightforward as she seemed? The latter seemed likely. Carmen no doubt thought Janice too old to consider courtship, or too much of a spinster for her brother-in-law to be interested. She shouldn't look for undercurrents that weren't there.

But Janice didn't think she could bear to be parted from Betsy for so long a time. Months, Carmen said. Tyler and Evie lived in Natchez when they lived anywhere at all. That was hundreds of miles away. Her heart lurched desperately at the thought. What if Betsy got sick? Who would see that she didn't overexert herself? Who would comb her hair in the mornings? And who would Janice have to talk to at night when that little bed in the corner was empty?

With guilt at that thought, Janice looked down at the frail child all the world thought of as her sister and swallowed hard.

Her one major mistake at the tender age of fifteen had

given her a gift and a burden she could no longer live without. Janice was too intelligent to believe that was healthy for either of them.

She smiled weakly at Betsy and looked back to Carmen. "We'll talk about it later," she managed to murmur.

# *Three*

Mulloney rode toward town through the shadows of the cottonwoods along a dry river bank. It was late. The moon had already reached its zenith and was on its downward path. He was tired, filthy, and numb from the long journey. He'd only stopped to rest for the sake of his horse, and the animal was fairly dropping on its hooves now. As much as he wanted to find the Double H, he would have to wait until morning.

He found a secluded place just on the outskirts of town where a trickle still ran in the riverbed. At this hour, few lights gleamed in the windows of this town sprawled along the intersection of two roads. No doubt a hotel awaited somewhere down that main street, but he was flat broke. It didn't matter. He was used to sleeping on the ground.

He took his horse down to the water, brushed it down, and unpacked his saddlebags. He lit a small fire to make coffee and ground his teeth around some beef jerky to pretend he'd eaten. The night was more than warm, and he kicked out the fire, buried it in dust, and scattered the stones to let them cool. Then he strode off into the bushes to take a leak before settling down for the night.

In the morning, he'd find some way of making himself respectable before heading for the Double H. He didn't know the Hardings, but his brother Daniel had given him their names as people he could rely on out here. People like that were rare, and he'd traveled a mighty distance to find them. He just hoped they were the sort who were willing to risk investing in a gold mine.

Buttoning his denims, Mulloney glanced in the direction of a light flickering from a nearby window. He wondered what emergency kept anyone up at this hour. Fingering the two weeks growth of beard on his jaw, he almost turned and walked away until he saw a silhouette appear between the curtained window and the lamplight.

He almost swallowed his tongue as he watched the silhouette drop the bodice of her gown and bend over what must be a basin of water. She moved with the grace of a sylph, supple as a willow as she swung a cascade of long hair over her head and dipped it into the water. Mulloney had to grab a branch overhead to keep from falling on his face. He knew it had been a long time since he'd had a woman, but he'd never strained his pants at the sight of a shadow before. He really must be in bad shape.

What in hell was the damned woman doing washing her hair at this hour of the night? He had half a mind to yell at her for her foolishness, but then he told himself he was being an idiot and tried to turn back to camp. He couldn't do it.

He was fascinated by the sight of long slim arms scrubbing and lifting the thickest hair he'd ever had the pleasure of seeing. He wondered what color it was. He'd never watched a woman wash her hair before. He'd never imagined what an erotic show it could make. His pulse throbbed as she squeezed the tendrils dry and stood up, shaking the long tresses over her shoulders. She had her back to the window, and he could see only the hourglass shape of curving hips and slender waist and supple back. He willed her to turn around.

She lifted her hair with a comb or brush, he couldn't see which, the thin muslin curtains concealed too much. He almost convinced himself he was a pervert probably watching some old lady who couldn't sleep. Then she turned slightly so her breasts were outlined against the flimsy material, and he felt his mouth go dry. She was perfect.

High full breasts sloped down to a narrow rib cage he could almost feel in his hands right now. Thick hair flowed loose and easy past a slender waist to well-formed buttocks that would fill a man's hands. Hell, he'd hold her if she were eighty. He would bury himself inside her if she were purple with pink spots. He didn't care what the hell she looked like as long as she had a body like that.

The lamp went out and he cursed. She must be sitting there brushing her hair in the dark. He wondered if she could use a little help. As exhausted as he was, he wouldn't be able to sleep for the rest of the night after that little show.

He ought to know better by now. Unless she was a whore, she wasn't available. He'd had his fill of whores for the moment. Catalina had been the last of a whole string of them. He didn't need the grief. Maybe when he was rich, he'd go back East and find himself a fashionable young lady and sweep her off her feet. Until then, he was better off tending to himself.

Loins aching, he curled into his bedroll. As he suspected, sleep eluded him. He wished there was enough water in the river to douse himself, but he suspected he'd need more water than it took to douse a major fire before he cooled off. He wasn't sure he would survive long enough to make a fortune and go back East to find a willing woman. He wanted one right now. He'd denied himself a great deal over these last years. Maybe he denied himself unnecessarily now. There had to be women out here somewhere who needed a man as much as he needed a woman. He just needed to find one who wasn't a whore.

Peter dozed briefly on the edge of sleep until a whicker from his horse made him push back to wakefulness. That's when he smelled the smoke.

Janice pulled her comb through a tangle of hair, wincing slightly as she worked it out. The task of washing and combing her hair had soothed her slightly, but not enough to make her face that empty bedroom. Even now, with the lights out and the whole world asleep, the little house echoed of silence. She kept listening for Betsy's breathing.

She had spent ten years listening for Betsy's breathing. In that first year she'd been terrified every time she couldn't hear it, certain death had come to steal her away. She had slept with the baby in her bed so she could reach out and touch her chest and reassure herself every time she heard the silence. And when she knew the infant was all right, she would weep herself to sleep, ashamed because she had almost wished the child had died.

There had been times since then when the burden of living had become so grueling and painful that she had wished the angels would come carry Betsy to a better place, but those times were long past. From that terrified, guilt-ridden fifteen-year-old she had grown into a woman who knew her own strengths and weaknesses and used them to her advantage. Betsy was her biggest weakness and her greatest strength. For her child, Janice would and could do anything. Should the world discover that Betsy was actually her bastard and not her sister, her reputation would be shredded and her means of earning a living lost. She would be forced to turn to prostitution to stay alive— the only suitable occupation for a fallen woman like herself.

She walked a tightrope every day of her life. Even Betsy didn't know the truth. That was the reason Janice had finally capitulated and let Betsy go with the Hardings to Natchez. A sister would be much more apt to let someone else take care of a younger sibling than a possessive mother would.

But she suffered for it. It had been nearly a week now, and Janice couldn't sleep, couldn't eat, couldn't occupy her mind with anything but worrying about Betsy. She had always been the one to see that Betsy got her rest, that she ate right, that she didn't overexert herself, that she took her medicine at all the right times. Betsy had always been too weak to run and play with the other children, so she had always been right there by Janice's side whenever possible. It was like losing her right arm not to have her here now.

But someday Betsy would have to learn to live on her own. Janice knew that was the healthy outlook to take. She just had a hard time accepting it. Ellen at the dry goods store was only sixteen. In six more years, Betsy would be old enough to be married and pregnant too. Janice couldn't bear to think about her life stretching on forever while Betsy went her own way, leaving nothing but this emptiness. But it had to be that way if Betsy was to lead a happy life, and Janice wanted that more than anything.

So she consoled herself that Betsy was happy now. She was with friends who didn't mind that she couldn't keep up with them. She had people to look after her. She had a teacher who could teach her to use the art set she received for her birthday. Janice smiled at the memory of Betsy's excitement upon unwrapping the gift. She had practically danced up the walls. It was worth the extra hours Janice had worked at copying pages of legal text for the lawyer's office.

Her eyes ached from staying up so late tonight finishing the task, but she might as well continue earning the money since she couldn't sleep anyway. Maybe she could save enough to offer to pay James Peyton to come into town regularly to give Betsy lessons. The older man was losing his eyesight and the palsy in his hand prevented him from holding a brush, but he still knew how to teach painting and drawing. His encouragement gave Betsy the kind of confidence she needed.

Janice pulled on her cotton nightgown and braided her still damp hair. Summer hadn't officially begun but the night was hot. She'd never in her life slept without clothing because she'd always lived in a house filled with people and no privacy, but with Betsy gone, she was almost tempted. Maybe as the summer moved on, she would try it. It gave her something else to think about.

She heard a horse whinny outside, and she frowned as she moved toward her narrow bed. There had been some problem earlier in the year with vagrants helping themselves to horses down at the livery and breaking into henhouses for their meals, but none had been seen lately. The sheriff had dealt quickly and firmly with the thieves, and word had apparently spread to avoid Mineral Springs. Somebody must have left their animal tied up outside for some reason.

She was just pulling the covers back on the bed when the pounding started on the door.

"Fire! There's a house on fire! Give me some pails!"

Fear jostled briefly through Janice's insides: a brush of panic at a strange male voice, the knowledge of what fire could do in a town of wood like this. But she had handled more than her fair share of emergencies in the past. Sliding on her slippers, she grabbed a wrapper and hurried for the water pail on the stove.

She barely noticed the shadowy figure filling her doorway as she threw open the door and thrust the pail out. Obviously, he had to be tall and broad to fill her doorway like that, but other than noting the bristly beard, she had no opportunity to see anything else. He grabbed the pail and ran for the pump, yelling for her to go find help.

He didn't have to remind her. She could see the flames leaping from the roof of the schoolhouse. The schoolhouse. Panic really did grab a lungful of air from her then. That was her livelihood, her main source of income, the reason she had use of this house. She set her slippers to running for the fire bell at the end of the road.

Men stumbled from houses and saloons and barns as the bell clanged and echoed and shattered the night silence. A rooster crowed. A donkey brayed. A shout went up from someone who saw the flames. Pretty soon the street filled with running men, most half-dressed and bleary-eyed. The last time there had been a fire, they had almost lost half the town.

Women and children staggered out after them. Boys pulling suspenders over nightshirts galloped down the road, their hands filled with buckets. The pitiful excuse for the town water tank was rolled out from behind the livery by the strongest men in town, and they raced down the street hauling it by the traces that should have held horses. They'd bought the fire engine after the last fire, but the town council had never decided whether to buy horses or ask for volunteers to pull it.

Janice grabbed another pail and washbasin and ran after them. Her house was closest to the fire, the most likely to catch next. The generosity of a trust fund from Jason's stepmother had allowed the school board to build the little house near the school when Janice had arrived with Betsy. Teachers with children to raise had been unheard of until then. The school board had only been willing to accept Janice because she was the only candidate available after a year's search. She'd had to sign a contract to stay on for five years when they offered to build the house. The five years were up, and if something wasn't done to stop the fire, so would be her job and the house.

She handed her containers to two children and grabbed the pump handle away from the man filling a bucket. He didn't argue but took his bucket and ran to where the fire was spreading to the grass around the school. Janice pumped the old handle up and down, filling every bucket and pan and bowl shoved beneath the spout. She was used to the old pump. She'd had to use it every day of her life for the last five years. Her arms no longer strained at the task.

She kept glancing over her shoulder at each shout and yell from the leaping fire. Her heart stuck in her throat as she saw the flames licking along the roof rail. There wasn't any chance of saving it now. They could only try to contain it.

The faces running up with empty containers were black with smoke, but she recognized most of them. She'd lived here long enough to know every man, woman, and child in town. The few she didn't know were most likely traveling drummers coming through town on the stage, stopping off long enough to sell their wares and moving on. The only one that didn't fit that description was the large man with the beard. He came back more times than any of the others, flying over the field with long strides and quick, incisive movements as he took charge of the most dangerous spots. He lined up women in a water line to the schoolhouse, sending boys to carry water from the women to the men closest to the fire. He was too impatient to wait for the containers to be passed along the line. He grabbed them out of waiting hands to throw their contents on flames licking along the dry grass and up the trees, heading straight for the house.

"A shovel," he demanded of Janice as he shoved a bucket into someone else's hands. He looked braced to run as soon as she gave him directions.

"Toolshed, back there." Janice nodded at the precarious lean-to attached to the privy.

He was off and running before the words left her mouth. Minutes later, she saw him digging a trench across the school yard, flinging dirt on trails of fire while ordering someone else to keep an eye on the cottonwoods. The man knew what he was about. Janice breathed a sigh of relief. It was good having someone who knew what they were doing.

The schoolhouse couldn't be saved. She knew that. The men futilely emptied the water tank on the blaze and succeeded only in sending billowing clouds of smoke into the air, making them cough and gag and fall back. The lines of women and children passing containers of water faltered as smoke and exhaustion thinned the ranks. Janice could feel her own shoulders and arms and back ache and moan with every pump of the handle. She would be stiff for a week, but she couldn't stop now. There was still a chance to save her house.

The man with the beard seemed to be working toward that goal now. He yelled at the ranks of faltering water carriers to cover the side yard between the two buildings. The schoolhouse was on the outskirts of town. The schoolteacher's house was the next closest building. Dry grass and the dry riverbed were all that separated her house from the rest of town. From the river, buildings scattered to the right and left, up and down the main street. They had to stop the fire here, where there was only grass to burn.

More men ran for shovels. Children ran to the puddles in the riverbed to fill their containers. Someone shoved Janice away from the pump and began to beat it with more vigor. She staggered backward, found a pail, and wearily filled it, hauling it toward a new line of flame licking beyond the trench.

She had no concept of time. She only knew the eastern horizon was spreading a red glow that reflected the dying fire before the schoolhouse crumbled slowly into a bed of embers. The wind died with the dawn, and the remaining small bonfires were quickly doused.

As her shoulders sagged beneath the weight of one more bucket of water, a hand reached out to take it from her.

"Go to bed. It's over. I'll bring your pail back when I find it."

His voice was raw from smoke and exhaustion, but the unfamiliar accents sent a shiver down her spine. They were crisp and precise, unlike the slow drawl of the town's inhabitants, more like the voices of her past. She took an odd comfort in that and nodded obediently.

She didn't even turn to look at him as she walked away.

# Four

Hell, some days it didn't pay for a man to get out of bed.

Peter Mulloney wiped his sleep-grimed eyes and propped himself on one elbow, trying to focus his blurred vision on the circle of men towering over him. One kicked his hip to induce him to wake more quickly.

"Get up. We got some questioning to do." The voice was rough and authoritative and not in the least reassuring.

Mulloney groaned and tried to sit up without tearing every muscle in his back loose from its mooring. Sleeping on the hard ground after a night of hauling buckets and shoveling an acre of dirt didn't make for much of a massage.

"I'm up. I'm up," he grumbled, untangling his legs from the bedroll. Damn, he stank. He reeked. He could almost feel the fumes rising from his smoke-saturated clothes. He'd been too tired to take them off when he'd collapsed at dawn. The way things seemed to go in this damned town, he was better off keeping them on. Maybe his stench would drive them off after a while.

"Grab his arms, boys. We'll haul him down to the jail. Maybe the sight of iron bars will set his tongue to flapping."

Wondering if this was his reward for trying to save the damned town or his punishment for his lustful peeping, Mulloney disbelievingly allowed his wrists to be tied together as they hauled him to his feet. Maybe it was all just a giant nightmare and he would wake up at any minute. The way his head felt, anything was possible.

At his suddenly upright position, he began to cough. He'd breathed in enough smoke to last a lifetime last night, and it felt as if it were all trying to escape at once. His captors took no pity on him. They half dragged, half lifted him from his feet as they hauled him from the trees and into the glaring sunlight.

Peter's last sight before he blacked out was of a woman appearing in the doorway of the little house he'd saved last night. The hair rippling down her back was a glorious pale yellow that rivaled the sun.

Janice clutched her wrapper and watched the sheriff and his men drag the bearded stranger away. She stepped out of sight the instant she saw them, but she had the uneasy feeling the stranger had seen her. He'd looked right in her direction before he fell and the men had to catch him.

Why had he been hiding in her bushes? Why was the sheriff taking him into town? She pushed her hair out of her face and turned swiftly toward her bedroom. She didn't believe in standing idly by and wondering, but she couldn't go into town looking like this.

She'd never slept this late in her life. It had to be almost noon. Still, she hadn't gone to bed until dawn. She felt as if she needed a full night's sleep yet, but she'd heard the sheriff's voice, and after last night, she wouldn't be able to lie in bed and speculate.

She grabbed a brush and began to pull her hair into a thick knot at the back of her head. She didn't have time to braid it if she meant to find out what the sheriff was doing to the stranger. Men were such idiots. That man might be another of the vagrants, but he had almost single-handedly saved her home last night. It might not be her home much longer if the school board decided they couldn't rebuild the school, but the bearded man's efforts ought to be rewarded and not punished. The sheriff didn't look like he was handing him a blue ribbon or the key to the city.

She shimmied out of her nightgown and struggled into her cotton combinations. Half the town must have seen her in dishabille last night. She couldn't afford to let them see her in anything less than proper garb now. She had to be the absolute epitome of the staid, old-maid schoolmarm today to wipe out their memory of last night. Her job hinged on it now that her contract was completed. They might just go looking for a male teacher who could stay with the families of students and use her little house as a school. It would save the town a lot of money, and soothe the ruffled sensibilities of those who believed only a man could teach their little darlings.

Janice jerked on her freshly laundered waist petticoat and reached for her corset, hastily pulling it around her and fastening the front clips. Thank heavens the laces Betsy had tied off had stayed fastened in back. She didn't want to have to struggle with them on her own.

The plain gray walking dress ought to be stuffy enough. There were days when Janice longed to wear pretty striped silks in cherry-red and apple-green, but they wouldn't be suitable for an old-maid schoolmarm. She indulged her desire for pretty things by adding bits of lace and a draping of nice material that almost made a small train over her bustle.

She straightened the horsehair pad over her petticoat, pulled on the gown, and hurriedly fastened the row of innumerable buttons marching down the front. Without Betsy to help her dress, she would have to forfeit the few dresses that fastened down the back. She might eventually fasten them all herself, but she couldn't guarantee they would all be in their proper holes when she got done.

Checking her tiny dressing mirror, Janice adjusted the drape of the skirt over her bustle, fluffed out the frill of white lace at her throat, and scowled at her hair. It looked like a field of wheat.

She brushed it back hastily and tugged a wide-brimmed hat over it. That succeeded in hiding everything but the thick lump of her chignon in back. She would never be blessed with fine curls to dangle at her nape or adorn her brow, but that suited her image just fine. All she needed now was the spectacles.

With the gold wire rims settled over her nose, she looked the part she played. It wasn't a difficult role. She'd been too old for her age for the better part of her life. After Betsy was born, she had attacked life with a steely determination that had left little time for laughter. She might have needed to disguise herself when she first came here at the age of twenty, but the years since had made her what she was: an old maid.

Lifting up her heavy skirt, Janice hurried out the front door and into the noon sunshine. She seldom had time to worry about the plights of others around her, but specks of Daniel's heroism had brushed off on her somewhere along the line, and she did what she could when she was able. There were times she cursed Daniel for ever befriending her, but she wouldn't be where she was now without him. It behooved her to act in a manner that would meet his approval.

Knots of people gathered throughout town, and from the expressions on their faces, they weren't discussing the weather for a change. The way some of them looked away from Janice as she approached warned of the topic of some of the conversations. She hadn't made friends of everybody in town. She was much too opinionated for that.

Ellen hurried out of the dry goods store to catch her hands. "Oh, Miss Harrison, last night was awful! Bobby wouldn't let me go out, but he came home all smoky and wore out and told me all about it. Mr. Holt said they might not have the money to rebuild the schoolhouse. How will my baby ever learn to read or write?"

Janice remembered Bobby leaning against the empty water tank, guzzling from a bottle as he watched the schoolhouse burn. No doubt he thought his heroics in hauling out the tank with the help of half a dozen others allowed him to rest while others worked. She'd called him a shiftless skunk in front of his face before, but she wouldn't talk behind his back now.

"You don't need to worry about that for a few years yet, Ellen. You just concentrate on keeping that baby healthy. There'll be someone to teach him when the time comes." She clasped the girl's hands reassuringly, then hurried on. Once she had a goal in mind, Janice didn't like to be distracted.

A few more women drifted in her direction to commiserate with her over the fire or to find out more gossip. Janice tried to smile at them, but she knew Mrs. Danner was one of the more vocal protesters against female teachers. Rumor had it that her husband had been smitten with Evie Monteigne back when she taught here. The randy old goat had tried to pinch Janice a time or two, but she hadn't grown up on the wrong side of the tracks without learning a few things. He hadn't touched her since she used a hat pin on him.

Janice had difficulty prying herself away from the clacking hens, but she finally managed it. Hat ribbons sailing in the breeze she created, she hurried down the street in the direction of the sheriff's office. She prayed the gossips thought she was going to identify the culprit or to press charges or to make inquiries. Surely they couldn't suspect her real intent or tongues wouldn't stop wagging for a month of Sundays.

She had to do this discreetly or they wouldn't stop wagging anyway. Checking her image in the glass of a store window as she passed, she tucked a straying lock back into her hat, straightened her shoulders, and marched into the sheriff's office.

Evie would have sashayed in. Georgina would have flown through in a flurry of ribbons and curls. Unlike her friends, Janice could only march like a stern soldier. Her prim gray walking dress had the effect of a uniform. She blinked her eyes to adjust them to the dusky light of the interior, ignoring the stares of the men at the desk.

"Miss Harrison." Ever polite, the sheriff rose from his chair. He was the closest thing the town had to an objective bystander. Even the newspaper held a biased slant on every news story in town. The sheriff never seemed to have an opinion on anything. He just arrested any man who crossed the fine line of the law and let the citizenry do the rest. This was the man she had to appeal to.

"Sheriff." Janice nodded her head stiffly. Now that the glare was out of her eyes, she could look over her glasses and recognize the other men with him. Mr. Holt was here. So was Jason. She exchanged looks with him, then scanned the rest of the crowd—mostly the school board. That answered volumes right there.

"I understand you have arrested the perpetrator of last night's fire." She had established herself as a no-nonsense type of woman. Old maids were allowed that privilege. She used it to her benefit now. Taking the offensive was always more effective than the defensive.

The sheriff nodded grimly. "We think so. He's a drifter, camped at the river behind your place last night. Don't think he did it deliberately. Probably got drunk and fell asleep and let his campfire get out of control."

"Is that the story he tells?" A moment of apprehension shook her. The story seemed very plausible. She hadn't intended to come rescue a drunk. She had meant to rescue the man who had saved her home.

"He swears he put out his fire before he went to sleep, but there ain't any other explanation. The school's been closed up this past week or more and there's been no fire in the stove that might have blazed up. There warn't anyone else out there but you and him. Facts is facts."

"Well, I certainly can't debate that," she assured him, but her mind spun quickly. She knew what she'd seen. That man had nearly killed himself trying to save the school. And she was quite certain that without him she wouldn't have a home today. The thought of losing those few precious possessions she had accumulated with such hard work over all these years made her shiver as she spoke. She didn't care if he was a drunk. He didn't deserve to be punished for what he couldn't help.

She turned her gaze to Jason. He had the money and

position in this town to make his voice heard. And he was her friend. "I saw the man they put in jail this morning. He's the same man who almost single-handedly saved my house last night. If he started the fire, I'm sure it was an accident, and he did everything humanly possible to put it out. What do you intend to do with him?"

"Well, Miss Harrison, I reckon it's up to a jury. Arson is a serious charge." The sheriff drawled the answer even though she wasn't looking at him.

Janice disregarded this nonsense and continued staring at Jason. He shifted his weight uneasily and ran his fingers through his graying hair. The gray made him look distinguished rather than old. He was still a handsome man, but he didn't seem aware of it. Jason wasn't aware of much of anything but his damned ranch.

"Now, Jenny, don't you go lookin' at me like that." The pet name he used for her had developed gradually over a period of years. "Janice" was just too clipped and formal for him. "There ain't nothin' I can do about it. We can't just let drifters roam through here, burning the town down."

"He didn't burn the town down, he worked to save it. You don't think I'd be here now if I thought anything else? That fire's likely to have cost me my job and almost cost me my home. If I thought he was responsible, I'd be the first person to say hang him." She hesitated about mentioning that he'd come to her first, warning her of the fire. Somehow, the fact that he'd been the first to see the fire made his presence all the more suspicious.

A couple of the men from the school board snickered in the corner. Janice managed to keep her jaw clenched against an urge to smack their hands with a ruler and demand that they tell the class what they found so all-fired funny. In this case, she had a suspicion she knew. The image of the old-maid schoolteacher come to save the virile young drifter would fire their limited imaginations.

One of them cleared his throat and poked Jason in the ribs. Out of habit, Jason leaned in his direction, and the man whispered something in his ear. Jason had spent years telling the school board what to do with his step-mother's trust fund. The habit of deferring to him died hard. His eyes narrowed thoughtfully as he listened to the suggestion.

"I don't know, Mick. You seen the man? He looks a scoundrel to me. Don't look to me like Miss Harrison would be safe with a man like that out there all day."

Janice felt her stomach plummet to her toes. Out where all day? What in the name of heaven were they cooking up now? She didn't like the look on anybody's face as Mick whispered his suggestion to someone else. If he'd been in her class, he would be sitting in the corner right now. Whispering wasn't polite.

"Sheriff, why don't you bring the man out here and let us question him? Maybe we got a suggestion or two that might solve a few problems." Pushing back his leather vest, Jason found a wooden chair and sat down, propping one boot on the sheriff's desk as if he owned the place. Which he no doubt did. His bank held the mortgages on every place in town.

Janice moved uneasily into a far corner of the crowded office. She hadn't meant to attract anyone's notice. She'd asserted herself much further than she had ever intended. She had just wanted the sheriff to know what the man had done. But now she didn't dare leave before she found out what they were up to.

"Doc said he's suffering from smoke inhalation and ought to rest. He passed out cold on us when we brought him in here." The sheriff shifted his big shoulders uneasily.

"Doc" was a euphemism for the pharmacist. He'd never had real medical training, but he claimed to have worked with a trained doctor some years ago. There weren't any other medical professionals around to argue with him. Janice waited impatiently for someone to make a decision.

"Well, we can't all fit back there. Just set him in that chair there and we'll be real quick." Jason shoved his foot against another chair no one had been bold enough to take.

When no one else offered any objections, the sheriff picked up his key ring and went to fetch his prisoner. Janice clasped her hands nervously in front of her. She didn't know why, but she didn't want the drifter looking at her. It was a quite irrational feeling, but she did her best to hide in the corner anyway, concealing herself behind a solid wall of men's bodies.

The prisoner came out peacefully enough. She could peek between Mr. Holt and Mick and catch a glimpse of him as the sheriff jerked his arm and shoved him into the room. He was a tall man. She remembered that much. The sheriff was the tallest man in town, taller even than Jason, and the stranger matched the sheriff's height.

He had wide shoulders and narrow hips. She didn't know what made her think that. She'd never noticed a man's hips before. She would have blushed had she not been hidden. The man couldn't possibly know what she was thinking.

The beard was an abomination and his stench reached her even back in this corner, but Janice didn't imagine it had occurred to the sheriff to offer him a bath. She wondered what he would look like once he was cleaned up. She thought he might look a good deal younger than she'd first thought. The way he had commanded the crowd last night, she had thought him an older man accustomed to authority. She could see that wasn't so now. She gulped when he turned and his eyes seemed to find her even through the solid wall of bodies. He had green eyes. And long lashes.

He didn't smile. He didn't take the seat offered. With his wrists manacled in front of him, he merely scanned the crowd without expression. He didn't even complain or question the reason for being brought here. She didn't think he cared why he had been brought here. It was as if he were calmly telling them all to go to hell, that he had better things to do. She had never seen anything quite like it.

"These gentlemen here want to ask you a few questions." The sheriff jerked his thumb in Jason's direction.

The stranger raised his eyebrows in that direction without comment.

"What's your name?" Jason demanded.

"Peter Aloysius Mulloney. And yours?"

Janice didn't hear Jason's response. With a gasp, she grasped the nearest wall and held herself up. It couldn't be. There couldn't be two men of that name. Peter Aloysius Mulloney had been the man who had fired her sister and caused Janice to lose her own job. His family had been responsible for the shantytown where her parents died and the rent collector beat them up. This couldn't be the man she hated as much as she could hate anyone.

The arrogance of his response said it could. And the glitter of those hard green eyes as they found her again were exact duplicates of the man she despised even more than this man. She stared into the eyes of Artemis Mulloney, the man who owned Cutlerville, the man who had destroyed her life.

# Five

Mulloney saw the schoolteacher slip out the door while the yahoo in the leather vest interrogated him. He knew she was the schoolteacher. He had heard the men last night discussing her, and he'd overheard her plea for reason this morning. He knew she was the nymph from last night and the blond goddess of the dawn he had seen this morning. She had just managed to disguise that fact behind those gawd-awful spectacles and an enormous hat.

He didn't know why his mind was on the woman who had just walked out rather than these asses bombarding him with idiot questions. If they would just stop and let him speak his piece, this would all go much faster. Maybe the woman had tired of listening to their yammering. He didn't think that was the real reason, though.

"What was your purpose in coming to Mineral Springs, Mr. Mulloney?" the man in the leather vest asked. He had disregarded Peter's earlier query as to his identity.

Peter raised a cynical eyebrow. "Why, I came to burn the schoolhouse down. That's what I do best. I travel around looking for schoolhouses to burn. It's a most rewarding occupation." He was getting tired of this. His head hurt, his throat was raw, and his stomach was about to eat his insides out. And these redneck cowboys were keeping him tied up here when he needed to be cleaning himself up and looking for the Double H. Maybe he ought to stop in and visit the schoolteacher if he got a chance. Better yet, he'd look for a whorehouse.

The sheriff yanked his bound arms and Peter winced.

"Better answer the question, boy. You're already in a heap of trouble."

Peter yanked his arm back. "Look, it would save us a great deal of time if you would just pay attention. I told you. I'm here on business. I got in late last night and camped out by the river. I cleaned up and got ready to turn in when I saw fire in the windows of a building down the road. I ran to the nearest house to get help and took a bucket to start pouring water on the flames. That's all there is to it. Did anybody notice which way the wind blew last night? Did anybody look to see what direction the fire followed, if it really could have blown from my fire toward the school? Did anyone even look at the remains to see if they could discover the cause of the fire? If you'd done any one of those things, it would be evident I'm not your man. I haven't got time to waste jawing with you."

Some of the men where whispering at the back, and Peter scowled in their direction. They were the same ones he'd heard whispering about the schoolteacher earlier. He probably shouldn't have mentioned he'd run to her house first, but he was trying to get the facts straight here. He'd have to worry about the teacher once he got himself out of these manacles.

"What is your business here?" Leather Vest inquired again.

Peter gave up. He might as well talk to a cage full of monkeys. It was a trifle hard adopting an authoritative pose while garbed in stained denim and cotton, smelling like a smokehouse, and unshaven, but he did his best. He pulled himself straight and glared straight into Leather Vest's eyes.

"I'm here on business with Jason Harding of the Double H. Does that satisfy your curiosity?"

Leather Vest remained unperturbed. "I'm Jason Harding, and I'm not expecting any visitors."

Well, that finished that. Might as well scratch the Harding brothers off the list. He'd have to move on to Natchez, if he ever got himself out of this hellhole. Cursing inwardly, Peter gave a stiff nod. "Glad to meet you. My brother Daniel told me to look you up while I was out here."

"Daniel? Daniel Mulloney? Damnation, it's a wonder you didn't burn the whole town down!" Slapping his thigh and roaring, Harding shook his head in disbelief. The others around him erupted in similar cackles. "That boy ever tell you how he blew up Main Street? Only a fool or his brother would admit to being Daniel's kin around here. Guess that makes you the real thing."

Jason Harding turned and pounded the sheriff on the back. "Well, Powell, if he is who he says he is, looks like we can solve this problem right enough. Why don't you have someone telegraph Daniel for identification while we settle this right here?"

Peter didn't allow himself to relax. He didn't like the way that was being said, and he liked it even less that they were notifying Daniel of his whereabouts. The older brother he'd never known until he was grown, the son their father had thrown away, had assumed more than the reins of Mulloney Enterprises upon his return to the family fold. He'd taken on the whole damned family. Peter didn't want to be another of Daniel's projects. He wasn't going to beg, but he turned a wary eye to Harding.

"You'll word that telegram just so he knows you're verifying my identity, won't you? His wife's expecting and I don't want them troubled with the rest of this idiocy."

Jason clapped his shoulder and grinned. "I already believe you are who you say you are. Nobody but Daniel's brother could cause such an uproar around here. Powell will do his civic duty and no more."

Peter held his manacled wrists up questioningly. The sheriff hesitated over the keys, turning to Harding for authority.

"Unwrap him, Powell. I'm sure once he understands our predicament, he'll be proud to help out. Where'd Jenny go? She ought to be here to explain." He glanced around and, not finding Janice, shrugged and turned back.

"She musta thought we were getting a little unruly. She'll probably smack our hands with a ruler if we don't do this right."

Several of the men guffawed, but Peter noticed several held back disapprovingly. "Jenny" wasn't friends with everyone, it seemed. He didn't know why it should matter to him, but she had tried to help at a time when no one else would. Few enough people in this world would do a thing like that if it wasn't necessary. He'd like to return the favor. He'd like to do more than return the favor, if he were truthful with himself, but he didn't have time for that now. He was going to have to get himself to Natchez.

The sheriff unfastened the handcuffs and Peter rubbed his wrists while he waited for whatever entertainment Harding had planned next. He didn't wait for long.

"Now, the way I figure it, all you need to do is build the schoolhouse back like it was, and we're even. We made Daniel and those friends of his fill the street back in, and it looks to me like we've got the same situation here. Jenny will have her school back, and we can do a little business when you're done. How's that sound?"

Not good. Not promising at all. Peter stared at him incredulously. "Build a school? I wouldn't know where to begin, even if I admitted to burning it, which I don't."

"That's not a problem. We can probably scrape together enough money for the lumber. There's plenty of broad backs around to do the labor. You just gotta get it organized and keep it going. Fellas tend to be shiftless a mite if someone ain't on them all the time. Know what I mean?" Jason gave a steely look that belied his friendly tones. "And if that ain't to your likin', we could always keep you locked up until the judge comes around. You can plead your case afore him, if you want. But that won't get Jenny her schoolhouse. Without it, she can't teach. There will be those who'll want to take her home away if she ain't teaching. Are you beginning to understand me?"

Unfortunately, yes, he was. Peter rubbed his brow where the ache just became a little stronger. "How much time you figure this will take? I've got business back in New Mexico that can't wait too long."

Harding shrugged. "Not more than a week or two. We don't need nothin' fancy. I've got to go into Houston on business anyway. I'll see what I can find in the way of books and things, but you'll have to have them put together desks and whatever else Jenny says she needs. When I get back, if all's well, we can have that little talk you wanted."

He had him pinned there. Harding wasn't such a yahoo after all. The man knew what Peter wanted, and he dangled it like a carrot on a stick. Peter sighed and nodded. "I take it the schoolteacher is the one I need to ask for details? If you're not going to be here, can I rely on her to give me the name of people who are supposed to help on this project?"

"Jenny can give you anything you ask, including cash from what's left of the trust fund for the lumber, unless you're willing to donate that yourself?" Jason raised an eyebrow as he prodded his prisoner a little more.

Peter smelled a hint of a threat there, and he rebelled. "If I'd done it, I'd be wiring for the funds now. The only reason I'm falling for your blackmail is because I don't want the teacher to lose her job and I'm in a hurry to get out of here. This seems the fastest way to take care of both."

Jason nodded. "Have it your way. Just have that school up when I get back. And don't think you can walk away. Powell's the best damned tracker in the territory. He'll find you wherever you go."

"Just tell me where I can get some breakfast and some hot water to wash in. I'm not doing anything until I've eaten and made myself presentable."

Jason grinned, all affability once more. "Powell takes care of his prisoners. He'll get you what you need. You'd better bathe some before you go see Miss Jenny. She's likely to send you home if you go up there smelling like a polecat."

They made her sound like a real tartar when all he'd

seen was a nymph, but Peter wasn't about to argue with
them over the local schoolmarm. He'd damned well have
that building up and be out of here before another week
went by. He couldn't afford delays like this.

Janice wheeled her cycle back into town as the sun
lowered behind her. The Double H had been quiet with
the kids and Carmen gone and Kyle out checking a fence
break. She'd arrived after Jason had already left for
Houston. His cryptic instructions for the time he was
away had left her vaguely puzzled, but that was nothing
new. She would just ask Kyle about them tomorrow.

She stopped at the law office and picked up another
packet of papers for transcribing. She wasn't looking forward to going home to that empty house, but at least she
would have something to keep her occupied through the
lonely evening hours. Nothing in Jason's notes had said
anything about the school board's decision regarding a
new school, so she assumed she didn't have to pack and
leave just yet. Knowing the board, it would take them the
length of the summer to decide.

She really didn't feel like going home and lighting a
fire to fix dinner for herself. She considered stopping at
the little restaurant beside the hotel and just ordering up
a meal, but that would cut into her finances, and she
wasn't pleased about sitting at a table by herself in what
was usually a room full of men. Maybe she could make
do with some leftover biscuits and jam.

When she rode up to the house, she was startled to notice a stack of lumber piled in the school yard. Her spirits
soared instantly. They were going to rebuild! Bless Jason.
He might be a blind, thick-headed numskull at times, but
his heart was in the right place whenever he could find it.
She would have to sew him a new vest for his birthday.
She was tired of that stained leather one.

She hadn't realized how worried she had been until her
spirits soared at the sight of that lumber. She couldn't
have felt better if the weight of the world had been lifted
from her shoulders. She'd had horrifying visions of Betsy

coming home and finding her living in the streets. Rental houses weren't readily available out here, even if she could afford one.

That called for a celebration. Maybe she would light up the stove after all. She would make a pie that would last her all week. Pies might not be real nutritious, but they kept well. She couldn't afford an icebox and didn't have a spring house. If she wanted to eat, she had to stop at the greengrocer's and the butcher's before coming home, and she hadn't. But she had some dried apples that would work just fine in a pie.

She had the stove heating and was humming to herself as she rolled out the crust when a knock at the door intruded. Frowning, she tried to clean off her hands on her apron as she went to answer it. With school out, she didn't have much company from students or parents. Maybe Ellen needed something.

Opening the door to find Mulloney standing on the other side caused her to step back, speechless.

She had managed to push him out of her mind all day. She hadn't expected a man like Peter Aloysius Mulloney to hang around long. She'd wasted her time trying to help him. He'd have lawyers from all over the country down here by daybreak if he was in trouble. She could just pretend that he didn't exist as long as she didn't have to look at him.

But she was looking at him now. He'd certainly made some major improvements since the morning. His beard was shaven to reveal a strong jaw with a cleft in the middle, and a mouth that didn't look like it turned up at the corners much. She remembered the humorless green eyes quite well and didn't need to meet them as she glanced over his shoulder for some explanation of his appearance.

"Miss Harrison?" He doffed his gray felt hat with the silver shells on the band. He'd changed into a clean white shirt and khakis and had obviously bathed, but Janice wasn't impressed. She started to close the door.

He shoved his foot inside. "Sheriff said you'd be recompensed for providing my meals while I'm working off my debt to society."

She stared. She wasn't certain she heard this right. Peter Mulloney was standing on her doorstep, asking for a prisoner's meal? *The* Peter Mulloney? He could have bought the restaurant and ordered them to make roast duck if he liked. She shook her head, certain that she had heard wrong.

"I'm sorry, Mr. Mulloney. What do you want?"

"Supper," he said succinctly. "I'm starved. I had beef jerky for lunch since you weren't here, but I could eat the wood off that table right now."

She did have an arrangement with the sheriff to fix meals for prisoners on a rotating basis with some of the other women in town. And this man had been a prisoner this morning. She just didn't think prisoners usually arrived at the door, hat in hand.

"You don't look like a prisoner to me, Mr. Mulloney," she reminded him, just in case he'd forgotten.

There was a suspicion of a curl to the corner of his lips as he looked her up and down in a blatantly sexual way that made Janice want to take her rolling pin to his noggin. "And you don't look like much of a cook to me, Miss Harrison. I'm just taking the sheriff's word for it. You want to talk to him?"

"I'll do more than talk to him. Nobody warned me about this arrangement. There's not a thing in the house to eat but apple pie, and that's not ready yet."

He had thick dark eyebrows that formed upside-down V's when he raised them. "You're planning on eating apple pie for supper?"

"That isn't any of your business. Since you're wandering around loose, why don't you wander down and ask the sheriff to come back here and verify your story? He'd better bring around the makings of dinner while he's at it." This time, she pushed the door so hard, he had to hastily move his foot before she crushed it.

Then she braced herself against the door and listened to the sound of his boots walking away. Peter Mulloney, a man richer than Croesus, begging at her door. She must be hallucinating. She had been working too hard and the loneliness was preying on her mind.

God might make miracles, but He didn't send gifts like that to her doorstep.

# Six

Janice turned the beefsteak over in the frying pan and leaned over to check the biscuits in the oven. Her stomach felt tighter than a bowstring, and claws of something irrational ripped at her insides. She had ordered Peter Aloysius Mulloney to stay out of her house while she cooked, but the knowledge that he was outside her door kept her off balance.

She'd heard him washing up at the pump earlier. She had sneaked a peek through the curtains sometime later and seen him pacing off the charred area of the schoolhouse. The sheriff had assured her that Mulloney would rebuild the schoolhouse for her. She ought to be relieved and grateful.

Instead, she was walking on hot coals. He didn't know who she was. There was no reason in the world that one of the grand and mighty Mulloneys would recognize one of his many impoverished and ill-treated tenants. Not that she had even lived in Cutlerville these last five years for him to recognize.

But she recognized Mulloney, all right. She could remember what he and his fiancée had looked like in his polished carriage behind those matched bay horses. They had been the epitome of everything she could never have. It hadn't broken her heart any when Daniel had come along and not only overthrown the heir apparent, but stolen his fiancée too.

Evie had once tried to explain how Daniel with his crippled leg and uncertain parentage had been cast out of the Mulloney family at birth, but Janice had just scored one more point against the wealthy, greedy Mulloneys. Daniel was her friend. She had cheered with the rest of the town when he'd taken over Mulloney Enterprises. She had never given a single thought to the brother whose place he had taken. She'd left Cutlerville too soon after that to hear the details.

She didn't know what Peter had been doing all these years, but she knew Daniel would never disown his brother as his family had once disowned him. So she couldn't fathom what Peter Mulloney was doing out here or why he didn't hire a fleet of carpenters to rebuild the school if that was what he had in mind. He'd announced his name to all and sundry, so he wasn't traveling incognito for some reason. Daniel would never have thrown his own brother out without a cent. She couldn't imagine why the fabulously rich Peter Mulloney was sleeping on the ground in filthy clothes not fit for a beggar.

The puzzle worried at her mind, but not as much as the thought of the man himself. The sheriff had said she would have to work with Mulloney to see the school rebuilt properly. She didn't know if she could stay in the same room with the man without killing him. Those years in Mulloney tenant houses had been pure hell. She'd like to return the favor sometime.

But she had learned to hide her feelings long ago. When supper was cooked, she called to the man kicking idly at a fallen timber. Standing with hands in pockets, silhouetted against the setting sun, he looked more lonely drifter than fancy financier. Janice didn't let her imagination take hold. She kept her face stiff as he hurried toward the house.

Mulloney ate like a starving man, but a polite starving man. He waited for Janice to sit before taking his place at the table. He knew how to use his napkin. He cut his meat into small bites and chewed hurriedly, but thoroughly. He didn't forget to compliment his hostess on everything from her cooking to her neat kitchen. She still wanted to kill him.

It took all her willpower to keep from telling him that

she knew who he was. Maybe he was planning on skipping town without rebuilding the school, saving himself a lot of money and trouble. That would be like the Mulloneys she knew. She would just hate to telegraph Daniel and tell him what kind of wretch his brother was, but that schoolhouse was her livelihood. She would do whatever she had to do.

"I'll tell you right now, Miss Harrison, I've never built anything larger than a tent before." Peter sat back in his chair, wiping his hands on his napkin. He hadn't eaten anywhere that used napkins in so long he couldn't remember the last time. He savored the taste of the tender steak lingering in his mouth and looked around hopefully for the apple pie she'd been baking. He hadn't realized how starved he had been until he'd sat down at this table to a selection of fresh vegetables and tender meat. It was plain fare, far plainer than the delicacies he had eaten at home, but he couldn't remember a better tasting meal.

"Then you'll have to rely on Jed to tell you what to do." The schoolteacher stood up and brought the pie out of the pantry.

Peter watched her cut a generous slice and felt his mouth water. He wasn't certain if it was from watching the pie or the teacher. When he'd first appeared at her door this evening, she hadn't been wearing her spectacles, and her hair had been tumbling loose from her chignon, making her look years younger than her present guise. Since then, she had jerked all that golden glory back into a knot and donned her spectacles and an apron three sizes too big for her. He wasn't fooled. Beneath that bulky cloth was a figure he'd die to clasp in his hands. He could barely keep his eyes on the food for waiting for a glimpse of the real Miss Harrison.

"Does this Jed live here in town? I suppose I ought to go over and introduce myself and get some idea of where we need to start."

She set the pie down in front of him and he caught a whiff of some light scent that made him think of soft skin and smooth sheets. He wondered what it would take to seduce a schoolteacher. From the frozen scowl on her face, he assumed it would take an all-out assault. She no doubt thought him lower than scum. He didn't have much time to prove himself any different.

"Jed lives on the far end of Main Street, in the blue house. He's working on the livery this week, so he's in town."

She sat primly across from him, sampling the tiny sliver of pie she had cut for herself. She hadn't eaten scarcely a bite all evening, Peter realized guiltily. He'd cleaned up everything in sight. He sought for some way to get past her reserve. She'd taken his earlier compliments without comment. He'd never fancied himself a ladies' man. He'd never had to be. But he wished he had the facile tongue necessary to reach this goddess.

"I'll go over and see him just as soon as I help you with these dishes, Miss Harrison. This has got to be the best meal I've ever eaten."

She scowled at him as if he had told her the meat stunk. Did she hate all men or just him?

"I can clean up, Mr. Mulloney. The schoolhouse is a good deal more important."

She stood up and began cleaning off the table, deliberately turning her back on him when he rose with her. Peter carried his dishes to the dry sink and poured hot water from the stove into the basin. She went outside to fetch cold water from the pump as if he weren't there.

When he picked up the towel and started to dry the dishes she set aside to drain, she grabbed the linen and glared at him.

"Go see Jed, Mr. Mulloney. My duty is to feed the prisoners, not keep company with them."

Not an ounce of emotion touched his face as he handed her the plate and the towel. "You're quite right, Miss Harrison. Thank you for dinner. I'll see you in the morning."

He strode off without looking back. Janice watched him go with an increasing knot in her stomach. Her mind was telling her one thing and her conscience quite another. Peter Mulloney was a ticket to wealth if she had ever seen one. A man like that could provide the best doctors for Betsy. He could ensure her daughter a life of ease so that she would never have to marry or bear the burden of grief and poverty her mother had known. For Betsy, Janice would do almost anything.

Could she force herself to respond to the blatant loneliness in Peter Mulloney's eyes in order to ensure her daughter's happiness?

He made it so easy for her. Mulloney showed up early the next morning, clean-shaven, hat in hand, his hair still slightly wet from washing. He didn't smile, but he complimented Janice on how fine she looked, then looked as if he had been handed heaven when she set scrambled eggs and bacon in front of him. A hungry man couldn't be wary when filling his stomach. Janice poured fresh coffee and sat down across from him.

There wasn't anything tender or soft in Peter Mulloney's face as he sipped gratefully at the coffee, but Janice had seen the desperation behind men's eyes often enough to recognize it. She didn't know what had caused it in this man. She knew nothing of the feminine wiles necessary to wheedle the knowledge out of him. She only knew what loneliness and hunger could do to a person. Reluctantly and with great caution, she plied that knowledge now.

"You eat as if you haven't seen food in a week," she murmured, pouring him a second cup of coffee.

"Longer than that, truth be told." He neatly scraped his plate clean with his fork and didn't protest when she brought him more toast and jam. "Beef jerky and train fare can't be called eating."

"Train fare? Have you traveled far to get here?"

He sat back and sipped at his coffee slowly now that his stomach was full. He still didn't smile, but Janice could feel his appraising look. She had left her spectacles off this morning. She only needed them for reading, but she'd found they added years to her age and made an excellent preventative against unwarranted attention. For the first time in her life, she found herself attempting to attract a man's interest. She shuddered inwardly at the thought, but kept Betsy's pale face uppermost in her mind.

"I've just come in from New Mexico," he answered casually. "And rode up here from the station at Fort Worth."

Janice nodded and rose to clear the table. Her stomach was so tense she feared she would have to throw up what little food she had eaten. She wasn't any good at this sort of thing. She despised this man. How was she going to catch and hold his interest without making a fool of herself?

"I understand you wanted to see Jason. Did you get a chance to talk with him before he left for Houston?"

"Only long enough to know I'd better get this school built before he gets back." Peter got up and helped her clear the table, although what he really wanted to do was sit here for the rest of the morning, sipping coffee and watching the odd shadows flit across the teacher's face. She had a soft voice that he suspected could carry a note of authority when she wanted. He'd heard a hint or two of that last night. He wondered what had changed her mind about him since then.

"Everybody around here pretty much lets Jason have his way. He and his brother own the biggest ranch in these parts as well as the town bank. They're fair men, but it doesn't pay to get on the wrong side of them."

Peter picked up the towel and started to dry the dishes she was washing. This time, she didn't stop him. "I kind of got that figured. I'm needing to talk to them about some business, so I'll try to stay on their good side."

She nodded and handed him a cup. "I didn't think you were the one to set that fire. You worked too hard to stop it. I tried to tell them that, but I'm only a woman."

Peter heard echoes of his past in that last statement. How many times had Georgie told him he wouldn't listen to her because she was "only a woman"? How many times had he actually ignored women because he thought them frivolous? For the most part, they were, he supposed. But over these last years, he'd met one or two who had taught him how to survive. He didn't think this fragile-looking schoolmarm could teach him anything about surviving, but he didn't intend to ignore her either. He had decided he needed a woman, and she was very definitely all woman.

"Women have been the cause of wars. It's not smart to ignore them," he heard himself saying. Georgie would choke and swallow an apple whole to hear him say that. He ought to gag on the statement himself, but he continued to calmly dry her dishes.

She sent him a telling glance that said she wasn't fooled. "You'd better go get Jed and the others to start hauling off that debris, Mr. Mulloney. I'm perfectly capable of finishing up here."

Well, he should have figured a schoolteacher wasn't stupid. He had just hoped an old maid might be easily persuaded. Now that he thought about it, it was a trifle odd that a woman as lovely as this one hadn't been snatched up long before. He would have to be a little more cautious in his seduction. Peter set down the cup and returned the towel to the rack.

"Will you be here for lunch?"

"I'm working over at the newspaper this morning. I'll come home around noon to fix something cold. If you're still working, I'll leave it out for you."

Peter nodded and walked out, but he was already counting the hours to noon. His stomach was full, so it wasn't the thought of a meal that kept him going. It was the flicker of something almost flirtatious in the schoolmarm's eyes—rusted from disuse perhaps, but still flirtatious. He'd had enough women look at him that way to know what it meant. He almost managed a smile as he started in to town.

Maybe the old-maid schoolteacher had a cold bed that needed warming.

Janice flinched as a gunshot rang out on the main street of town. Looking up from the legal papers she was working on at the kitchen table, she noticed the sun had set some time ago. Her gaze went to the stew cooking over the stove, and her belly rumbled. Mulloney should have been here hours ago. Maybe he had decided to run off while the sheriff was occupied with the rowdies in town.

Even as she thought it, she heard a light knock at the kitchen door. It swung open before she could answer. He stood silhouetted there against the blue-black evening sky, his hat tipped back off his forehead. In the lamplight, he was every bit as handsome as she remembered, just a world older.

Another gun fired somewhere beyond the thin walls. Mulloney closed the door behind him, his gaze never drifting from the woman seated at the wooden kitchen table. "Is it always like this around here?" His hand unconsciously fell to his holster when a yell and a rifle blast sounded farther down the road.

Janice hastily stacked her papers and began to clear the table. "Just on Saturday nights when the men come in from the ranches. Sounds like the sheriff has his hands full tonight. It's dark. I thought maybe you'd found somewhere else to eat tonight."

Peter set his hat aside and reached for the dishes in the high cabinet while Janice busied herself setting the meal on the table. "You mean you thought I'd skipped out while the sheriff wasn't looking."

Janice sent him a swift look, but as usual, his face was expressionless. "It was a possibility," she admitted.

"I can't go anywhere until I talk to Jason Harding." He took her hand off the heavy stew kettle, and she jerked away as if his touch rather than the pot had burned her. "I can fill my plate from the pot. There's no sense lugging it around."

She backed away and let him fill both their plates. Suddenly, in the dim light of the lantern, he was larger and malevolently more masculine than she remembered. She didn't like men to get too close. This man was not only too close, but too big, too overpowering. In her head, she knew Jason was wider and probably stronger, but Jason never infringed on her territory like this. She hurriedly took the seat Peter pulled out for her.

"It won't hurt any for me to see you get your schoolhouse back while I'm waiting," he said, as if there hadn't been any silent tug of wills between them.

"Since you didn't set the fire, that's gentlemanly of you." The touch of irony in her voice was subtle. She hoped he didn't hear it.

"I've been looking into that," he replied, undeterred by her sarcasm or oblivious of it. "I'd say from the path of the fire that the wind blew toward my camp that night, not away from it." He reached for the bread and cut off a slice.

He opened his mouth—whether to continue his discourse or to eat the bread, Janice would never know—when a rifle blast shook the walls. Glass shattered in the front room.

Outraged, Janice leapt to her feet, but Mulloney grabbed her waist and pulled her down. Before she knew what was happening, she was lying on her kitchen floor with a strange man half on top of her while what sounded like a band of Indians whooped and hollered in the street outside.

# Seven

"Get under the table and keep your head down." He didn't have time to consider how good she felt beneath him. He'd learned about keeping his priorities straight years ago. Saving his skin took precedence over a surge of lust.

Peter shoved Janice to safety while his hand instantly went to his own gun. The sheriff had said nothing when Peter claimed the revolver earlier today. A man just didn't live without a gun out here.

Crawling rapidly to the doorway between the kitchen and the front room, he surveyed the damage. No lamp burned in here, but he could see the glitter of broken glass from the reflections of the kitchen light. The front curtains blew slightly in the draft created by the broken window. The noise outside had grown ominously quiet. Peter got to his feet, and keeping out of sight of the window, he crossed the room.

Outside, the sheriff had already roped two of the drunken cowhands and jerked them to the ground. He had his knee in the back of one and the other trussed tighter than a turkey. If there had been more, they were long gone. Peter had no intention of getting involved if there was no further danger. He checked the rest of the street, and seeing nothing he could do, he holstered his pistol and headed back to the kitchen.

Janice had already come out from under the table and was going to the closet for her broom and dustpan. She glanced over her shoulder as he entered. "Sheriff Powell take care of them?"

He noticed she kept the distance of the table between them as he came into the room. It was unnatural for a beautiful woman like her to be so wary of men. Peter had enough experience in the ways of women to know that much. He didn't have enough experience to know what to do about it.

"He's hauling them off as we speak. You can't be safe out here alone with renegades like that running loose." He was eager for the stew cooling on the kitchen table, but he was more eager for the woman bending over the shards of glass in the other room. He followed just to keep an eye on her.

"I stay out of the front room on Saturday nights," she responded absently, sweeping the glass into the pan. "Mostly, they leave me alone. I suppose Bobby Fairweather had a little too much and got into it with his wife again. Whenever Ellen complains about his drinking, he blames it on me."

By now, Peter had heard enough of the town gossip to know about Bobby and his exceedingly pregnant wife. He took the dustpan from her hand and carried it off to the trash. He heard Janice washing her hands in the basin, but instead of being afraid for her, he was remembering what it had felt like having her under him for those few brief minutes. He needed a woman real soon, but he had a feeling that town gossip would tell this woman the instant he frequented one of the whores. Not that he had any money for whores.

He didn't tell her that he had decided the sheriff would have a full jail and wouldn't miss him if he stayed here for the night. He let her sit back down at the table as if everything was normal between them. But it wasn't. She flinched every time he looked directly at her. She nearly dropped a bowl when they both reached for it at the same time and their hands touched. She kept sending him surreptitious glances when she thought he wasn't looking. By the end of the meal, her hands were shaking ever so slightly as she removed the dishes from the table.

He didn't want to crowd her. Obviously, she didn't usually have men around the house. He didn't know how to let her know he was harmless. He wasn't completely certain he was harmless. He wanted her enough to ache.

The sheriff pounded on the front door while they were putting the dishes away. Drying her hands on a towel, Janice hurried to answer it. She smiled in relief as Powell took off his hat and nodded politely.

"Sheriff, come in. You took care of those rowdies real well. I do believe Mr. Mulloney thought we were under attack." She stood back to let him in.

He remained in the doorway. "Jason would have my head if anything happened to you, Miz Harrison. Just checking to see you're all right. I'll have someone out to fix the window in the morning." He glanced up to see Mulloney, his arms crossed, leaning against the kitchen door frame. He nodded warily in the other man's direction. "You might be better off camping out tonight, Mulloney. The jail's kind of crowded."

Mulloney nodded. "I was figuring that. Any objection if I pitch camp outside Miss Harrison's here? It doesn't seem safe for her to be out here all alone."

The sheriff frowned. "She's been safe all these years. Reckon she's safe now. Harding won't like it if you go messing with the schoolteacher."

Janice frowned as this conversation took place over her head. "I'll have you remember I'm standing right here, gentlemen. I'm a grown woman, and if I want Mr. Mulloney to camp in my yard, I'll tell him so. And if I don't want him there, I believe I'm capable of telling him that also. Now, Sheriff, go on back to your duties. I'm just fine." She threw a glance over her shoulder to Peter Mulloney and tried not to shiver at what she was certain was a predatory gleam in his eye. "And, Mr. Mulloney, you can put your bedroll out in the lean-to if you want. It looked like rain earlier."

Both men exchanged glances over her head, and Janice gave a muffled oath. It was like having two adolescent boys sizing each other up before a brawl. Firmly she moved the door to shut the sheriff out. "Good night, Mr. Powell. I'll see you in the morning.."

With the thickness of the door between the two men, Janice turned and glared at her guest. "You may leave now, Mr. Mulloney. Dinner is over."

He straightened but made no effort to leave. Stretched to his full height, he towered over her by a head. Janice didn't get any closer.

"Is Harding always so protective of his schoolteachers that he has the sheriff keep an eye on them? Or is it just you who raises his better instincts?"

She didn't like what he seemed to be insinuating, but she didn't intend to give him the pleasure of a reply either. She pointed at the back door. "Good night, Mr. Mulloney."

He gave her an enigmatic look as he turned around and walked out.

Janice didn't sleep any better that night knowing he was out there. Not even a hint of breeze stirred the sticky, humid air as she lay stiff and uncomfortable in her long gown and her narrow bed. The lean-to was quite a few yards away from the house, but she imagined Mulloney sitting outside of it, smoking a cheroot, watching her windows. She didn't know why she imagined him doing such an idiotic thing, but she couldn't keep the image out of her head.

When the first heavy drops of rain hit the tin roof overhead, she felt a pang of guilt. The lean-to leaked. She should have urged him to find better shelter.

She didn't feel relieved when the rain started to pour and she heard the sound of boots on the back porch. She didn't need to check out her window to know Mulloney had decided the porch was drier. She could hear him moving the tin tub and mop while looking for a dry corner. She ought to go out and offer her kitchen, but she was damned if she would. She had guarded her reputation zealously these last years. Not even Peter Mulloney would slip under her defenses.

By morning, she feared her defenses weren't as strong

as she thought. All night she had listened to him stirring restlessly outside her window. She didn't think she'd had a wink of sleep. She couldn't say she felt guilt at leaving Peter Mulloney sleeping on the porch in the pouring rain. After living in Mulloney tenant houses with snow drifting in the windows and mold growing up the walls, she felt no guilt at all. She just knew her nightgown felt too warm and she didn't dare take it off.

She stayed far away from her bedroom window as she dressed. She could hear him take the bucket out to the pump, heard him as he splashed in the cold water to wash. She ought to give him some warm water from the stove, but she didn't want him to know she knew what he was doing. It seemed so intimate somehow, knowing he stood on her porch, probably half naked and shaving. She would prefer to remain in ignorance.

She was dressed and standing over the stove when he came in carrying a load of kindling. She managed a "Good morning" while not looking at him, but she couldn't help noticing him when he brushed her skirts to get to the kindling box. She caught a glimpse of the way his dark shirt strained over his shoulders when he bent over the box, and she hastily looked away.

"Will hotcakes be all right this morning?" she asked—foolishly, because she already had them cooking.

"I'd just about get down on the floor and beg for hotcakes. Is there anything I can do to help?"

She was having a hard time getting used to having someone underfoot in her kitchen besides Betsy. She had her own routine, her own procedures that kept everything moving smoothly and quickly. She had difficulty slicing off part of that routine and handing it to someone else. But she'd rather keep Mulloney on his toes and moving than sitting at the table watching her.

"Get the dishes down and set the table. And there's syrup in the pantry. These will be ready in a minute."

She thought it might be a trifle unusual for a man to help with these chores. Even after her mother died, her father had seldom trespassed in the kitchen. Janice had always had that one room at her command. She couldn't think of any of the men she knew actually setting a table. She watched from the corner of her eye as Mulloney carefully laid out plates and silverware. He didn't seem certain where to put each utensil, but he did seem to recognize that they had certain places. She held a smile as he lined all of them up on one side and hid them with a napkin.

"Is there any place around here that takes in laundry? I'm down to my last clean shirt." He threw this over his shoulder as he went to the pantry for the syrup.

Janice waited until he was back in the kitchen before answering. "Molly Magee does laundry, but she comes high. I'll be doing my wash tomorrow. Why don't you leave your things on the porch and I'll get them when I do mine?"

He took the heavy skillet from her hand. When confronted directly with him like that, she could only stare at the buttons on his shirt. He hadn't fastened the top one. She could see a patch of sun-darkened skin and the edge of a dark curl. She shivered and stepped hastily backward.

"I can't let you do that without paying for your services. I don't imagine the sheriff will go so far as to pay for a prisoner's laundry."

He carried the empty skillet to the sink, and she breathed a sigh of relief as the distance between them widened. "You can help me haul water and empty the tubs." She almost said that she wasn't used to doing that without Betsy's help, but something made her hold her tongue. She wasn't ready to explain about Betsy yet. "That's the hardest part."

Mulloney pulled out a chair for her. His eyes held a questioning glint as she sat down. "That sounds fair, but I'm not sure a maiden lady ought to be doing for a man. It's not just shirts that need washing."

She colored. She actually grew red. She hadn't been embarrassed since she was fifteen years old. This was ridiculous. Firmly setting her foolish emotions in check, she reached for the stack of hotcakes. "Don't be foolish,

Mr. Mulloney. I've washed my younger brother's clothes for years. There might be women out there silly enough to sort a woman's underthings from the men's so they don't mingle in the water, but I haven't time for that nonsense. Whatever needs washing, put on the porch."

He sat across from her and helped himself to a generous stack of the hotcakes. "I didn't know you had a brother. Where is he now?"

She couldn't say "Cutlerville, Ohio." Then he'd know she knew who he was. She sliced a neat wedge in the steaming stack of hotcakes. "He's back East learning to be a newspaperman."

"Any other brothers and sisters?"

He was bound to hear about Betsy sooner or later. Janice shrugged. "Two sisters. One is staying with friends this summer. The other is going to be married shortly."

He looked around with curiosity. "They live here?"

She was beginning to get annoyed with this line of questioning. "Betsy does. How about you, Mr. Mulloney? Any brothers and sisters?"

He chewed his hotcakes slowly, hesitating over the answer. He found himself inordinately relieved to know that the schoolteacher was staying here alone for the moment. He'd heard something of the sort back in town, but he'd wanted to verify it for himself. She was looking at him now as if he were a particularly repulsive specimen of cockroach, but he didn't think she found him unattractive. He'd apparently just grazed too close to a subject she didn't want to talk about. She'd evened the score by asking about his family.

"I come from a family of four boys," he replied evasively. The fact that he'd grown up with only two of his three brothers didn't have to be mentioned.

"That should have made your father a proud man."

Was that a note of sarcasm he heard? Peter gave her a sharp look, but she was serenely cutting her pancakes into tatters. He had the feeling this woman didn't particularly like men. "My mother would have liked it better if there'd been a few girls."

She smiled faintly at that, whether recognizing it as the riposte it was or not, he couldn't tell. He was having difficulty balancing the sharpness of her wit against his lust for her body. He was used to separating the two. The women who usually decorated his bed didn't have much more going for them than big breasts and long legs. He wasn't inclined to talk to women who considered themselves his equal, but when he did, he generally didn't consider them as candidates for his bed. He couldn't say he was attracted to the schoolteacher's rather sour outlook on life, but her attitude did add a little spice to the contest. He really needed to find some way to get between her sheets soon. He could scarcely keep his eyes away from the slight V formed by her unbuttoned collar.

They both managed to get through breakfast without revealing more of themselves than necessary. Peter thought their relationship might be like two caged dogs sniffing around each other and waiting for the other to make the first move. He wasn't certain how dogs decided whether to fight or hump, but he definitely hoped to make it the latter.

A little while later Peter was slightly disconcerted to discover that he was expected to attend church services since all of his workmen had abandoned him for the Sabbath. He hadn't seen the inside of a church since he'd left home, and these weren't exactly the kind of churches he attended. When the schoolteacher offered to take him to her church, he almost declined in favor of working on the school by himself. Instead, seeing her all fancied up in hat and gloves, he warily agreed and went to fetch his wrinkled coat and cravat.

Walking down the street beside Miss Janice Harrison, schoolmarm, Peter gradually felt the collar around his neck tighten. Everyone in town turned to greet her as they entered town. All the women looked at him with knowing glances. The men restrained themselves to soft snickers and quickly hidden grins.

They thought he was courting her. Peter saw his error immediately. He gave the schoolteacher's composed oval face a hasty glance. He couldn't tell what she was thinking.

But he knew—as certainly as the sun rose in the morning—that this woman could not be had for anything less than a ring around her finger.

And a noose around his neck.

# *Eight*

"Miss Harrison! I understand you've been entertaining our resident convict." The good-looking cowboy bowed ostentatiously over Janice's hand, sending Peter a mischievous look that would have better suited a twelve-year-old boy than a grown man.

Janice primly removed her gloved hand from his. "Kyle, I'll tell Carmen you're misbehaving again. Mr. Mulloney hasn't been convicted of anything."

The cowboy didn't look a bit abashed as he tilted his ten-gallon hat back on his head and grinned. "Now you do know he's Daniel's brother, Jenny? You and Evie being close, you got to know about Daniel."

The sudden silence that ensued didn't precisely answer his question, but Kyle drew his own conclusions and gave a soft whistle. "Well, now. It seems the two of you have got a lot to talk about. See you later." With a broad grin and a swaggering stride, Kyle headed for the church doors.

Peter broke the silence first. "Who was that?" he demanded, watching the cowboy swagger away, wondering if it would do any good to shoot him. The man had been all too familiar with the schoolteacher, and certainly more than conversant with his own connections.

"Kyle Harding, Jason's younger brother," Janice answered simply as she walked toward the church.

"How do you know Evie and Daniel?" Peter didn't think he wanted to hear the answer to this. Evie was his brother Daniel's adopted sister and alter ego. The pair had been inseparable as children and were still close as adults.

He'd been doing fine thinking of the schoolteacher as just another stranger who'd crossed his path, one for whom he held little or no responsibility. He could have taken her to bed and headed off for New Mexico as soon as the loan was in his pocket without a qualm. It began to dawn a little too forcefully on him that he may have underestimated the situation.

"That's a long story." She stepped inside the church and found her pew without making any attempt to explain further.

He was afraid to sit by her. He didn't want the entire town writing Daniel and telling him he was seeing a schoolteacher, particularly if that schoolteacher happened to be a friend of Daniel's and Evie's. Why hadn't it occurred to him earlier that Daniel and Evie had once lived in this town, that they had friends here?

Probably because it hadn't mattered before. All he'd expected to do was ride in, obtain a loan from one of those friends of Daniel's, and ride out again. Now he was in the company of a respectable spinster the entire town had probably been trying to marry off for years, and the whole damned town knew who he was. Hell, he couldn't have walked into the trap more surely if he'd planned on it.

He couldn't do much about it now. He couldn't marry anybody until he had that loan and the gold mine in his hands. He'd been looking for a wife. The schoolteacher might do, but she might take exception to living in the wildness of a New Mexico mining camp. He would just have to unravel himself from this knot as quickly as he could, get the school built, get his loan, and hightail it out of here. If the Hardings actually owned the bank, he shouldn't have any difficulty getting the loan right here rather than going on to Natchez. Maybe when he came back to pay it off he could take another look at the teacher.

When the service ended, Peter was anxious to get back to work, but the townspeople seemed more interested in gathering to gossip. He cornered a couple of the men supposed to be volunteering their labors, and they gave him vague answers as to when they would get up to the schoolhouse. Frustrated, he looked around for Janice and found her talking to the pregnant girl from the mercantile.

Their conversation seemed intense, but he wandered up to them anyway. He caught the girl saying, "No, Bobby was with me all evening. He doesn't do those kind of things anymore," but something in her face told Peter she was covering up for her drunken husband. Remembering Janice's calm statement that Bobby Fairweather tended to take out his hostilities on her, Peter understood the reason for the lie.

"Good morning, Mrs. Fairweather. You're looking in fine fettle today." He doffed his hat and bowed politely at the flustered young girl.

She gave him a beaming smile. "Mr. Mulloney, you do look a sight in that fancy cravat. Is Miss Harrison seeing to your Sunday dinner?"

He lifted an eyebrow in the teacher's direction and she gave a curt nod. "It seems there is no rest for the wicked, Mrs. Fairweather. It doesn't seem quite fair that Miss Harrison should be punished for my sins, but there it is. Where is your husband this fine morning? I need to have a word with him."

"Fine" wasn't exactly the word for the morning after a storm. The street was a sea of mud, and horses splashing through puddles threw up a constant wave of wet and dirt to be dodged. Janice glared at this blatant falsehood, but he didn't seem to notice.

"I was just telling Miss Harrison, Bobby is a bit under the weather this morning. Could I give him a message?" The anxiety was back in the girl's eyes again.

"Tell him I need some help in repairing Miss Harrison's windows, and the sheriff promised Bobby knew how to do it. I'll be up at the schoolhouse this afternoon. He can come by there to get me."

The girl flushed and nodded and soon hurried away. Janice sent him a discouraging look.

"That wasn't necessary, you know." She started away

from the church crowd, looking neither to the right nor left.

"If he's going to shoot them out, he's going to learn to put them back." Peter fell into step with her.

"There were others involved. Mr. Powell will see that they make reparations."

"Yeah, but will Powell see that it won't happen again? You could have been hurt."

"I told you, I know better than to go into the front room on Saturday night. You can't lasso every cowboy in town. You embarrassed poor Ellen. She has enough on her hands right now."

Peter couldn't believe they were arguing right here in full view of all of Main Street. Where he came from, women didn't do that. He reached to untie his cravat. "How do you know Daniel and Evie?"

Janice had had plenty of time to think her way around that one, and her response came easily. "My brother is working on Daniel's newspaper. Evie's family lives here. Kyle's wife is her cousin. She visits frequently."

"You should have told me you knew Daniel." That was an idiotic thing to say. He knew it as soon as he said it. The look she threw him confirmed it.

"Then you should have told me you were his brother." She gathered up her long skirt and stalked ahead of him.

There didn't seem to be any answer to this impasse. Peter shoved his tie in his pocket and threw his coat over the porch railing when they reached the house. He headed up the hill to the schoolhouse when he heard Janice enter the kitchen and slam the door. It didn't make sense to argue over a man living a thousand miles away—especially a man neither one of them knew very well. He'd obviously been working in the hot sun too long. He didn't know what the schoolteacher's excuse was.

She fixed chicken and dumplings and spring peas and corn pudding for dinner. By the time he finished eating, Peter was ready to bury the hatchet, but there were men outside already arguing over the best way to repair the front window and others were heading up the hill to the

schoolhouse. Peter shoved back his chair from the table
and gave Janice a look of apology.

"I hate to eat and run, but it looks like duty calls. I
don't want any harsh feelings between us. Why don't you
come up and help supervise this afternoon, get out in the
sun a little instead of working so hard in here?"

A faint smile crossed her lips. Her lips were naturally
pale, like her complexion. She really couldn't be called
pretty, but he didn't know what else to call her. Her gray,
piercing eyes turned her fair features into something more
arresting. When she smiled, she made his heart quake. He
couldn't remember a woman's smile ever doing that.

"You want me to fry my brains as you have yours? No,
thank you. I think I'll just stay in here and see that the
windows are replaced properly. I'll have a cold collation
when you're ready to eat."

He liked that thought. Slamming his hat on his head,
Peter wandered off to the work site, enjoying the idea of
a woman sitting at home, looking after the house, preparing a meal just for him. Now if he could just imagine her
lying in bed, waiting for him . . .

But that would mean marriage. He could see that now.
He had been so desperate for a woman he had almost
tricked himself into thinking an old-maid schoolteacher
might be willing to fool around a little. But she wasn't as
old as he had first thought, and she was a good deal more
innocent than he wanted. Warning sirens screeched in his
head.

When Bobby Fairweather finally showed up later that
afternoon, he was already halfway drunk. Peter gave him
a look of disgust. "You'd better get a hold of yourself,
Fairweather. You've got a wife and kid to look after now.
You can't be drinking like you're a free man."

The cowboy gave him a belligerent look and belched.
"What the hell do you know about it? She was the one
that got pregnant. If Holy Harding hadn't held a gun to
my head, I'd still be a free man today." He cackled slyly.
"You start fooling around with that schoolteacher, and

he'll have a gun to your head too. Only he's likely to shoot it instead of waiting for the preacher."

Peter had already got that impression from the sheriff. He didn't like it being reinforced now by this two-bit banty rooster. "Go get a hammer and start nailing that frame up there. They've already fixed the windows."

Fairweather frowned. "I don't like the way you said that. I didn't have nothin' to do with them windows. It wasn't me the sheriff arrested out there."

Peter walked off to yell at a man about to nail a board to another man's foot. With the danger averted, he turned and gave the ropy cowboy a look of disgust. "You want me to go in and talk to the men the sheriff arrested? What kind of story do you think they'll tell? Just keep away from the schoolteacher, understand? You go raise hell anywhere else you want to, but keep away from her."

Bobby growled something obscene and walked away without offering to join the others. Peter was just as happy that he was gone. He didn't need a drunk falling off the roof and putting a kink in his schedule.

The frame was up and the roof half done by the time Peter called a halt for the day. He gave the partially constructed building a look of satisfaction before he started back to the house. A few more days with this many men at his disposal and he could finish up and be out of here before the week ended. He hoped Jason Harding was on his way back from Houston by now.

Peter walked in to find Janice bent over a sewing machine, humming happily to herself. The late afternoon sun highlighted the soft blond tendrils escaping from her chignon, and he was struck by the exquisite portrait of vulnerability posed by her slender neck. When she looked up with happiness dancing in her eyes, he was struck by something a good deal more earthy. His loins strained against the fabric of his pants, and he had to walk to the window to keep his back to her.

"You keep this up, and you'll have the school better than new before the week's up," she chirruped. Peter gritted his teeth at her cheerfulness.

"You'll need to help us with the interior, tell us where to put the stove and what all you need in there."

"Shelves. I would dearly love some shelves for books. Not that we have any books, mind you, but someday . . ."

"Harding said he was bringing back books. Why don't you write Daniel for the ones you don't have? He's got a complete library at his disposal."

He sensed the stiffening of her posture even as the cheer went out of her voice. "I don't ask for charity, Mr. Mulloney. When the townspeople are ready to raise the funds to buy books, they'll raise the funds."

What put the starch in her, took it out of him. Peter turned around to meet her gaze. "That's a fool way of thinking, Miss Harrison. Daniel has enough money at his disposal to furnish an entire library and not miss it. Why should he keep it when he doesn't need it and you do?"

"As Daniel's brother, you are just as capable of funding a library if you so desire," she said sweetly, turning her back on him and walking out.

That drew the line where it belonged. He wasn't any more capable of asking for charity than she was. When he walked out five years ago, he had taken out every penny he had ever earned from Mulloney Enterprises. He wasn't likely to ask for more now.

Now that seduction was no longer a possibility, Peter found it easier to back his hostess into a verbal corner. He wanted to know more about the haughty Miss Harrison. She was more than attractive. She was hardworking. She could cook and keep house. So why in the name of all that was holy hadn't some man snatched her up years ago? He followed her into the kitchen, determined to find out.

"When I'm as rich as my father, I'll fund your library." He took the plates out of the cabinet. "But in return you're going to have to tell me why a woman with as many attributes as you hasn't ever married."

She didn't even bother looking at him as she sliced the cold chicken. "Because I have more brains than most women, Mr. Mulloney, and I know better than to shackle myself to some lying, no-account layabout. Does that answer your question?"

"I'm not sure it will win you a library. If you're as smart as you say you are, then you know the entire male population can't be burdened with those characteristics."

Her knife moved on to slice sharply through a loaf of bread. "No. Some are pigheaded and arrogant. Others are self-righteous idiots. Then there are those who think they're God's gift to women. Should I go on?"

He smiled wryly. "I think I get the idea. Does that mean you're so perfect that you never get lonely in the middle of the night?"

She set out the platters of meat and bread and the left-over apple pie. "That's none of your business, Mr. Mulloney. I've seen enough suffering in my lifetime to know when I'm well off."

He held out her chair, and after she finally took it, he seated himself across from her. "There aren't many women who would forgo the pleasures of matrimony, Miss Harrison. You are taking an isolated stand."

Those piercing eyes lifted to fasten firmly on his face. "I never said I wouldn't marry, Mr. Mulloney. I meant that I'd have to be offered one whale of a lot of money before I'd consider it."

That neatly put the subject in a package and wrapped a bow around it.

# Nine

Janice knew she shouldn't have said it the minute the words were out of her mouth. Peter Mulloney no doubt had women chasing after him for his money since he was twelve years old. Her comment would give him a thorough disgust of her and neatly dissolve any fragile hopes she might have had of leading him into matrimony.

Well, the hopes had been built on little more than the desire she had seen in his eyes. They had been foolish hopes from the very first. All he wanted was what all men wanted, and that certainly wasn't the legal commitment of marriage. At least she had the courage to be honest. That was more than he had.

He looked as if he had been struck by lightning. Janice felt an odd sense of satisfaction that she had said something that had really hit him where it hurt. Generally, men were too full of themselves to believe anything she said or did mattered. She picked up her empty plate and carried it to the sink.

The action must have stirred him back to the moment. He helped himself to another piece of chicken. "Does Jason Harding know your opinion of men, Miss Harrison?"

He was too quick by half. Janice poured hot water into the basin and added enough cold to be comfortable. "He never asked me, Mr. Mulloney."

She thought she heard him chuckle. She'd never known him to even express humor before. He scarcely knew how to smile. She turned and gave him a suspicious look.

He met her look impudently. "Remind me not to ever ask your opinion unless I'm ready to hear it."

For a minute she almost managed a smile. He made her feel warm inside, as if he understood her. And then she realized the impossibility of such a notion, and she turned back to her dishwater. "I'll do that, Mr. Mulloney."

Surprisingly the conversation didn't dwindle from there. Janice wondered if her declaration had released him from some obligation he had felt toward her. He seemed more congenial than at any time since she had met him. When he asked her what she had been sewing, she felt no hesitation in answering.

"I'm making new curtains for Betsy's room. I want to surprise her when she returns. She wants those ruffled kind that Melissa Harding has in her bedroom. My only problem is that this place doesn't come equipped with curtain rods and I'm not certain how to go about hanging them."

Peter pushed his chair back and carried his plate over to the sink. "I don't know much about curtains, but show me what you want and I'll try to figure out how to hang them."

She was slightly embarrassed to show him the plain muslin nailed to the walls in Betsy's room, but he didn't seem to notice anything odd about the arrangement. When she explained how the new curtains were supposed to be gathered up on a rod, he caught on quickly.

"You just need some kind of stick to go through that pocket you've made there, and then the stick needs to hang on some kind of bracket, right?" He showed her what he meant by cupping his hand against the wall and balancing one of Betsy's paintbrushes in it.

Janice nodded dubiously. "I think so. Mr. Holt probably sells the rods down at the mercantile. Do you think he'll have the bracket things?"

"There's no need to give Mr. Holt your money. I bet I can whittle out what you need from some of that wood out back. Let me take a look at what you've got."

If anyone had ever told her that the arrogant, fabulously wealthy Peter Mulloney would be sitting in her front room whittling curtain rods, she would have laughed herself to death. But as she carefully ran the gaily-colored gingham through her sewing machine, there he sat at her hearth, shaving away at a piece of wood. He seemed quite at peace with himself, and not at all the impatient, irritable gentleman she had seen back in Cutlerville, Ohio.

The sight of a handsome male at her hearth was doing terrible things to her insides however, and Janice tried to keep her attention on her work. But as companionable as their silence was, she couldn't resist this chance to find out a little more about this man who so easily filled her empty evenings.

"Once you've discussed your business with Jason, what are your plans, Mr. Mulloney? Will you be going back to Ohio?"

He cast her a swift glance, but she didn't see it. "I've not been back there in years, Miss Harrison. I'm thinking of making my home in New Mexico." He wasn't about to tell anyone about the gold, not until it was his. He'd seen disaster strike too often once the whispers of gold escaped. He noted with interest, however, that she wasn't close enough to Daniel to know that Peter had left home years ago.

"New Mexico? Santa Fe? I've heard that's an interesting town."

"The mountains. You ought to see them in the spring. They're covered in flowers and wildlife, and a man can look as far as the eye can see and not find another human being."

"Sounds lonely. I find it hard to picture a city man living like that for long."

"I don't find it hard at all. I had a place up there for the winter, raised mustangs. Never saw a neighbor from one day to the next. Can't say I'd do it for a lifetime, but it suits me fine right now. What about you? Do you like teaching out here where the cowboys shoot up the town every Saturday night?"

"I like living where people respect me for what I do, and I can make something of myself. A woman can't do that easily back East."

It seemed to him that women got plenty of respect back East, but Peter had the feeling he was missing something here. He began sanding the rod he was working on. "It seems to me there are more rich men back East than out here."

"I never said I was looking for a rich man, Mr. Mulloney. I'm perfectly capable of looking after myself. You're the one who thought I ought to be married."

Her answer was quite complacent and not the least bit angry. He found it hard to believe that any woman didn't consider marriage her lifetime goal, but he didn't mean to argue. She did seem to be getting along quite well without a man of her own, whereas he grew mighty tired of living without a woman. The difference might be that she didn't know what it felt like to have a man in her bed. It gave him something to think about while the conversation drifted desultorily on.

They were trying out the new curtains and rod in Betsy's bedroom when the knock sounded at the front door. Startled, Janice froze. All she could think of was that it was the middle of the night and she had a man in the house. The man in question gave her an impatient look when she didn't hook the rod in the bracket. Seeing her expression, he peeked between the curtains to see who the visitor was.

"From the shape of her, I'd say it was your friend from the mercantile. Want me to see what she wants?"

Janice instantly recovered her aplomb. "No! Heavens no. Ellen is a good girl, but she gossips dreadfully. Stay in here. Don't let her know you're in the house."

She fled the room, leaving Peter helpless to do anything else but sit on the bed for fear he would make a noise that would alert the visitor of his presence.

Janice flung open the door and caught Ellen's arm, pulling her into the house. "Ellen! Whatever are you doing out at this hour?" A dozen possibilities danced through her mind, but only one was logical. Ellen's reply confirmed her suspicion.

"You haven't seen Bobby, have you? Mr. Harding said

it would be all right for him to stay in town with me now that I'm so close to my time, but he didn't come home tonight."

"Sit down. Get yourself off your feet. Let me make you some hot tea. You haven't been all over town looking for that scoundrel, have you?" Janice pushed her guest into a chair and looked quickly about to be certain no evidence of Peter's presence lay about. The whittling knife lay by the hearth along with a clump of shavings. There wasn't any way she could disguise them. She'd have to think up a story if Ellen noticed.

Ellen looked uneasy. "I just stopped by. I don't need anything. It's just . . . Well, Bobby was complaining about that Mr. Mulloney. And I thought . . . You know how Bobby is. He's got this quick temper . . ."

Janice patted her shoulder. "Mr. Mulloney can take care of himself, I assure you. And as much trouble as he's in with the sheriff right now, he won't hurt Bobby if he can help it. Don't you worry about a thing. Bobby's probably just out with the boys somewhere. He'll be home soon." She wanted to offer the girl the bed in Betsy's room. Bobby's temper was notorious, but so far he hadn't been known to take it out on Ellen. Normally, she wouldn't take any chances, but she couldn't see any easy way to get Peter out of the bedroom so Ellen could go in.

Ellen struggled to her feet. "I'm sure you're right. I just worry all the time these days. Isn't that silly? Mrs. Danner says it's because of the baby. I sure will be glad when it's born. I'm sure Bobby will be glad too." She shrugged slightly with embarrassment. "He can't . . . you know. Not while I'm like this."

Janice was afraid she very much did know, but she didn't feel inclined to comment upon it. After all, she was supposed to be an old maid. She hugged Ellen's shoulders instead. "Bobby will be so proud when he sees that baby, he'll have that new house built in no time. Do you need me to walk you home? I don't like for you to be out alone like this."

Ellen giggled. "Then you would have to walk home

alone, and I'd be obliged to walk back with you. We'd be walking all night."

Janice got the girl to the front door, but Ellen wasn't eager to leave yet. They talked a few minutes more, standing on the porch in the warm June air. Most of the town had retired for the night. Being Sunday, even the saloon was closed. Janice breathed a sigh of relief when she noticed a familiar figure striding down the street.

"There's Sheriff Powell. Let me get him to help you home. Then we won't have to walk back and forth all night." Reassured by Ellen's giggle, she hurried down the path to signal the sheriff.

Powell immediately hurried toward her. "Anything wrong, Miz Harrison? Did that Mulloney fellow go back to your lean-to tonight? I been looking around for him."

"He was helping me hang curtains, Sheriff. I'm sure he's sleeping by now. Would you escort Ellen home? We got to talking and it's kind of late and I hate for her to be out there alone."

Five years of teaching school had not only taught her how to speak with authority, but to cover up what wasn't being said with a firmness that left her audience completely convinced she'd answered their question. She'd covered many gaps in her education that way. It served her well tonight.

Powell took off his hat and offered his arm to the girl standing in the shadows of the porch. "Come along, Miz Ellen. Let's get you on home. Your fella will be wondering where you are."

As they walked away, Janice could hear Ellen rhapsodizing over how hard Bobby had worked today and telling the sheriff that her husband was no doubt sound asleep in bed already. If that was true love, Janice wanted no part of it. If she were Ellen Fairweather, she'd have the sheriff out looking for her drunken sot of a husband and hauling him off to jail for criminal neglect, at the very least.

But she would never be as naive as Ellen Fairweather, so the point was moot. She entered the house and firmly latched the door behind her. It was time to call it a night. Just because she had taken to staying up late, filling the empty nights with work, didn't mean she ought to be entertaining a man like Peter Mulloney while doing it. She marched promptly to the tiny front bedroom.

And found Peter Mulloney sound asleep on Betsy's narrow cot.

She stared at him in perplexity. He was too large for the cot. His boots hung over the edge. He was lying flat on his back with his hands crossed over his chest as if he had just been lying there contemplating the ceiling while waiting for Ellen to leave. If he turned over, he would fall off the bed and flat on his face. But he must have been exhausted to fall asleep so quickly, and she really didn't have the heart to wake him and throw him out. She'd heard the rumbling of thunder when she was outside. It didn't seem quite fair to wake him and send him to sleep on the porch again.

The sheriff thought he was sleeping in the lean-to. Knowing Powell's regular habits, he'd head on to his own house now that he'd made his rounds. Who was to know or care if Mulloney fell asleep in Betsy's bed? Common sense told her he wasn't harming anyone.

It wasn't common sense making her nervous as a June bug when Janice went to her own room to prepare for bed. She didn't like the idea of a man sleeping in the other room. That's all it was, she told herself. But she couldn't get the image of Peter Mulloney's sprawling length out of her mind as she pulled on her nightgown. What if he got up in the middle of the night?

He wouldn't do that. He was a gentleman. He wasn't a crude youth to take advantage of a helpless woman. And she was far from helpless, anyway. She'd been helpless at fifteen, but she wasn't now. Grimly she shoved a chair under her doorknob and checked the shotgun under her bed. She'd never had to use it, but Jason had shown her how.

Oddly enough, she didn't have any difficulty going to sleep this time. The knowledge that Mulloney slept in the next room was somehow comforting, providing a security she hadn't felt in years. She drifted off to sleep as soon as her head hit the pillow.

She shot right out of that pillow the moment the fire bell began its excited clamor.

Running to the window, she checked the partially finished schoolhouse first. No flames leapt from the rafters, and she breathed a momentary sigh of relief. The rain the other night had made the possibility of a flash fire less likely, but the wind from the approaching storm didn't bode well. She reached for the gown she had discarded a few hours before. This time, she meant to go out properly attired.

She heard Mulloney's boots hitting the floor in the other room. She had almost forgotten about him. She hurriedly buttoned her bodice over her nightgown and pulled the chair from under the doorknob. He was already heading for the front door when she caught him.

"Out the back!" she whispered, as if someone would hear her. "I told the sheriff you were in the lean-to."

He nodded curtly and turned in the other direction. Seeing her disheveled attire, he frowned. "You stay here. I'll send someone back if they need more help."

"Don't be ridiculous." As if that were argument enough, Janice hurried back to find her shoes. It was too late in her life for any man to take to ordering her around now.

He didn't hang around to argue more. Giving her a steely frown, he hurriedly strode for the back door.

By the time Janice was appropriately dressed, most of the excitement was over. As she hurried out in the street, she could see the dying flames of the fire in the old shack on the outskirts of town. The men on the fire wagon pumped water over the last burning timbers. There hadn't been enough to the shack to burn for long.

She knew some of the town men gathered at the shack on Sunday nights. She'd been told the old man who lived there sold illegal liquor. A sudden frisson of horror struck her as she remembered Ellen's tearful plea. That was just the sort of place Bobby would frequent. And there could have been others. She hurried toward the silent crowd.

They carried out a blanket-wrapped body just as Janice arrived. She clutched the arm of the woman nearest her. As much as she despised Bobby, she couldn't wish him dead for Ellen's sake. Even as she thought this, she saw Bobby helping wind up the fire wagon hose. He was all right then. Janice turned to the woman next to her.

"Do they know who it is? Or what happened?"

"It's Old Man Samuel. Sheriff says the place smells of kerosene. He thinks somebody lit it."

As the other woman spoke, Janice looked up in time to see Sheriff Powell clap a pair of handcuffs on a tall, familiar figure at the front of the crowd.

Powell was arresting the only suspected arsonist in the county—Peter Mulloney.

# *Ten*

Stunned, Janice didn't move as Powell jostled his prisoner past the expectant crowd. A man had died this night. The town would require justice. She imagined a cloud of righteous satisfaction rising from the people around her as they watched Peter Mulloney hauled off to jail. He wasn't one of them. There would be no weeping widow or grieving children to mourn his departure when the jury found him guilty and ordered him hung. She could almost hear their thoughts as Mulloney was dragged to his fate. There had been two fires since the stranger had arrived in town. That was evidence enough for them.

As the last of the fire was quenched, the crowd dissipated. The woman whose arm Janice clutched looked at her queerly, then gently disengaged herself. She walked off, leaving Janice standing there alone.

She had to do something. She couldn't just stand here and let everyone think Mulloney had murdered an old man in his bed. It didn't even make logical sense. What in heaven's name would a man like Peter Mulloney get out of murdering some old man he didn't even know? Maybe she could use logic to get him released.

She knew better than that. Logic didn't explain the wildfires that swept the town or the floods that inundated it in spring. Logic didn't explain the senseless use of guns on Saturday night. Logic explained very little of life out here on the plains of Texas. Vengeance was the only recognized logic. No one would question why a man would set fire to a shack. The shack burned and a man died.

That was fact. Someone had to pay for it. Mulloney was convenient.

Janice wondered how soon Jason Harding would come home. He wasn't likely to get caught up in the emotional melodrama that would seize the town now that the scent of a hanging hung in the air. She could talk to Jason. She shivered at the thought of how he would take it when he learned Mulloney had been sleeping in Betsy's bedroom. He wouldn't believe her claim of innocence for a minute. Neither would anybody else. But Jason would more likely keep his mouth shut about it.

But she would lose her job whether she told Jason or the sheriff. Female schoolteachers did not allow men to spend the night in their houses. That was another fact of life. To give Mulloney the alibi he needed, she would have to lose her job. She would have to leave Mineral Springs entirely. Betsy would never see her new curtains.

Janice had been terrified more times in her life than she could count, but these last years had been relatively comfortable ones. She didn't want to go back to the terror of living from one day to the next, never knowing where the next meal would come from or if she would have a roof to keep over their heads. Panic froze her insides, as it always did at times like this, and she walked woodenly toward home.

It wouldn't do any good to go to the sheriff now. Maybe they would turn up a new suspect before dawn. Maybe Peter would tell them a believable lie. Maybe he would tell them the truth and they would come to her for corroboration and everyone would believe them. Maybe pigs could fly.

There wasn't a chance of getting back to sleep now. She went in and filled up a bucket and began scrubbing the kitchen floor. She could show them the wrinkles on Betsy's bed. She would show them the new curtains and the wood shavings on the hearth and they would have to believe her. They would have to believe Mulloney was innocent and let him go. They wouldn't have to believe the same of her.

The panic she had experienced as a pregnant unmarried fifteen-year-old came back as clearly as if it were yesterday. Janice vividly remembered the buckets of tears her mother had wept, the stony anguish on her father's face, the uncertain looks she had received from her younger siblings when she broke the news of her fall from grace.

To hide her shame, her parents had made a disastrous move to Cutlerville, a move that eventually destroyed the lives of everyone in her family, right before Janice's eyes. She had watched her mother starve to feed her children, watched her father grow old and weak in the years of scraping by after that. She had spent years bending over backward to make some kind of reparation to her brother and sister for the misery she had caused. Only to have it happen all over again like this.

Hot tears hit her hand as she scrubbed—tears ten years had failed to heal. She would never rid herself of the hideous memories of those years of poverty and guilt. She wept harder at that thought, wept for the child she had never been, the parents she would never see again, the years of deprivation and suffering that followed their deaths. She had tried so desperately to keep her little family together. And she had succeeded. She had succeeded despite everything. They were all healthy and nearly grown now. They would be happy.

Except for Betsy. Wouldn't God ever forgive her for that one mistake? Why did He have to make Betsy suffer for what her mother had done? It wasn't fair. Life wasn't fair. Why should any of them have to suffer for what was as much Betsy's father's fault as anyone's?

The thought of Betsy's father made Janice sit up and wipe her tears. They'd both been young and foolish, she more so than him. He'd known precisely what he was doing, but she'd only been madly in love and eager to display her affections. Things went too far too fast. She had tried to stop him, but he was older and stronger. She remembered the piercing pain, the helpless struggle, and the humiliation. But when he was done with her, she remembered her foolish pride that this handsome man had chosen a girl like her for his wife. Except they never quite made it to the altar.

And she placed that blame squarely on the shoulders of Artemis Mulloney, Peter's father. Janice hastily wiped her face with her sleeve and tried to remember she was a grown woman now. Artemis Mulloney was a crippled old man. He couldn't ever hurt her again. He didn't even know she existed. All he had done was fire Betsy's father from his job on the railroad. Actually, he fired most of the employees so he could hire cheaper labor—Negroes from the South and indigent immigrants. The town they'd been living in was a railroad town. It had become little more than a ghost town after that. And Stephen had left for parts unknown along with dozens of others.

Leaving her with Betsy, an aching gap in her middle that could never be filled, and a terror that never quite went away. Stephen had taken all the joy from her life that day. She'd never known happiness since. These last years she had learned contentment, and that had been enough. It had been more than enough. The peace of having a roof over her head and a regular income and the respect of her neighbors was sufficient to keep her going from one day to the next. She didn't know what she would do if she had that taken away from her again. And taken away from her because of Artemis Mulloney's son.

Janice got off the floor and dusted her skirt. She walked across the still wet floor to get hot water from the stove and pull out the tin tub. She would take a bath and put on fresh clothes and think about it later.

While she bathed, she heated more water. She had promised to wash Mulloney's clothes today. He would need fresh clothes in jail. She could do that much for him.

She fixed breakfast and wondered who the sheriff had cooking for his prisoners today. No one came to collect a meal from her.

No one came as she filled the wash bucket and scrubbed the light-colored clothes. Would Mulloney really keep quiet about where he'd been last night? It didn't seem possible. It wasn't within the realm of her experience with men. She methodically wrung out the light clothes and hung them on the line, then started on the dark. She had to rummage through Mulloney's saddlebags to find his things. They were pitifully few.

She hung up his long johns in the lean-to where she hung her underclothes. The heat would dry them just as quickly as the sun.

By noon, Janice had come to the decision to wire Daniel. She didn't like to disturb Georgina, but Daniel had to know. Surely they knew some fancy lawyer in Houston or somewhere who could come out and put an end to this farce. There really wasn't any evidence against Mulloney. Surely they couldn't hang him on the basis of nothing? That thought brought back the edge of panic, and she carefully blanked her mind and returned to her routine.

She ate one of the biscuits she had made for breakfast that no one had come to collect. Her stomach wasn't really prepared for food, but she got it down anyway. She tucked her hair neatly beneath her hat, donned her spectacles and gloves, and started down the street. She had the appearance of a very proper, very respectable old-maid schoolteacher. No one would believe she was a weeping, hysterical fifteen-year-old inside.

She stopped at the grocery to order some more flour and sugar sent up to the house to replenish her supply. Talking hushed as Janice entered, but one of her older students rushed up to whisper that she thought the prisoner was the handsomest man she had ever seen and she didn't believe for a minute that he did it.

That gave her some indication of which way the wind blew. Janice nodded politely and inquired after the girl's mother, then sailed out to visit the pharmacy, where she partook of a sarsaparilla to quench her thirst. There she was confronted by Mrs. Danner, who declared Mulloney ought to be hung immediately and demanded that Janice agree with her in front of a store full of attentive ears. Janice smiled politely, informed her antagonist that the Ten Commandments said "Thou shalt not kill," and walked away. Ambiguity was rapidly becoming her forte.

She didn't want to wire Daniel unless absolutely necessary, but it was becoming more and more clear that absolute necessity had arrived. She didn't dare look to the sheriff's hole-in-the-wall office and jail, fearful she might see Mulloney's accusing eyes looking out at her. He was keeping quiet. The least she could do was see that he got the help he deserved.

She ran into Jason Harding just before she walked into the telegraph office. So grateful was she to see him that Janice grasped Jason's shirt sleeve and looked up at him with genuine relief. She had never touched him before, scarcely ever looked him in the face, and his reaction was one of shock when she did.

"Jenny, are you all right? My word, I had no idea this had hit you so hard or I would have been out to see you sooner. What did that bastard do? So help me, if he hurt you—"

Janice shook her head violently and interrupted. "No. No, that's not it. They're going to hang an innocent man, Jason. You've got to stop them. I was just going to wire Daniel. Mr. Mulloney could not possibly have done it."

Jason relaxed slightly and patted her hand. "I know he's been friendly to you and all, Jenny, but the fact is, he could have done it. There's no one to say he was in that lean-to all night sleeping. It's almighty suspicious that there were two fires in town directly after he came here. I don't want to believe it either, but the sheriff has to do his duty. I'm sure a jury will consider all the evidence."

Deflated, Janice pulled her hand away. "Samuel could have fallen asleep with a cigarette in his hand. He could have got in an argument with some of the drunks that hang around over there. Almost anything could have happened, Jason. You can't pin simple coincidence on Mr. Mulloney."

"It wasn't simple coincidence that Mulloney was the only one in the vicinity of the schoolhouse when it caught on fire. I don't believe in coincidences, Jenny. Let me help you word that telegram to Daniel. I think his brother is in a heap of trouble."

He caught her elbow to escort her in, but she couldn't do it. Georgina was expecting their second baby. Daniel would be torn apart wanting to come down here to rescue his brother and needing to stay with his wife. She owed it to Daniel to tell the truth. Daniel had rescued her when her whole world was falling in. She hated to have to turn to him again. She hated being obligated to anyone. But she was obligated to Daniel, and she couldn't repay that debt by putting his brother through the mockery of a jury trial.

"No, Jason. I can't worry Daniel and Georgina like that. Come with me to the sheriff's office. I only mean to tell this story once."

She didn't even ask to see the prisoner when she swept into the sheriff's narrow office with Jason trailing behind her. If she were Peter Mulloney, when that jail door opened she would run from this town as fast as she could go. She wouldn't be seeing him again.

Mentally, as she faced Sheriff Powell, Janice counted the coins she kept in her cookie jar and the savings she had in the bank. There should be just enough for her to make it to Natchez and Betsy. What she would do after she got there, she would worry about later. She didn't have a doubt in her mind that she was destroying her life and her home by rescuing Peter Mulloney. She despised herself as much as she despised him for having to do it. She just kept telling herself she owed Daniel.

"Sheriff, I don't mean to cause anybody any trouble, but you're holding the wrong man," she said, facing him with determination. "If that fire really was set, the arsonist is still on the loose, and I can't allow that to continue."

The sheriff looked her over carefully, then looked to Jason hovering behind her. He hawked and spit a wad of tobacco juice at the spittoon. "Miss Harrison, I believed Mulloney was as innocent as you did the last time this happened, but I can't let him go just 'cause hc's used a few honeyed words and made you think he's something he's not. I got a wire from Daniel saying the last time he'd heard, his brother was in New Mexico. That might not even be Peter Mulloney in there. When I asked him a few simple questions Daniel wanted me to ask, he couldn't answer them."

"Couldn't, or wouldn't?" Janice asked wearily. "The man is precisely who he says he is. I can positively identify him. You forget, I'm from Cutlerville too. He's simply protecting his family, like he's protecting me. I can't say as I've met any other man with that much arrogant stupidity in my life, but there's no doubt that he's a Mulloney. He fell asleep in Betsy's bed last night while Ellen Fairweather was over at the house. We'd been hanging new curtains, and it was late, and I didn't have the heart to wake him. He was right there, sound asleep, when the fire bell went off."

Janice heard Jason's angry intake of breath, saw the doubt in the sheriff's eyes, and knew it was going to happen all over again. The last time, she had been guilty as sin. This time, she was only trying to do a good deed. But people believed in sin a lot easier than good. They wouldn't believe Peter was hanging curtains. They wouldn't believe an old-maid schoolteacher would allow a man to sleep in her sister's bed. And if tongues started wagging fast enough, they just might assume Betsy was just exactly what she was: a bastard. She would have to get out of town before that happened.

The sheriff asked flatly, "You willin' to testify to that in court?"

Janice sighed and held her gaze on her neat white gloves. "If it comes to that."

"Go ask the bastard for his version of the story," Jason ordered from behind her. "That one's too farfetched for him to make up."

"He claims he slept in the lean-to," the sheriff protested.

"Tell him the schoolteacher's in here telling different."

The sheriff nodded at the wisdom of that and disappeared through the doorway to the jail. Janice didn't turn around to look at Jason. He was generally a fair man, but he had the prejudices of most men. She could see his point of view. A healthy, virile man did not normally hang curtains for a young woman without reason. And to a man, there could only be one reason. Right now, she couldn't even think of another one herself. She didn't know why Peter Mulloney had helped her hang those curtains. Maybe he had thought he was seducing her. Maybe that's why he had the sense to keep his mouth shut. She would never understand the male mind.

Raised voices came from the other room. Jason took a step toward them, heard the angry clang of tin against iron followed by normal tones, and waited. The sheriff appeared a few minutes later, shaking his head.

"Mule-headed son of . . ." He stopped, glanced apologetically at Janice, and continued, "He tried to tell me she was just protecting him because of Daniel. When I said she was prepared to testify in court, he got kind of upset. Then he asked if she'd have to go to court if he told the truth now. I promised she wouldn't if she didn't want to. Then he told the same exact damned story as she did."

He talked as if she weren't here. Janice was used to that, and she was too emotionally drained to care right now. Peter had verified her story. That was that. She turned around to leave.

Jason caught her arm. "I'm sorry, Jenny. I shouldn't have let them send him up there to work on the school. I just didn't think . . ."

"Just leave it at that, Jason. You just didn't think." Janice shook him off and tried to get around him. He just didn't think an old-maid schoolteacher would be attracted to a young good-looking man like Mulloney. He just didn't think she had a life or feelings of her own. He just didn't think she was anything more than a machine like his fancy typewriter. She was the one who had let him think that. She couldn't blame the man.

"Jenny . . ." An uncertain plea tinged Jason's voice as she skirted around him and opened the door.

Janice didn't look back. She had overreached herself. She could have had Jason if she'd really put her mind to it. But no, she had dallied with delusions of marrying the fabulously wealthy Peter Mulloney. She had encouraged him, if she was truthful with herself. She had been prideful and greedy and now she reaped her just reward.

For she knew as sure as God made little green apples that the gossip would be all over town before day's end: the schoolteacher had slept with the prisoner.

# *Eleven*

Peter felt the sweat pooling under his arms as he walked out of the makeshift courtroom. He disguised the damp by keeping his arms down and bending his neck to don his hat. He straightened and nodded politely at a staring young girl as he passed by.

He felt the stares everywhere. He dusted an invisible dust mote off his freshly laundered coat sleeve. His garments had arrived that way at the jail: all scrubbed and smelling of fresh air, pressed and folded neater than any laundry had ever done them. He'd accepted it as the farewell it was and hadn't tried to contact the teacher in any way since.

The trial had been a farce, just as he had known it would be. He hadn't any money to pay a lawyer, so he had been assigned a young man fresh out of school. There wasn't much either side could say. Once Jason had stood up in front of the courtroom and repeated the teacher's account of the evening, the prosecution lost all interest. With Jason Harding on the defense side, there hadn't been a case. Not in this town, anyway.

Peter stood hesitantly in front of the local livery. The sheriff had told him his horse was boarded there. His impulse was to ride out of town and keep riding until he reached Natchez. But he'd already used up over six weeks of his three months. The ride to Natchez might take him another month if he ran into bad luck. If he got the loan there, he'd have the money to take the train back, but the tracks ran out at the foot of the mountains. That would be cutting the timing a little close. And if he didn't get the loan in Natchez . . .

That didn't bear thinking on. He would have to tackle Jason Harding. The man owned a bank. He knew Daniel. He'd stood up for him in court. There might be some possibility that he could convince him to part with a few lousy dollars. Then he could go home to New Mexico and get rich and come back and see if the schoolteacher was still talking to him. She'd said she would marry a rich man. He'd have to hope she didn't settle for Harding first.

Peter walked past the livery. He hadn't intended to do that. He was organized and efficient, a man who set his eyes on certain goals he meant to attain in a logical order. That order demanded that he get on his horse and head for the Harding ranch. Instead, he was walking in the direction of the little house at the end of town. He noticed no one had worked on the school since he'd been thrown in jail.

Peter heard the titters first. Without seeming to, he glanced from beneath his hat brim to discover two young girls lingering in the shadows next to the pharmacy. They were looking at him. There had been a time when he wouldn't have believed they laughed at him, but that had been knocked out of him recently. Stoically he walked on.

He wished he could stop in the pharmacy and buy her a box of candy or something. It was the least he could do for the woman who had saved his life. She hadn't come to visit him once throughout the wait for the trial. She hadn't been in the courtroom. He could understand that. The neatly laundered clothes had told him all he needed to know. She didn't harbor any ill feelings toward him, but she couldn't afford to make a spectacle of herself. He still wanted to thank her.

He wandered into the pharmacy wondering if he couldn't arrange to pay the bill later. It was a truly foolish idea, but he needed to at least try. He lingered over the fancy wrapped packages of chocolate bonbons and wondered if the prim little schoolteacher would like such decadence, or if she wouldn't prefer the little sewing kit with the shiny scissors and needles and pincushion.

He didn't know how long he'd stood there, lost in this decision, before he heard the voices coming from some corner of the room. The acoustics in here were rather odd. He could barely see the women out of the corner of his eye, and he would swear they were too far away for him to hear, but he heard them just the same.

"That's the one, Isabelle. That's the one I told you about. It's easy to see how she fell for him. Isn't he the handsomest thing you ever saw? Of course, you haven't met the schoolteacher yet. She's a mousy little thing, just as prim and haughty as they come. You wouldn't think it of her, but those are the ones who fall the hardest, they say. The school board's voting tonight, but there isn't a chance they'll extend her contract. Mr. Danner means to see to that. And Mr. Holt never was for a woman teacher, no how. I heard they've found a man over Obion ways willing to move here. It doesn't do for a woman like that to be teaching our young, now does it?"

Peter considered crushing the pretty box of candies in his hand, but he couldn't pay for them and he'd only make a scene. He set them carefully back on the shelf and walked back to the street, his mind churning.

She was prim and haughty, all right, and probably as cold as the devil. She had a way of looking at a man as if he wasn't any more than a cheap piece of glass not worth picking up. She was a calculating bitch who planned to marry for money.

She was the woman who had saved his life.

Pretending to light a cheroot, Peter stopped near the open barbershop door. The men inside didn't even see him. Their voices carried clearly. Their message was the same. The schoolteacher would lose her job tonight. They didn't believe for a minute that the arsonist had just accidentally fallen asleep in one of her beds. They weren't entirely convinced he wasn't an arsonist. The next logical step to these theories was set forth by the surly voice of

Bobby Fairweather: the schoolteacher and arsonist were no doubt in cahoots.

Even the men in the barbershop found that hard to swallow, but Cutlerville, Ohio, wasn't so different from Mineral Springs, Texas, and Peter knew how it was in his hometown. Once a nugget of gossip got rolling, it snowballed fast. The schoolteacher would be out of a job and a home and not a soul in town would dare to help her.

She could wire Daniel, maybe. Daniel would send her enough money to go to her sister or brother or someone. Peter crushed his cheroot under his boot and kept walking out of town. He remembered her refusal to accept charity, even for her bull-headed neighbors. She wouldn't like wiring Daniel.

He smiled as he remembered the day he had seen her flying through town on her tricycle, ribbons flying. He'd never seen a woman on a cycle before. And she knew how to type. She wrote a perfect hand, and she was educated enough to teach. A woman like that could have any number of uses. A mining business needed good secretarial help.

He didn't think she would be much interested in going to New Mexico on the basis of a prospective job in a business that didn't exist. But he wanted her there.

His footsteps quickened. He could see the advantages. He was a practical man. She was a practical woman. They would work well together. He didn't think she could be any more cold than the ladies he had considered courting back East. He'd once planned on marrying Georgina, and she'd never even kissed him.

All he had to do was offer the schoolteacher wealth. She wouldn't refuse him. He had found just what he wanted in a woman, just a little sooner than he had anticipated. He had wanted a woman to cook and warm his bed, one who wouldn't cheat on him behind his back. He could almost swear on a stack of Bibles that Miss Janice Harrison would never even look at another man. And she could cook better than any woman he'd ever known. He was a little uncertain as to the warming his bed part, but he rather thought she would do her duty, and that was all he needed, wasn't it? He had never expected more.

Peter's heart beat faster as he approached the little house where the new ruffled gingham curtains blew in the open window. He had never expected to find a wife who could also help him in his business, but he was coming to like the idea. It would be nigh on to impossible to find qualified help in the wilds of New Mexico. And then, when they had children, she could teach them.

The thought of having children gnawed a little worriedly at his stomach, but he figured if Daniel could handle it, he could. He was thirty years old. It was past time that he start a family, now that he was going to have the wealth to raise one. If he had the wealth to raise one. He couldn't dwell on that right now. He had to persuade one Janice Harrison that he was going to be a rich man indeed.

Janice shook her head at the big man standing on the braided rug in front of her chair. Jason Harding wasn't used to sitting still, but he made her nervous with his pacing up and down. She wished he would light somewhere and quit towering over her.

"I'm sorry about the school board, Jenny, but you've got to understand their thinking. You swore in a statement to a court that you let a man sleep in your house. A schoolteacher just can't do things like that. It don't look right. Their hands are tied, Jenny."

He wasn't telling her anything she didn't already know. The tension that had held her back straight ever since Jason had appeared at her door began to seep out of her. She had hoped he'd come here to rescue her, to swear that he knew she was innocent, that he wanted her to be his wife. She had been prepared to accept him too, even though she was terrified of what it meant. The idea of sleeping in a bed with a man twenty years older than herself didn't bother her so much as his size. Jason Harding was a large man. He could easily hurt her with his awkward clumsiness. But for Betsy's sake, she would have married him and escaped the horror of homelessness.

But it didn't look as if she would be making the sacrifice. Harding was an old-fashioned man. He thought a woman should be sweet and pure and all that nonsense. She hadn't known how she would tell him about the impure part anyway. He would never understand. Maybe it was better this way.

She hid a grimace as Jason generously offered to find her a job elsewhere. He didn't even mean to offer her a better position at the ranch or a place to stay. If Carmen had been here, she would have made the obtuse man see the necessity, but the only thing Jason understood was cattle.

Cold fear began to creep around Janice's heart as she promised to consider his offer of help. She really and truly was going to have to leave her home. That knowledge hadn't begun to sink in until now.

She watched Jason ride away with her heart in her throat and panic in her eyes.

The schoolteacher looked so startled at Peter's presence on her doorstep when she opened the door at his knock that he had time to study her, to reassure himself that he was doing the right thing. She hadn't bothered with those silly spectacles, and her hair was escaping from its prim knot as seemed to be its wont. She was much too pale, and her eyes appeared to be red-rimmed. That gave him an unwanted jolt. She'd been crying.

Peter didn't bother to continue his inspection. He shoved open the door with one arm and caught her waist with the other, dragging her into the front room with him and slamming the door behind them. She went without protest, still staring at him. He'd heard about people being in shock. He rather thought she suffered it now.

"I've given this a lot of thought, so don't think I'm acting on impulse. I know your opinion of men. I know you're perfectly capable of taking care of yourself." He pushed her into one of the straight-backed chairs that were the room's essential adornment. "But I hate taking care of myself. I'll never get used to it. I want a wife. I've put it off until I have the wealth to support one, but I've almost got it, Janice. All I need is that loan and I can buy a mountain of gold. I'll be rich. I'll be wealthy beyond all your dreams. Tell me you'll marry me now so we can go to New Mexico together. I don't want to go back alone."

Damn, but he was making an impassioned fool of himself. Peter flung his hat to the nearest chair with disgust. He hadn't intended to reveal so much. He hadn't even known that much about himself until he'd said it. He winced at the way he must sound to this unflustered woman who could sit through a performance like that and keep her hands crossed in her lap. He felt like an idiot, but he didn't know how any man could ask a woman to marry him without sounding like a candidate for an asylum.

Janice dropped her gaze from his face to her lap. "Don't you have to ask the permission of your family or something? I'm not exactly the type of woman they would expect you to marry."

Peter didn't know if it was joy burning along the edges of his veins, but whatever it was, it was heady and frightening at the same time. He crouched at her feet and reached for her hands. "I'm thirty years old, Janice. I think I can make my own decisions by now. You're exactly the kind of woman I expect me to marry."

Her lips trembled slightly, and he had to bite back a tremble in his own. In a few minutes he ought to have the right to kiss those lips. That thought nearly undid him. He had difficulty focusing on her reply. She hadn't said no. She seemed to be saying yes. She just seemed to be as confused as he was.

"Betsy is only ten," she murmured, biting her bottom lip and looking away from him. He could feel her stiffen slightly as he squeezed her hands, but he didn't say anything. He waited for her to go on. "I can't leave her behind. She has to go with me."

Betsy. The sister. In Natchez. Not good, but possible.

Peter clasped her hands tighter, realizing they were un-gloved. He began to explore them with his fingertips. Her hands weren't soft, but they weren't callused either. She had firm hands, with neat nails. Carefully he phrased his reply. "Your sister is welcome to stay with us. I haven't sold my ranch yet. The two of you could stay there until the mine is producing and I have time to move you up the mountain. It would probably be good for you to have company. But I have to get back there quickly. There may not be time to bring your sister back from Natchez just yet."

She nodded, biting her bottom lip. "She's with Kyle's family and Evie and Tyler. I could wire them, ask them to keep her a little while longer." She frowned slightly. "I just hope the journey out there won't be too difficult for her."

That was when he knew he had her. Peter didn't think he'd ever felt true elation before. He didn't know if he felt it now. He didn't see how it could be. It was too sur-rounded by doubt. But just for one wild moment, he felt the exultation of freedom.

He threw his arms around her, dragged her up against him as she stood, and kissed her soundly.

She stiffened harder than a maple board. Peter didn't care. She was in his arms. He had won. She was going to be his. He felt triumphant enough to grin down at her. Gray eyes returned his stare with uncertainty.

"It's going to be all right ... Janice. May I call you Janice now?" She didn't answer, but Peter took her si-lence for consent. Wonderingly he touched a strand of golden hair gleaming in the sun from the window. In a few short hours he would have the right to touch her any-time he wanted. She would be his. He felt a sense of sat-isfaction at that knowledge.

"I know this is sudden, Janice. I hate rushing you like this. But I've only got six weeks to get back and claim the option on that land. We could get married today and I could leave you here to get ready, but I can't promise to be back real soon. I'd rather you came with me, but I'll leave the choice to you."

He could almost see the wheels turning in her head. It could be months before he got back here again. The town would have found another teacher. They would want her out of this house. She would have to endure the whispers and stares and the speculative glances. He didn't know how much that meant to her, but he had guessed it meant a lot. He could see the decision in her eyes when she looked up at him.

"How soon will we have to leave?" she whispered hoarsely.

"As soon as I get out to talk to the Hardings. Tomorrow, or the next day." He felt her shiver in his arms, but he didn't try to hold her closer. She was resisting his touch as it was.

She nodded. "I can pack my clothes by then. What will happen to the rest of our things?" She glanced around at the neat front room, the sewing machine that was her heart and soul, the carefully accumulated pillows and crocheted doilies and other accessories that made this house a home.

Peter didn't know. He couldn't promise her anything until he'd had time to talk to the Hardings. He'd been a fool to come here before he had the money in his hand. But for her, he smiled and spoke reassuringly. "We'll hire someone to pack everything and store it for us until we can come back and claim them. I'll have to build you a respectable house to put them in. They're going to look too grand for my cabin."

She almost smiled then—a teary, wavery smile, but it was more than she'd offered before. Peter felt something within him clench oddly at that look. She was trusting him. He didn't think this woman had ever trusted anyone in her life. He didn't know why she consented to this madness, but he wouldn't disappoint her. He would do everything within his power to keep his promises.

"I never thought my poor things would ever be considered grand, Mr. Mulloney. You must lead a very Spartan life."

He dared to touch her hair. "Peter. You must learn to call me Peter. And yes, my life has been positively barren these last years. I'm enjoying the idea of having someone to decorate it. Do you think your sister will like me?"

A shadow of uncertainty passed over her face. Peter felt the cold draft of it before it dissipated. Her face was closed and calm when she turned back to him.

"Betsy has never met a soul she didn't like, sir. She will be thrilled to meet you."

He didn't know why those felt like fatal last words. He dropped his hold on her and progressed to the detailed planning of his wedding day. Planning was what he did best.

# Twelve

Janice watched Peter Mulloney stride off down the street as if he owned it. His broad shoulders filled the seams of his perfectly tailored frock coat. His Stetson sat on his head at just the right angle to indicate wealth and position and authority. Somehow, even his boots managed to gleam in the late afternoon sunlight. No one would doubt he was just exactly who he said he was: a rich man about to become richer.

She shuddered a little and clasped her hands in front of her as she turned from the window. She didn't know what she had done, but she had done it. In the days and weeks to come, he might come to despise her for consenting to his proposal, but he was the one who had offered. She hadn't tricked him into it.

She just hadn't told him the whole truth.

Nervously she brushed back a straying strand of hair and tried to apply her usually calm mind to the tasks ahead. Her thoughts swirled restlessly instead of lining up in progressive order. She had to get dressed. Peter was going to fetch the preacher. They would be married in a few short hours. She had to find something to wear. She had to put clean sheets on the bed.

She considered her small bed dubiously and brushed that thought aside. She didn't have anything for a wedding dinner. She needed to decide what to pack in her trunk. How would they get to New Mexico? She couldn't remember if trains ran in that direction.

Why hadn't she told him about Betsy?

That thought ran under and around all her other

thoughts as she tried to concentrate on one task at a time. She heated water for a bath while searching through her wardrobe. She found one of Betsy's hair ribbons in the pocket of one of the gowns she considered.

She poured water into her tin tub and stripped to her bare skin, and her fingers scraped along the pale stretch line from when she had carried Betsy. She soaped hurriedly, but nothing could wash away the lie she had left in the mind of the man she was about to marry.

It shouldn't matter, she told herself throughout her bath and as she settled on the royal-blue gown with the extravagant lace on the sleeves. She donned her best linen and eyelet drawers and the matching chemise, but the refrain still danced in her mind. She should have told him. It shouldn't matter.

She was going to be his *wife*. He was going to take these clothes off of her and lay her down in that bed and put himself inside her, and he was going to *know*.

She couldn't bear to think about it, and it wasn't just her lie that she couldn't bear to consider. She had just agreed to be a man's wife, to give him full possession of her body, to allow him to do *that* to her. She didn't know how she would endure it. Other women did, so she supposed she would learn, but all she could think of now was the pain and humiliation.

She briefly entertained the thought that he wouldn't be interested in that way in an old-maid spinster. He was just rescuing her out of gratitude and he would be satisfied with the best secretary his money could buy. Even her mind wasn't strong enough to buy that reasoning for more than a minute. She'd seen the lust in his eyes and knew it for what it was. Somehow, he had seen through her disguise to the sinner she was. He wasn't marrying her for any reason other than the one men usually married for. She would get his money and he would get the use of her bed and body.

She would just have to concentrate on his money and let the rest come as it would. Betsy would be taken care of for life. After what the Mulloneys had done to her family, she deserved that much. Betsy could go to the best doctors, go to private schools, have her own art teacher if she wanted. She would never have to suffer the horrors her mother had known. She would never have to suffer a man in her bed, either, if she didn't want. Betsy wasn't strong, but Janice was. She could carry the burden of life's troubles and let her daughter be free.

That knowledge helped her get through the rest of the afternoon. She had told Peter she would meet him at the church at five. She didn't want to excite the interest of the town any more than necessary until the deed was done. Then they could gossip and whisper as they wished, but she would be the respectable wife of the wealthy Peter Mulloney and none of it would matter anymore. She would never lack for a roof over her head again.

Janice knew the dress she wore was too elegant to go without notice as she started down the street, but she was determined to make her wedding day all that it should be. Irish point embroidery tumbled from her collar and adorned the edges of her fitted elbow-length sleeves and the fashionable Marie Antoinette overskirt. The lace embroidery had been a gift from Georgina for her birthday last year. She'd never had a place to wear the gown before. She had made it for the sheer satisfaction of owning something beautiful. Janice wore it carefully now, holding it up out of the dirt as she entered town.

She wished she had a parasol or one of those English bonnets with roses on it to cover her hair, but she couldn't make those things herself. She had changed the ribbons on her straw hat to ones of blue to match her gown. That would have to suffice.

She didn't see Peter waiting for her at the church door, but he was no doubt being discreet. The preacher wasn't, however. The church bell rang out just as Janice stepped up on the wooden porch. The bell only rang for services. Everyone would know something was going on.

But it would be too late for anyone to do anything about it. Janice opened the heavy oak door and stepped into the dim twilight of the small wooden church.

When her eyes adjusted to the dusk, she distinguished the figures of the preacher and Peter standing by the altar. To one side waited the preacher's wife. To the other side stood Sheriff Powell shifting nervously from foot to foot. Janice almost smiled at the irony of Peter's choice of best man.

She approached unhurriedly, enjoying the rustle of her satin skirt and stiff petticoat in the still hush of the church interior. The last echoes of the bell outside were dying by the time she reached the altar. Peter held out his hand, and she laid her gloved one in it. His grasp was firm and reassuring as the preacher greeted her.

She scarcely paid attention to the words of the ceremony as they sailed over her head. Love and honor were only words. They had little to do with scrubbing floors and working to dawn to put bread on the table. She was quite willing to do anything her husband wanted her to do as long as he kept her family fed and clothed. That's what she had been doing all her life. It wouldn't be any hardship to continue now. She gave her vows calmly, without inflection.

She was somewhat surprised when Peter didn't have a ring for her but pried off the one on his smallest finger to use when the preacher called for it. It was merely a thin gold band with some worn decorations on it, but she supposed there hadn't been time for him to look for anything suitable. Jewelry wasn't important to her. She'd never owned any.

When the service ended and Peter bent to kiss her chastely on the lips, she felt a smidgen of relief. His earlier kiss had nearly paralyzed her. It had been hot and demanding and more than possessive, and she hadn't known how to respond. But she could deal with this polite caress. She held his hand and pressed her lips to his and managed a rather crooked smile when he pulled away at the sheriff's nervous cough.

They turned to face their audience and accept congratulations. Several people had trickled in to see the cause for the bell, and they hurried forward to pick up any tidbits to be used as gossip.

As Mr. and Mrs. Mulloney, they signed the register and the license along with the witnesses. The preacher's wife hugged Janice while the sheriff shook Peter's hand. It almost seemed a perfectly normal, respectable wedding as they descended the aisle through the small crowd of well-wishers. Janice just wished Betsy could be here.

The feeling of isolation didn't surround them until they reached the street. People turned and stared at the sight of the schoolteacher and the recent prisoner dressed in their best clothes walking up the dusty street. Peter increased his pace to hasten them past anyone appearing to want to talk to them. Janice was in full agreement. She simply didn't have anything to say to any of them.

But there didn't seem to be anything she could say to her husband, either. They remained silent until they reached the house and Janice remembered she didn't have a special dinner waiting. Her first night as wife and already she felt her inadequacy.

Unfastening her bonnet ribbons, she turned and met her husband's gaze steadily. "I didn't have time to prepare anything for dinner. I'm sorry. Will eggs and potatoes be enough?"

He seemed almost as nervous as she was. They had eaten together in this house the better part of a week. There shouldn't be anything strange about it. But he was wearing a fancy black frock coat and black tie and looked at her from beneath the broad brim of his gray hat, and she suddenly realized she had married a total stranger. The uneasiness of earlier returned with a vengeance.

"Eggs will be just fine. Whoever did the cooking for me this past week wasn't nearly as good as you."

The low rumble of Peter's voice so close to her nearly made Janice jump out of her skin even though she was looking right at him. Why hadn't she noticed before how his voice licked across her skin like that? She hurriedly pulled off her gloves.

"Very well. Make yourself comfortable. If you're not too hungry yet, I can make some fresh biscuits."

To her chagrin, Peter followed her into the kitchen, shrugging off his coat as he did so. She wanted to tell him to stay out of her kitchen, that this was her sanctum, but he had been welcomed here before. She couldn't throw him out now that they were married.

He didn't even ask how he could help. He just started adding wood to the stove, lifting down dishes, and carrying water. It made her nervous as all get out every time he brushed near her, but she wasn't about to complain when a man wanted to help. All too soon the newness would no doubt wear off and he would revert to normal. She might as well take advantage of his willingness while it lasted.

"Tell me more about New Mexico," she asked as they sat down to the table at last.

He helped himself to a generous portion of the eggs and fried potatoes as he spoke. "There's not much out where we'll be going. Even the Apaches have left us alone. There're a few ranches, and a town down at the base of the range. It's not as big as this. There's no railroad nearby. I won't lie to you. It's lonely as hell. But once we start toting gold out of that mountain, things will change. We'll hire miners, preferably ones with families. We'll build a town for them. We'll have to put in a rail line down the mountain and install a processing plant. That will bring in more people. The stage will have to come through more regularly. Once there are enough people out there, maybe we could get a railroad spur into town. You'll have to imagine the future when you see the place."

Except for the mention of Indians, it sounded better than she could have imagined. She wouldn't have any difficulty dealing with miners and their families. They were her kind of people. She was more than relieved that he didn't intend to return to Ohio and the civilized snobbery back East. The part that worried her most was the current lack of railroad.

"How will we get to this place if there isn't any rail line yet?"

He'd rolled his shirt sleeves up when he had carried in the wood. His tie had departed with his coat. He could be any hardworking man that she knew sitting across the table from her, not the wealthy financier she knew he was. Except she could see the confidence in the strong lines of his face and knew this man had never accepted defeat. She didn't know too many working men who could say that.

"There's a railroad out of Fort Worth that takes us up through El Paso. Once we reach Gage, though, we'll have to take the stage to carry your trunks into Butte. From there, I guess we'll have to rent a wagon to get your things up to my place. It will be a long while before those roads are ready for fancy carriages."

Fancy carriages didn't worry her. Betsy did. The journey sounded long and tedious and dusty. Janice frowned and bit her lip. "How far away is Gage from this place we're going?"

Peter gave her a careful look. "I'd say fifty miles or more."

Janice's stomach churned. It sounded as if they would have to do a lot of traveling by stage and wagon. Maybe if she could find someone to keep Betsy until the winter when the dust and heat weren't so bad . . .

"It's a good thing it's summer. We can travel faster. When the snow falls, no one gets through." Peter reached for the pan of biscuits again.

Janice's hands fell in her lap and she stared over his shoulder at the last ray of sun coming through the doorway. She'd really gone and done it now. How was she going to make the best of this new disaster?

It worried her all evening. They cleared the table and washed the dishes together, and she asked questions and listened carefully as Peter talked, but all the while, the predicament of transporting Betsy across desert territory worried at her. She had married this man to protect Betsy. She couldn't let her decision end up killing her child.

But the well-charted territory of the kitchen soon gave way to the next step in her new position, and she had other things to worry about.

There was a moment of awkwardness when they had the last plate dried and put away. Janice ended it when she left the kitchen for the front room. The sun was just setting, and she lit the lamp to fend off the growing dusk. She felt more than saw Peter as he followed her in and watched her move about the room.

"It's early yet. What do you usually do in the evening?" She tried to sound bright and serene, but the effort cost her.

She turned and saw her husband leaning against the door frame, arms crossed over his chest as he watched her. She knew she couldn't run from the gleam she detected in his eye. She had never tried to imagine what lay beneath the smooth linen of his shirt, but she was aware of how it strained over certain portions of his anatomy. She didn't dare look to his trousers. They weren't cheap cotton denims but made of some rich material that draped neatly over his narrow hips and clung almost indecently to his thighs. She actually found herself trying to imagine how the material would outline his buttocks, but he was turned the wrong way. She had to turn back to the window to keep him from seeing the flush in her cheeks.

"Read. Play cards, I suppose."

He had taken so long to answer that she had to remember the question. She crossed her hands in front of her and nodded absently. The rumble of his voice seemed to touch her somehow. Little prickly footsteps were rising up and down her arms and creeping around inside of her. She would have to get this over with before she made it any worse than it was.

"Jenny."

The sound of Jason's pet name for her on Peter's tongue made her start, but not so much as the fact that he was right behind her. She jumped when he laid a hand on her shoulder, but he did no more than that. She tried to quiet her quaking nerves.

"We're neither of us children anymore, Jenny. We're man and wife. I think we're both levelheaded adults. We walked into this with our eyes wide open. We may have a lot to learn about each other, but I don't think there's anything to fear. Pardon my asking, but I need to know how careful I have to be. Have you ever known a man before, Jenny?"

He made it so amazingly easy for her. Janice nodded silently, and she could almost swear he gave a sigh of relief. His words confirmed her impression.

"Good. I didn't think I would have enough control to do it right if you were a virgin. It's been a long time since I had a woman, Jenny. I need one real bad right now. Would you mind too much if we skipped the preliminaries and got on with this?"

What a romantic declaration. Janice had to smile at his practicality despite the terror seizing her insides. He was a man after her own heart, going straight for what he wanted without letting anything get in his way. The fact that what he wanted was her had an almost reassuring touch to it.

"I'm ready when you are," she murmured obediently, turning in the direction of the bedroom.

"I'll give you time to get ready," he said to her back. And then, as she walked away, he added, "Don't bother with a nightgown."

# Thirteen

Peter watched the graceful sway of Janice's bustle as she walked away and almost felt himself drooling. He was perfectly aware that he was nearly desperate for the relief of a woman's body beneath him, for the physical release that would come with the heated sheath of her surrounding him. But he was also aware that he had always been able to control these physical reactions before. He'd never in his entire life *ever* wanted to fling a woman to the ground and jerk her skirts up. But that was how he felt right now.

He didn't even care who the man had been before him. He didn't care if it had been "man" in the plural. He was merely relieved that she knew what to expect and wouldn't be shocked when he took her with a great deal less care than he ought. There would be time enough to do it properly once he got some relief from this tension.

He knew part of the tension was worry over getting that loan and what would happen if he didn't, but he could scarcely think of that right now. Every time he tried, his mind strayed to the delicate sashay of Janice's shapely rear end or the narrow span of her waist. She had never worn a gown revealing enough for him to guess the size of her breasts, but he was quite content with the swell of the curve he'd seen beneath the tight corseting of her wedding gown. She was small-boned and slender as any lady, but he already knew she possessed solid steel for a backbone. She would need it where he was taking her.

He wished for a drink while he listened to the subtle

rustling of silken clothes in the other room. Maybe he should have offered to help her undress. He rather imagined her elegant gown would have wound up a crumpled ball on the floor if he had. This was the proper way of doing things on a wedding night, even if the bride and groom weren't exactly innocent.

When he heard the squeak of the bed springs, Peter blew out the lamp and started unfastening his shirt. He had it undone by the time he crossed the room.

The room was dark when he entered it. He pushed the door closed and dropped his shirt where he stood. His knee bumped a chair, and he sat down to pull off his shoes. He could scarcely hear her breathing for the pounding of his own heart. This was his wedding night. The woman in that bed was his to have and to hold until death did them part. He was damned well terrified, but his body was taking care of that terror quite succinctly. He had to unbutton his trousers to ease the pain of constriction.

He was grateful for the darkness. She would no doubt faint if she could see him now. He'd never felt so huge in his life. He stepped out of his trousers and, completely naked, approached the bed.

He hit his shin on the low bed, but Peter scarcely noticed as he pulled back the thin sheet she'd covered herself with. The June heat filled this airless room, so she didn't need the cover for warmth. He found her modesty endearing, if a trifle unnecessary.

Her skin was smooth silk as he climbed in next to her. He felt her flinch when he first touched her, but she didn't move away. Whoever the man or men had been, they hadn't made her into a whore. She was as rigid as a frightened virgin beside him.

He'd scarcely even had a chance to kiss her or hold her, and here he was reaching to caress her breast. Peter prayed she would forgive him because he couldn't help himself. His fingers closed around the soft yielding mound and he gave a sigh of pure pleasure. She was perfect.

He kissed her then, or tried. She didn't seem to know to open her mouth. He teased his tongue along the seam of her lips and caressed her breast until she shivered and tentatively circled his shoulders with her arms. That convinced him he was welcome. He moved his kisses along the line of her jaw rather than force her to do something she apparently found unseemly.

She made a soft little moan when he teased the tightening crest of her breast. Peter couldn't resist trying to capture that moan with his mouth. She froze up on him again, but it didn't matter. He was about to explode with need. He would teach her about kissing later.

He found the soft triangle between her legs and slid his hand deep between her thighs. She moaned again and stiffened, but her hips rose toward him when he pressed her there. She wasn't exactly moist when he inserted his finger, but he hadn't prepared her very well either. That was something else that would come with time.

He spread his hand and forced her to part her thighs. He held them apart with one knee while he bent to suckle at her breast. He could feel the shock roll through her, and he almost chuckled. The prim schoolteacher really didn't know much at all about lovemaking. He applied himself more diligently to this pleasure and was rewarded by the increasing moistness where his finger worked slowly in and out.

She shivered uncontrollably and he thought he heard his name whisper between her lips. He really couldn't wait any longer. He'd surprised himself by showing this much restraint. Beads of moisture coated his brow from the effort. The time had come to claim his wife.

Peter knelt between her legs and pushed her knees up when she didn't seem to know to do it herself. He was so engorged he feared he would hurt her otherwise. But then he lost any remaining restraint or courtesy. She was open and waiting and his for the taking.

She made a muffled noise when he pushed into her. He hesitated, but no membrane blocked his passage. He couldn't register more than that. Despite her passive protest, his body screamed "Now, now!" and his hips moved instinctively in the same compelling rhythm. Thrusting repeatedly in and out, he lost any remaining fragments of control, breaching her surely and thoroughly and so completely that he exploded within her in one final thrust that left his whole body throbbing. Not until he collapsed against her did Peter realize she was whimpering and weeping beneath him.

When her new husband finally rolled off of her, Janice turned on her side with her face toward the wall. She felt Peter awkwardly caressing her bare shoulder, and desperately she tried to halt her sobs, but they were instinctive and from somewhere deep inside her.

It had been the same violation all over again. She had hoped and prayed that it would be different this time, but in ways it had been horribly worse. Her breast ached where his beard stubble had scraped her, and she buried her face in her hands as she remembered the other humiliating thing he had done to her. His finger! He had used his finger where she scarcely dared touch herself.

It had to be proper. Peter Mulloney was more gentleman than she was lady. But she couldn't help this repulsion. It had nothing to do with him and everything to do with Stephen, but she couldn't explain that to him. Peter's terrible weight had held her pinned just as Stephen's greater strength had held her then. She had fought Stephen when he had shoved her legs apart. With Peter, she had fought herself. Still, she hadn't been able to fight the paralyzing terror when her husband had entered her. He had shoved his body up inside hers repeatedly, far more than she could remember Stephen having done, and it hurt. She felt raw and used and . . . She didn't want to think about the last thing she felt. She could feel the sticky liquid of his seed seeping down her thigh. At least this time it wouldn't contain her blood. But this time, she knew what it meant. In nine months she could be full to bursting with his child.

She cried in earnest now. Every humiliating day of her last pregnancy came back to her with a clarity she couldn't escape. The nausea, the dizziness, the sympathetic looks and shamed silences, followed by the swelling, the gradual bloating and swelling until she was certain she resembled one of the hot air balloons she'd seen at the fair. Would her husband do like Ellen's husband was doing now? Look at her in disgust and go elsewhere for his needs?

She cringed when Peter's hand slid caressingly down her arm. Surely he couldn't want to do that again so soon? Even Stephen had waited awhile before forcing his attentions on her again. Oh, Lord, but she remembered now how often he had taken her that night. Her whole body shriveled up with the memory. She hadn't been able to walk the next day. It had been a good thing her family hadn't been home. Of course, if they'd been home, it never would have happened.

"I'm sorry if I hurt you, Janice. I didn't mean to. It's just been so long ... Damn." He let her go when she cringed away.

She could feel him lying flat on his back, taking up most of the bed. She ought to say something. A wedding night wasn't supposed to be like this. There was something wrong with her. She had always known it. Stephen had told her so when she had cried and asked him to stop. Now Peter would be just as disgusted. For Betsy's sake, she had to do something to show him everything was all right. But even for Betsy's sake, she couldn't make herself roll over and touch him.

Janice shoved a corner of the sheet in her mouth and stopped crying though. The place between her legs ached, but not with any real pain. She just felt hollow, and very aware of where he had been. She had better get used to the idea of having children. She didn't think Peter Mulloney was the kind of man to give up when confronted with a little resistance. He would be back again tomorrow night, if not again tonight. And she would bear his children. That was what she had agreed to do when she had accepted his ring in front of witnesses. The pretty words of the wedding ceremony just disguised the ugly truth of marriage. With the placement of that ring, the man owned the woman, could use her body when and as he willed, and in exchange for his protection, she must bear his children. It would make much more sense if the preacher would just say that and make it clear.

They both must have finally given into the exhausting emotions of the day and slept, for the sun crept in the window when next they became aware of each other.

Janice woke to find her back against the burning furnace of her husband's chest and his muscular arm wrapped solidly around her waist. When she gently tried to wriggle loose, his grip tightened, and she felt the heat of his male parts pressing along her posterior. She went rigid immediately.

His hand moved to caress her breast. "We need to learn what brings each other pleasure, Jenny. Do you like this?"

She didn't like anything. She wanted out of this bed, and she wanted out of it now. Panic careened down her spine and spread through her veins. She gritted her teeth and nodded her head in a blatant lie.

"Good, because I like it too. You have a beautiful body, Jenny. There's this lake back at the ranch. It's crystal blue and you can see clear to the bottom of it. And there's this little waterfall that trickles into it in summer and pours in spring. I want to see you standing there naked in that waterfall, Jenny, your hair wet and streaming all down your back, your breasts glistening with water. If we're lucky, we'll have time to do that when we get there. I'm going to make love to you in the grass and sunlight, the way nature meant it to be."

The soothing sound of his voice completely disarmed her. The image he created was the first erotic thing she'd ever heard in her life. She could picture the lake and the waterfall, but she couldn't picture herself naked. She couldn't picture him at all. But she still liked the image and the way his voice made her feel.

But he couldn't leave the image just to words. Janice realized his hand played with her breasts, and whatever he was doing made her very conscious of an odd sensation between her thighs, as if the two places were somehow connected. He seemed to know it too, because he slid his other arm beneath her to continue the caressing while his hand slid proprietarily to the place that tingled.

She wanted to stiffen but found that she couldn't. She ached and she tingled and she felt all hollow inside. He pressed his finger into her and she instinctively arched against it until it slid deeper.

"That's it, Jenny. That's the way I want you. Look at how your breasts have swelled for me. Look, Jenny. It doesn't hurt to look."

Peter moved his arm beneath her breasts and pushed them up until she couldn't help but glance down. His arm was brown and covered with black hairs and contrasted vividly with the pale smoothness of her breasts. She had never really looked at her breasts before. They did seem to be alarmingly round and full and the tips were flushed and extended into hard points. When her husband's thumb brushed against one, a rush of something intoxicating swept through her middle, and her hips surged against his finger again. Her eyes widened as they stared down at where Peter had his hand.

"I want you, Jenny. I want to be inside you again. But I don't want to make you cry. Will you let me try again, or shall I stop?"

He was giving her a choice! Amazement flooded through her. He was asking, not demanding. She could feel the thick length of him pressing between her legs, knew the muscular strength of the arms wrapped around her. He could force her with ease. They both knew it. But he wasn't taking that advantage.

"Could we wait?" she whispered. She knew the way people could manipulate each other by seeming to give in or pretending acquiescence only to gloat when they grabbed the advantage to get what they wanted. She knew he was hoping that if he asked, she would say yes. She ought to say yes. He was her husband and her duty was to say yes. But just this once, just once, she would like to feel that she really had a choice.

He kissed her temple and reluctantly moved away. "Will you tell me sometime why you cried? I'm not going to be able to stay away from you as much as you might like. I'd like to make it easier for both of us."

He was actually getting out of bed. Janice was so surprised that stupidly she turned over to watch him. She saw a good deal more than she was prepared for.

There was enough light in the room to see the muscles bunch in his back and buttocks as Peter stood up and reached to brush the hair from his eyes. He was tanned down to the line of his trousers, and her curiosity couldn't keep her from staring at the tight muscles below his waist. And then he swung around to look down at her when she didn't answer, and she was confronted with the swollen male part of him. She backed hurriedly against the wall.

He had put *that* inside her? Her eyes grew round in disbelief and she continued staring even when he reached hastily for his trousers and drew them on.

"Janice? Are you all right? You did say you'd been with another man before, didn't you?"

He seemed more anxious than angry, and she didn't know whether to nod her head or shake it. She just suddenly realized that she was as naked as the day she was born, and she jerked the sheet up around her.

"I'm sorry," she whispered. "I didn't mean ... How ..." She couldn't get the words out. She didn't think she'd been embarrassed in years, but now she stuttered like an adolescent. She watched as he gingerly tucked himself inside his trousers. He didn't attempt to fasten them entirely, and her gaze was distracted by the dark swirl of hairs disappearing into the V beneath his trouser band.

He leaned one hand against the wall behind her and gazed down at her in puzzlement. "You weren't a virgin, Janice. How could you not know how men are made?"

She averted her eyes. "Please, I don't think I can talk about this."

He tipped her chin up until he had captured her gaze

again. "We're going to have to, but not right now. Feed me one of your bountiful breakfasts, and then I'll go out to face the Hardings and get that money I need. Then we'll have all the time in the world to learn about each other."

"Money?" She watched carefully as he crossed the room, evidently meaning to wash before he dressed.

He stopped in the doorway and looked back. Long lengths of flaxen hair tumbled across her bare shoulders and down the white sheet barely covering her full breasts. He almost forgot the question. Gray eyes sharpened quizzically, and she pulled the sheet a little higher.

"Money." Peter straightened and shoved the hair off his forehead. "I told you. I need money to buy that mountain. I'm down to my last red cent. I'm hoping the Hardings will loan me what I need."

She emitted a tiny whistling sigh and her face lost what little color it possessed.

"The Hardings haven't got any money. They spent every last penny on buying that government land, and the bottom fell out of the cattle market. Their bank is likely to go belly up any minute."

# *Fourteen*

Peter stared at her, uncomprehending. "Belly up?"

"Broke." Janice jerked the sheet tighter around her as she looked around for something decent to pull on. "Everyone is. People began fencing their lands so the herds couldn't range free. Those cows need a whale of a lot of land to range. So like everyone else, the Hardings had to start buying that government land they'd been using for nothing. Then they had to buy fencing. The Double H was lucky to have a free source of money in the bank, but when the bottom fell out of prices, they couldn't pay back the loans. If they borrow any more, they'll be tapping into the funds of little old ladies and schoolteachers like me. Jason won't do that."

His wife's pragmatism had a way of taking the starch out of Peter. The desire that had been burning so heatedly in him just moments before died rapidly. What she was saying couldn't be true. The Double H was the richest ranch in this part of Texas, everybody said so. And the Hardings owned a damned bank. There had to be money there somewhere.

Peter watched her reach for a wrapper. He took a deep breath. "I still have to go out and talk to them. It would be much simpler if I could get the money here. Time is running out."

He turned and left the room. Janice could feel her hands trembling. Surely he hadn't meant what he said about not having a red cent. He was a Mulloney. Mulloneys had more money than anyone could possibly spend in a lifetime, Daniel had told her so. Not having a cent probably meant something different to Peter than to her.

She washed hastily in the cold water in the washbowl, pulled on a wrapper, and went to the kitchen to start breakfast. Now that she was married, her only responsibility should be the house and the children they didn't have yet. Her husband could worry about the money situation. That was the way it was supposed to be. She didn't want to worry about where the next meal came from anymore. That was the reason she had married. Peter would have to hold up his end of the bargain. She didn't see any reason why they should own a mountain of gold. She would be quite content with just a house of her own.

Peter came in the back door, clean-shaven, with flecks of water still glittering on his face and chest. Without a word, he picked up his clothes and returned to the bedroom to dress.

Janice felt the tension in him, and it multiplied the anxiety eating at her stomach. She told herself not to worry, but she had spent a lifetime worrying. She didn't know how to break the habit.

When he came back, fully dressed and looking the part of a wealthy financier again, she wanted to ask him why he couldn't just wire Daniel for the money. Instead, she set a plate full of sausage and biscuits in front of him and made small talk about the kinds of clothes she should pack. She hadn't figured out how to fit herself into the mold of wife yet. She had this vague idea that wives didn't question their husbands about finances. She didn't want to insult Peter this early in the game. She would just have to hope he knew what he was doing.

"If we're coming back through here for Betsy, you don't need to pack your warm clothes yet," he answered absently. "Just take whatever you need to be comfortable right now. We'll be traveling light this trip."

She could tell his mind wasn't on the conversation. She wanted to ask him how broke was one red cent, but she didn't have the courage. She was strong and she had her own opinions about many subjects, but she had never learned to intervene in other people's lives. Tight-lipped, Janice poured more coffee and brought him a piece of hot sweet bread. She had coated it in honey and pecans left from last fall, but he didn't seem to notice.

He cleaned his plate and went to the dishwater in the basin to wash the stickiness from his hands. "I shouldn't be long at the ranch. I'm going to check at the stage office to see what times they leave. Will you be all right out here?"

He looked over his shoulder at her. It was a perfectly ridiculous question, but Janice rather liked the concern behind it. It had been a long time since anyone had showed concern for her.

"I have more than enough to do," she reassured him. "Go on and get your business done."

He dried his hands, caught her shoulders when she turned to pick up a pan on the stove, and pressed a kiss against her temple. "Thank you," he murmured into her hair.

Startled, she looked up to ask him what he was thanking her for, but he had already gone out the door. In wonder, she stared after his departing back. Peter Mulloney was nothing like she had expected. Actually, she had never even thought he was human. She didn't know if she wanted him to be a man with all the failings of a man. It was much easier to dislike a devil. But it had been a long, long time since someone had touched her with such easy familiarity. She could come to like the sensation.

When the sun rose toward noon, Janice set out for town. She didn't need to spend the entire day packing her few meager summer dresses, and without knowing how long they were remaining here, she couldn't pack everything yet. Her time would be more wisely spent in running a few other errands.

With great trepidation, she went to the bank to draw out her carefully hoarded savings. She didn't want to rely on her husband for everything.

She offered smiles and hurried excuses to the women stopping her in the street to offer their congratulations. She didn't even have time to listen to Ellen's wails about losing her schoolteacher. Janice merely made her purchases, patted the girl reassuringly, and hurried on to the butcher's. She had to make something for dinner, and maybe supper. It was difficult to know how much she needed.

She hastened back to the house and had time to discard her bonnet and gloves and start the meal before she heard a horse riding into the yard. A hasty glance told her Peter had come home, and her heart skipped an erratic beat. Her husband made an imposing presence even when there was no one about. He sat straight in the saddle, hands firmly on the reins as he brought his mount to a halt. She couldn't see his face beneath the hat brim, and nothing in his posture as he swung down warned of his state of mind. She hurried back to the stove.

She heard him washing the dust off his face and hands before he came in. To Janice, that alone was a sign of his good upbringing. But she couldn't bring herself to smile when he came in. She just watched him through worried eyes.

He didn't smile either. He hung his hat on a hook by the door and ran his hand through his crushed curls. When he saw that she was cooking, he fell into their usual routine, reaching for the plates in the high cabinet.

"Tell me when I overstep my bounds," Janice murmured softly, her back to him. "But I've spent my life worrying about money. I can't just turn it off now. What happened?"

"They gave me the names of a few banks where I might use them as reference. Did you say your sister was staying with the Monteignes?"

Tension emanated from him in waves. She could almost hear his teeth clenching. Nervously Janice stirred the creamed corn. "Yes, but I thought you said it would take too long to go get her."

"I'm going to have to go east anyway. I'd rather go to

a friend than to a bank where I'm not known. Can you ride?" Peter didn't want to ask her this. He didn't want her sleeping on the trail like he had. His personal preference would be to leave her here, but he didn't think either sister would appreciate it if he went to Natchez without her.

Janice looked up, incredulous. "Wouldn't the train be faster? There's a station at Fort Worth. The stage will take us right there."

Peter's expression was hard and unreadable. "I told you, I have no money. I left most everything I had with my partner back in New Mexico so he could buy supplies."

Janice stifled her growing fury and fear at the words "no money." Her stomach churned as she fought for control, a control she had tended carefully these last ten years. Ten years ago she had learned that love was dangerous; hysteria and anger, worse than useless; happiness, ephemeral. Emotions could not deal with reality. She would not give into that disabling panic and anxiety now.

But her hand went instinctively to that part of her abdomen where even now a child could be growing. She had a choice to make. She could take her few coins, go to Natchez, collect Betsy, and find a job elsewhere. Or she could offer what she had to her husband and pray that he would make the best of them. It was a terrifying choice, one she didn't feel qualified to make. She knew little or nothing of this man she had married. What little she had thought she knew seemed to be wrong.

Cautiously, she inquired, "Won't Daniel loan you the money?"

Peter's mouth hardened into a grim line. "I'm doing this on my own. I'll thank you to keep my family out of our affairs."

Startled at the anger in his tone, Janice didn't inquire further. Daniel was her friend. That didn't mean he was Peter's. Under the circumstances, she could understand Peter's resentment. Daniel, after all, had usurped the place Peter had once thought was his.

She covered her faux pas by saying, "One of the women down in town offered to buy my cycle." She was merely thinking out loud, searching desperately for some way to satisfy the conflicting needs of supporting Betsy and making this marriage work. "I won't be able to use a cycle in New Mexico, will I?"

Peter looked at her with curiosity. "No, I suppose not. I don't think those things work well on mountains."

"I'm sure I could get enough for train fare, and maybe a little extra. And I have enough saved to buy a round-trip ticket. We can get to Natchez. I don't know if there'll be enough to go any farther."

Peter stood still, frozen with his hands full of plates while he contemplated her suggestion. She could tell it went against his grain to take money from her. She could almost see the battle of wills going on inside of him. He wanted to refuse, but he was too practical to allow pride to make that decision. Janice didn't know if she ought to be relieved or not. She ought to feel triumphant at stinging the arrogant pride of a Mulloney. Instead, she just felt frightened and uncertain.

"I'm your wife," she reminded him gently. "I didn't bring much into this marriage but myself, and I'm not much of a prize. If we're going to be partners, you're going to have to let me contribute what I can."

He took a short breath and set the plates on the table. "I'll accept only because I can't leave you here. I want you somewhere safe, with friends."

She didn't like the way he said that, but she began dishing out the meal without saying a word. She had learned how to ignore orders and go her own way a long time ago.

They rode the last train out of Fort Worth that night.

Janice stared at the ill-matched curtains of her bunk and thought what an odd way this was to spend her second night of marriage. The bed had room for only one, and Peter had chosen to take a cheaper seat. She was relieved for that in one way, but in all others, it didn't bode well.

Unreasonably, she found herself wanting him near. The bumping, grinding, and rolling of the train were taking her away from the home she had known these last five years, a home where she had been content and relatively secure. The train carried her to an uncertain destination, an uncertain future, a life she had never anticipated. She wanted reassurances. She knew Peter had none.

She clutched her fingers in the linen covering her abdomen. She knew only one thing for certain: she didn't want a baby until she again had a home to call her own. Peter would have to understand that.

She didn't think he would be very amenable to her decision. It didn't matter. He was the one who had married her under false pretenses. He was supposed to be *rich*.

When Peter walked down the aisle of the sleeping car some time later, he found his wife sound asleep, clutching her sheet to her breast. There was something vaguely defiant in her expression, but he attributed it to her dreams. So far she had been so wonderful about all this that he wanted to pinch himself to be certain he was awake, only he feared he really would wake up.

He brushed a straying strand of hair from her cheek and felt her stir restlessly beneath his touch. He liked knowing she was his, that he had the right to touch her like this. This journey was going to put some serious dents in his plans to teach her how to make love, but they could make up for lost time when they reached Natchez. Time was running short, but by taking the train, he saved a great deal of it. They would be able to spend a few days getting to know each other.

He just didn't know how to let her know he wouldn't have time to take her back with him. He was going to have to ride flat out to make up for these lost days. He wouldn't have time for the luxury of a stage on the last leg of the journey.

But she would be with friends now. She would understand. He had married a reasonable woman.

Peter let the curtain drop and wandered back to his lonely seat. He could amuse himself by counting the hours until he had his wife back in his bed again. And when that failed to amuse him, he could picture the number of different ways he would make love to her. He'd learned any number of useful and pleasurable things these last few years. He thought with time Janice would come to learn to appreciate them.

They couldn't afford the time or the luxury of taking the train into New Orleans and a steamboat up to Natchez. They got off at the first station in Louisiana nearest the Mississippi, rented a wagon, and transported themselves to the dock. From there, they took the first boat going north.

If she weren't so worried, Janice would have almost enjoyed the journey. The scenery through East Texas and Louisiana was so lush and green that she wanted to reach out and touch all of it. The wagon part of the trip gave her the opportunity to smell the rich magnolias. Peter even obligingly stopped once so she could run up and touch one of the waxy blossoms. She had seen them on her first trip out here, but no one had ever given her the opportunity to really drink in their scents.

And she felt like royalty on the steamboat. The last time she had come through here, she'd rode on the lower deck with the humbler passengers. When she'd suggested they do the same now, Peter had to be told about steerage. He had barely been aware of its existence. When he discovered it meant they would have no access to the luxurious salons of the main deck, he'd been adamantly opposed to his wife traveling in such a manner. She could tell he debated the possibility for himself, but she refused to go above unless he was with her.

That had settled it, and their brief journey to Natchez was done in style. Self-conscious at first that her plain traveling gown could not compare to the rich silks and laces of the rest of the company, Janice quickly forgot herself in the myriad amusements to be seen around her. Lavish crystal chandeliers danced in the sunlight, sending rainbows reflecting against mirrored walls. A piano player made soothing music to converse by while uniformed waiters circled among the passengers, taking orders for drinks. Peter indulged her with a glass of champagne, and for the first time in her life, Janice felt the frivolous bubbles tickle her tongue.

This was how she had expected life to be with Peter Mulloney. She was well out of her depth, she knew, but just this brief glimpse served to smother some of her immediate worries. She sipped the champagne, admired the view, and smiled at her husband as if she had lived in this world all her life.

"I wish you'd do that more often."

They stood outside at the rail, watching the muddy river pass beneath the slowly turning wheel. Peter's request came out of the blue. Startled, Janice gave him a puzzled look.

"There, I've gone and done it now. It's gone again. You have the loveliest smile, Mrs. Mulloney. Why don't you use it more frequently?"

The sultry summer breeze licked at her hat, and Janice grabbed it more firmly as she studied her husband's face. She hadn't thought Peter Mulloney the sort of man who flirted. "My smile?"

There was genuine puzzlement in her voice. Peter had continually found himself astonished in these last few days by the amount of tenderness he could summon when faced with this extraordinary creature he had married. He had known she was strong and determined and practical. He hadn't known that she was not only completely unaware of her beauty, but innocent of all forms of feminine guile. She was refreshingly straightforward, so that he always knew where he stood with her.

"You have the loveliest smile I've ever seen, but you seldom ever use it. You're not a schoolteacher any longer. You don't need to be stern and forbidding. I like to see you smile."

She still stared at him with more puzzlement than pleasure, but obligingly she managed a smile. Peter laughed at her blatant attempt to please him.

"You're going to be a marvelous wife, Mrs. Mulloney. I'm going to like having you to come home to."

Her smile grew more genuine with that, but before she could express her pleasure, a shattering thunder split the air.

In the dusky sky over Natchez, a dozen skyrockets exploded, and then before the startled eyes of the passengers rushing to the deck, the sky erupted into brilliant red and gold flowers of flame welcoming their arrival.

# Fifteen

"Tyler and some friends just bought a fireworks factory, and he's been eager to find some way to show off for weeks now. I couldn't persuade him that the Fourth of July is just a little way off. He wanted to surprise you and celebrate your wedding. No doubt if you'd married here, the donkey would have kept you up all night with the display." Hugging Janice, squeezing a surprised Peter, Evie Monteigne chattered unrepentantly. Her magnificently plumed hat had no ribbons to keep it tied on, and she kept grabbing for it in the mild breeze off the river. Or allowing others to grab it for her.

"Betsy is just a little bit worried. I made her wait in the carriage. I've told her everything I know about you, Peter, and a lot you probably didn't know yourself, just so she would sleep since you sent that telegram. I figured you had already wired Daniel and Georgina, but I sent them another when you said you were coming here. I'm sure they won't be able to travel this close to Georgina's time, but I thought they'd like to know you were going to be with family."

Tyler Monteigne listened to his wife's prattle with a hint of amusement. Some ten years Peter's senior, he still had the lean figure of his youth, only slightly broadened by the years. His golden brown hair glinted in the sun, and the laugh lines around his eyes deepened as he looked from his wife to Daniel's overwhelmed brother.

He caught the hint of a frown on Peter's face when Evie mentioned her family penchant for telegrams, but Janice seemed serenely unworried by the news. Tyler had liked the schoolteacher the few times he'd met her. He couldn't imagine anyone being more different from his excitable, story-telling wife than the imperturbable, steadfast Janice Harrison, but he was charmed by the difference. From the few glimpses he'd seen of the newlyweds already, he rather thought the bridegroom felt the same.

Once Evie released the poor man, Tyler held out his hand. "Good to see you again, Peter. It's been a few years, but I remember you well. Someday you're going to have to tell me the story of how two residents of Cutlerville, Ohio, had to go all the way to Texas to meet each other."

This time, it was Janice who frowned, and Tyler had the distinct feeling that his words somehow perturbed Peter. He couldn't figure where he'd gone wrong, but he sent a signal to Evie that she interpreted immediately. Something was out of kilter here, and they were going to have to get to the bottom of it.

But for the moment, the Monteignes could only stand back and watch as a child broke through the crowd emerging into the street above the bluff. She was so fair and fragile that it seemed she would almost certainly be trampled by the much larger adults around her, but the crowd seemed to part to allow her to sail gracefully through. At the sight of Janice hurrying forward either to rescue or meet her, she smiled and waved with delight, and the very air around her appeared to shimmer with gold.

Tyler caught the expression of astonishment on Peter's face as he watched this fairylike child approach. As Janice hugged the girl and the two of them came forward, swinging their hands between them and chattering, the astonishment turned into something else, something very like enlightenment, and it was Tyler's turn to study the two. He couldn't see what the other man obviously did.

Both Janice and Betsy had hair as fair as moonlight, but Betsy's had a curl and shine that Janice's straight, straying tresses would never attain. The little girl's eyes were an angelic shade of blue rather than the disdainful gray of her sister's. Janice was small-boned, but in no way as small and fragile as her younger version. There was a family resemblance, yes, but Tyler could see no more than that.

Peter's expression softened even more as he knelt before the child to take her hand. Suspicion flickered in the girl's eyes at first, but then he said something to her that made her laugh, and the suspicion disappeared as if it had never been. Tyler shook his head as Betsy hugged her new brother-in-law's neck. The child never knew a stranger. He prayed life would never teach her anything different.

"Evie says you're to be my new brother." Betsy stood beside Peter as he handed Janice into the waiting carriage, then scrambled in to take the place beside her sister. Her small face looked up expectantly for Peter to sit on her other side, so that she sat sandwiched between them.

Peter hesitated over the answer, throwing Janice's impassive expression a quick look before answering. "Yes, yes I am. Shall you call me Peter?"

The child's smile was as bright and winning as Janice's. Again, Peter looked between the two faces. He could be mistaken. He'd never asked Betsy's age. For all that matter, he didn't know his wife's. It was possible . . .

He wouldn't speculate. He didn't like to think that his straightforward, honest wife would keep a secret of this magnitude from him. Betsy was just as Janice had said, her sister. The family resemblance was strong, as were the expressions and gestures, but Janice had raised the child. That was to be expected. He smiled as Betsy murmured "Brother Peter" under her breath, as if to taste the sound of it.

"How long will you be staying? We have a real whopper of a fireworks display planned for the Fourth. The town's having a parade, and the women have been planning food for weeks."

Peter had felt Tyler studying him since they arrived, and he did his best to reply in a manner that would satisfy all the interested ears turned in his direction. "I haven't seen a Fourth of July parade since that one Georgina manipulated back home. I'm almost relieved I don't own any factories around here so we won't have half the town marching under my windows demanding better working conditions."

His audience laughed, and Peter sent a surreptitious glance to Janice. The Monteignes knew about that incident. They had been there. Had Janice been living in Cutlerville on that Fourth? It had been one of the worst days of his life, the turning point that had sent him out into the world. Would she have been one of the people storming his father's estate in protest against his unfair labor practices? It didn't matter. If she were from Cutlerville, she had known who he was all along. Everyone in Cutlerville knew the Mulloney family. Why had she never told him she knew who he was?

He sank back in his seat and considered this new aspect to his wife. He had thought her so open, but he could see now that he had only been fooling himself. People were seldom what they seemed on the surface. That didn't mean there was anything wrong with them. It just meant that Janice was a little more complex than he'd bothered to find out. He wished there would be more time to explore before he had to go back to New Mexico, but he was going to have to wait.

The knowledge that Evie had wired Daniel about their marriage sat uneasily inside him, also. He hadn't bothered even writing a letter telling his family about his marriage yet. There hadn't been a lot of time for writing. He'd wired the Monteignes out of necessity. That was business. Wiring the brother he barely knew ... Peter sighed and turned his attention back to the chatter around him. Common courtesy required that he at least inform his parents of his marriage. He hadn't even done that—but now Evie had. He didn't wish to consider the consequences.

The child between them kept Peter from reaching for Janice. He wanted the reassurance of her fingers wrapped in his right now. He felt like he was running along a cliff and one wrong step would send him stumbling over the precipice.

"We cleaned out the bridal suite for you," Evie said, turning dancing brown eyes to Janice. "I've been meaning to have that tower cleaned out for years now. The view is just gorgeous, but there are so many stairs ..."

Tyler laughed. "There are so many stairs that only newlyweds would be crazy enough to climb all of them to go to bed. Of course, once up there, who wants to come down again?"

Janice squirmed uneasily in her seat and managed a nervous smile that had their host and hostess exchanging laughing glances. "A tower? The house has a tower? Like in a castle?"

"An observatory, actually," Tyler replied. "My grandfather built the house before the war. He had a fascination with astronomy. He kept his telescope up there and could watch the sky even on the coldest nights. But all those stairs even deterred him when he grew older, so the tower just became a place to store things we didn't need right away. It was used as an observation post during the war for a while, but we're too far out of town to provide an effective warning system. The Yankees moved in anyway."

There was still a trace of bitterness in his voice, but it disappeared behind Tyler's white smile and laughing words. "The birds thought it belonged to them for quite a while, but you don't have to worry. We've put the glass back in the windows."

Janice gasped as she gazed out and caught a glimpse of the house as the carriage turned up the drive. Through a curtain of live oak leaves and hanging moss could be seen patches of brick and soaring white columns and banks of glittering windows set among riotous blooming bushes and magnolias.

"Oh, my. Daniel told me you lived in a mansion, but I never ..." Janice went quiet, unable to say the polite thing.

Tyler chuckled. "It's looking better than it did. We're

taking it one room at a time. There used to be chickens
nesting in the dining parlor and pigs corralled in the family salon. Now we mostly have kids swarming over every
inch of space. Enjoy the pristine aspect you see now.
When you get up closer, you'll see the real house."

It was almost full dark by the time the carriage pulled
up in front of the house, but the gas lights in the yard and
on the wide veranda threw the front of the house into
shadowed illumination. The air erupted with an explosion
almost as loud as the earlier fireworks when Peter stepped
out of the carriage, only this time the racket had almost a
musical rhythm to it.

Tyler groaned as he leapt out of the carriage to stand
beside his guest. "I told those damned boys not to . . ."

The distinct sound of a horn trumpeted through the
night until the dissonant racket of drums threatened to
overcome it. Peter thought he detected the rattle of Mexican gourds, a flute, and a guitar intertwined in the riotous
rhythm. The music itself seemed to veer between primitive African and provocative Spanish. He shook his head
in disbelief as an owl hooted in disapproval from the tree
above them before flying off into the night.

Betsy leapt down from the carriage without assistance,
running off in the direction of the noise without a word
of explanation. Even Janice smiled slightly as she took
Peter's hand and climbed down. Evie laughed out loud
and shook her head at her husband, who rolled his eyes in
disbelief.

As they started up the stairs, childish laughter exploded
overhead in the same instant that the air around them
burst into thousands of tiny colored pieces of confetti. Paper rainbows in reds and blues and yellows fluttered and
flew and drifted and coated their hair and clothes and the
stairs around them, blowing off into the night and deco-
rating the azalea bushes lining the drive. The music
reached new crescendoes of delight.

Evie and Tyler laughed and yelled and shook their fists
at the balcony overhead, all at the same time. Peter caught
Janice's hand and she turned an unwilling grin up to him.

A piece of pink confetti clung to her nose, and he grinned back, wiping at the paper he felt adorning his own cheek.

"Do they always live like this?" he asked, indicating the unusual couple now running up the stairs and into the house.

Janice tried to manage a demure smile, but every time the reckless band above broke into a new rhythm, she couldn't prevent a grin. "I think it's supposed to be a shivaree. I hear the fine sound of a Rodriguez behind this. Be prepared for anything."

Rodriguez. Peter sought the memory of that name as he assisted his wife up the stairs and out of the last spiraling bits of colored snow. He heard the distinct sound of childish laughter lilting through the air above them as they reached the safety of the door. Rodriguez! Of course. Evie's cousins, Daniel's companions in crime. He shivered with a premonition that this was not going to be the quick and businesslike meeting he had anticipated.

The noisy band seemed to come crashing down from the open hallway above the magnificent stairs in the main floor gallery. Before the visitors could catch sight of their serenaders, a gray-haired black woman in voluminous skirts stalked down the polished hall clutching a wooden spoon she waved like a sword when she advanced up the staircase.

"I told you young beggars not to mess my carpets up there! If you done got any of that there mess in my parlor, I'm agonna wring your necks and serve you up for dinner! Now get yo'selves down here right this minute or see if I don't come after you."

Laughter and running footsteps clattered through the upper hall, accompanied by the occasional toot of a horn or beat of a drum as the culprits scattered. Peter was still staring up the stairs in astonishment when the Monteignes reappeared in the hallway from the rear of the house, followed by a tall, thin black man and a lovely woman with skin the color of creamy coffee.

"I can't keep an eye on those cretins every minute of the day," the black man was complaining. "That'd be like askin' me to part the Mississippi. Where's Carmen? She's the responsible party here."

As if summoned by the mention of her name, the responsible party appeared at the top of the staircase, followed by her two children and Betsy. Laughing, she lifted her skirt and ran down the stairs to greet Janice.

"There you are! How does it feel to be an old married woman now?" She didn't pause in her speech as she turned to Peter and held out her hand. "Evie tells me you're Daniel's brother. I had the maddest crush on Daniel when I was just a little older than Betsy." As Peter's hand enveloped hers, she sent Janice a mischievous look and whispered loudly, "You were smart to wait for this one to come along. He's much better-looking than Daniel."

Peter found himself totally outnumbered and thoroughly at sea as the lovely Spanish/Mexican-looking woman holding his hand was introduced as Carmen Harding, Kyle Harding's wife and Evie's cousin, the black man and woman as Benjamin Wilkerson the Third and his wife, Jasmine, and the large gray-haired woman as Grandmama Sukey, Ben's grandmother. He assumed the boy and girl clinging to Carmen's hands were the Harding children, and the two young men and a girl slipping into the hall from various directions were some other relation to Carmen—and thus to Evie—although Evie bore no resemblance to their Mexican good looks. He was grateful that Janice seemed to be familiar with them all. Maybe sometime in the next decade he would straighten out all the names and faces and relationships.

Right now, he couldn't do more than note that this was a radically peculiar household, a far cry from the sterile mansion of his own childhood. As Peter and Janice were escorted into the best parlor, Benjamin sprawled against the fireplace as if he were as much owner of this house as Tyler. Benjamin's wife consulted with Carmen and Grandmama Sukey and the three of them disappeared into the bowels of the house as a herd of children ranging from the age of two on up to Carmen's sister's approximate seventeen ran in and out of the parlor and up and down the stairs, toting musical instruments and streaming confetti behind them. The children ranged in color from Betsy's pale fairness through the Hardings' tanned bronze to a toddler's gleaming black. He would never straighten out the menagerie, but he was fascinated by the fact that Evie and Tyler treated every one of them as their own. Actually, Peter couldn't quite decide which ones actually did belong to the Monteignes.

Peter gave up the pursuit of knowledge some while later when he noted the lines of fatigue marring Janice's smile. They had sipped rich wines and coffee, nibbled at cakes and breads and meats that would have rivaled those of the best restaurants Peter had known, and the conversation had whirled furiously from the mundane to the outrageous. The time had come to put an end to the welcoming ceremonies. This was their honeymoon. Someone needed to remind the company of that.

Without fanfare, Peter wandered over to his beautiful hostess as she gave instructions to a young girl called Maria he assumed to be Evie's youngest cousin. The girl hurried off to locate the last of the children and send them on to bed, and Evie turned expectant eyes to her guest.

"Janice looks a trifle weary. You will be wanting someone to show you to your room, won't you?"

If Janice were half as beautiful as Evie Monteigne in ten years, he would be a lucky man. Peter smiled gratefully at his hostess. "The last days have been a trifle hectic, and traveling is always difficult. As much as we are enjoying the company, I think perhaps we ought to think about retiring for the evening."

Evie's laughter bubbled from her lips and into her eyes. "You've spent too much time with your father and not enough time with Daniel, Mr. Mulloney. You're in danger of becoming a pompous man. Come, I will show you the tower stairs, but do not dare to tell me that it is only your weariness that inclines you toward bed. I have seen how you look at your wife."

Her laughter carried them to where Tyler and Janice sat

side by side, discussing the need for expanding public education. Evie's last words fell into a sudden silence, and the flush on Janice's cheeks indicated she had caught their drift. Peter smiled at the bloom of color. Finally, he could take her to bed again.

Janice looked away from his eager gaze.

# *Sixteen*

They used candles to light their way to the top of the long staircase leading into the tower room. The Gothic qualities of the approach to their bedroom held a vague appeal at the moment. Janice thought perhaps she'd had too much wine if she was finding humor in this situation.

She smiled in genuine delight when they threw open the door and entered the outer chamber. The tower was far enough above the trees for the moonlight to shine in far stronger than the faint candles they carried. A silvery cast glittered over an old-fashioned love seat in gold velvet and mahogany, a towering armoire that could date back to Revolutionary War days, a delicate writing desk sporting a silver tray and crystal champagne glasses—and a bottle of champagne. The Monteignes were obviously romantics.

Behind her, Peter laughed. Janice couldn't remember if she'd ever heard him laugh. The sound was vaguely delicious, sending a thrill through her middle. She knew she'd had too much wine when she thought that. She didn't have the courage to face her husband just yet, and she wandered to the magnificent bank of windows to look out at the stars. She was much too aware of the closed door on the other side of the armoire.

She heard Peter pop the cork on the champagne and fill their glasses. Trepidation filled her along with the sound of the wine in the crystal. Here was the perfect setting for a honeymoon seduction, a second chance to see if she could overcome her flaws and become the kind of wife

her husband craved. But even had she wanted this opportunity, she couldn't take it. Embarrassment as much as
anything else overcame her as Peter came up beside her
and handed her a glass.

"To a lifetime together, Mrs. Mulloney." He struck his
glass to hers and the crystal chimed in the silence.

Janice sipped the intoxicating bubbles and dared lift
her eyes to study her husband. Carmen was right. Peter
was far more handsome than Daniel. There had been a
time a long, long time ago when she had fancied Daniel
as the hero of her dreams. Peter's broad build was far
more suited to the hero image than lanky Daniel, but
Janice rather thought that Daniel's character was probably
far more heroic than Peter's. Still, she couldn't really resist the pull of her husband's dark good looks when he
smiled down at her. She hastily took another sip of champagne.

"I don't want you to be afraid of me, Janice," he murmured, tucking a straying strand of hair behind her ear. "I
should have treated you better the other night, I know, but
I thought you more experienced. I know better now. I'll
do what I can to make it good for you."

She blushed, a painful hot flood of color that seared her
cheeks. She couldn't look at him. She admired the way
the moonlight played across the champagne bubbles instead. "We can't," she whispered at the glass.

Peter's hand halted its caress. "Can't?"

"The train," she murmured nervously. "When I
travel . . ." She couldn't get the words out. She was
twenty-five years old and had never had to explain personal functions to a man. She didn't know how to do so
now, especially to a man who had grown up in a household of boys and no doubt never thought about such
things. "It's my time," she managed to get out before giving up.

She felt him studying her, working her words through
that encyclopedia of a brain of his. She was quite certain
the section on feminine hygiene would be extremely
small. Peter's reputation back in Cutlerville had little to

do with women despite his good looks. He was known as a thorough, humorless, highly intelligent, driven autocrat. She was beginning to understand that he may have been expecting his employees to keep the same kind of hours and work as hard as he did himself, but that was neither here nor there at the moment. What she needed him to understand had nothing to do with business, but Peter knew very little outside of business.

"I see," he finally said, although his tone voiced less than certainty. "Perhaps you'd rather go on to bed then. I'll stay out here until you've had time to get to sleep. I'm still a trifle restless."

Janice interpreted that easily enough. She might not know a great deal about men, but she understood the source of their restlessness. She felt a twinge of regret at disappointing him, but she shoved it away with the knowledge of how much he had disappointed her. She wouldn't forget that they had made it to Natchez on her money, not his. He had a lot to prove yet.

She turned to leave and felt even more regret that this wonderfully romantic setting wouldn't be the beginning of something beautiful. She had always known she wasn't meant for the kind of love and passion that the Monteignes enjoyed, but that couldn't keep her from wishing. She felt a tear pressing at the corner of her eye as she watched moonlight reflect off the crystal prisms on the desk lamp. She was almost afraid to look in the bedroom.

Unable to leave so easily, she asked over her shoulder, "You didn't wire Daniel about our marriage, did you?"

He was silent for a moment before answering, "No."

Janice nodded and started to walk off. She refused to speculate on whether he had been ashamed of his marriage or just too contrary to tell his family. Peter's voice behind her made her halt again.

"I'll write them before we leave. If you come from Cutlerville, you'll understand that I'm not very close to my family."

There was a challenge in his voice, and Janice turned

to meet it. He still stood in the window, his broad shoulders in the dark suit jacket outlined against the moonlit night. Something in her stomach clenched at the sight, but she had already rejected him and he had accepted that rejection. She no longer had to worry about that. Not tonight, anyway.

"I'm from a town down by Cincinnati. My parents were immigrants. We just ended up in Cutlerville by default. I wouldn't say I was from there, any more than I would say I was from Texas."

His face was too shadowed to read his expression. "You knew who I was though. Why didn't you tell me from the first? There must have been any number of opportunities."

Janice shrugged. "I knew your name, and I owed Daniel a great deal, and I knew you were innocent of arson. I did what I had to do. I can't say that I liked it." She thought he almost smiled at that. She couldn't tell for sure.

"I guess that gives me a better idea of where I stand. You despise me for being a Mulloney and married me because I am a Mulloney. I'm just concerned what will happen when I don't live up to your expectations."

"So far, you've shot down every one of them. That doesn't make us any less married. I'm not completely certain why you married me unless it was out of pity or gratitude, but I knew what I was doing when I accepted you. I'll honor my vows." She hesitated, then finished bravely, "I just don't want to have to raise another child in poverty."

She entered the bedroom then and closed the door after her. Peter stared at the closed door with more confusion than he'd ever felt in his life. There had been a time when he'd been confronted with the extent of his father's perfidies that he'd been furious and without direction, but that hadn't been the same kind of befuddlement that he felt now.

He understood, even if he didn't accept, his father's

callousness. But he couldn't ever come close to under-standing the woman he had married.

Janice was a beautiful woman he'd thought would stand gratefully and loyally at his side for the rest of his years. Instead, he'd found an enigmatic puzzle who in all probability despised him for what he had been and had married him for the money she despised him for having. That made no logical sense at all.

And there was still the matter of the child. Her parting words had been telling, a warning he didn't want to heed. She didn't want to have to raise another child in poverty. The words didn't mean Betsy was more than her sister. It was the way she said them.

Peter turned back to stare out the window at the dark shapes of the trees below. He felt a hollow where his stomach should be. From a few terse comments Janice had made, he'd gathered she had grown up in poverty. He'd never known the specters of poverty himself. They'd never haunted his sleep. Even now, so broke he used his wife's money, he knew he had only to make a few visits and he could be working again, making good pay. He could wire Daniel and have funds within days. His children would never starve. His pride might, but not his children. How did he explain that to a woman who had watched her family starve while his own got wealthy off their labors? For that was no doubt what had hap-pened if she grew up in Cutlerville. He knew his father's villainy and cutthroat hold over the working citizens of his hometown too well.

When he finally had enough wine in him to make it safe to follow his wife to the bedroom, Peter found her sleeping on the far side of a bed draped in finely woven netting. The breeze through the open windows lifted the edges of the netting and fluttered them in a soft dance around the ancient four-poster bed. The bed dominated the chamber, but he found a chair to lay his clothes across. He had difficulty undressing while he watched his wife sleep, but he somehow managed to get all the but-

tons through their holes and his shoes off. Janice slept
without moving.

He didn't own a nightshirt, and the formal shirt he
wore with his suit was too stiff for sleeping in. His spinster wife would have to become accustomed to waking up
with a naked man in her bed. That gave him a moment's
satisfaction as he slid between the sheets.

The satisfaction died the instant he felt her linen gown
against his legs, but he forced his thoughts to the discussion he meant to have with Tyler in the morning, and
gradually his body relaxed. Moments later he slept.

When Janice awoke in the morning, she found the
sheets had fallen off the bed. The room was too warm to
miss them, and she regretted her long nightgown, until
the instant she realized the greatest source of heat—the
man beside her.

She had her back to him, but she knew he was naked
as soon as she realized he was there. She remembered
clearly that other morning when she woke in his arms to
find him fully aroused and ready to take her again. Her
cheeks burned with the memory, and a previously unknown tingle stirred inside her.

But the knowledge that their one time together hadn't
left her with child gave her the strength to move away.
She might like to know what it would feel like to have
Peter's hands touch her breasts again, but she was quite
certain a man wouldn't be satisfied with just that. So the
fact that the bodice of her gown suddenly felt tight while
she remembered how his hands felt against her skin held
no meaning. She started to move her legs over the edge of
the bed.

His hand caught her arm and slid around to her waist,
pulling her backward against him. Janice stiffened, trying
to avoid the dangerous territory of her husband's hips, but
that was an impossibility. She could feel his arousal pushing against the thin material of her gown, but he merely
kissed the nape of her neck.

"I'm surprised our hosts haven't bestowed us with a
fairy godmother bearing champagne and strawberries for

breakfast, or at least installed an orchestra playing Mozart so we can waltz down the stairs," he murmured into the thick braid of her hair.

Janice giggled. She couldn't help it. She was so tense she thought she might break in two at the slightest wrong move, but the image of fairy godmothers and waltzing down stairs was so far removed from her current worries that her only recourse was laughter. She swore she could feel him smile behind her, and some of the tension slipped away. He was only human. She would have to remember that.

"I'm certain there's champagne left, and I'll look into the strawberry situation, if you like. I'm rather afraid the music will more likely resemble a hoe-down than a waltz, though."

He chuckled and moved his hand upward, brushing the undersides of her breasts. Janice tensed again, but he didn't seem to notice.

"With the Monteignes as the influencing factor in his growing up, I can see why Daniel turned out as he did. They're enough to make anyone believe in fairy tales."

Janice couldn't help smiling, even as Peter's thumb moved determinedly to caress her nipple through the soft cloth. The tender touch felt good, much too good, as long as she ignored the hard male length of his body behind her. That was hard to do when the place between her legs moistened just from the rumble of his voice near her ear.

"The Monteignes aren't quite real, are they?" she answered. "I think they're rather like a heady wine, too much and you're in trouble."

"I've had quite enough wine, thank you. My head is hurting from last night's abundance." Peter's fingers found the erect tip of Janice's breast beneath the cloth and tweaked it gently. She gave a tiny gasp, and he smiled in satisfaction as he slid his hand back to the safer territory of her waist. The hand rebelliously kept on moving to her hip, where it pulled her slightly closer to him. He gave a moan of frustration. "I'm hurting in any number of places, Mrs. Mulloney. If you don't mean to tend to me personally, perhaps you could bring me the rest of that bottle."

She practically jumped out of the bed, leaving Peter to grope the warm sheets. Her trunk had been transported to this room but not unpacked. She grabbed the first things that came to hand and fled for the far room.

Peter sighed and rolled over, giving the stiff flagpole of his manhood a disgruntled look. That was the reason he'd got into this mess, he had no doubt about that. His wife might not comprehend why he had married her, but he hadn't any doubts at all. He wanted to bury himself inside her and stay there for about six months at least.

But if he understood the calendar of human events, he wouldn't even be able to have her once before he left.

Damn.

He slammed his feet to the floor and reached for the well-worn contents of his saddlebag.

Tyler's study had more the appearance of an eccentric garden shed than an office. On the wall over the fireplace he had mounted a rifle and pistols, but someone had hung a shiny Valentine heart over the barrel of the rifle and a red paper rose stuck out of one of the pistols. The shelf of books to one side had obviously well-read volumes stacked haphazardly everywhere, interspersed with objects too strange for Peter to discern without obviously ignoring his host and studying them.

A rake rested in one corner of the room, several games of patience had been left in various states of disarray on a side table, and Tyler shuffled another deck of cards back and forth as he listened to his guest. Peter experienced some difficulty remembering why he had come in here. He kept waiting for the flying cards to leap into the air or scatter over the worn carpet.

"So you can see the loan would only be temporary," he heard himself saying. "We could repay it as soon as the deed is in our hands. You can practically name your terms."

Peter thought he'd said all that he'd come here to say.

He was usually pretty thorough in these kinds of matters. Business was his strong point, after all. But Monteigne seemed to be looking somewhere over Peter's shoulder, and his cards kept flying back and forth between his hands.

The cards suddenly piled themselves up in a neat stack on the cluttered desk, and Tyler leaned back in his chair—so far back that Peter thought he would tumble over at any minute. Instead, the other man swung his boots up on the already scarred wood and grinned.

"I've got just the solution for you," he agreed. "This place eats up every piece of cash I ever get or I'd give you the money right out. I like gambling on sure things. But seein' as how that kind of cash ain't readily available, we'll have to wager for it."

Peter stared at him as if Tyler had just said they would have to go to hell and dig it up. "Wager for it?"

"Yep. I've got a horse that I've been meaning to race for some time now. We'll enter it into the holiday sweepstakes."

Peter grasped that notion well enough. He didn't like it, but he understood it. He raised his eyebrows uncertainly. "Holiday?"

Tyler grinned broadly. "Fourth of July."

That would give him less than five weeks to get to New Mexico. Peter felt sweat break out on his forehead. "If the horse is a sure winner, won't the odds be rather low? That would take a lot of cash."

Tyler swung his boots down and stood up, the very picture of a man eagerly setting out to meet a challenge. "The horse never won a race in its life. Come on, let's go look at it."

Wincing inwardly, Peter followed the madman out of the house. He could feel his entire future sliding down the drain, and he had the awful feeling he could do nothing at all about it. God meant to punish him for his sins, unintentional or not.

# Seventeen

A tall man with the stooped shoulders of age stood beside Betsy's easel while the child painted the paddock scene before her. The man's hair was the same chestnut as Evie's, only faded and gray with time. Up close, Janice could see the dark eyes of Carmen and her brothers. James Peyton was the man who brought the separate heritages of Evie Monteigne and the Rodriguez family together. Janice smiled as Evie's father and Betsy launched into some argument over an object in the painting in front of them.

Her smile disappeared as her gaze traveled to the paddock and the men standing at the fence. Peter had discarded jacket and vest in the summer heat and leaned his shirt sleeves against the rail. He studied the horse in the paddock so intensely that he didn't even notice her approach. The man on the other side of him, however, turned immediately and gave her his famous smile.

Janice shook her head, indicating that he not interrupt their conversation for her. Tyler grinned and returned to watching Benjamin cinching the horse's saddle, then grabbing the reins and hanging on while his mount flailed the air.

Peter protested, "The animal isn't even broken yet! Monteigne, you're out of your mind. Just look at it! I've never seen a more pitiful excuse for a horse. It's practically wall-eyed, and look at those flanks! Geld him and make him a plow horse, maybe, but race? I'll just end up owing you a thousand bucks with nothing to show for it."

Janice's eyes went wide at this startling information,

but she kept her mouth shut. She hadn't heard the whole conversation. She may have missed something.

"Ben's had him out. The brute has the devil in him, but if anyone can handle him, Ben can. Just keep an eye on him." Tyler propped a boot on the bottom rail and pushed his light-colored frock coat back to shove his hand in his pocket. Even in the steamy afternoon heat, he looked cool.

Janice shook her head in dismay at this discovery. She wore her thinnest gown and not enough petticoats to be decent, and still she felt like a steamed ear of corn. She eyed the raging horse with trepidation and eased away from the fence. She didn't like horses, and she definitely didn't like the looks of this one.

"That young fellow certainly knows his horses," Peyton commented behind her. Unconsciously she had gravitated in the direction of Betsy and her tutor.

She didn't know which young fellow Peyton referred to, but she didn't think she agreed with his comment either. She merely nodded and kept at least the corner of her eye on the tableau in the paddock while she turned to admire Betsy's work.

She stared at the striking ebony horse leaping off the canvas. "Betsy, that's marvelous! That's not watercolor. However did you learn to do that?"

Too intent on trying to capture a particular gleam in the horse's eye, Betsy didn't even look up. "Mr. Peyton taught me. He let me use his paints."

Janice had a sinking feeling that the oil paints were considerably more expensive than the pitiful child's colors she had bought Betsy for her birthday, and she sent Peyton a look of gratitude. At least, she thought she was grateful. When Betsy had to leave the luxury of these new paints behind, she might be of a different mind.

"The girl's talented. She has a good eye. She's got a lot to learn when it comes to animals and such, but there's plenty of time. She's about outgrown watercolors already. I couldn't keep her painting clouds and flowers forever."

This last was almost an apology, as if he understood Janice's financial predicament.

"I'm grateful for all the help you've given her, sir. I only wish I could reimburse you for your efforts."

Peyton grinned, a charming grin reminiscent of Evie at her worst. "Just send me the proceeds of her first sale, and we'll call it even. I'd only drink it up or gamble it, anyway."

The horse squealing from the paddock caused them to turn and watch the athletic display of man against beast. Ben was on the stallion's back, clinging to the saddle and the reins as the animal reared and circled and screamed in protest. It was an admirable contest, but Janice felt only fear as sharp hooves slashed the air daringly near to the men at the fence.

As Ben brought the horse under control, Tyler ran to throw open the paddock gate. Peter was already moving away from the fence in the direction of the little group beside the easel, instinctively placing himself between the horse's path and his family. Janice hadn't thought he even knew they were there. Perhaps he didn't. Perhaps he was just sensibly removing himself from the path of danger.

It didn't matter. Nothing could have prevented what happened next. It was just one of those quirks of fate that one of the Monteigne youngsters chose that moment to dash out of a mock-orange thicket in pursuit of a puppy that had escaped his care, just as Ben and horse sprang through the paddock gate.

A scream split the air. Tyler jerked his head up in time to find his son on a collision course with death. He ran for the boy at the same time as Ben tried to wheel the horse away. It all happened too fast for Janice to ever put together completely later.

Tyler grabbed his son and rolled out of the way of sharp hooves. The horse reared. Ben went flying from the saddle. And the stallion broke loose from all restraint. The animal's path to freedom led directly toward the little party at the easel.

Janice knew she was screaming as she grabbed Betsy

and started to run. She had never screamed in her life, but she couldn't stop now. The horse was bearing directly down on them, breathing flames for all she knew or cared. She could hear Peter's shouts, but they were meaningless to her. All that mattered was rescuing Betsy from the tearing hooves of the beast racing toward them.

And then the horse screamed, and the yard suddenly filled with people racing out of nowhere. Somebody grabbed Betsy out of her arms. Someone else caught Janice and held her trapped. Everyone froze, staring in the direction of the paddock, with no one running to help Ben or Tyler. Terrified, Janice turned and looked over her shoulder.

Peter had the stallion's reins. He hauled on them as hard as he could, but the brute was terrified and furious. Even as Janice watched, the horse nearly lifted Peter from his feet. And then in amazement she saw her husband get his foot in the stirrup and throw himself on the horse's back. The scream in her throat died as the world seemed to come to a standstill around her. The only movement was man and beast. The horse bolted.

She realized Peyton held her. His old arms couldn't keep her steady as she sank to her knees and watched her husband race across the tree-studded yard on the back of a beast from hell. Her heart tore from her chest and raced after him, carrying with it all the frightened screams that froze in her throat.

The horse aimed directly for the low branches of a magnolia, but Peter jerked it to the outer edge and ducked. They avoided an oak, and even the stallion had sense to stay out of an enormous holly. And then they hit the drive and disappeared from view.

Shaking, unable to move, Janice stayed where she was as Evie and Carmen ran to Ben and Tyler. Tyler climbed to his feet, carrying his son back to Evie, but Ben was down. Betsy came to hold Janice's hand, tears streaming down her cheeks, but neither said anything as they watched the place where Peter had disappeared. A wail went up from a different direction as Jasmine came running out of the smaller house toward the rear of the mansion and saw the figures bending over Ben. Disaster was strewn in the path of the stallion, and Peter was on its back.

"The boys and I will go out after them. Get her in the house."

Janice heard Tyler's voice somewhere in the distance, but she ignored it. She resisted the hands coming to pull her to her feet. She had lived through more disasters in her life than she ever wished to contemplate. She always found it easier to meet them on her knees. Beneath her breath, she prayed fervently while her fingers worked at the handkerchief someone had handed her.

"Leave her be," Carmen spoke sharply over Janice's head, overruling the patient understanding murmurs urging her to stand. "We'll wait out here. Betsy, go fetch your sister some ice water."

"At least get her out of the sun," Peyton muttered. "There's a bench under that oak."

The bench faced in the direction that Peter had gone. Janice accepted this new position. If she could just keep watching, he would return safe and sound. She knew he would. He had to. The alternative stretching out before her if he did not was too bleak to consider. She wasn't ready to be a widow. She wasn't even a wife yet.

She didn't cry. Tears were ineffective in the face of disaster. She had learned that a long time ago. Panic held her frozen, but steadfast concentration sometimes worked. If she could focus every inch of her being on the person endangered, sometimes they came through. She'd done that for Betsy more times than she could count. It hadn't worked for her mother and father, but they had lost faith in her. Peter didn't know to doubt her. All she had to do was sit here and concentrate and will him to be all right.

She heard the other horses riding out, but in some dark part of her mind Janice realized the men would be as useless as tears. All they could do was pick up Peter's broken body if he fell. She bit her lip and focused her mind more fiercely. He wouldn't fall.

The ice water went ignored when it came. Betsy's hand in hers was a help. Two minds focused on the same situation couldn't hurt. She squeezed Betsy's fingers and prayed harder.

It took a moment before Janice could accept the cheers when they finally rang out from the road. She kept praying, hoping the noise meant what she needed to hear, terrified she dreamed it.

But Betsy jumped up from the bench and cheered with the rest of them, and Janice dared to scan the road hidden behind the trees. Betsy couldn't race down the drive like some of the boys were doing now, but she obviously had confidence that the cheers meant good news. Even Peyton limped toward the road as fast as his arthritic legs would carry him.

The horse and rider bursting through the shadows and into the sunlight were the most beautiful things she had ever seen in her life. Janice held her breath as Peter brought the glistening black to a smooth canter and then a walk. His shoulders strained beneath the confinement of his white shirt, and his legs clung powerfully to the animal's sides until she couldn't tell where man began and horse ended. She let out her breath in a grateful sigh of relief as he guided the massive beast back into the paddock and someone slammed the gate after him.

Picking up her skirts, Janice ran as quickly as she was able toward the man who had risked his own life to save them all. How could she have ever thought him anything less than hero material? She must have misjudged him terribly. She'd finally found a man who could save her from the lifetime of drudgery she had faced, and she had almost turned her back on him.

Peter was off the horse and climbing over the fence when she came close enough to hear him yell at Tyler as the other men rode up to join him: "I'll take that wager, Monteigne! You've got a winner here."

Janice halted in her tracks, staring from the man she'd thought racing toward death to the grinning men still on horseback. Surely she hadn't heard right?

"Only if you ride him," Tyler yelled back, sidling his horse in closer. "Ben's turned his leg. He's out of the running."

To Janice's absolute horror, Peter walked up to Tyler and held out his hand. "That should increase my percentage. Who's going to circulate the rumor the beast is uncontrollable?"

Tyler laughed and shook Peter's hand. They weren't paying any attention to her at all. They behaved as if this whole thing were some kind of cosmic joke fate had played into their hands. People had almost died today, and they were calculating how to fix the odds on a horse race!

She swirled around in a fury and walked right into Evie.

Evie caught her arms, steadied them both, and, glancing over Janice's shoulder to the men slapping each other on the back, started back to the house beside her.

"Well now, you can't say that wasn't exciting. That husband of yours rides pretty well for a Yankee, I must say. I think we could all use a fresh lemonade after that. Ben's already inside complaining about all the women hovering over him. Maybe you could persuade Peter to come in and apply the reins to Ben. He really shouldn't use that leg for a while."

Janice had never really felt fury until now. Terror was an old friend, but fury was something usually as senseless as tears. But it seemed better to be furious than to break into the hysterics she had felt earlier. If the horse hadn't killed him, she would. He had risked his life, their future, for a horse race? And he was going to do so again? And all this to obtain the money for a gold mine that might not even exist? She practically shook with rage.

She didn't think she could stand it. She had married a madman, a gambler, a bankrupt ne'er-do-well who would no doubt spend his life sponging off his friends and chasing rainbows. She would have to leave him. She would have to find a job and start all over again. She wanted a house of her own. She wanted a future. She didn't want grandiose schemes involving horse races and gold mines. She didn't want Peter Mulloney.

Suppressing her fury, Janice stopped in the parlor to console an impatient Ben. She sipped the lemonade someone handed to her. She gave Betsy a hug and sent her out to play. And when Peter finally entered in a circle of triumphant men, she turned her back on him and walked out.

Peter watched her go with bewilderment. He had done what needed to be done. He'd thought he'd returned the conquering hero. He'd even found the means to make the money to buy the gold mine. He'd thought she would be proud of him. He had expected kisses and hugs. He hadn't expected an icy glare and the echoes of an unslammed door.

Behind him, Tyler and Evie exchanged glances.

"You men are such fools," she whispered.

"Fools? What did we do?" Tyler's expression reflected the same bewilderment as the man in front of him.

"You tear up dreams like bits of paper and walk on them," Evie declared. Then smiling at the child running to her for attention, she went in pursuit of the required cookies.

# *Eighteen*

"**Y**ou've been avoiding me all day. What is it?" Peter finally cornered his wife on the gallery later that evening. The scent of the magnolias was overpowering with the onset of darkness, but the fresh air felt good after the stifling heat of the lighted interior.

"I've been busy," Janice replied stiffly. "I need to see if Betsy has gone to bed. Let me by."

"Like hell, I will. Betsy's old enough to put herself to bed, and even if she isn't, there's enough people in there to help her along. The whole damn place crawls with people. There hasn't been a minute when I could get you alone."

She arched her eyebrows in imperious question. "Why would you want to get me alone? I'm perfectly capable of speaking in company."

"Don't give me that schoolmarm attitude, Mrs. Mulloney. I wasn't born yesterday. You're avoiding me, and that can only mean one thing that I know of. You've got a bee under your bonnet about something. Now let's get it out."

"Why? It's my bonnet." Smiling pleasantly, Janice attempted to skirt around him.

He grabbed her bustle and pulled her back. When she turned to smack him, Peter trapped her against the railing, placing his arms on either side of her to keep her from swinging at him. "You're my wife now. Everything that's yours is mine. So that's my bonnet and if I want to find out what's under it, I will."

"This is a ridiculous ..." Janice screamed slightly as

the small hat she had donned when she came outside went sailing into the bushes. "You can't do that! I haven't but two hats and that one has to do me . . ."

"Until I buy you a new one. And I will buy you a new one. That one looks as if you found it in a cow pasture. Now tell me what's wrong or I'll assume that bee is stuck in your hair and start on it next."

He reached for the pins and combs holding her hair in place. Janice smacked at his hands. "Nothing is wrong. Now stop that. I'm not a child. I'm entitled to my own thoughts and actions."

It only took the removal of a pin or two to collapse the first smooth loop of hair. It straggled over her shoulder in a limp mass, and she shoved it back nervously.

Peter wrapped it in his fingers. "You promised to honor your vows. Didn't they include honoring and obeying?" He purposely deleted the first part of the vow. She may have promised to love him, but he knew as well as anyone that wasn't possible. He didn't doubt that women were capable of imagining the emotion of love. He just knew that this woman would never love the man who represented all that she despised. He knew she had to despise his family. He despised them. She had talked of poverty and starvation, and he knew the man responsible. He didn't expect her to differentiate between himself and his father. There wasn't a world of difference between them. So he would just be content with honoring and obeying.

"There are limits, you know," she informed him. "If you told me to jump off a cliff, I wouldn't do it. And if you turn into a drunk who wallows in the mud, I won't honor you. Vows may be pretty, but they're not practical."

"And you are. You are nothing if not practical. Now tell me, my practical wife, what is it that I have done to upset your practical soul? Should I have let the horse loose to trample where it would? Should I have conveniently broken my neck so you could go weeping home to Daniel and live in luxury for the rest of your life? Just what exactly is it that I did wrong?"

Janice shoved ineffectually at his imprisoning arms.

"You married me, that was what you did wrong. Now let me go, Peter. I won't be treated like this."

Instead of releasing her, he circled her waist with his arms and pulled her up against him. "That wasn't wrong. Insane, maybe, but not wrong." He bent his head and pressed his lips against hers.

She went stiff against him again, but the day had left Peter churning with too many unsettled emotions to let her get away with that. He teased his tongue along the corner of her mouth and felt her lips part slightly. With a sigh of satisfaction, he took instant advantage. She gasped and tried to shove away when his tongue took possession of her mouth, but the move only gave him easier access to her breast. He captured it with one hand between them while he made a leisurely exploration of the sweet hollow behind her lips. He had longed for this for a long time. He couldn't be easily persuaded away.

Her corset hampered his explorations in other areas, but he managed to slide enough of his hand along the ridge to feel her nipple swell against his palm. He caressed it gently while stoking the fires with deepening kisses. He was rewarded when she moaned and shuddered against him.

That moan was almost his undoing. He grew hard and aching and could think only of what it would be like to be inside her again. He forgot his question. He forgot where they were. He forgot everything but the woman melting in his arms.

Janice clung to his coat for support, and then her hands slid beneath the hampering material to wrap around his back. Peter could feel the burning heat of her fingers through the layers of waistcoat and shirt. He wanted to strip off her gown and taste her skin, but he had enough sense left to realize this was the wrong time and place.

He knew if he let her go, she would retreat. He knew he couldn't go forward. So he stayed where he was and enjoyed what he was given.

A door slammed and small feet pattered across the wooden gallery and down the stairs in accompaniment with childish laughter. Peter pulled Janice deeper into the shadows thrown by the morning glory vines rambling up the post. A woman's voice called from a nearby window, and he gritted his teeth as Janice tried to pull away. Lord, what would he have to do to kiss his own wife?

Another door slammed. This time adult feet traversed the boards, and they didn't conveniently go running off into the darkness. Peter cursed beneath his breath as the steps drew closer. Pulling himself away, he attempted to right the damage he had done to Janice's clothing.

Breathlessly she pushed his hand away and straightened her lace, but the hairpins were long since gone. She tucked her hair up the best she could while Peter stayed in front of her as shield.

The intruder struck a match to light a cheroot, and the brief illumination revealed their hiding place. Tyler chuckled and calmly went about tending his cigar. "You're allowed to go up in the tower anytime you want. You're sure not keeping us company by staying out here."

"We just thought we'd go for a walk before we retired. I trust Betsy wasn't one of the rapscallions that just took off through the bushes?" Peter had learned the polite art of conversation at an early age and with good reason. He employed his talent now, accepting that Janice wasn't in any state to respond. He was rather proud of himself at bringing her to that point. The lady wasn't as cold as she pretended.

"No, that's the boys. They think they're going to find night crawlers. Most likely all they'll catch is mosquitoes, but at that age, who notices? If you're going to walk after dark, I'd recommend carrying a citronella lamp with you. Those critters will carry you off if you don't."

"Thanks for the warning. After all the excitement of the day, I think we'll just go on upstairs." Peter wrapped his arm around Janice's waist, guiding her past Tyler through the shadows so her dishevelment wouldn't be noticed.

She called a soft good night to their host as they passed, and he returned the greeting warmly. Just as they reached the door, Tyler's syrupy drawl called out, "You might want to stick that fancy cravat in your pocket, Mulloney. It's going to look mighty awkward where it is when you get inside."

Peter glanced down, found the offending article half tucked down inside his collar and half off, and jerked it hastily from his shirt. Beside him, Janice giggled. It wasn't much of a giggle, but it was enough to let him know she wasn't angry. Hopes soaring, he shoved the cravat in his pocket and practically pulled her into the house.

"We can't retire this early," Janice whispered as he steered her directly toward the stairs.

"I'm sorry, but I've seen all the people I want to see today. That tower is beginning to look mighty good to me." Peter kept a firm grasp on her waist.

Janice tried to twist away. "I've got to say good night to Evie and Carmen. And I ought to ask after Ben. It's rude to go to bed without telling anyone."

"They'll understand, I assure you." Peter hauled her closer to the staircase.

"But we can't . . ." She stumbled over the words but not the steps. He held her too firmly for that.

"All right, so we won't. But there're other things we can do."

Janice looked interested and wary at the same time. "Such as?"

Peter relaxed and hurried her up the stairs. "I'll show you."

But by the time they traversed all the landings and stairs and reached the top of the tower, Janice was stiff and nervous beside him again. Peter bit back his impatience and wished he'd had the forethought to have another bottle of wine brought up.

As soon as they entered the room, she pulled away from him and wandered to the window. Peter struck a match and lit the lamp on the writing desk, but he didn't see the need for a great deal of illumination for what he had in mind. Their shadows flickered across the ceiling as he moved the lamp.

He suddenly felt awkward and ill at ease. He'd never had the need to learn the art of seduction. In the past, when he had needed a woman, he'd simply bought one. These last years, when his funds were tight, he'd gone to places where he knew his looks would attract women willing to dally awhile. He'd worked at many things in his life, but he had never worked at persuading a woman to like him.

Peter walked up behind her and rested his hands on her shoulders. She jumped slightly but didn't move away. Before he could say anything, she did.

"This isn't going to work." She spoke so low, he didn't know if he'd heard her correctly.

"What isn't going to work?" Peter rubbed his thumbs into her shoulders, hoping to work the tension out of them. He hadn't married an easy woman, but he hadn't wanted an easy one. A willing one would have been nice.

"Us," Janice whispered at their reflections in the window. "I'm grateful that you thought to rescue me from the scandal back there, but we're not suited. When you find your mountain of gold, you can buy a divorce, I'm sure. In the meantime, I think I'd just better see if I can't find a job somewhere."

"No."

She turned and stared at him over her shoulder. "What do you mean, 'no'?"

He began pulling the remaining pins from her hair. "Just what I said. No. There won't be any divorce. And you won't be finding a job elsewhere. You have one. Once I buy that mountain, you may have more jobs than you can handle. Now quit worrying and let me kiss you."

She jerked away from him, turning to glare at him fully. "You said you were going to borrow the money and we would leave here at once. What happened to the six weeks or whatever you said we have left? I don't see you making any effort to get back to New Mexico."

"There's been a slight change of plans." He was growing angry now. He didn't like explaining himself. But she looked so lovely standing there, the moonlight glinting off the pale strands of hair tumbling to her shoulders, that he found himself offering what he could in hopes of gaining more. "Tyler doesn't have that much cash right now."

Janice's lips set in grim lines, and Peter hastened to relieve the anxiety flickering in her eyes. "He can get it. There's just going to be a slight delay." He hesitated to explain the reason for that delay. Peter had a decided feeling that his wife wouldn't approve of the means of obtaining that cash. He wasn't thrilled with them himself.

"I see. And I don't suppose that delay has anything to do with waiting for the Fourth of July races, does it?"

So that was it. She knew. Well, there wasn't anything that could be done about it. "It doesn't make any difference what the reason is. I've got to have the money and Tyler is my best source. This will all be over shortly, and in a few months we can set up housekeeping just like I promised." He knew as soon as the words were out of his mouth that he'd said the wrong thing.

The cool gray of her eyes glazed colder. "A few months?"

He was a man who could deal coolly and authoritatively with all aspects of business and potential disasters, but that cold flicker of her eyes infuriated him. Conquering a flare of anger, he replied, "I will have less than five weeks to get back to New Mexico. There won't be time to take a wagon and trunks. You'll have to wait here until I can get back for you." She might as well understand now that first things came first, and he was the one who made the decision as to what came first. There could only be one man in a family.

"Very well." Janice picked up her full skirt and started around him. "You go your way, and I'll go mine. That's what I meant to do anyway."

She didn't slam doors. Peter appreciated that fact. She shut him out quietly and effectively with just the gentle click of the latch on the door between the two rooms.

That way, the whole household wouldn't know the practical, mature, composed newlyweds were ready to tear each other's throats out.

# Nineteen

"**Y**ou're girls! You can't go with us."

"That's not fair, you beasts! We want to fish too."

The childish voices drifted in through the open window, and Janice couldn't help glancing out to find the source of the argument. Betsy and Melissa Harding stood beside one of the porch columns in their short dresses covered in flounces and bows, watching with disappointment as a group of boys raced down the drive carrying fishing poles and gear. But it was the two older girls, Maria Rodriguez and fourteen-year-old Alicia Monteigne who were doing the shouting. Janice shook her head in dismay. They were old enough to know better.

Betsy didn't say a word when Janice joined them, but the youngest Monteigne girl, Rebecca, was sitting on a swing, wiping tears from her eyes. At the appearance of an adult, she wailed. "I'm gonna tell Mama on them!"

"Hush, Becky. We'll get even with them. Just see if we don't!" Alicia scowled after the departing boys. "They think they're so great just because they're boys. A lot they know."

Janice bit back a smile. The eldest Monteigne girl sounded just like her mother. No doubt Evie would have a brilliant solution to this situation, but she was busy putting the finishing touches on one of her children's books and wasn't to be disturbed this morning. The boys had probably counted on that particular piece of information.

"The best way I know to get even in a situation like this is to have an even better time than they have," Janice said casually, wondering if she was getting in over her head. She had learned to deal with rooms full of school-children by wielding her authority. She had never really learned to be friends with them.

All the girls looked up at her with interest. Betsy was the first to question. "How? They took all the fishing poles."

"We can make fishing poles easy enough." Janice hoped that was true. She had never gone fishing in her life, but poles and string seemed simple enough. "But you need to make it more fun than what they are doing. What is more fun than sitting on a bank and fishing?"

She hoped they would come up with something re-motely within her areas of expertise, but it wasn't likely they'd say "baking a cake" or "sewing a shirt." She waited with some trepidation for the reply. She didn't have long to wait.

"Sitting in a boat and fishing," Alicia and Maria both answered decisively and at the same time. At Janice's questioning look, Alicia said, "Daddy took us out on a flatboat last summer. He's promised and promised to do it again, and he even had Ben get the boat out and make it ready, but he's been too busy with the darned fields to take us out. And now that Ben can't get around so good, he'll never get away."

"Get around so well." Janice corrected her absently. "A boat. Well, that does sound better than sitting in mud. Why don't I see what I can do? And just in case I can't round up a boat, think of something else that's even more fun than what the boys are doing."

She left the girls chattering excitedly as she returned to the house. She had to be out of her mind to agree to put together a fishing expedition, but she had never been able to disappoint Betsy in any way if she could possibly avoid it. Betsy wasn't outspoken like Alicia and Maria. She would never complain. But Janice knew only too well the childish heartbreak of being denied the pleasant pastimes other children enjoyed. She couldn't remember a time when she hadn't worked, but she distinctly remembered all those times while she was working that she had heard the laughter of other children playing in the streets. She had never learned how to kick the can with them, or jump rope, or play dolls. She would deny Betsy none of that, even if it meant taking her fishing.

Entering the dim parlor, she nearly walked into Peter. He caught her arms to steady her and didn't let go. They had slept in the same bed last night, but he had made no further effort to touch her until now. Somehow, standing this close, feeling his fingers dig into her arms and his breath against her hair, even though they were fully dressed, was more tantalizing than lying on opposite sides of the bed with an ocean of sheet between them. Janice made a slight effort to escape, but Peter didn't even appear to notice.

"Can you and Betsy swim?" he asked, not gripping her arms hard but running his fingers up and down her sleeve. "Do you know anything about poling boats?"

He'd heard. Janice shrugged. "The Hardings taught Betsy to swim a little. I'd hoped I could find somebody who knew something about boats. I just couldn't see any reason the girls had to be stuck in the house all day if the boys didn't have to."

"I rather thought that was what girls were supposed to do," he said wryly. "I thought they liked sitting inside in their ribbons and bows, sipping tea and playing with dolls."

She would have liked to have done that once upon a time. But then, she would have done anything just to have the ribbons and bows when she was a child, up to and including drinking tea. That was no reason Betsy should be confined to such a role. Janice met her husband's gaze squarely. "Girls can do almost anything boys can do. They can ride bicycles or play tennis or go fishing, if that's what they want. These are modern times, sir."

Peter glanced to the open window where the sound of excited chatter began to dissipate. He had the suspicion that their argument had an audience. Out of sheer devilment, he whispered in her ear, "What will you give me if I take you boating?"

He had pulled her so close that Janice had to rest her hands on his chest to keep a space between them. He was a tall man, and his height and breadth made her feel small and vulnerable. At the same time, she felt protected rather than threatened. It was an extremely odd feeling, and one she didn't want to investigate too closely. She held him where he was and considered his question.

"I don't have anything to give you," she finally decided.

Peter kissed the tip of her nose. "Yes, you do. But I'll let you decide if my efforts are worth your favors. I'll go check with Tyler about the boat." He said the last sentence loud enough to bring cheers from their unabashed listeners.

Janice felt herself grow warm, but when Peter went off to see about the boat, she regained her schoolteacher image and went out to order the girls to don suitable clothing. They scampered off immediately.

By the time the girls returned in old skirts too short for them, simple shirtwaists, and broad hats that tied under their chins, Peter had located the boat and an additional poleman, the eldest Rodriguez male, Manuel. And Jasmine had practically pleaded with them to drag Ben along to get him out of the house and from underfoot. He just wasn't allowed to stand on his injured leg.

"You can put the wiggly worms on the hooks," Betsy assured Ben when he complained at being made to sit in the back of the wagon like an invalid.

"We don't have worms!" Maria cried out in dismay as she helped Becky into the wagon bed.

"Biscuit dough works just fine," Ben assured her, holding out a hand to help Betsy and Melissa in beside him. "We got us a whole basket of goodies here. You just got to leave some for the fish."

They laughed and giggled all the way to the river. Janice sat between Peter and Manuel on the wagon seat, and the two of them teased her with horror stories of fish leaping out of the water to wriggle in the laps of ladies, but she didn't mind their laughter. She could hear Betsy's laughter intertwining with it, and her heart soared joyfully. If she had learned nothing else in this lifetime, she had learned to grab the few moments of joy God gave her and make the most of them. This was one of those moments.

The July sun was merciless, but the breeze off the river was refreshing. Childish laughter mixed with the wild notes of a mockingbird, and the aroma of fried chicken from their lunch basket competed with the earthy smells of mud and river as they found a place to stop the wagon. Even the strong male presence of Peter at her side was a source of pleasure right now. Janice took his arm after he tied off the reins, and when he looked down at her questioningly, she gave him a smile in return. She felt it deep in the pit of her stomach when he smiled back.

That feeling didn't go away as they pulled the boat into the water and managed to guide the excited girls onto it without dumping anyone into the idle current. Every time Janice looked at her husband, she somehow felt him. Was that what happened between husband and wife? Was that physical joining also a permanent tie that bound her to him forever? It felt that way. The hollow inside her deepened and ached when he discarded his coat and rolled up his shirt sleeves. As if he knew what she was thinking, Peter looked up at her and held out his hand to help her onto the boat. The touch of his bare palm against hers sent a tremor rippling through her.

The girls didn't leave Janice much time to worry over this new awareness of her husband's presence. They had to be made to sit still while Ben attached strings and hooks to their poles and baited them with wadded-up biscuit dough. The older ones attempted to do it themselves, under his direction while Janice helped the younger ones to lower their hooks over the boat's side. Manuel and Peter kept the simple flatboat near the river's edge, poling it just to keep it out of cypress knees or partially submerged cottonwood trunks.

Alicia spotted the boys on the riverbank at the same time as Maria saw the low-lying island ahead.

"There they are, the skunks! Look, they're not even fishing. They're just jumping in the water and chasing the fish away."

Mildly alarmed at that announcement, Janice hastily attempted to distract their attention by pointing out Maria's discovery. "Do you think we could row over to that island? There's a tree on it that would give adequate shade for a picnic." Firmly she directed Betsy's attention away from the riverbank. She didn't have any illusions about what the boys were doing while "jumping in the water and chasing the fish." And she didn't think they were wearing anything particularly appropriate while doing it. The muggy heat made skinny-dipping almost essential.

The boys shouted when they discovered the boat, and the girls smugly agreed that the island would be just fine. The boys wouldn't be able to reach it without a boat of their own.

Behind Janice, Manuel chuckled as he pushed the boat into deeper currents. "This isn't going to work, you know. José isn't going to let Maria and Alicia get the better of him. He may have just finished that fancy college, but old habits die hard."

Janice threw a look over her shoulder. Sure enough, José was striking out toward the island on his own. And the younger boys seemed prepared to do the same. She glanced worriedly at Peter. "How dangerous is that current?"

Peter frowned and kept a close eye on the race. Ben was the one to answer. "Current changes from day to day. It ain't been raining, so it should be gentle if they don't fool 'round none."

The girls yelled and screamed and scared off any fish they might have caught as they realized the boys were racing toward the island ahead of them. Nine-year-old Melissa Harding jumped up and down and hurled childish curses at her younger brother while Alicia Monteigne scowled and watched her brothers divert their course and head for the boat.

"Manuel!" Peter's shout jarred the carnival atmosphere. "Catch that log!"

Janice glanced to where Peter was looking and saw the rotted log riding the current just beneath the water. She knew very little about rivers and swimming, but she could see that there would be unexpected dangers like this one. She glanced worriedly toward the smaller boys still struggling to swim toward the boat.

Manuel couldn't stop the log with just a slender pole. It bumped the pole, floated around it, and kept on going, straight for the young boys. The older girls realized something was amiss, and their screams silenced as they looked from the boys swimming toward the boat to Peter, whose face was set and grim. On the island, even José seemed to sense something was wrong. He stood on the bank, straining to see what the others saw.

"Them boys don't see it coming. Give me the pole and I'll hold the boat," Ben said quietly.

Peter nodded, handed over his pole, and began to strip off his shirt and shoes. Janice held her breath. It had never occurred to her to ask if Peter could swim. She had never seen him in anything less than a suit back in Cutlerville. Surely, somewhere along the way he had learned to swim as she never had.

He dived into the water and reached the log in a few powerful strokes. She breathed again, but only until she realized he was riding the log to steer it from the boys. He could be washed out into the middle of the river at any moment. It didn't seem to concern anyone else. They were cheering and shouting and jumping up and down, and Janice could only watch her husband's dripping hair and wide shoulders float further away.

Manuel and Ben tried to pole the boat closer to the boys. The youngest seemed to be growing weary, and Janice leaned over the edge in an effort to reach him. Her arms weren't quite long enough.

Sending the log past the boat, Peter let it go and began

the swim back against the current. Janice's cries as one small head bobbed beneath the water caught his ear faster than all the other yells. She was nearly half out of the boat and reaching for the Monteigne boy struggling up for air. With a curse of his own, he struck out faster.

He grabbed the boy's hair just before he could go down again. Hauling him up, he shoved him toward Janice's waiting arms. She caught the boy and with the help of all the others managed to haul him into the boat.

He glanced around to make certain the other two boys pulled themselves up, then grabbed the side and climbed back in.

Janice immediately left the boy to Alicia and came to kneel beside Peter, using her handkerchief to mop the water from his eyes. "I was afraid you couldn't swim," she murmured.

Peter sprawled on his elbows against the boards to catch his breath. The sun's rays heated his skin and turned the drops of moisture on his chest to steam, but the concern behind his wife's voice made his insides boil. It was all he could do to keep from pulling her down on top of him.

"I'm not an idiot. I wouldn't jump into a river if I couldn't swim."

"Or grab a half-broke horse unless you could ride. I know." She mopped his face with the damp cambric. "But I'm used to worrying."

"And I'm giving you just one more person to worry about." Peter added another layer to his understanding of this complex woman he called wife. "I don't suppose it will help to tell you not to worry anymore, that I'm going to take care of everything?"

"Our ideas on what constitutes 'taking care of' tend to differ, I'm afraid. It's too late to change my ways," she admitted reluctantly.

Peter pulled her head down until their lips met. Janice only resisted briefly, then kissed him back to the cheers of their audience. When he released her, he whispered, "It's never too late, Mrs. Mulloney," in a voice that only she could hear.

Janice blushed and moved away to scold the adventurous trio.

# Twenty

The day progressed with much hilarity after that. Janice was unaccustomed to spending even one day—and certainly not several—doing nothing but enjoying herself. She packed and unpacked picnic baskets, took off her shoes and waded out into the water to help pull in fish caught by small hands, and did her best to keep her unruly charges clean and dry. But it was still more like play than work, and she found herself often enough just sitting at the river's edge, laughing at the antics of the children.

During one of those moments, Peter dropped down on a rock beside her. "I love hearing you laugh," he murmured, adjusting her broad-brimmed hat to better shade a nose rapidly turning pink. "You ought to do it more often."

"Ho! Listen to the pot calling the kettle black." She turned an impish grin up to him. She had never grinned at a man in her life, or at least not in the last ten years, but something about the way Peter looked at her made it easy. These idle days were corrupting her rapidly. Or maybe it was her husband. She had actually giggled at him last night when Tyler had caught them kissing on the porch. And she had actually been *kissing* him. She had been contemplating a lot more than kissing him until she remembered herself. She would do well to remember herself now, but it didn't seem necessary on this tiny island filled with children. She was safe here.

"I laugh," he demurred. "I laugh all the time."

"You most certainly do not, Peter Aloysius Mulloney.

That's a whopper of a fib. You hardly even smiled when we first met. And I can only remember you laughing once since then."

"Hmmm." He propped his chin on his fist while he pondered that thought. "That makes me sound like a proper stuffed shirt."

"You are. You always have been. I can remember going down to meet my sister at the store, and you would be officiating some argument between the clerks or pompously steering some rich old lady to her carriage. You always looked as if your spine were made of steel."

He gave her a look of amused incredulity. "And you married me anyway? What does that say about you?"

"Not very much, I'm afraid," Janice admitted willingly. "I was scared and I took the easy way out. I'm not particularly proud of myself."

The amusement fled his face. "Do you really despise me that much?"

If she didn't look at him, she could almost answer affirmatively. She had spoken lightly, but she could remember other things about those times she had seen him back in Cutlerville. She could remember standing in the street, dripping wet from the rain, afraid to enter the hallowed doors of Mulloney's elegant department store. Instead, she had waited outside to walk her sister home and watched as Peter rode off in his fancy carriage, his top hat virtually untouched by the weather since his carriage driver had held an umbrella over him. He hadn't even been aware of her existence then. She was just another one of the town's pathetic poor.

There were other things to despise him for, like the rent collector who beat women. Or the derelict houses his family refused to repair. There were the low wages and the hideous working conditions. The list could go on into eternity if she really wished to work at it. But she didn't. She couldn't quite match the man beside her with her list of grievances. The man she had despised in Cutlerville couldn't be the same man who had dived into the filthy river to save a boy he scarcely even knew. She didn't know who this man was that she had married.

"I don't know you well enough to despise you," she finally answered.

"But you lived in Cutlerville, and your sister works at the store. You lived in those houses that belonged to my father, didn't you? Even my fiancée hated me when she found out about those houses, and she didn't have to live in them."

Janice looked up at him with curiosity at the tone of bitterness she heard underlying his words. "Did you love her very much? Is that why you left town?"

Peter picked up a flat stone and skipped it across the water. One of the boys yelled in appreciation and attempted to better his feat. A stone-skipping contest erupted not yards away from them, but he didn't seem aware of the fact.

"I didn't even know her. Our fathers wanted us to marry, and I saw the opportunity to get out from under my father's thumb if I acquired her share of the factory. She suited what I thought I would need in a wife. It didn't take long to figure out that I didn't know what I wanted, but I knew it wasn't Georgie. I left Cutlerville because I was tired."

"Tired?" Janice could scarcely keep the surprise out of her voice.

"Tired of trying to keep my brothers away from my father's tirades. Tired of trying to protect my mother from the truth. Tired of fighting his battles. Tired of doing what he told me. Tired of losing my self-respect. I should have fought harder after I learned about those tenant houses. I should have quit Mulloney's when I realized I couldn't stop my father. I'm sorry I dumped it all on Daniel, but he seemed much better prepared to deal with all of it than I was at the time."

"And he wanted it," Janice responded. "He loves having the family he never knew. He's thriving on what you considered punishment. You needn't feel guilty about leaving your family to Daniel." She had only come to know Daniel those last few months before she left Cutlerville, but Daniel was an easy person to get to know. Perhaps Peter's brother had been fortunate in being raised as a bastard orphan instead of being ground under the relentless thumb of Artemis Mulloney as Peter had.

Peter managed a smile. "Daniel's certainly got our father over a barrel, anyway. Anytime the old man wants to do anything against Daniel's high and mighty principles, Daniel threatens to expose him in the newspaper. And the old man can't fire him. The boys are too young and don't have Daniel's experience, and Dad still can't get about without the help of a wheelchair. So he's stuck with Daniel. I'd almost like to go back there someday and watch them in action."

Janice worried at a loose thread in her skirt. "That's one of the reasons we'll never suit. I couldn't go back with you."

The stone Peter had started to skip fell with a loud plop into the water. The boys jeered at his failure, but he didn't notice. He stared at the woman by his side. "Why in hell not?"

Janice broke off the thread and twisted it around her finger. "I've made it from slum to schoolteacher, but I don't think I could make it as far as high society. My parents came from respectable but poor families. They taught us to speak correctly and use proper manners and such, but we never moved in the kind of circles that your family belongs to. If we'd met back in Cutlerville, you would never have looked at me."

That was probably true, but if they'd met in Cutlerville, he wouldn't have been sitting in a jail cell charged with arson either. Texas and Ohio were worlds apart in more ways than one. Peter picked up a handful of stones and skipped them methodically, one by one across the water, each one taking more leaps than the next.

"If that's the way you feel about it, we won't go back to Ohio," he announced after several minutes of thought. "I don't belong back there anymore either."

"That's ridiculous. Your family is back there," Janice objected strongly.

"So is yours." He threw her a look. "I won't fit in with your family any better."

Well, that was no more than the truth. Her brother would probably try to strangle him and her sister would spit on his shoes. Janice couldn't help a curt laugh at the thought.

The laugh went unnoticed when one of the younger Monteignes took that opportunity to fall into the river. Both Janice and Peter were on their feet and running toward this latest disaster before their differences could sink in.

Manuel fished the boy out of the water without mishap, but Janice declared it was time to head back home. Two of the youngest fell asleep with their heads in her lap before the boat had poled from shore. Janice leaned against the boat railing and stroked their heads. For the first time in a long time, she felt an odd contentment. She watched Betsy and one of the Harding boys carefully compare the treasures they had collected on the island, and she smiled. Betsy didn't even know what the words "high society" meant. She would remember very little of the first five years of her life as time went on. But she would remember riding with the Hardings and fishing with the Monteignes and playing tag with Benjamin's cousins. The fact that all of them had far more money than Janice would never occur to any of these children any more than the fact that they were white and black and brown. That was the way it should be.

Peter and Manuel carried the sleeping toddlers to the wagon when they reached the shore. Judging by the lack of noise, the whole lot of them were ready for naps. Most of the boys elected to walk back to the house rather than ride in the wagon with "girls," but the youngest settled in beside Ben and demanded a story. Janice sat next to Peter on the wagon seat and listened with quiet appreciation as the horse slowly pulled them home and Ben spun a tale of talking rabbits and foxes.

The day had been an illuminating one in many respects, but Janice was afraid to consider what the repercussions might be. Nothing had changed. She had a husband who was broke and without a job, and she wasn't in much better shape. Peter was still set on borrowing money to gamble on a horse race so he could sink the proceeds into an even bigger gamble—a gold mine. Maybe she couldn't despise him as she ought, and maybe he was a stronger man than she thought, but that didn't change the basic situation. They couldn't even introduce each other to their respective families, for pity's sake. What in the world had she been thinking when she married the man?

She had been thinking she would be rich, that's what she'd been thinking. She wasn't at all proud of that decision. Of course, she'd been terrified of being thrown out on the street without a job too. It had only seemed fitting that Peter be made to pay for what she suffered. And he wasn't hurting any from her decision. He had wanted a wife who could cook, and she could do far more than cook. He'd got a good end to his bargain.

Except for the one little matter that she didn't want to think about just yet.

Evie and Carmen came running out of the house to carry their young ones off to their beds. The older ones ran off to new mischief. The men helped Ben to a rocker on the porch and settled down to swap fish stories until supper.

Peter caught up with Janice as she started up the stairs to the tower to change clothes and freshen up.

"There's time for a little nap before supper," he murmured suggestively, leaning one arm against the wall and pressing a kiss to her temple.

Janice felt the heat creeping up in her cheeks, and she looked at anything but the man beside her. "Not yet. Not tonight." She knew she couldn't put him off much longer, but the decision she had to make was an enormous one. It was one she should have made before she agreed to marry him. Of course, circumstances were different now.

Peter brushed his knuckles against her cheek. "Tomorrow? They're having a barn dance tomorrow night. We've never danced, Jenny. You can dance with every man there and pretend you're free for a while. I'll court you. I'll punch out any man who dares dance with you twice. I'll sweep you off your feet. And then we'll come back here and I'll make love to you all night long."

His voice was a seductive velvet that crept up and down her spine. He did this deliberately, Janice knew, but she couldn't fault him for trying. He hadn't protested all week when she'd held him off. He was giving her another day. But that was the day before he meant to leave. They would have one night together. Wouldn't it be better to wait?

She didn't think he would. She shivered as Peter's mouth found the corner of her lips. He took her silence as acquiescence. His lips swallowed any protest she might have made.

Janice gave herself up to the luxury of his kiss. She was coming to like the fiery touch of Peter's mouth and hands too much. She closed her eyes and let the heat surge through her, felt his palm mold itself to her breast, and understood the spiral of need curling through her middle. In only a matter of time, he would be inside her again. He wouldn't let her escape this time.

The effect of Peter's kisses didn't fade with the passage of time or the light of a new day. The fact that he didn't lose a single opportunity to refresh her memory didn't help. He had decided tonight was the night he would stake his claim, and he was a lot like a child at Christmas. Or a stallion straining at the bit, Janice thought, watching the animal in question in the paddock as the men ran it through its paces. Her husband was every bit as impatient as that animal.

Just that knowledge made her blood stir as it hadn't in more years than she cared to consider. She was alternately hot and cold, thinking of Peter's kisses and then considering where they would lead. She would be a puddle of frazzled nerves before the day ended.

She didn't have much time to fret. The children practically bounced off the walls in excitement at the thought of the dance tonight and the Fourth of July celebrations on the morrow. The kitchen exuded aromas of baking pies and cakes and frying chicken. The barn was being cleaned, tables set up, and the house generally spruced up for the crowd of party-goers. Every corner of the yard and mansion was a beehive of activity. Janice found herself firmly drawn into the hectic bustle no matter where she turned.

Not until the heat of midafternoon settled in and things slowed down did Janice even consider what she would wear for the dance. She went in search of Evie to consult on the proper attire.

Evie waved a fashion magazine like a fan to cool herself off in the family parlor. At Janice's question, she laughed. "Wear the coolest thing you can find. I wouldn't advise silk, though. Some of the boys get a little rowdy and you're likely to land up in a haystack or drenched in punch. That's why we hold it in the barn. We were lucky the house was a shambles that first year we tried to hold it inside. Fortunately, they only set fire to draperies that needed burning anyway. We just keep the horse troughs full now. If you have a light cotton gown, that will do just fine."

Janice had cotton gowns, but they were all of the schoolmarm variety. Drab grays and browns didn't seem exactly appropriate for a dance. Maybe she could take a little white lace off one of her church gowns.

As if reading her guest's mind, Evie exclaimed, "I know!" She looked Janice up and down carefully. "You're about the same size I was a few kids ago. I never throw anything away. The styles have changed some. How good are you with thread and needle?"

"Pretty fair," Janice said carefully. Evie's flair for fashion was well known. She found it hard to believe her hostess would have something so mundane as a cotton gown, even one several years out of fashion.

"Excellent! Between us, we can concoct a gown that

will bring that husband of yours to his knees. It's about
time the two of you learned to enjoy yourselves." With
that pronouncement, Evie sailed toward the stairs and her
attic wardrobes.

Janice stood in awe as door after door was thrown open
to reveal gowns of silks and satins, wool and foulard,
eyelet and lace. Evie moved knowledgeably from one
gown to the next, rejecting one after another until she
found the one she wanted. In triumph, she jerked out a
midnight-blue and ivory-striped cotton faille and held it
out for inspection.

"A bustle will take up a lot of this old-fashioned train,
and we can strip off the bottom flounce to shorten it even
more. You don't want to be dragging all this material
through straw. I think you're a little taller than I am, so
that should bring the hem just about where it belongs for
this year's style. If not, we can always pin it up a little beneath the polonaise. The color is perfect for you. I love
redoing old gowns, don't you? It makes me feel so cre-
ative."

Janice hesitantly reached out to touch the rich material
of the elegant gown. The cotton was soft as silk, and the
ribbing appealed to her sense of touch. Most of all, the
cascade of flounces down the back and ribbon trimmings
in the front made her ache to try it on. She had never
owned anything half so elegant. The expense and labor of
all that extra material and trim had always been beyond
her means.

"Are you sure?" she murmured uncertainly, trying to be
polite while dying to grab the gown and run.

"Of course. Look at this waistline! I couldn't get in it
again in a million years. Come on. Let's get it on you and
see what we can do."

Before the afternoon ended, Janice was standing on a
chair, modeling the marvelous gown as Jasmine added the
finishing touches to the hem while Evie and Carmen hastily transformed the removed train into flounces for the
bustled overskirt. The blue bow of the neckline had been
converted to hold up the overskirt, and now the bodice

opened at the throat with a touch of ivory lace to adorn it. Janice kept smoothing the rows of material on the skirt and wondering how anyone could think anything so marvelous could be perfect for a barn dance.

"Très élégant," Jasmine murmured, stepping back to admire their handiwork. "The hair, now," she added reflectively. "We must do something with the hair."

"Gardenias," Carmen announced decisively. "She must wear gardenias. They'll match the ivory stripes to perfection."

Janice's protests were swept aside.

"I will have Kitty press the hem while we all bathe," Evie agreed. "Janice, after you wash your hair, you'll have to come down here while your hair is still damp. We can put a little curl in it with rags and give it some body."

"You'd better keep that husband of hers out of the house," Carmen intruded. "He's been panting after her like a hound all day. I'll get Manuel to distract him."

Laughing, the women plotted the evening, and quite wittingly, Janice's own seduction.

# Twenty-One

**P**eter watched the vision of loveliness descending the stairs, barely aware that Betsy stood beside him. Except for their wedding day, he had never seen his wife in anything but the drab colors of her old-maid wardrobe and in the plain styles her budget could afford. He wasn't one to spend much time noticing a woman's clothes, and he had paid little heed to her lack of feminine finery until now. He had to raise his hand to his jaw to make certain his mouth didn't hang open.

Janice practically floated down the stairs. The gown foamed around her, dipping and swaying with each step. The light color of the ivory set off her radiant complexion, and the deep blue contrasted with her fair coloring. The effect was such that the gown became part of the woman, and all he could notice was the long-lashed slant of her eyes and the exquisite line of her nose, and the pink tilt of her lips, provided he didn't look lower and lose himself in the full thrust of her bosom and the small circumference of her waist. The surge of lust to his loins made him gulp. He would have a damned difficult time making it through this evening, knowing what awaited him.

As she approached, the exotic scent of gardenias enveloped him. Peter knew she didn't own perfume, but he didn't question the miracle. He circled Janice's waist with his arm and pulled her close, pressing a kiss to her brow despite their interested audience.

"I take back everything I said," he murmured into her

hair. "You're not dancing with anyone but me. I'm damned well not letting you out of my sight."

"I can't dance," Janice replied under her breath as a smattering of applause broke out from the audience hidden in the shadow of the parlors. She held out her hand to Betsy as the hall began to fill with people congratulating her and themselves for their success.

Peter chewed on this new piece of information while his host shook his hand and commented on the loveliness of his wife, the latest odds on the morrow's race, and the number of wagons and carriages already pulled into the yard. Despite the insistence of the Rodriguez boys that they ought to go out and check the consistency of the punch, Peter stayed right where he was—with his arm around his wife.

As the small party gradually filtered out the front doors, Peter took the opportunity to lean over and whisper in Janice's ear, "Tonight, I'll be the teacher. Is that all right with you?"

She raised her eyes to meet his and knew dancing wasn't the only thing he meant to teach her. The impact of that knowledge shattered what remained of her composure. She had never been the object of a man's attention. She had never been the object of anyone's attention. She was frozen with nervousness. The heat of Peter's gaze cracked the ice, leaving her with no defense at all.

She felt as vulnerable as a newly hatched chicken, but the protection of Peter's arm around her kept her moving in some semblance of normality. She managed to answer a gay sally of Carmen's, smile at James Peyton's old-fashioned gallantry, and respond with some pleasantry to Manuel's very Latin flirtation. The knowledge that none of these people had ever looked at her as they did now kept her sufficiently off-balance to be grateful for her husband's support. She had always been the old-maid schoolteacher. It wasn't easy to grow into this new persona.

"It's all right to be beautiful, you know," Peter said casually when they stepped outside and found themselves a distance from the others. "You can't be condemned for the assets God gave you."

"Yes, I can. People do it all the time." Janice answered nervously and without thinking, in automatic response to an argument she'd had with herself for years. It had been her fault that she'd got pregnant, she'd heard people say. She shouldn't have flaunted her looks for a young man like Stephen. Men were easily led astray. A woman should at all times be modest and unassuming. She had got what she deserved. Her stomach clenched uneasily as she realized the accuracy of those words. She was going to pay tonight for flaunting herself like this.

Peter gave her a quick glance but mercifully didn't question further. "Friends don't," he answered bluntly. "Hide from strangers, if you must, but not from me, not from your family, not from these people here. We know you're lovely, inside and out. No one will condemn you for it."

Janice had her doubts, but it was too late to do anything about it now. Betsy was looking at her as if she had been transformed into a goddess. Perhaps she ought to let her know that it was all right to be beautiful. Betsy had more potential beauty than any person Janice knew, including Evie. Her daughter would need something to keep her strong. Somehow, Janice would have to show her the way. She felt horribly inadequate for the task.

The barn was already filling with people, most of them strangers to Janice. The ones to whom she was introduced seemed friendly and accepting enough. Still, she was grateful that Peter didn't stray from her side. She didn't know how she would manage if he left to join the crowd of men by the refreshment table. She didn't know how she would manage when he left for New Mexico.

But she refused to think about that tonight. She had never been to a dance or a party before. It was one of those things she had longed to do all her life but been denied because of circumstances. If nothing else, Peter was introducing her to a life she had previously only dreamed of—even if she only had this one brief glimpse. She meant to enjoy it while she could.

The musicians launched into a rollicking reel at some signal from Tyler. Janice contentedly stood on the sidelines and tapped her toe, smiling as the crowd slowly formed into figures and picked up the beat and began to dance. She knew nothing about music or dancing, but she loved watching the gay parade of colors and rhythmic motions. Everyone looked so happy that she couldn't help but feel happy too.

"I hope you're wearing comfortable shoes; I mean to dance your feet off tonight."

Before Janice could glance up in surprise, Peter grasped her waist and swung her into the nearest circle of dancers.

"It's not the kind of dancing I learned at home, but it looks easy enough to pick up," he said as he followed the other dancers through the motions.

Astonished that he was as ignorant as she was of these steps, Janice could do nothing but focus her attention on the couples beside them and lose herself in the music and concentration. The dance ended just as she thought she had a grasp on what was expected of her.

It didn't matter. The musicians instantly struck up another tune, and Peter whirled her across the floor again. Janice laughed at the speed with which they moved. He scarcely allowed her to touch the floor. He carried her and she was flying. Peter had the strength and agility to carry her through her ignorance of the world around her. It was the most amazing feeling, and Janice met his eyes with more than gratitude.

"You give in so beautifully, Mrs. Mulloney," he declared, grinning down at her. "Will you always surrender to my charms like this?"

"I'm not surrendering," she protested breathlessly as he swept her down the line. But she was surrendering. Even as the musicians began a slow tune and Peter guided her expertly into his arms for a waltz, she followed his every lead. She amazed even herself. Had any other man attempted to hold her like this, she would have been as stiff as a board, but Peter had succeeded in destroying all her barriers. She floated in his arms, with no more will of her own than a butterfly on the wind.

Her concentration on the dance steps kept her from complete awareness of her husband's masculine proximity for a while. But as she became comfortable with the rhythm of the dance, Janice found herself noticing the firmness of Peter's hand on hers, the way he held her waist so that she could feel the sway of his hips, and that achingly familiar shiver began to take root in her middle. She wasn't comfortable enough with the steps to look away, and her vision was either filled with the breadth of his shoulders and chest or the sight of his smile if she looked up. He didn't take his gaze off her, and after a while, she had difficulty looking away. By the time the dance ended, she thought she might be glued in this position forever, with Peter's arm pulling her close and his gaze devouring her.

Luckily for them, Betsy came running to demand some small favor, and they were forced apart. But the awareness of that moment lingered as they moved through the rest of the evening.

Occasionally, Janice allowed herself to be swept into a circle of gossiping women or into a fracas of children at the punch bowl, but as soon as any other man approached her, Peter appeared at her side again. He didn't say anything, didn't touch her, didn't pull her away. He merely waited while she exchanged pleasantries and made up her mind whether or not to accept the gentleman's offer to dance. She didn't know what he would have done had she accepted their offers, but she didn't. She had no interest at all in dancing with any other man.

As Peter slowly accepted that fact, his desire seemed to multiply. He only touched her in the socially acceptable manners of the dance, but Janice could feel his gaze burning against her breast, felt the jolt of heat as his hand skimmed her back, and knew the reason he hid himself in her skirts and moved with some discomfort when they waltzed. He was doing his best to be a gentleman, but his thoughts were on the bed they would share when this was over.

As were hers.

The knowledge that she would have to surrender herself entirely this night made her even more edgy as the night progressed. She had never really made the decision that this was for the best. She had never come to an acceptance that she might bear a child from this encounter. She wasn't even certain that they ought to be married. She only knew that as husband, Peter expected her to be his wife in every sense of the word. And she was no longer averse to having physical knowledge of her husband's body.

That thought struck her sharply as Peter pulled her into the shadows for a light kiss out of the sight of others. Not that anyone watched anymore. The plentiful supply of beer and liquor had heightened the jollities, and those not seeking the privacy of sheltered corners like themselves were reeling in dizzying whirls on the dance floor. They could be completely alone for all the crowd cared, and Janice didn't protest when Peter pulled her closer until she felt the rigidity of his desire through the protection of her skirts. Even through her fear, she knew the thrill of that desire.

"The children have gone off to bed. How soon can we follow?" he murmured hoarsely against her ear.

"Peter, we have to talk." She tried to worm her hands between them to hold him away, but she found herself clutching his shirt instead. His vest and coat had been discarded much earlier in the heat of the evening.

"Talk isn't a solution. We're married, Jenny. It's time we start acting like it. I don't think you're afraid of me anymore, are you?"

She was terrified of him, but not in the way he meant. Her vulnerability terrified her. What he could and would do to her life and to her future terrified her. But what he would do to her body no longer held her in trepidation. She wanted to try that closeness again. She craved the intimacy. She needed to know he desired her. But none of that was strong enough to overcome all her other anxieties.

"You're going to leave me," she protested weakly.

"I'm going to come back for you." Inexorably, he captured her waist and drew her toward the dark outline of the barn door.

"I can't be certain. Peter, this isn't seemly!" Panicking, Janice tried to resist as he dodged a circle of laughing guests and dragged her toward the shadows nearest the exit.

"It wouldn't be seemly to take you in that haystack over there, either, but that's what's going to happen if we stay in here. I've given you time, Janice. Do you still find me that repulsive?"

Shocked by this question, she allowed him to pull her outside where she halted and looked up at Peter's face. The handsome features she was coming to know so well were shadowed now, but she sensed some hurt in them. She touched her hand wonderingly to his cheek. "Repulsive? How can you ask that?"

"It's easy when I have a wife who darts out of my hands every time I touch her. Maybe we ought to talk. Maybe you ought to tell me what happened with that first man. Did he hurt you, Janice? Is that what this is all about? Or is it just me?"

"No, it's not you. It's us. We've gone about this all wrong. It isn't going to work. You'll leave me, and I just can't go through that again. I just can't, Peter. Go buy your silly mountain, but don't touch me. It's better this way. You'll see."

She tried to pull away from him, lifting her skirts and straining against his firm hold while she spoke. Her own words heightened her sense of panic. She couldn't go through with this. She just couldn't. He would go west and she would never see him again. She had vowed never to be left in that hideous position again, swelling with child and no man to care for her. Never, ever again.

She emitted a brief scream as a tall shadow loomed out

of the bushes. Peter shoved her behind him when the figure stepped menacingly closer.

"I believe the lady wants to go, son. I'd let her, if I was you."

"Who in hell do you think you are telling me what to do with my wife?"

She heard Peter's astonishment. It would have matched her own had she not already been in a panic. She didn't know whether to run for help or run from herself.

"I'll tell you only once, sir. Let the lady go."

The stranger had to be inebriated. Janice started to scream, but she saw the familiar shapes of Tyler and Manuel emerging from the darkness. Her one goal now was to remove herself from the scene as quickly as possible. Peter would be fine. She wouldn't be if she allowed him his way.

Peter released her arm and swung at the stranger all in the same move. Janice gave a start of surprise at the swiftness of his action. She cringed at the sound of flesh hitting flesh.

Tyler gave a shout and started loping toward them. The stranger reacted with the same brute force as Peter, swinging with a powerful undercut that caused Peter to stagger but not to fall. Janice backed away, horrified. They were fighting over nothing, over absolutely nothing. They certainly couldn't be fighting over her.

Tyler grabbed the stranger from behind and tried to jerk him around. The man drove his elbow backward and connected roughly with Tyler's midsection before launching himself at Peter again. Peter dodged and drove his fist at his opponent's chin, narrowly connecting.

More men ran out of the barn to join the fray. In the darkness, she doubted that any of them knew who was fighting or why. Manuel shoved someone away and received a fist in his face for his efforts. Someone else attempted to pull Peter back from the stranger, and Peter struck out in self-defense. The stranger turned and plowed into Tyler when Tyler tried to retaliate for the earlier blow. The fracas escalated rapidly into a battle.

Janice eased away from the fray in disbelief. She was still shaking inside, but she couldn't readily identify the reason. She was terrified for Peter, but he didn't seem terrified for her. She had thought him a gentleman incapable of this sort of mindless violence, but his fists flew faster and harder than anyone else's. She ought to do something to break up the fight, but her instinctive urge was to run and hide while she could.

With the appearance of Evie and a band of women bearing buckets of cold water from the horse trough, Janice fled, leaving the field in the hands of better warriors than she.

In her heart, she knew this was the beginning of the end. She could only hope Peter accepted the fact gracefully.

# Twenty-Two

Peter knew the instant that Janice fled. Distracted, he didn't see the fist coming until he was on the ground. The fist couldn't hurt any more than his wife's flight.

Evie waded in then with her water battalion, and Peter rolled out of the line of battle. Already covered with dust, he didn't need the mud that would result from a horse trough full of water. What he needed was already across the lawn and disappearing inside the house.

He cursed himself for allowing the stranger to interfere. He knew his own pent-up frustration had caused him to lash out, yet he had to wonder at the stranger's intrusion. He glanced over his shoulder, but whichever of the mud-covered warriors was his nemesis, he couldn't tell from here. It would serve no purpose to seek him out now. He had to get back to Janice before she shut him out completely.

He wished he knew what he was doing wrong. She was his wife, for heaven's sake. Maybe he'd been a little crude that first time, but he'd done everything he knew how to make it up to her since then. Did she intend to put him off forever? He didn't have forever. He only had tonight before he had to ride out. He could be gone for months. He couldn't wait for months.

He raced across the lawn and into the house, knowing without thinking about it that Janice would be headed for the safety of the tower. He might know very little about the woman who was his wife, but he knew the illusion of strength that she wielded against the world was just that—an illusion. She had learned to wield it very well and it was an effective disguise, but he had caught glimpses of the broken little girl behind the facade. The little girl was the one who ran.

His breath came in short pants as he reached the top of the tower. He breathed a sigh of relief at finding the door to the suite still open. He still had time to convince her of whatever it was she needed to hear.

The sitting room wasn't lit, but he knew she was here. Peter crossed the room and reached for the door to the bedroom—and found it locked.

He stared down at the knob in astonishment. He hadn't even known the thing possessed a key. Despite all their arguments and disagreements this past week, Janice had never once locked him out of their room. He had slept beside her every night—horny as hell, maybe, but he'd been in the same bed with her. He couldn't believe that after everything had gone so smoothly, she would lock him out now.

If he was any kind of man, he'd tell her to go to hell, leave after the race, and file for a divorce as soon as he had the money. No woman was worth this kind of trouble. There was obviously something wrong with her in any case. She'd been willing enough earlier, he'd wager. It wasn't as if he were in the habit of forcing her. She'd just been an old maid too long, maybe.

But he wasn't any kind of man, he guessed. He'd married this woman and he meant to have her. He'd allowed too many things and too many people to slip through his hands in the past. He didn't intend for it to happen again. He didn't know what he would have to do to hold her, but he knew he wouldn't allow her to hide from him anymore.

As his mind churned with these decisions, Peter inspected the window overlooking the trees. The moon was on its way out, but its light still illuminated the side of the tower and the flat roof of the gallery below. He glanced over at the other window, the one leading into the bedroom. It would have to be open like this one to let in the air. It would be too hot to breathe otherwise.

He had to be insane to contemplate what he was contemplating. The Monteigne mansion was two stories tall with a walk-up attic above that. The tower stood another story above the attic. It was a damned long way down to the ground. But right at this minute, Peter didn't see any other course.

He had no intention of begging and pleading at the door. And he damned well wouldn't sleep on any couch. He meant to sleep with his wife, where he belonged.

The party was still going on when he came downstairs. Peter sent a pair of sleepy children peeking out the curtains back to their beds, checked to make certain Betsy slept, then headed out to the yard. He'd seen a ladder thrown against the stable when they cleaned out the barn.

It wasn't easy maneuvering the long ladder through the front doors to the second floor, but it wasn't long enough to reach from the ground to the tower. Alicia Monteigne peered out her bedroom door to see what he was doing, but Peter was beyond caring what other people thought. Let the girl tattle tomorrow. By then, he'd have settled this matter with Janice.

He left the ladder lying in the second-floor hall while he ran up the stairs to inspect the attic windows. As he'd thought, the dormer window overlooking the second-floor gallery roof was just barely big enough to allow the ladder through.

He retrieved the ladder and carried it up the second flight of stairs. By this time, he knew he was crazy. He wore his best trousers and shirt, and they were ruined with dust and sweat. His jaw throbbed where the stranger had hit it. He probably looked as mad as he felt. But he was determined to have the woman lying in the bed just above this floor, just like he would have that mountain if he had to kill himself doing it. A man had to set his sights on some goal and pursue it. He'd rather make an ass of himself going after what he wanted than to sit around complaining that he couldn't have it.

It wasn't easy getting the ladder out the narrow window, but he managed it. It rested quite nicely on the gallery roof, but it came somewhat short of the tower window. Peter eyed the distance and wondered if Janice was asleep yet. He hoped he hadn't left his guns in the bedroom. If she wasn't asleep, she might think him a burglar and shoot him.

That thought didn't deter him. He swung out the attic window to the gallery roof, moved the ladder into a stronger position, and began to climb.

Lying in bed with the mosquito netting pulled back to allow in every breath of air, Janice heard the scraping noises but paid them no heed. She had heard Peter follow her into the suite, heard his footsteps outside the door, heard the knob turn. She had held her breath and waited for his cries of outrage, but they'd never come. He had simply walked out again.

She didn't think she wanted to cry. She was accustomed to being alone. It was much better that things ended this way, before they did or said things they would regret later. Peter would come to understand that he was better off without her. He might even be grateful for her decision sometime in the future. She just wasn't entirely sure about herself. She didn't know how she would survive. But it would surely be much easier to go on now, before she came to rely on a man who wasn't reliable.

The scraping noises grew odder. If the wind had picked up to brush branches against the house, she ought to feel a breeze by now. The tower caught more of the evening breezes off the river than the rest of the house, but it still held the heat of the day. She was sweltering.

It didn't take but a moment's defiance to pull off her nightgown and throw it to the floor. There wouldn't be anyone here to notice, that was for certain.

The sheets weren't much cooler than the gown, but the air against her skin felt delicious. She felt bold and daring and more in control of her life than she had been for longer than she cared to think. She shoved back the top sheet and stretched grandly in the huge bed, pushing the covers off with her toes and reaching her arms above her head. The action caused her breasts to rise, and she had a sudden vision of Peter pushing them up and telling her how beautiful they were. She lay still, and almost felt his tender caress. Her nipples grew hard and ached in response.

She was suddenly painfully aware of her body. She had never thought of it as more than a department store dummy to be dressed and kept clean. Now she had breasts that tingled and a hollowness on her inside needing to be filled and an ache where she couldn't mention. She curled into a ball to try to shove all these parts back into the numb whole she had once been, but it didn't work.

Peter had brought her to life again.

She didn't like it. She didn't want to feel. She didn't want to give in to these intruding sensations. They had led her to do mindless things once before, and the result had been disastrous. She couldn't allow herself to ever give in again.

But it was too late.

Even as her hand covered her breast in a futile attempt to erase the ache, the noise at the window drew her attention. Janice stared as dark shoulders emerged above the open window frame. That wasn't possible. The room was far above the trees. No one could come in from outside.

The open window went from floor to ceiling. Seemingly effortlessly, powerful arms and shoulders pulled the figure of a man through the opening to a kneeling position on the floor. Then he stood and stepped through the flimsy muslin curtains. Janice lay motionless, disbelieving. She wasn't afraid. She knew who it was. She just couldn't believe he'd done it.

"Peter?" she finally got his name out, although it was colored with astonishment. Perhaps the figment would disappear at the sound of a voice.

He didn't disappear. He moved closer to the bed, and Janice could see him unfastening his shirt. That sent a frisson of something through her, but she wasn't sure it was fear. She didn't entirely comprehend what was happening here.

"You must have locked the door by mistake. I didn't want to wake you."

She heard the lie in his voice. He wasn't angry. His tone was wry, as if he could scarcely believe what he had done, either. Janice stared from the window back to the man who now sat on the edge of the bed, removing his shoes.

"You climbed in the window?" That was a stupid question, but she was too amazed to think of another. Her mind wasn't quite functioning yet.

"Tyler's going to wonder about that ladder if he gets up before we do in the morning, but from the sounds of it, the party will go on until dawn. I don't think we have to worry."

This was insane. They sat here having this perfectly normal husband and wife conversation, and he had just climbed up four stories to come in her bedroom window. Janice stared at him as if he were crazed.

"If there hadn't been a ladder, would you have climbed the vines?" she asked, still incredulous, but her incredulity now wasn't so much for the fact that he had been able to do it, but that he had done it to get to her. She could see him shrug as he stood up.

"Probably." He began to unfasten his trousers.

He was unfastening his trousers, and she was lying here naked. And she wasn't doing anything about it.

She didn't know if Peter could see her in the moonlight. But she could certainly see enough of him to know what he was doing. And how he was feeling.

She stared as the patch of dark curls emerged from the unbuttoned material, and she couldn't look away when the rest of him emerged. The vigorousness of his arousal didn't leave any doubt as to what was in her husband's mind. Janice moved slightly away as he stepped out of his trousers and came to the bed.

"We're going to talk," he told her. But what he did next didn't feel like talking.

He climbed onto the bed and on top of her.

Janice sucked in her breath as she felt Peter's knee

come between her legs. He didn't do anything more than prop himself on his elbows above her, but she was frantically aware of the heat of his arousal rubbing low against her abdomen. She wouldn't be in any condition to talk like this.

Neither was he. He hesitated briefly, then bent to place a kiss at the corner of her mouth. "We'll talk, but not now," he whispered against her lips.

Not now. Not ever. It didn't matter. She was on fire.

Janice opened her mouth for his kiss, and found herself drowning in sensations with just the touch of his tongue. He caught her head and held her still while his tongue probed and explored and her body arched helplessly upward in some instinctive resistance to his possession. The move was a mistake, because now she was aware of the hardness of the male thighs capturing her own, of the length of the male organ searing her skin, and the need of her breasts to be touched.

Peter obliged this last without being told. His hand cupped her fullness while his thumb tortured the tip, driving her mindlessly to deepen their kiss. She returned the caress of his tongue, grasped the straining muscles of his arms, and lifted herself invitingly to his touch. She felt him groan and shudder above her, and then his mouth moved from her lips to her breasts and she writhed in ecstasy.

She didn't know how she could reach this state so quickly. It didn't seem possible. She didn't want it. She wanted nothing to do with what he was doing to her. But she rubbed her hands up and down his arms, kissed his hair, and groaned helplessly as he ravaged first one breast, then the other. She was behaving shamelessly, for she knew of a certainty where this would lead, where she wanted it to lead.

He was too impatient to make her wait for long. Janice cried out when Peter's fingers slid between her thighs, but she spread them willingly at his caress. She ought to be fighting him, protesting, but he'd sapped her will and left her spineless. She parted her legs and cried out in delight when his fingers pierced her and she raised herself eagerly for more.

"Tell me when, Janice. I'll not leave you crying this time."

The whisper against her ear startled her. She had been so caught up in the sensations of her body that she had left her mind behind. She lifted her eyes to see Peter's hovering just above her. His fingers were doing unspeakable things to the lower part of her while his gaze followed the expression on her face. She ought to be embarrassed beyond redemption. Daringly she touched the muscular ridge of his chest. She felt the tension in him, knew the willpower that held him back, and knew she wouldn't fight him. She would curse herself in the morning.

"When, Peter," she whispered, and felt him crush her in his arms in reply.

She was going to regret this, she knew, but nothing short of death would stop her now.

# Twenty-Three

Peter kissed her—a kiss so deep and full of longing that it released the locks on her own carefully shielded emotions. Janice thought she would drown in the flood of unleashed desire, and she clung tightly to Peter's shoulders as her only anchor in a tide of uncertainty.

But the flood quickly found an outlet in the things he did to her body. All the tension and passion rushed to her loins, building up a powerful flood tide that waited only for the dam to be breached. Touching wasn't enough. She needed more.

And he gave it to her. With a muffled groan of triumph, Peter surged into her, and she no longer had any need to hold back. Janice cried out her joy and pain as he filled her, stripping away all the ache and loneliness, penetrating the vacuum that she had been.

He was fast and fierce in his possession, as if fearful he would be denied again and determined not to be. He wasn't any faster or fiercer than Janice wanted. She had no knowledge of the joy of this joining until now, when it welled up in her and built with every stroke of Peter's hard body. She reveled in the power of this happiness, understanding it wasn't just her own joy but his also that came with this blending of their bodies.

And then he erupted inside her, burying himself so deep and with such passion that he forced open yet another lock. Janice screamed at the explosion overwhelming her, carrying her along with him, shaking her right down to her toes as her womb seemed to take on a life of its own. As her insides clutched him and pulled him deeper, Peter laughed and moaned and held her close, until they were both too weak for more.

He finally found the strength to roll his weight off her, but he gathered her close against his side. Janice went willingly, not yet ready to return to a state of separateness. As long as she sprawled along Peter's side, her perspiring flesh stuck to his, she could remain part of him. She was so very tired of being alone.

His hand skimmed her side, touched her gently at the hip, moved upward to curve around her breast. Janice sighed and snuggled closer. She would undoubtedly regret this later, but not now.

"You're more generous than I ever dreamed, Mrs. Muloney," he murmured near her ear. "And so good that I want you again already."

She ought to be frightened at the thought, but she wasn't. "I didn't know it could be like that. You'd think we could hurt each other."

His hand trailed down to the apex of her thighs and rested there lightly. "I didn't want to hurt you. I suppose it's kind of hard for two people living together not to sometimes hurt each other, but I didn't want to hurt you this way. I don't want to just use you."

This time what he said and not just the sound of his voice caused a warm little shiver in her middle. She understood now that she had been used before, that what they had just done was so completely different that she couldn't grasp the whole of it yet. She ran her fingers daringly up his chest, exploring previously forbidden territory.

"You didn't hurt me," she said slowly, looking for ways to explain. It wasn't easy. What they had just done was a topic never spoken about to her knowledge, and it certainly wasn't a subject she had ever dared to think about. Finding words for it now seemed an impossibility. "I didn't know . . . I thought it was different for a woman than for a man."

The hand under her stroked her hair. "It doesn't have to be, although I'll admit my experience in that department is limited. With you, I know the pleasure isn't faked. I don't think any woman has ever made me feel so good. I want it to be the same for you." Peter turned his head to look down at her. "Will you tell me about that first man? Is he the reason you were afraid?"

Even now, feeling so relaxed it was a wonder she didn't melt, Janice could feel the old protective barriers snapping into place. But they didn't snap quickly enough to keep everything out. "How do you know there hasn't been a dozen men?" she asked with a hint of anger. "Isn't that what men usually think? Once a woman has fallen, she's eager to sample everything that comes along?"

Peter snorted and shoved her over on her back, trapping her there with one strong leg. "I probably would have thought something equally asinine about any other woman but you. You don't know a damned thing about making love. You didn't even know how to kiss. And you did your damnedest to hide behind that schoolmarm disguise so no one would ever attempt to teach you. You're hiding something, all right, Mrs. Mulloney, but it isn't a trail of lovers."

He was coming much too close. She could see no reason in the world why he should know the whole truth when no one else did. It would serve no purpose. As a mother duck will protect her young by leading intruders astray, Janice gave him enough to lead him away from more dangerous shoals. "I thought I was in love once. I was very young and he was very selfish. That's all there was to it."

Peter brushed her hair back off her face. "He must have been more than selfish. He must have been crude and stupid. How could he hurt a beautiful young girl and then walk off and leave her?"

She could tell him that part easily enough. Peter had just said people living together would occasionally hurt each other. She had a bushel basket of hurts to distribute. If it would keep him away from Betsy, she would willingly stab herself.

"Stephen was young too, young and ambitious," she

answered slowly. "When your father fired all the railway workers, Stephen lost the only employment he knew. He went in search of work. He never came back." Even after all these years she didn't know what had become of him. She had thought he would write. There had been six terrible months while she waited to know where he was so she could tell him about the child they'd made together. But she'd never heard from him again. He could be dead now for all she knew. She didn't mourn him.

Peter fell silent at this admission. He teased her hair with his fingers, drew soft circles on her cheek, then drew one hand downward to fondle her breast. The tip rose in instant response, and he shifted his weight slightly so he could look at her there. Just his look brought a rush of desire to her midsection. Janice shuddered and tried not to rise to meet the press of his fingers.

"My family destroyed a lot of lives," he admitted sadly. "I can't bring them back. I can't even mend them. If it were up to me, I'd give all the money back, but the money was never mine. Did you love him very much? Should I have Daniel look for him?"

"I was fifteen years old," she whispered as his hand took a more possessive hold on her. "What does a child that age know of love?"

Fifteen. Peter shook his head, whether in denial or disbelief, he couldn't say. Fifteen. Then it was possible. Betsy could very well be the product of that union. He leaned over and kissed the corner of her eye. The tear he found there chose his course. He didn't want to hear it if Betsy was more than a sister. He wasn't prepared for that knowledge. He just knew Janice belonged to him now, and it would be his child that grew within her. His kiss lowered to her lips.

This time, they made love slowly, with more care, seeking those places that brought the most pleasure. The first time had left her so enervated that Janice didn't think she could ever respond again, but Peter taught her the fallacy of that assumption. And she learned the joy of bringing him pleasure. She hadn't known it was possible to excite herself by exciting him, but she trembled with need by the time Peter moaned and finally surged into her, unable to hold himself back any longer. She felt vaguely triumphant that she could reduce him to the same quivering need that she suffered.

The climax was much more intense this time, closer and more intimate now that they knew what to expect. Janice bit back her cries as Peter's seed exploded inside her. Her traitorous body accepted the liquid heat, opening and welcoming it as he sank deep inside her. But her mind was still terrified of what was happening to her. As pleasurable as this moment was, she knew the horror of what could follow.

She could never explain it to him. She could never tell him how terrifying it was to be left pregnant and alone with no means of feeding her child. She had hoped to persuade him to go off without touching her. Now that he had not only touched her, but taught her to crave that touch, she didn't want him to go.

"Couldn't we stay here?" she murmured sleepily, hoping he was still awake.

"And do what?" Peter rolled her against his side and tucked her head into the curve of his shoulder. "Go to sleep, Jenny, and quit your worrying. I'll be back."

He knew she worried, but he did nothing about it but give her promises. Just like a man. Sighing, Janice gave up the battle for the moment. Sleep had to come first.

Morning didn't make it any easier. She came awake the instant he did with the awareness of her nakedness and his arousal coming together at the same time. The sun spilled across their bodies, indicating the lateness of the hour. Janice looked up as Peter leaned over her and knew she wouldn't stop him. Her hand caressed his stubbled jaw, and she smiled at the prickly feel of this man she could call hers.

He kissed her cheek, then her breast. His beard chafed her skin as he drank hungrily at her growing arousal. She touched him every where she could reach, wondering at the strength rippling beneath tanned skin, marveling at the hardness of his torso. He could hold her pinned to the bed with ease, do as he wished with her, and she wouldn't be able to stop him. She wouldn't want to stop him. She parted her legs at his urging and lifted them to give him ease of entry. She rocked her head back and moaned with the deep-seated bliss of his filling. For this brief moment in time, she was his.

Later, when they lay satiated among the rumpled sheets, Peter covered her breast with a possessive hand and grinned at the canopy over them. His elation was difficult to ignore.

"We're going to make a pair, Mrs. Mulloney. As soon as I wire you that I have that mountain, I want you to start buying yourself some pretty dresses and all the things you're going to need to set up a fancy home. Buy a train car full of furniture, if you like. It might take us a while to haul it all up the mountain, but we'll get it there. I want you to have the best."

She'd heard dreams like this before. Stephen had gone off to make his fortune with the same kind of promises. Janice looked at Peter sadly, slipped from his hands, and rolled out of bed. She was sore between her legs. She knew what that meant. She could still feel him deep inside of her, knew even now his seed would be taking root. Stark terror kept her moving.

"I don't need the best, Peter. I need a home. I like it here. Couldn't you use Tyler's money to start a store or something? I'll be more than happy to help. Maybe there's a building back in Natchez with rooms above the store where we could live until we get on our feet." She wrapped a robe around her nakedness and swung to plead with him face-to-face. "I don't need gold, Peter. We could be happy here."

The expression on his face revealed his shock. "You want me to be a storekeeper? Janice, I've spent five years of my life looking for an opportunity like this. I can't just up and throw it away and pretend it never happened. Besides, I've got a partner back there waiting for me to come back and help him buy that mountain. He's count-

ing on me. We've been through a lot together. I can't let
him down."

He climbed out of the bed and gathered up his clothes.
He held them in front of him as he met her stoic gaze
with a smile. "You're worrying again, Jenny. I told you to
let me do the worrying from now on. We're going to be
rich. I'll only be gone a little while. I wish I could take
you with me, but I can't leave you at the end of the line
while I ride like mad for Butte. I'll come back and we'll
do it in style. That will be better for Betsy."

He was so damned confident that everything would go
his way. That's what happened when a person was raised
with riches and given everything he wanted. He didn't
know the meaning of failure. He didn't know the meaning
of tragedy. Anything could happen out there, but Janice
couldn't make him see that if he was too blind to look.

She wasn't a person accustomed to argument. She had
always gone her own way, done what she thought best.
She would continue to do so. While Peter was out galli-
vanting across the countryside, she would be looking for
a job and a place to stay. If he left her pregnant, she
would just have to turn to Daniel for help. At least this
time she was married, and her husband had a family she
could turn to.

They met Tyler coming in the front door as they came
down the stairs. He raised a knowing eyebrow and
smirked but only wished them a "good morning" as he
headed for the breakfast table. Janice gave Peter a questioning look.

Peter shrugged. "I didn't get the ladder down in time.
You'll have to grow your hair long like Rapunzel if you
mean to keep locking me out of towers."

Janice blushed and he grinned. "Go on and get something to eat. In this household, one entertaining story
more or less isn't going to matter, but I'll get the ladder
down before Betsy sees it. She might not be quite old
enough to understand." Peter brushed a kiss across her
hair and pushed her lightly toward the dining room.

Despite the late hours everyone had kept the previous

night, the whole household seemed to be up and running about. Janice met with numerous winks and grins from people coming and going through the dining room, but the talk was all of the big parade and horse races scheduled for the afternoon. Janice wished she could work up the same enthusiasm, but she felt as if the minutes to doom were ticking away when they talked of the race.

For a few brief moments she almost wished Peter would lose. They would be a thousand dollars in debt to Tyler, but they could earn that back somehow. She just didn't want Peter to go. But that was selfish of her. Some poor man back there in New Mexico waited for him to show up and save the day. And Peter wanted it. She couldn't begrudge her husband for having dreams just because she had given them up long ago.

Well, she might begrudge them, but she didn't have to complain about it. Janice put on a happy smile as Betsy came racing into the room talking excitedly of the race that her "Uncle" Peter was going to win. Brother-in-law was just not a concept she grasped yet, not with all her friends calling the adults "uncle" and "aunt."

The women spent the morning packing enormous baskets of food for the picnic that would follow the parade. The children, as well as Carmen's brothers, Manuel and José, spent the time perfecting the tunes they meant to play as they marched. The cacophony arising from the yard was alarming, sending the hens into the bushes and the horses into nervous circles, but it kept the children out from underfoot.

Betsy's delight at being able to slam two pieces of tin together in time to the beat was worth every minute of the noise. When the baskets were packed and the proud mothers crowded onto the gallery to watch their children play, Janice had difficulty hiding her own pride. Betsy looked like a golden princess this morning with her hair curling in tendrils around her small glowing face. Her white eyelet gown only came to her knees and already her white stockings were sagging and dirty, but Janice thought her the most beautiful child she had ever seen.

Just as she realized she might already be carrying another child to be sister to this one, Peter came up behind her and placed his hand on her shoulder.

"She looks just like you, you know," he whispered in her ear. "If our daughter is only half as beautiful, I'll be twice as proud."

Shocked, Janice glanced up to meet her husband's eyes. He knew.

# Twenty-Four

I f he really knew that Betsy was her child, Peter didn't seem very concerned about it. He wrapped his arms around Janice's waist and pulled her back against him. She thought he must surely feel her shivering from the shock, but he was grinning and exchanging comments with Tyler on the possibility of using firecrackers to replace the erratic drummer.

Surely he wouldn't say anything to anyone else. He couldn't know for certain. Betsy mustn't learn from idle gossip that her adoring older sister was actually her mother. Janice wouldn't have her ever learn that if at all possible. The child had enough difficulties in her life without learning she was a bastard, that the father and mother she could scarcely remember were actually her grandparents. Janice would deny it until the end of time, but there would be no difficulty in discovering the truth if someone wanted. Everyone in the town she lived in before Cutlerville knew her shame.

She would have to speak to Peter. He would understand. Taking a deep breath, Janice tried to enjoy the moment. The Fourth had dawned brilliant and hot. Heat waves shimmered above the dust. But the children didn't seem to feel it. They raised their joyous noise and laughed and broke into spontaneous dancing when Benjamin's toddler—too young to hold an instrument—began to wiggle and clap in time to the music. Soon, the lawn sported an impromptu reel in imitation of their elders, and everyone was laughing.

"We'd better get the rascals loaded into the wagons and

into town before they look like ragpickers," Tyler commented as the reel deteriorated into a giggling heap of wrestling children. He turned to Peter. "You going to ride that brute over there or save your strength for the race?"

Peter didn't hesitate. "I thought I'd ride him. When we get close enough to be seen, he's guaranteed to raise a ruckus for the audience. That ought to shoot the odds up even more."

Tyler grinned. "I didn't take you for a gambling man, but I can see it's in the blood. You catch on real quick. Odds are already at fifteen to one. Think we can make it to twenty?"

They wandered off to the paddock, making their plans, and Janice bit her lip to keep from crying out her protest.

Evie came up behind her and gave her a hug. "You might as well get used to it. You wouldn't want a man who would do everything the way you wanted it done, would you? He'd be no man at all. Working out those compromises is the hardest part of being married until you get used to it. I think that's why God gave us beds. Sometimes, that's the only thing that keeps you together at first. There were times when I really thought I would have to kill Tyler to get him to listen to me. Now I just make him give in on the really important things, like not naming the baby Fannie Mae after his favorite aunt."

Janice couldn't help but smile at this eccentric assessment of marriage. Evie was ten years older and had been married since she was twenty. Maybe she ought to be given credit for a little experience. But Evie had always led a protected life, going from a loving home to Tyler's strong arms. Janice felt like she had a vast amount more experience in the ways of the world than her hostess. But none of that experience told her how to deal with a husband.

The laughter and the noise carried them into Natchez, where crowds had already begun to gather. Janice did her best to hide her apprehension. She could do many things to improve her lot in life, but she had never learned how to fight fate. If Peter won the race, she would kiss him farewell. If he lost, they would be bankrupt and in debt over their heads. Neither alternative particularly appealed to her. It was too late to do anything about it.

They stood on the sidelines and watched the mayor and his wife go by in their grand carriage decorated for the occasion. They watched the Confederate soldiers in their faded uniforms march and ride and show off their medals. The town band strutted and performed a stirring marching song. And the children rollicked in between, performing their song when Manuel got their attention, laughing and giggling when he did not. It was a grand day for a parade, and the onlookers laughed and clapped for everyone.

Janice could manage happiness just by watching Betsy. Betsy couldn't run in the three-legged sack race, but she almost won the egg contest, tripping at the last minute and splattering her egg all over the winner. The loss didn't seem to bother her. Just the fact that she had been able to play thrilled her. Perhaps, at long last, she was growing out of the bad spells.

The time for the horse race came soon enough. Peter grabbed Janice, kissed her hard for luck, and ran off to join the others. She clenched her fingers into fists and watched him go without raising a word of protest when what she wanted to do was scream and rail against the fates.

"That man of your'n is riding a mighty mean stallion, ain't he?"

Janice looked up in surprise at the tall stranger leaning against a nearby walnut tree. His grizzled beard probably hadn't been cut in weeks, and his worn leather vest was probably more disreputable than the one Jason Harding wore. Still, he looked like a relatively harmless old man, until he shifted his stance and she could see the guns he wore on his hips.

Except for this one, the men were all around the paddock or the track. Carmen and Evie and Jasmine were all concentrating on keeping the children away from the horses and out from under the feet of the men. No one heard the question but herself. She ought to ignore him and walk off, but she couldn't. Something compelling about the stranger's gaze kept her from dismissing him.

"I don't know much about horses," she offered carefully, moving toward the other women and away from him.

"Reckon he can keep the brute on the track?" the stranger inquired, undeterred by the distance she created.

He must be trying to decide on a wager. Janice wasn't precisely certain how betting worked, but she couldn't be less than honest with the man. She nodded. "Peter can ride him. I've seen him."

The old man grinned and fished in his pocket for a cigar. "Oh, I saw him all right. Put on a pretty show for the greenhorns, he did. Had that animal on his back feet like a dancing bear. Odds are twenty to one against his winning and five to one he'll get himself killed out there. I wouldn't want to see the boy killed. If you say he can ride him, I'll take your word on it."

Killed? She hadn't considered that alternative. With rising panic, Janice searched the paddock for some sign of Peter and the horrible animal he'd chosen to ride. She had considered his winning or losing, but she hadn't thought he'd be foolish enough to get himself killed. Surely Tyler wouldn't let him ride a horse that dangerous.

She couldn't see anything but a blur of milling horses, riders, and dust. When she looked back to the tree, the man was gone.

The stranger appearing and disappearing like that made her even more nervous. She didn't like it. Checking to see that Betsy was safely sitting on the carriage seat, bouncing up and down with Melissa in an attempt to see the track better, Janice forced herself to walk closer to the railing.

She knew the race was over a mile long. The track was little more than a field that had been used once too often for racing. Over the years, distance markers had been tacked up haphazardly, and today a form of starting gate had been built. The grass was thick and dry, and there didn't seem to be any obstacles in the way. Janice couldn't see anything that would pose a danger, other than the horse itself. She might know nothing of horses, but surely the men did. They would know if it was safe to race the stallion.

Manuel materialized at her side, and she sent him a quick glance. He was probably a year or so older than she. He'd been running his uncle's ranch back in Mineral Springs until Peyton had sold it to the Hardings. Now that Manuel had seen his kid brother through college, he was footloose and fancy-free, figuring José could support their youngest sister Maria and uncle now that he was going to be a lawyer. Manuel's Mexican good looks were an oddity here in Natchez where everyone seemed to be blond and fair, but he didn't seem to have any trouble attracting girls. If she wondered why he'd chosen to stand beside her and not one of the Southern belles looking his way, his first words answered the question.

"Pete said I'd better keep an eye on you. Can't quite tell if he expects you to throw something at him or to faint. I told him you're more likely to take a ruler to his hand, but he ain't seen you behind a school desk, and he doesn't believe me. Are you going to do anything rambunctious, Mrs. Mulloney?"

His dark eyes laughed, but they watched too. Janice smiled at his concern. "I'll wait until after the race if I mean to do anything rambunctious. That pretty girl with the blue ribbon is looking over here. Why don't you go entertain her with your wild tales?"

Manuel pulled on his hat, studied her face one more time, then grinned. "I just might do that. Do you think she'll believe the one about me blowing up the town?"

"That one gets bigger every time someone tells it. I thought Daniel was the responsible party."

Manuel shrugged and started to walk away. "Don't think there were any responsible parties at the time, but it's a great attention-getter."

Janice laughed and returned her gaze to the track. She should be thankful Peter wasn't like Manuel, with his eyes always following a different lady. She swallowed hard when she saw the horses already lining up at the gate. She suddenly felt very uncertain if following gold was any better than following the ladies.

When the gun went off to start the race, she jumped, startled, and grabbed the railing to steady herself. Peter's stallion was equally startled by the noise. The animal reared and whinnied and lost ground to the steadier participants. Janice gave a small cry of frustration and pounded the fence, which shocked her even more when she found herself doing it.

Peter jerked his mount back to order and sent the animal after the rest of the pack. The horse's heavy muscles rippled under a shiny coat of black. Janice couldn't see any of the physical faults Peter had noted that first day. The stallion was huge and fast. Had he not delayed his start, he would be way ahead of the others by now. As it was, he had already passed the slower horses and gained on the heaviest part of the pack.

Janice discovered she was digging her fingers into the fence post, but she didn't bother trying to pry them loose. She sensed the little crowd forming behind her, knowing the women by their perfumes, hearing the loud shouts of the men as Peter pulled the stallion on the far side of the track. That maneuver meant his horse would have farther to run, but it was safer than forcing his way through the pack.

Tyler screamed instructions Peter couldn't possibly hear. Benjamin simply yelled in some relentless rhythm that duplicated the pounding of the horses' hooves. Janice dug her fingers farther into the railing and prayed.

She screamed with the crowd when Peter's stallion pulled ahead of all the others but one. She screamed as the two lead horses came around the stretch, neck and neck. She screamed herself hoarse when Peter's mount pulled ahead by a nose. And she screamed hysterically when a gun went off near the gate, sending the stallion wheeling in panic, flinging his rider to the ground.

Janice was over the fence before anyone could stop her. The pack of horses racing down the track were no more than a horde of insects to her ears. People screamed as the stallion flew across the finish line, riderless. Others scrambled over the fence to grab Peter out of the rush of hooves pounding his way. They had him on the edge of the track at the railing by the time Janice reached him. She fell on her knees and pulled his head in her lap and bent over him just as the last horse flew by.

Peter managed a lopsided grin as Janice's face bent over his. "I told Manuel to keep an eye on you. That boy can't do anything right."

"I hate you, Peter Mulloney," she whispered where no one could hear. Not that anyone could hear for the screaming and shouting and cursing going on all around them. "If you haven't broken your neck, I'll do it for you."

He moaned slightly as he shifted position, and he closed his eyes. "I knew you were the kind of woman who would give me wifely consideration. I did a good job picking you, didn't I?"

She wept then. Tears crawled down her cheeks, and she despised herself for them, but she couldn't stop. She buried her fingers in Peter's hair and held him close while a doctor climbed over the fence to examine him. She was behaving like an hysterical female, she knew, but she hadn't been prepared for this. She could plan so many things, but she couldn't plan disasters.

"You're goin' to have to let him go, ma'am. He needs to sit up so I can see if there's any bones broken." The doctor had already done a thorough inspection of Peter's legs, now he waited impatiently for Janice to release his patient.

Peter lifted one eyelid to peer at the physician. "Don't you think I ought to just rest here awhile longer? My wife won't kill me if she thinks I'm dying."

The side-whiskered physician harrumphed and bit back a grin. "You pretty durn well near killed yourself, I figger. Maybe she'll take that into account."

By this time, Tyler and Benjamin were shoving back the crowd and bending anxiously over the fallen rider.

When Peter managed to sit up without falling over, they stepped back with relief. Janice wrung her hands together to keep from striking out at all of them. They'd lost the race and had nothing to show for it but a thousand-dollar debt and a lump at the back of Peter's head.

Peter gave her a wink and tipped her cheek gently. "Quit fretting, Jenny-belle. I'll live." He looked up to Tyler. "Don't suppose a horse crossing the finish line without a rider counts, does it?"

Tyler snorted. "I'm going to find the damned cracker that shot that gun and ram him down the barrel. Are you going to get up from there or are we going to have to carry you?"

Peter tentatively stretched his legs, and finding them still in working order, he wrapped an arm around Janice's shoulders. "You look beautiful even when you cry, Mrs. Mulloney, but you're not going to get rid of me this easily. Help me up, and I'll find us some way out of this."

Janice wiped hastily at her tear-streaked face, then wrapped her arm around her husband's back. She didn't think he really needed her help. He was just looking for some way to hold on to her a little while longer. It didn't matter. It was all over. They had lost. She didn't know what the future held, but she had married this man for better or worse. They would make the best of it somehow.

Peter limped slightly once he reached his feet, but he steadied himself on Janice's shoulders and kept his arm there as he headed off the track.

"I'll wire Daniel to get you the money I owe you if it's going to leave you short," Peter told Tyler as the other man walked alongside of him. They both watched as Benjamin went over to take the reins of the stallion that had cost them so much.

"I'll not be short," Tyler answered absently, watching a man in top hat and frock coat come up to pat the stallion's neck. "I had me a few side bets."

Peter turned to stare at him. "Side bets? You bet against your own horse?"

Tyler's grin was lazy and disarming as he continued

watching his animal. "Never put all your eggs in one basket, Mulloney. That's the key to successful gambling. The odds weren't great, but they paid back the original bet."

Peter nodded. "Lesson learned. Well, if you don't mind then, I'll wait a while to pay that debt. I'm going to have to go into Houston and see if I can borrow from those banks Harding told me about."

Janice looked up, startled at this new development. He still meant to try to buy the gold mine?

Tyler stopped a few yards short of the crowd gathering around the stallion. He tipped his hat back, looked around to make certain no one listened, then answered, "No need to do that. I've got the cash."

Peter shook his head as if the fall might have worked something loose. "You've got the cash? I thought . . ."

Tyler shook his head and grinned proudly at the stallion rearing back at all the sudden attention. "I've sold that devil, Mulloney. The damned fool man gave me enough to buy a gold mountain. You interested?"

Peter coughed, grabbed Janice tighter, and looked from his host to the wild horse. "You sold him?"

Tyler pulled a pocket full of bills from his shirt and handed them over. "When his new owner gets tired of trying to tame the devil, I'll get him back, for a third of the price. Get yourself back here before I do. Next time, I mean to win that race."

Janice looked in wonder at the huge stack of bills. She'd never seen so much money in her life. She looked up at her husband's astounded face and saw the excitement building there.

He was going to leave her for a damned gold mountain.

# Twenty-Five

Dusk colored the landscape with blue and golds. Janice wandered through the dark shrubbery, feeling more lost than she had in years.

Peter was upstairs packing his valise. He meant to catch the train that left at midnight. She had come looking for Betsy, but Betsy was busy catching lightning bugs with the other children. Janice supposed she could search out the other women, but she didn't think she could handle their sympathetic expressions without weeping.

She wanted to be happy. She had meant to be. It had been a glorious day with sunshine and flowers, laughter and music. She ought to occasionally be allowed a carefree day where all she had to do was sit back and enjoy herself. She supposed that was the day of the island picnic. She would pay for that day for a long time.

She pressed her fingers to her abdomen and tried not to envision what might already be happening there. Other women were married for years without having children. She knew in her head it didn't always happen. Just because it had happened once after a night with a man didn't mean it would ever happen again. She was just borrowing trouble.

She was so edgy she almost screamed when a man rustled through the bushes to find her. Janice made herself smile when she recognized Peter, but she knew it was a pitiful excuse for a smile.

He knew it too. He bent over and kissed it away. "We still have a little time, Mrs. Mulloney. I found the perfect place to watch the fireworks."

Janice took his arm and glided through the shrubbery, holding up her skirt as if used to having a man around to support her. Were anyone looking, they would see an elegant gentleman in his frock coat and vest, carefully tending to a lady with upswept hair and a summer gown shaped by proper corset and bustle. She should be feeling like a lady at a tea party and not like a bereft fifteen-year-old girl.

Peter guided her to a latticed pavilion on a hill overlooking the river. The breeze off the water cleaned the air of the usual summer miasmas, and they had a clear view of the surrounding countryside.

"Tyler promised to keep everyone out of here. He's taking the kids out on the boat to see the fireworks, and everyone else is watching from the gallery." Peter led her to the softly cushioned bench lining the walls. "I wanted you to myself for just a little while. Do you mind?"

Nervously Janice clasped her hands in her lap and stared down at them. "Of course not. How long do you think you'll be gone?"

Peter pulled up a wicker chair in front of her and reached to take her hands. "Depends on how the trains run. I mean to make Butte in two to three weeks. I'll need to spend a week or two at the camp getting things moving. The nearest reliable telegraph office is over fifty miles from the camp." He didn't warn her about the renegade Apaches and outlaws and the various other detriments of his chosen path. Those were his problems to worry about. Janice already worried too much.

"Why don't I wire you when I'm ready for you to come? I've talked to Tyler and Manuel. Tyler says you can have his private car, and Manuel said he's interested in coming to work for me, so he can ride along with you. You can have the car sidetracked at Fort Worth, get your things loaded on it, say your good-byes to the people in Mineral Springs, and take the car to Gage. By the time you get there, I should be waiting for you. That will save us a few weeks. We can be together again in less than three months."

Three months was all eternity to a fifteen-year-old, but Janice tried to look at it as an adult. "Will the weather hold? You said the winters were bad."

"If you buy a mountain of furniture, I won't guarantee we'll get it all home before winter. Will you mind terribly living in a crude cabin until I can haul in the necessities?"

That was the very least of her worries. Janice shook her head emphatically. "I just want to know there will be a roof over our heads and food in our stomachs. I don't need a lot, Peter, but you're leaving me helpless to make my own way while I wait for you. I don't like being helpless."

Peter shifted his seat to sit beside her and pull her into his arms. "I'm sorry, Jenny. I know I've put the cart before the horse. I should have waited to marry until I had the money, but I couldn't let you go. If you'll have faith in me for just a little while, I promise everything will go smoothly after that."

Janice gave a curt laugh and buried her face in his shoulder. "You don't know life like I do. Nothing ever goes smoothly."

Peter ran his hand into her hair and began to scatter the pins. He knew from the experience of these last five years that money was the grease to make life smoother, but she'd never had money. She wouldn't believe him until he showed her. He couldn't show her just yet, but he would. He kissed the fascinating shell of her ear and felt her shiver.

"I love the way you shiver like that," he murmured. "You know I'll send for you as soon as humanly possible because I don't think I can last very long without you in my bed. I need you now, Jenny. I'll need you every night that I'm away. You'd better be well rested when we come together next, because I'm not going to let you out from under me until we're both exhausted."

Peter's words shocked her, but not as much as what his fingers were doing. He had the bodice of her gown undone and her corset unhooked before Janice knew what he was about. She gasped as his warm fingers slid beneath the confinement of the corset to caress her breast. He silenced any protest by covering her mouth with his.

He was promising he wouldn't have any other woman while he was away. She understood what his words didn't say. It had never occurred to her until now that he might, but her husband was a virile man, one accustomed to having women whenever he needed them. Still, she didn't find it hard to believe that Peter would wait for her. He would be too busy with his damned mountain to do anything else.

Janice tried to push him away. "Peter! We can't . . ." Her words caught in her throat as her corset gave way and he bent his head to lick gently at the peak of her breast.

"I thought I'd already proved that we can." He bit lightly at the sensitive bud, then moved his marauding mouth to her throat. "No more proper schoolmarm, Jenny. I want the woman inside this getup."

He had her, there was no doubt of that. As he laid her back against the cushions, Janice reached to unfasten his buttons. She was actually unfastening a man's shirt buttons. She had never dreamed of doing such a thing, but her fingers ached for the feel of something more satisfying than linen. She gave a sigh of contentment when her palms finally rested against his chest.

"You're a good student, Mrs. Mulloney," he murmured appreciatively, nipping at her ear and spreading his kisses inexorably downward again.

Janice held her breath as he worked his way closer to her breast.

"There are a lot of other things I mean to teach you once we're snowed into those mountains." Fondling one breast, Peter lifted the other to his mouth.

Janice felt the swirling sensation of his tongue clear down through her middle.

"But tonight, I don't have time for the niceties. Just be grateful this isn't a haystack."

Without another word of warning, Peter rucked her gown up to her waist. Janice gave a soft gasp and tried to fend him off, but he was already untying her drawers and the warm night breeze stirred what only his fingers had stirred before.

"Peter, please . . ." She couldn't finish the plea as his fingers parted the soft cotton of her underwear and touched her.

He suckled lightly at her breast once more, then moved his mouth to hers. "Please, what, my love? Tell me what you want. I'll move mountains for you."

His voice was thick with desire, and Janice had a vague understanding that she could ask for nearly anything now and he would give it to her. But she wanted only one thing right this minute, and her body was singing for it. She arched her hips slightly and reached for the buttons of his trousers.

Peter chuckled and helped her. "That's what I wanted to hear. This place will make heathens of us both if we stay much longer."

He was right about that. The heavy sweet scent of magnolias permeated the breeze blowing through the pavilion, adding a perfume to the erotic game they played. Just the feel of the warm night air on parts of her never before uncovered to the outside was enough to stir her senses and make her crazy. But what he did with his mouth and hands was more than she could stand. She wanted all their clothing gone, but there didn't seem to be time enough for that. The urges were too strong.

Their combined hands freed Peter from the confinement of his trousers, and for the first time Janice found her fingers in contact with that male part of him. She almost pulled away, but he caught her wrist and held her there until she realized he wanted to be touched. She did so wonderingly, caressing him and feeling him respond vigorously to the caress.

"You have the sweetest hands," he groaned against her ear. "I'm not going to be able to wait much longer."

She couldn't speak the words like he did, but she could show him. She had never known what it meant to be wanton. Perhaps the wine of summer, the heat and the laughter had unloosened these urges. Perhaps it was just the fear of parting. Whatever it was, she couldn't bear to be separate from him any longer. She guided him gently to where they needed to be together.

Peter moaned in delight, grabbed her mouth with his and kissed her deeply, then surged forward until he was all the way inside her. Janice found her cry of delight drowned in the sudden explosion of gunpowder on the river.

It took a moment and Peter's chuckles to realize what was happening. The burst of golden light crossing the night sky confirmed it. They were going to miss the firework show.

"Ahh, Mrs. Mulloney, I knew you would make me see fireworks that first night I saw you," he murmured in her ear.

Another explosion drowned out any reply she might have made. The tension of their bodies made any other words unnecessary. As the sky filled with golden stars, they coupled like the two young animals they were and had been too proud to admit. Nature brought them together and dissolved any lingering pretense. They were meant for each other, if only in this way.

Peter took her and filled her and brought her to the point where Janice couldn't discern the difference between the explosions of light on the outside and the tremors erupting on her insides. Either way, he left her as shattered as the multicolored stars spilling across the black sky.

She knew he felt it too, but words didn't exist for what they felt as Peter's body emptied itself into hers. They could only cling to each other and lay upon the bench, wrapped in the tangle of their rumpled clothing, watching the dying explosions of light overhead.

As the final round of gunpowder died into the night, Peter brushed her hair from her face and kissed her lips gently. "Whatever happens in the days and years to come, I'll never forget this moment, my love. I'll hold it with me forever."

And so would she. She just hoped it would be in her

memory and not any more concrete fashion. Her hand came between them to the place where they joined and pressed there, as if to ward off the evil spirits that had filled her once before. There could not be a child. Not yet.

They dressed slowly, mostly in silence. The euphoria of moments before became something else, something bittersweet in the knowledge of their parting. It had to be this way, they both knew. He had to see that she was safe and protected. He had to know that she was with friends and not strangers while he rode to claim their future. In return, she knew she couldn't follow, couldn't stay by his side. She couldn't risk the child that might come of it. She couldn't risk Betsy. She had to cling to what little she had.

But for the first time these reasons were somehow as thin and insubstantial as the paper moon Evie had painted for one of her children's books. A larger version hung in one of the windows now, illuminated from behind. As they crossed the yard into that crescent pattern of light, their fingers intertwined. They knew it was too late to do anything else, but their souls cried out for a different solution.

Still, they had both lived alone before. They knew how it was done. Gradually, as the magic of the night seeped away with the appearance of the house and lights and voices, the moment disappeared, and they were two separate persons once again. What had brought them together in the pavilion was still too new to withstand the parting to come.

Peter went to fetch his valise and say his farewells. Janice remained hidden on the porch, not yet willing to give up the magic of the night air. When he joined her again, he was mercifully alone.

He kissed her temple lightly, not daring to do more. "I'll wire you by the end of August, Jenny, I promise. I couldn't bear anymore."

He meant it now, but would he mean it then? Janice straightened his tie, smoothed his sleeve, and sent him on his way. It wasn't as if they'd exchanged words of love. He was a man, and she was his wife. He would send for her when the time came simply because she belonged to him. She would be a fool to think he would send for her for any other reason, no matter what had gone on between them tonight. Tonight had been a fluke, a moment of desperation. She would remember it always, but she had to be practical.

She would look for a job first thing in the morning.

First thing in the morning, Evie woke her with the news that Betsy was running a fever and couldn't breathe.

Life never went the way one wanted it to.

# Twenty-Six

Betsy was well enough to travel a few weeks later when the Hardings were ready to return to Mineral Springs. In the hours sitting over Betsy's bed, wiping her sweat-soaked brow, listening to her cough, Janice had had plenty of time to think. It only took Carmen's invitation to set her thoughts into action.

"Why don't you come back with us for a spell? Jason's complaining the office work is out of hand. He sure could use your help. And you would be that much closer when it comes time for you to go to Peter." Carmen folded one of her daughter's lace-edged dresses into the trunk she was packing.

Janice put the finishing touches on the hem she was letting out on one of Betsy's dresses. Despite her weakness, Betsy was still growing. She would need a whole new wardrobe before long. And she didn't have a dime to spare to buy one.

"I've been thinking about that myself," Janice admitted. "I suppose Tyler can send a telegram when Peter's message comes through. I don't like to impose on the Monteignes' hospitality any longer than necessary."

Carmen hooted. "Impose? I don't know how they're going to do without you, if the truth is told. They'd keep you in a minute. Evie isn't one for cooking and mending and cleaning. Even when you're sitting up with Betsy, you somehow manage to get people to do the work that needs to be done, and you've mended all that drapery at the same time. They're going to raise a cry of protest when I take you home with me."

Carmen's words proved accurate, but Betsy's smile of delight at returning to her hometown was all the encouragement Janice needed. The Ridge had made a delightful temporary haven from reality, but it wasn't home. Janice exchanged hugs with Evie and Jasmine, accepted Tyler's fulsome praise with a grain of salt, and shook Ben's hand in farewell. These people would always be dear to her, but they would never be family.

Janice wished briefly that she could return to Ohio to see her brother and sister and Daniel and Georgie, but she didn't have money for that. Tyler offered the free use of his private railroad car to take the Hardings back to Texas. She would have to take what was offered. Besides, she could be useful in Texas and perhaps make a little money. There would be nothing for her in Ohio but the idleness she was escaping here.

"Daniel is going to be disappointed that he missed you," Evie commented as they waited for the train to pull into the station. "Peter should have taken you up to see him before he left."

Janice smiled absently while keeping a careful eye on Betsy and Melissa playing among the trunks. "There wasn't time. Peter only had a few weeks left to buy that land. Maybe we'll come back next spring. I imagine there are all sorts of supplies he'll need to have by then."

A tall man in a battered cowboy hat caught her eye briefly where he leaned against the station wall watching the crowd. Janice thought he seemed familiar, but she was distracted by Carmen's approach, and when she looked again, he was gone. She frowned slightly, then turned her attention back to the matter at hand.

"Are you sure you shouldn't have bought some of the furniture and things Peter said you would need? Tyler's credit is good. We can always forward a few things to you if you change your mind."

Janice took the lunch basket from Carmen and smiled politely at Evie. "I haven't learned to deal with credit yet. I was raised to pay for what I wanted. I'm sure we'll have enough to get by for a while."

The train whistle wailed as the boilers heated, and steam filled the station. Tyler sauntered into view, directing a steady stream of porters to the luggage. When he had events in motion to his satisfaction, he wandered toward the women.

"The car is at your command, ladies. Manuel's already on board to see that everything gets loaded safely." He kissed Carmen' cheek, then turned to Janice. "I don't believe in farewells. We'll see y'all back here come spring, I imagine. Daniel arranged for a little wedding present to go with you, so don't make a fuss when you find it. Peter's likely to be living in a sod hut for all we know. We want you to start out with something nice."

Janice managed a smile as she shook Tyler's hand and accepted his token kiss on her cheek. She felt tears burning at her eyes. She hadn't imagined this parting would be so painful, but she almost felt as if the Monteignes had become part of her family.

"I'm going to miss you," she murmured as she hugged Evie again, then bent to hug and kiss whichever of the Monteigne children came running to say farewell. This had been a special slice out of time, like visiting a fairy-tale palace. She would never know its like again, but she was grateful she'd had this opportunity to see a different world than she had ever known. It made it easier to go to the one Peter meant for her to share.

Betsy and the Harding children ran blithely to climb into the railroad car. They had come to expect these uprootings as a natural part of their lives. Janice wasn't so blasé. She had never yet returned to a place she had left behind. Every move was like leaving a part of her self.

But this time was different. She was actually returning to a place she had never expected to see again. Maybe it was the start of something new. With renewed confidence, Janice joined Carmen and the others at the window, waving to the people standing on the platform watching them go.

By the time the train pulled out of the station, Janice had forgotten Tyler's words about the wedding present.

With a car full of energetic children, she had little time to think of anything at all. This ride was amazingly different from the one she had taken with Peter. Instead of hours staring out the window, worrying about the night to come, she was busy entertaining children, seeing to their meals, conversing with Carmen and Manuel and the others, and more than ready for her own private bed when she reached it. She didn't remember the wedding present until she went to open her carpetbag just prior to entering the Fort Worth station.

Inside she found one of Daniel's latest dime novels, a copy of the Cutlerville *Gazette* with the announcement of her marriage to Peter, a letter from Georgina, and an envelope with a $100 bill. Janice stared at this wealth with incredulity. It was nearly as much as she had earned all last year. She resisted her urge to send it back, and reached for the letter before deciding if she ought to be insulted or pleased.

Daniel's wife, Georgina, was everything that Janice was not: effervescent, spontaneous, incapable of worrying. Her new sister-in-law had been born with a silver spoon in her mouth and had never had to work at anything in her life. The fact that she did work at helping others was a credit to the generous person that she was. Janice read her letter with mixed degrees of emotion.

She read that the baby was due the end of August, that the Fourth of July picnic was a huge success sponsored by Mulloney's Department Store. Georgina described the wedding dress she was helping Janice's sister make and declared that Janice's brother, Douglas, would soon be editor of the *Gazette*, if Daniel could be persuaded that he couldn't do everything himself. And somewhere near the end, Georgina confessed that she and Daniel were terribly worried about Peter, worried that they had somehow wronged him, that he would never return to Cutlerville or his family. She pleaded with Janice to take care of him.

After Georgina's scrawl came a postscript in Daniel's hand: "I couldn't think of a better wife for Peter than you. Our mother sends her gratitude and wishes that you can soon visit, that you *will* visit. If there is any way at all that you can persuade him back here, please do so. She misses him. Peter is too proud to accept money, and it is possible that he doesn't need any. He doesn't tell us. But Georgie assures me that a woman can always use a few secret dollars with which to surprise her husband. So we send this gift with the knowledge that you will use it to make Peter's life a better one in whatever way you deem necessary, if it's only to buy him a new hat for his birthday. Write when you can and let us know how you fare, and give Betsy a hug from all of us."

Tears streamed down Janice's face before she finished. She read the letter a second time, then carefully folded it and slipped it between the pages of Daniel's book. It was like carrying a piece of home with her. Georgina and Daniel were gifted in that way. Even on paper, their words sounded like themselves. Whenever she got lonely, she could pull the letter out and read it again.

It made the decision about the money much easier. Peter might be too proud to accept money for himself, but she wasn't. She knew in the months ahead there would be dozens of uses for a few extra dollars.

She pinned the crisp bill inside her corset and went to join the others as the train pulled into the station. She had more confidence in this homecoming now that she had the means to leave again.

Not until she stepped off the train and onto the platform did Janice realize the traveling hadn't brought on her monthly courses as usual.

She stared in dismay at the unloaded luggage, oblivious to the sounds and sights around her. It had only been a few weeks. There wasn't time to know for certain. She couldn't be. Not yet.

Her gloved hand went instinctively to the draping of cotton twill over her abdomen, but her mind refused to accept the possibility. She looked around to find Betsy. There were things to do, places to be. She didn't have time for imagination.

\* \* \*

Mineral Springs hadn't changed any since they left. Jason greeted their return with gruffness, grabbed Janice's arm, and dragged her off to his office to show her some correspondence he didn't want to cope with.

She couldn't believe she had once imagined she might marry this man. He was a good man who lived for his ranch, but he scarcely knew she existed except as a tool like his typewriter. Peter might be wrapped up in his work, but he knew she existed all right. He didn't look at her as if she were a typewriter. Janice was beginning to desperately miss those heated looks he bestowed on her when they were surrounded by people and he could do nothing else. She wouldn't consider how much she missed what he did when they were alone.

In their absence, Ellen Fairweather had had her baby. Her husband had hung around long enough to put a roof on the house he had started building for her, but a week of the baby's squalling had apparently put an end to his connubial responsibility. Jason spat in the dust as he told of Bobby's disappearing in the middle of the night, leaving no one to mend the fences on the south range.

Janice had to smile at this typical Jason manner of speaking. He related his disgust to the ranch and not to the wife and child abandoned to their fate. But she knew without being told that Jason had made some arrangement for Ellen and her baby. He just didn't talk about those things.

As soon as she had settled into the room the Hardings made up for her and Betsy, Janice went to work. She disliked being a burden or accepting charity, but she knew the ranch and the work that needed doing. She could be useful here.

As soon as she had some of the chaos in the office brought under control, she asked to accompany Carmen into town. She needed to handle some ranch matters there, but most of all, she wanted to see Ellen, to see how she was managing. Janice wouldn't admit to herself that she wanted to see the baby.

Ellen greeted her arrival with delight. The house Bobby

had built was little more than a shack, but it smelled of
new wood and fresh laundry. A wooden crate made the
baby's bed, and Ellen's bed was little more than a mattress on ropes hanging in the corner of the house's one
room, but Ellen had covered every bare surface with colorful scraps of gingham patchwork, and the result was
cheerful in the August sun. Janice hugged her former student, catching even herself by surprise. She wasn't normally one to give hugs.

"Oh, Miss Harris . . . I mean, Mrs. Mulloney!" Ellen
giggled and led her toward the infant's bed. "It's so good
to see you again. I thought you were gone forever. That
new schoolteacher they've hired has come to town, and
he's an old wart! I don't want him teaching Mary Jane."

Janice knelt beside the makeshift cradle. The infant
slept soundly on her stomach, one fist bunched up at her
mouth where she could suck it occasionally. Her hair was
a ring of sparse dark curls that Janice couldn't resist
stroking. The baby stirred, exposing tiny bare feet beneath her thin gown, and Janice felt an odd tug of envy.
She had never found herself wanting a child before. She
hadn't wanted Betsy. She had hated the responsibility and
the constant demands and the draining away of her own
life. But she wanted to pick this child up and hug her to
her breast and pretend she was her own.

"She's beautiful, Ellen," Janice murmured, scarcely
able to tear her gaze away. "Does she eat well?"

"Like a little pig," Ellen declared proudly.

Janice felt her own breasts ache at the thought. That
had been the only pleasure she had known when Betsy
was a baby. She had loved holding the infant to her breast
and feeling her suck. It had been a quiet time of fleeting
contentment. It could be even better this time, with a husband to share her joy and to take away the worry.

She was having crazy notions. Peter would only now
be arriving in Butte, if his luck was good and the tracks
and trail were clear. It would be months, maybe years before he could see a profit, providing the gold was really

there. They couldn't afford a child. There wouldn't be any joy, just worry. She couldn't live through that again.

Her monthly courses were just late. The upheaval of moving probably had that effect. She wasn't real regular. There wasn't a baby. She touched the infant in the cradle again and stood up.

"Is Mr. Holt going to let you go back to work for him?" Janice asked casually, as if she hadn't a worry in the world.

"I think Mr. Harding told him he'd better. He said I could take Mary Jane with me and keep her behind the counter. I know I can do it. I'll work twice as hard and prove it." Ellen's eyes gleamed defiantly.

"I know you will. He ought to be glad to have such a good worker. Maybe now that you've been away for a while, he'll have learned to appreciate how much you do for him. Have you heard anything from Bobby?" Janice took the stool Ellen offered and didn't object when she was given a cup of coffee without a saucer. She might use some of the wages Jason had offered her to buy a few dishes as a baby gift.

The militant light left Ellen's eyes. She took her seat on the bed beside the cradle. "I don't reckon I will. Bobby just wasn't cut out for married life, I guess. I should have thought about that when he was courting me."

That wasn't something most young women in love thought about, Janice knew from sad experience. She sighed and sipped the weak coffee. Every woman ought to be told to think what kind of father a man would make before they went to bed with him. Maybe that would cool their ardor some.

She tried to imagine what kind of father Peter would make, but she couldn't say. He'd got along well with the children at The Ridge. He seemed to be a responsible person. But she couldn't fathom how he would respond to the knowledge that he was about to become a father. He just might take it as his due and her problem and go on.

"Well, marriage takes some men that way," Janice responded. "It's better to know right off, before you start depending on them. You'll make a fine mother. And everyone hereabouts will look after you. I don't think you need to worry." Fine thing to tell a mother. Mothers always worried. But Ellen was smiling again and Janice didn't feel guilty for the lie.

"Were there any more fires after we left? Did they ever catch who did it?" She changed the subject before she was led any deeper into sin.

Ellen immediately looked worried again. She fretted at her apron strings and didn't look Janice directly in the eye. Finally, she admitted, "There wasn't a one after you left. They never did catch anyone. A stranger poked around town a few weeks after you left, asking questions, but there wasn't any fire."

Janice frowned, trying to determine what Ellen wasn't saying. It was obvious that people still thought Peter guilty, but there was more to it than that. "Questions? What kind of questions did the stranger ask?"

Ellen shrugged, then forced her gaze back to Janice. "You might as well know. He was asking after you and Mr. Mulloney. He talked to Bobby a whole bunch. He said he came from back East, that he knew you when you was a girl." She looked a little more nervous. "He said he knew about Mr. Mulloney too, said he wasn't to be trusted. He was kinda upset that you and him married. He was going to set out after you. I guess he didn't find you."

Janice felt fear grip her stomach and turn it inside out. "Did he say what his name was?"

"Stephen. Stephen Connor."

The blackness hit before Janice knew it was coming.

# Twenty-Seven

"**I**'m all right. I'm quite all right." Janice was still protesting that evening. Ever since she had fainted and Ellen had screamed for help, there had been someone hovering over her, fussing around her. They didn't leave her time to think.

"I hear tell the ladies back East faint real regular, but you don't strike me as the type." Carmen's husband, Kyle, stood back upon command, but he was posed as if expecting her to fall off the couch at any moment.

"It was just the heat, and probably Ellen's terrible coffee," Janice insisted. "Now go away and let me get some work done."

Carmen tugged her husband's arm and pointed to the door. "We will call if we need you. Your fussing always made me dizzier."

Husband and wife exchanged significant glances, then nodding at Janice, Kyle left the room.

Carmen watched her husband go with a loving smile, then turned back to Janice. "Well, this changes everything. You cannot keep working so hard. And if that husband of yours does not come after you soon, you will have to stay here for the winter. There will be no traveling for you before long."

"I am not pregnant," Janice insisted, rising from the couch. "It was hot and Ellen gave me some shocking news. The sheriff still thinks Peter is guilty. I don't like the sound of that at all." She couldn't name the real source of her shock. There would be too many explanations demanded and too many lies she would have to repeat if she named the stranger in town as the source of her consternation. She hedged her story a little.

Carmen gave her a knowing look. "It is too soon, I know. But time will tell. In the meantime, you will rest. I will take a whip to that Jason if he drives you too hard. Now go and lie down until supper. Betsy is just fine where she is."

The children were in the orchard looking for the last of the summer peaches. Janice nodded agreement and went off to her room, but not to rest. She couldn't rest. Why had Stephen Connor stepped back into her life at this late date?

She hadn't heard a single word from him in all these years. She had thought him dead. There had been occasional rumors during those months of her pregnancy, but once she had left her hometown for Cutlerville, none knew of the association, and the rumors had stopped. In that first year she had corresponded erratically with a few friends from her former home, but they had never mentioned him. Work and marriage and children had gradually eroded even that fragile connection with the past. She hadn't heard from anyone in her prior hometown since Betsy was a toddler. No one in Cutlerville knew Stephen or Janice's history.

So she had thought him gone from her life. Had she been wrong? Had he actually been searching for her all these years, only to find her when she finally married? Fate couldn't be that cruel.

The Stephen she had known had been only twenty years old, whip thin, with eyes that alternately laughed and brooded. Even at twenty he had been tough and hard and ambitious. He had tried to form a union when the railroad had laid off all its old employees, but the new employees were too interested in keeping their jobs to listen. He had gone off in search of greener pastures with scarcely more than a farewell kiss a few weeks after he had taken Janice to his bed. She had been devastated at the time, but even more so a few months later.

She didn't want to know a man who could do that to a

young girl. She despised his memory. With sudden conviction, Janice changed her course and went to Jason's office for pen and ink. She would write Evie and Tyler and tell them not to reveal her whereabouts.

That was easier said than done. She would have to explain about Stephen before she could warn them about him. She could try to tie him in with the fires and make it seem as if he was after Peter. That would worry the Monteignes, which would worry Daniel and Georgina.

Janice sat at her desk and stared at the blank paper. It might already be too late. Stephen had plenty of time to travel to Natchez and talk to Tyler. She just couldn't believe he would do it. She couldn't believe he was actually looking for her. Ellen knowing his name convinced her that Stephen had actually been here, but she would be willing to wager a month's wages that Stephen had just accidentally stumbled across the town and heard someone mention her name. The rest was all talk, and probably half Bobby's. He wasn't looking for her.

Just as a precaution, she wrote a long chatty letter to Evie and mentioned the fact that someone had been in town asking after Peter. She added that she didn't like the kind of people he asked, and women's intuition told her that it would be better if he didn't know their whereabouts. Peter preferred to be secretive about his gold.

Janice read this last over with satisfaction. That would make them think twice about talking to strangers without worrying them excessively. Tyler and Evie were past experts at telling tall tales. If by any strange chance Stephen should show up in Natchez, they would lead him all around the bush and send him packing to the North Pole.

After the letter went out the next day, she wondered if she had done the right thing. Keeping Betsy from her real father could be the wrong thing to do. Did Stephen even know he had a child? Surely he must if he'd gone back to look for her. Everyone she knew in their hometown had known about Betsy and had guessed the father. He might be looking for her to make amends to his child.

It was too late now. Betsy thought her father had died.

For all intents and purposes, he had. Janice's father had been more father to her than Stephen ever had. And now they had Peter. Peter could be the father Betsy had never known. There was a bond between them already, Janice could tell. Betsy asked after him constantly, and Peter had displayed more than the normal amount of patience with Betsy's imagination and curiosity. He didn't even seem to mind that Betsy was sickly and couldn't help much around the house. Not many men in this world had patience with invalids.

So it was better if Stephen got lost and never found them.

Janice fretted at the slowness of the days as August dragged on. The heat was too intolerable to go outside. Betsy set up her easel in the doorway to Jason's office and spent hours between the shade of the porch and the house, catching what little breeze came along while painting things only she could see. Janice liked having her near. It kept some of the fears at bay.

Nighttimes were the worst. She lay in her empty bed trying not to remember how it had felt to have Peter lying next to her. But there were nights when she couldn't make herself stop thinking how it felt to have him inside her. With Betsy in the bed, she couldn't tear off her gown, and her skin seemed to swell and heat beneath the friction of the linen. She remembered the pounding of his heart, the flick of his finger against her nipples, the piercing sweetness of his possession, and her body ached in hollow yearning for his.

When she forced these images away, others replaced them. She dreamed of a child growing within her, Peter's child. She imagined a little boy with curls as dark as Peter's. She tried to imagine how Peter would greet this stranger in their life, but she could only hear an infant's wails of hunger and pain and see herself alone again. That terror stalked her even through the daylight hours.

She heard nothing from Peter. She had not expected to. There were no telegraph offices through much of the territory where he was going. Pen and ink and paper would

be hard to come by. The nearest town probably had a mail
service of sorts, but he'd said that was fifty miles away.
No, he wouldn't try to reach her until he had his mountain and his gold. He'd said he would send for her by the
end of August.

By the end of August she still hadn't heard from him,
and she still hadn't had her monthly courses.

She was pregnant, without a home, and her husband
was missing.

At least she had a husband, Janice consoled herself. That was an improvement over last time. She had
the money still pinned to the inside of her corset, so she
wasn't completely penniless.

But those practical consolations weren't what she
needed. She needed Peter.

As August became September, Janice realized that
more strongly. She needed Peter to reassure her that everything would be all right. She needed him to come
home at night and hold her. She needed him to laugh at
her fears, to admire Betsy's artwork, to compliment her
on her cooking. Most of all, she needed him to look proud
about the child she carried, to feel its first kicks, to know
that he would be there to hear its first cries. She didn't intend to go through another pregnancy alone.

She needed this man she had married, and she needed
him now.

She wasn't a proud woman. She had learned to bend to
necessity. She would crawl on her knees right now if it
would bring him home. But it wouldn't.

Desperate anxiety entered into the complex formula of
her erratic emotions the day Tyler's letter arrived. It had
been mailed just after the beginning of September, and
he'd had no word from Peter either. But he had heard
from the stranger Janice had warned him about. He'd sent
the man back to Cutlerville and warned Daniel to divert
him to the ends of the earth, but Tyler wasn't at all certain
the man had believed him. He urged Janice to show his
letter to the Hardings to see what they thought best.

Janice wavered one whole day trying to decide. Only

she knew Peter wasn't in danger from the stranger, but maybe that was for the best. Her greatest fear right now wasn't for Stephen, it was for her husband. Something was wrong. She felt it in her bones. Maybe it was her natural pessimism, but she knew Peter wouldn't leave her waiting without word unless something was wrong.

She threw the letter on the dinner table the next day.

Jason picked it up and read it through, then handed it to Kyle. He gave Janice an expectant look, as if knowing she already had the solution. Kyle gave a soft curse as he finished the letter, then looked from his brother to their guest.

"Well, what do we do? I can't believe some greenhorn could have made his way out to New Mexico already, but there's a chance. How could he have heard about the gold?"

Jason shoved a fork full of potato in his mouth, waiting for Janice to reply. He understood her a little too well. Janice kept her eyes on her plate.

"I think I'd better go out there. I can warn Peter there's someone sniffing after him so he won't be caught by surprise."

Jason snorted, glared at her while he finished chewing, then gave the reply she more or less expected. "And if this character is a thief, you're going to hold him off single-handed while Betsy looks for Peter. Don't be a blamed fool, woman."

Janice set her napkin down and pushed back from the table. "I'm not a fool. Something is wrong, and I'm going to find out what. You can't stop me."

"We could hog-tie you," Kyle said idly, shoveling up his corn.

Carmen kicked him under the table and answered, "We will send Manuel. He is nothing but trouble these days. He can make himself useful for a change."

Jason rolled his eyes ceilingward. "You should have thought of that yesterday. He got into a speck of trouble with Doc Hankins last night. I had to send him down to

Mexico to look at some calves just to get him out of town."

Carmen shrieked. "Trouble? What trouble? Why did you not tell me? It's that daughter of the devil, is it not? Never could Doc make her mind, and now she has her devil eyes on Manuel."

Her tirade threatened to continue in an accent more Spanish with each word until Kyle clapped his hand over her mouth. He shrugged as if to excuse his behavior to Janice. "She protects Manuel like he's still a small boy. Small boys don't get caught doing what he was doing."

Knowing Manuel's roving eye, Janice didn't have to stretch her imagination far to gather Manuel and the rather amorous daughter of the pharmacist had been caught in compromising circumstances.

"It is understandable. I would do the same for my little brother. However, I do not need Manuel. I am quite capable of managing on my own. All I need do is take the train to Gage and take a stage from there. It is not as if Indians are going to attack the train or anything. Travel is very civilized these days." She said that lie boldly, knowing full well only recently Geronimo's band had been rampaging through the territory the train crossed.

"A woman cannot travel by herself," Jason proclaimed as if he were Moses with the Ten Commandments.

"This woman traveled all the way here from Cutlerville by herself," Janice informed him calmly. "I'll manage. Besides, it is better if I leave now, before the weather turns bad."

The protests were many and varied but none of them swayed Janice's determination. She had wavered long enough. Now her mind was made up, and no one could divert her. Betsy's health was the only mitigating factor, but Betsy seemed stronger than ever. When told of the impending journey, she was more than ready to go. Peter had told her about the mountains, and she wanted to see them for herself.

"You're making a mistake, Janice. That's wild country out there. Not all the Apaches are on reservations. If you can't wait for Peter to meet you, I'll have to go with you. I can't let you go alone." Jason stood up and started for his office.

"You can't leave this blamed ranch and you know it, Jason Harding." Janice aimed these words at his back. "You need to move those cattle to the southern pastures and someone's been cutting the fences out there. Someone has to decide how many cows you're going to ship out before winter, and there's that bull over in Houston you need to look at. Kyle can't do it all. You'll stay here, where you belong. I'll be fine on my own."

Jason turned around and glared at her. "You know too damned much about my business."

"And you know too little about mine. I'm going, and that's final."

Jason growled and glanced around as if trapped. Carmen came to his rescue.

"We will buy your railroad tickets. You can wire us when you reach Gage and let us know what stage you will be leaving on and when you expect to arrive. If we don't hear from you at the expected time, we are all coming after you. I think we must tell Daniel of your plans also. He will be worried about Peter."

"I can buy my own tickets, but I will agree to the rest. Do not say anything alarming to Daniel, though. He's likely to do something foolish like hiring a gunslinger to come after us." Janice rose from her chair as if the discussion was over.

Before she could escape, Kyle went red and fished around in his pocket for a piece of paper. "I forgot about this. It's from Daniel. Georgie had her baby. It's a boy—seven pounds seven ounces. They're calling him George Mathias."

The room erupted in questions and excitement and the topic was quite neatly changed.

Janice returned to her room and packed what few items she had unpacked a month before.

* * *

Peter swiped the sweat from his dirty brow and glared bitterly at the mountain of rock towering above him. "It's in there, Townsend. It has to be."

His partner lay his pick down and leaned his aching muscles stiffly against the nearest outcropping. "If it's there, we'll have to dynamite it out. That'll cost."

Peter took a firm hold on his pick handle and swung furiously, unleashing his frustration on the crumbling rock. After a few strikes, the dent he'd made in the mountain was negligible. Panting, he leaned against the handle and stared at the opening in the rock through the sweat streaming down his face. "It's got to be there, Townsend. I've got to find it or die trying."

Townsend sent him a concerned look but said nothing. Both men knew what he meant. They were broke, head over heels in debt, and this pile of stone was hiding its treasures. It wasn't the best time to take on the additional burden of a wife and child. Somewhere out there a lovely woman waited for Mulloney, her hopes and future solidly in Peter's hands—hands that were raw and bleeding from this hopeless task. Townsend shook his head and swung his pick again.

Beside him, Peter scarcely heard the renewed echo of steel against stone. With every strike of his pick he saw Janice's eyes wide and soft and waiting. He felt her trust as she gave herself to him. He had promised her a future with him if she would give up her home in Texas, and she had accepted because she trusted him. He had some understanding of how difficult that had been for her. Mulloneys had destroyed her life once already. He couldn't do it again. He had to go back to her a rich man.

Or not go back to her at all. Daniel would take care of his brother's widow.

But he wouldn't give up yet. He was on the verge of having it all: the wealth, the woman he craved, and the knowledge that he could do it all on his own.

Right now, he wanted the woman more than anything. With frustration, he sent the pick ringing into the stone again.

# *Twenty-Eight*

Mesmerized, Betsy gazed out the train window as it approached her new home. So far, Janice wasn't the least bit impressed by the scenery, but Betsy seemed to find just the brilliance of the air fascinating. Despite the dust and heat, she was holding up to the travel very well, and Janice gave thanks for that.

What she didn't give thanks for was the attention they attracted. It would seem men out here hadn't seen women in a lifetime. At first, she had accepted their little attentions with gratitude. They knew where to find a glass of water or which stations would have food and they helped her on and off with her baggage whenever the train made an unscheduled stop. The haste with which the railroad had been built guaranteed there were a number of these, even when natural disasters or man-made ones were the immediate cause.

But as they rolled across the Texas border into New Mexico, the passengers all seemed to be men, and Janice felt exceedingly conspicuous. They vied for the privilege of bringing her water. They argued over the seat behind her. They even fought for Betsy's attention.

She was tired and worried and hot and dusty. She wanted to hit them all over the head and knock some sense into them. And she wasn't pregnant.

In the first days of travel, when she'd had to rummage in her bag for a rag she hadn't expected to need, Janice hadn't known whether to laugh or cry at this unexpected news. She had been nervous about the baby at first, but as the weeks went on, she'd been comforted by the thought of having a small piece of Peter inside her. She had painted mental pictures, dallied with boys' and girls' names, contemplated sewing infant gowns, dreamed of sharing this new life with her husband as she hadn't been allowed before.

Now there was nothing. If anything had happened to Peter, she would have nothing of him. She tried not to think these thoughts, but the closer they came to the rough territory of his new home, the more she understood how dangerous this land was. A man could die out here and there would be no one around to know or care. She didn't want to think of that happening to Peter.

Janice transferred her worries about the baby she wouldn't have to the husband she barely knew. Or perhaps she knew him much better than she thought. She understood his driving need to make his own way in the world, to be self-supporting and dependent on no one. And more than anything else, she understood the loneliness that created inside him. They had both left friends and family behind to satisfy their ambition. There wasn't time to cultivate friends while working day and night.

But they had each other now. She hoped that was enough for Peter. It was more than she had ever dreamed of having. Despite all the obstacles of their backgrounds, she really wanted to make this marriage work.

The porter walked down the aisle screaming "Gage!" over the noise of the brakes squealing and the whistle wailing. As Janice reached for her carpetbag, three men tried to help her with it at once, and a scuffle ensued. Janice gave a long-suffering sigh while Betsy chewed on her ribbon and watched the proceedings with curiosity.

Janice adjusted the stylish hat that dipped over her forehead and swirled up in back. She and Carmen had created it out of some old castoffs, and she felt quite regal in it. When the porter approached again, she held up a coin, and he immediately threw himself into the scuffle, emerging triumphantly a minute later with her bag.

She was learning how the rich did things. Being around Tyler and Evie must have been a bad influence. But she felt quite proud of herself when she descended to the station platform with a porter and her baggage in tow. Her disgruntled rivals descended hurriedly after them, but Janice tried to ignore them as she gazed at her first sight of New Mexico from something besides a train window.

Nearly the entire town could be seen from the railway station. The boards on some of the storefronts were still so new the sap ran on them. The storefronts concealed the crude adobe walls of the actual structures. The town had no boardwalks or macadamized streets. Within her immediate view she could see three saloons and no churches. If this was the big town that the train ran though, she hated to see what Butte would look like.

Holding firmly to Betsy's hand, Janice approached the station master to ask directions to the stagecoach office. She now had four men hanging on her skirts, willing to direct her. It was a rather overwhelming experience for an old-maid schoolteacher.

With more help than she could manage, she found herself sitting in the stage office, sipping lemonade with Betsy while listening to her retinue top each other with tall tales. Someone had gone to find them a box lunch while someone else saw to it that all her luggage was carted from the station. Janice wondered idly if she ought to go shopping in the local store while she was here, loading up on the supplies she might not be able to find farther into the interior, but she feared no one on the other end of the line would help her with the packages.

She asked questions about Butte, but her companions seemed to know nothing about it. In fact, her admirers pretty well ignored everything she said while showing off their own eloquence. Even Betsy began to grin at their antics when Janice asked if Butte might have a general store and one of the men responded with his version of the robbery of the Santa Fe train. Janice thought possibly the connection between the question and the answer was the supplies that didn't reach town, but she couldn't be certain.

She watched the arrival of the stage with a great degree of relief. A brief surge of hope traveled through her at the sight of a top-hatted man climbing out and reaching for his suitcase in the baggage carrier, but that died instantly when the man turned around to reveal a full beard and a stout stomach. She really couldn't expect Peter to arrive to meet her. She hadn't even been able to send him a wire to tell him she was coming.

They watched their luggage being loaded, then entered the narrow confines of the stagecoach as soon as the driver assured them he was ready to go. Janice let Betsy wave at their admirers as the horses lurched forward. Her nerves were in too much of a panic to do anything but clutch her bag and pray.

Their only fellow traveler was an older woman with a stomach as large as the lunch basket she carried. The woman opened the basket as soon as the stage reached the edge of town.

"We'll be lucky to get there without being raped and scalped," the woman said into the silence. She didn't seem disturbed by her words as she bit into a chicken leg.

Betsy's eyes went wide, and Janice gave a mental curse. "I didn't think Indians were a problem anymore," she answered calmly, hoping a practical point of view would reassure Betsy.

"Geronimo's on the warpath again. It's a wonder the train got through. Mark my words, he'll kill us all in our beds."

There wasn't any point in telling the woman that she was frightening a child. The woman wouldn't care and Betsy would only worry more. Janice set her lips in disapproval. "I thought Geronimo had returned to the reservation."

The woman shrugged her massive shoulders. "Can't keep an Apache in one place unless they're dead. They'll have to kill them all."

Malevolently, Janice wished the woman would choke on the chicken skin she was shoving into her mouth. "I understand the reservation conditions are not suitable for farming. I don't think I would like to be told where I must live."

Beady eyes glared at her. "When they rape you till you bleed like they did my daughter, you'll be sorry the army didn't shoot them all."

"I don't think this is a suitable topic for a child," Janice announced firmly. If the woman didn't shut up, she would have to personally strangle her. Betsy was so pale her freckles looked like brown splotches across her nose.

The woman grunted and went back to her feeding.

That wasn't a glorious start to their new life. The day didn't improve when it became clear that they wouldn't make Butte by nightfall. No one had informed her that she would be spending the night in an adobe hut in the back of nowhere.

Staring in dismay at the flea-infested sheets they were supposed to sleep on, Janice gave a moment's consideration to turning back. No wonder Peter rode a horse rather than use the "conveniences" of modern transportation. She might have to force herself to do the same.

It was too late to change anything now. The driver had promised they would be in Butte by noon the next day. They had only fifty miles to travel after that.

Fifty miles. Janice groaned as she lay down on the floor wrapped in her mantle rather than sleep on the bed. When her husband decided to desert civilization, he didn't do it halfway.

He didn't do anything halfway. Remembering the times when he had taken her to his bed, Janice quivered. There had been nothing lukewarm about Peter's desires. He might not love her, but he definitely wanted what she had to offer. The knowledge made her feel more feminine than she had in all her years. She was a woman now and not an automaton. The layers of tough defenses she had built were melting away, like calluses disappearing with soothing balm and disuse. To her surprise, she was discovering she liked being a woman.

And so she must find him. It was as simple as that. Her need might not be as physical as Peter's, but it was just as strong. She needed to be a woman again. She needed a family. She would do whatever it took to have one. And

she would enjoy every minute of the pleasure it required
to produce one.

Surprisingly Janice felt bright and refreshed when
morning came. Birds quarreled outside the station, and
the air felt fresher and cooler than it had for some while.
Betsy chattered incessantly as they picked at the remains
of yesterday's lunch basket and gathered their belongings.
Today they would arrive in their new home.

The morose woman was running low on food, and she
recited a catalog of complaints as the stage jolted along
the rocky trail. Janice tried to ignore her while she and
Betsy pointed out the sights from their respective windows. Neither of them had ever seen mountains before,
but they could see a range of them coming ever closer.
Betsy excitedly pointed out a white peak and asked if it
might be snow.

The woman didn't answer and Janice didn't know. This
was barely mid-September. Would there be snow in the
mountains then? What if Peter was up there and couldn't
get out? What if she couldn't get up to him?

She wouldn't let the panic take over. She would do
whatever she had to do when the time came. Panic had
driven her to extreme measures more than once. She
wouldn't let it direct her now.

They arrived in Butte without incident. Janice gave a
sigh of relief at seeing some form of civilization again
and no sign of wild Indians. Betsy jumped from the coach
eagerly, causing their fellow passenger to grumble about
unmannerly heathens. Janice deliberately pushed in front
of the woman to descend next. She didn't mean to miss
an instant of this new home.

Betsy swung in circles and stared up at the mountains
hovering over the tiny town at the foot of the range. Her
pale curls flew around her face, and Janice smiled at her
daughter's natural exuberance. It was good seeing Betsy
breathing freely and behaving like any normal child.

But she couldn't spend her time idling away the minutes. With dismay, her gaze roved the narrow strip of
weathered buildings perched on the hillside. She knew

something of mining towns, and this one had the looks of abandonment. Whatever the miners had hoped to find here hadn't materialized in any degree sufficient to support a town. Whoever remained must be lingering out of laziness or lack of ambition.

She found the ubiquitous saloon, a barber/doctor/ pharmacist, and a general store. She didn't know if any of these establishments were occupied. A few dwellings boasted curtains in the window. A structure on the outskirts of town looked like it might hold grain, so livestock might be raised in the area. But there obviously wasn't any way to ship cows out. Finding a job here didn't look promising. She would have to hope she found Peter before her dollars ran out.

Jason had insisted on buying the train ticket since Tyler's car had returned to Natchez, but Janice had paid for the stage and their food along the way. Back in Mineral Springs, she could live on the balance of her funds for six months. She wasn't at all certain the same held true out here.

There was no hotel. Janice made this discovery as soon as she looked for a livery to hire a wagon. There was no livery. How was she going to go the fifty miles up into the mountains to Peter? How would she know where to go?

It had seemed so easy when she set out. She would hire a wagon and a driver at the livery. In Mineral Springs everyone knew where everyone lived. She had just assumed the driver would know where to take her.

But the reality didn't seem so easy. She didn't even know if anyone lived here, and she doubted sincerely that anyone knew who their next-door neighbors were. It looked like that kind of town.

With some degree of trepidation she asked the man at the stage office if he knew where she could hire a wagon.

"A wagon? What you be needing that for? Ever'thin's in walkin' distance." He was lean and stoop-shouldered with a hank of greasy black hair in his eyes. When he lifted his eyes to her, Janice could see the lack of intelligence in them. She hoped this wasn't the telegraph operator. She needed to send word that she'd arrived safely.

"My husband lives in the mountains. I need some way of getting up to him," she tried explaining.

"Can't take a wagon up them trails. Most folks ride. Know where to get a horse, if you need one." He didn't look particularly interested in imparting the information.

She couldn't ride. Betsy couldn't ride. They would need a pack train to haul their luggage. She hadn't brought everything she owned, but she'd brought everything she could think of that she might need in the middle of nowhere. And she had planned on stocking up on some supplies before she set out. She needed a wagon.

What if he was right? What if a wagon couldn't go up those mountains? Janice sent a panicky look at the blue shadow looming over the town. She had never been on a mountain before. Did they go straight up? Were there even roads or just rocks?

Peter had said bring furniture. There had to be roads.

Stiffening her shoulders, she tried another tactic. "I need to send a telegram. Could you direct me to the telegraph office?"

"This here be the telegraph office. Where you want to send it?"

Oh, Lord, give me strength, Janice murmured to herself. With her luck, this greasy toad was the barber/physician/pharmacist too. She had brought a supply of Betsy's medicines, but what happened if they ran out? She curled her gloved fingers into her palms and tried to word the message to the Hardings.

Somewhere up the road a man's voice yelled a stream of epithets. A horse screamed in terror. The unexpected sound of wagon wheels suddenly rattling downhill made Janice jerk around to look.

An empty, unhitched wagon bed reeled wildly down the hill—directly toward the stagecoach office where they stood.

# Twenty-Nine

S he didn't even have time to think. Grabbing Betsy, Janice dived for the open doorway into the office. The greasy telegraph operator ran for the farthest corner away from the window where he had been standing. Betsy screamed as Janice threw her to the floor behind the wall and covered her with her body.

She waited for the explosion of the wagon smashing into the rickety building, the tumble of debris that would bury them. Instead, she heard the report of a rifle, a creak, and a gentle bump against the wooden porch supports.

Astounded more than shaken—there hadn't been time to really panic—Janice pried herself from the floor and Betsy and dared to peek out.

A tall, grizzled man in a disreputable high-crowned cowboy hat strolled down the middle of the dusty street, his rifle still smoking. He kicked at a wagon wheel wobbling in the roadbed and settled it down. The wagon itself rested half on the office porch, its back half buckling one of the posts. Janice stared in disbelief at the axle where the wheel should have been. The man had shot the wheel off.

She stared at the man now approaching the office. He seemed vaguely familiar, although she couldn't place him anywhere in her memory. He was easily twice her age with a graying stubble of beard and a ragged haircut that straggled around his ears. His face was as lean and rawboned as the rest of him, and he moved with a deceptive casualness. As he drew closer, Janice could see the blank curtain of his eyes, and she shivered slightly. She'd had

enough experience with living in frontier towns to know
this wasn't a man she wanted to cross.

"Are you all right, ma'am?" His voice was gravelly
and lacked any real concern.

"Yes, thank you, sir." To her dismay, her voice was little more than a gasp. Betsy appeared at her side, and
Janice pulled her into her arms and hugged her, needing
the reassurance that she was all in one piece. She tried to
regain a little more of her composure. "You saved our
lives, sir. I don't know how to thank you."

The stranger didn't even bother removing his hat. "I
warned the boy about that wheel, but he didn't listen. You
lookin' for someone?"

Since the telegraph operator was still cringing inside,
murmuring curses and nearly weeping, Janice took a bold
chance. "I'm looking for my husband, Peter Mulloney.
Do you know him?"

The stranger scowled, pulled his hat farther over his
forehead, and spit into the street, away from her. He shifted uneasily from one foot to the other. Finally, he turned
his head back in her direction, but the shadow of his hat
hid his eyes. "Know of him, I reckon," he reluctantly admitted.

Janice's insides went empty. She'd been around these
shy men who were easier with guns and horses than
women. She knew when one of them didn't want to tell
her something. And she could think of only one good reason why he didn't want to tell her about Peter. He knew
something bad had happened.

She refused to panic. She was going to be calm and not
let her imagination run away with her. Clutching Betsy to
her side, she asked, "Could you tell me how I can get to
his cabin?"

He shrugged, looking around as if he might find someone else to supply the answer, then nodded slowly.
"Reckon."

She was recovering from her panic rapidly. She wanted
to bounce something off the man's skull and draw a complete answer out of him. Perhaps he was a simpleton. She

tried to keep patient. "Is there somewhere I can rent a wagon to take me out there?"

The man eyed the heap of boards with wheels that now supported the porch as much as the post. "If it can be fixed."

Janice gave the pile of lumber a resigned look. "This is the only wagon available?"

The man spit again. "Reckon."

Janice really thought she would have to scream to catch his full attention. Instead, while she gathered her wits for a more precise question, Betsy let go of her hand and hopped down the steps to stare up at the stranger.

"Are you a gunslinger like my Uncle Daniel writes about?"

The child's golden hair gleamed in the sun. Her pale face was one of transparent innocence. Blue eyes looked up at him through thick lashes in unblinking fascination. The man rested his rifle on the ground and stared back with equal fascination and a great deal less boldness. He seemed terrified.

"He writes all about Pecos Martin. Do you know Pecos Martin?"

Janice had never seen Betsy behave so boldly. She was almost as amazed as the stranger. She wasn't so amazed that she didn't hear his answer.

"Reckon."

If she didn't kill the man, she was going to roll on the ground with laughter. Stifling a giggle, Janice noticed the young man running down the hill toward his dismantled wagon.

"Thanks, old man. Help me get that wheel back on, will you?" The boy grabbed the lone wheel and rolled it up to the porch. At sight of Janice and Betsy, he went to pull at a hat that wasn't there, then made an awkward nod. "Afternoon, ma'am. Sorry for the inconvenience."

Sorry for the inconvenience. She thought she might be hysterical any moment now. They'd almost been killed, and it was an inconvenience. She was amazed that this dirty, half-grown boy even knew what the word meant.

This was the strangest place she'd ever been in. She felt the telegraph operator appear at her shoulder, and she wondered if he might transform into a pumpkin or a king.

"Could I persuade you to loan me the use of your conveyance to haul my luggage to my husband's place?" Janice asked in her best schoolteacher manner.

The boy stared at her as if she were the one to convert into a pumpkin. The cowboy elbowed him sharply and removed the wheel from his grip. The boy jerked back to attention.

"Yes, ma'am. It'd be an honor, ma'am. Let me and Martin put this wheel back on and hitch up Bossie. We'll take you out in no time." He hesitated slightly, a frown forming on his forehead. "Uh, just exactly where is your husband at, ma'am?"

The cowboy came to her rescue. "I'll go," he said gruffly, lifting the wagon bed up from the porch. As an afterthought, he added to Janice, "You might want to get out here in the street, ma'am."

Janice had just about decided that for herself. Hurriedly she ran down the stairs and pulled Betsy farther into the road. The telegraph operator did the same. As the men pushed the wagon off the porch, the broken post creaked, sagged, and gave way entirely. The wooden overhead crashed to the ground in a puff of dirt, directly where they had been standing.

Janice sighed and pointed out the obvious. "That was my luggage under there, gentlemen."

It looked like the day could only get longer. While the men scratched their heads and drew a relatively small crowd, Janice took Betsy's hand and led her toward what she hoped was the general store. Betsy chattered excitedly the whole way about the stranger and gunslingers and "Uncle" Daniel's heroes. Janice thought she really could use a hero about now, but she didn't think the stranger called Martin was him.

Inside the general store she found a weary man in a red-checked gingham shirt leaning against the counter, staring out the dirty window. When she entered, he laconically began to rub the wood.

"They'll be all day straightenin' that out," he advised her sorrowfully. "Best get you a sarsaparilla and set a spell."

That sounded an excellent idea even if the stranger's pessimistic outlook sounded familiar. Sure enough, as soon as she and Betsy settled on a crate with a bottle of sarsaparilla, a complaining voice called from the interior, "Henry, ain't you done that polishing yet?"—the voice of the fat woman from the stage.

Janice was familiar with Lewis Carroll's works and she wondered idly if she'd fallen through a rabbit hole or a looking glass. If Tweedle-dum and Tweedle-dee ran the general store, was the laconic stranger the Red King or the White Rabbit? She hid her giggles from Betsy and resolved to remain mature about this. Or at least she wouldn't give in to hysterics unless she saw a cat disappear without his grin.

"I got a customer, Gladys," Henry called back. "I'll be with you right shortly." Resting on his elbows and not appearing overly interested in selling her anything, he turned to Janice, "You just in on the stage?"

Perhaps she could use this opportunity to learn about Peter. Janice sedately adjusted her hat and smiled in her best imitation of what she thought a lady like Peter's wife ought to use. "Yes, sir. I've come to join my husband, Peter Mulloney. Do you know him?"

Henry idly swiped at his counter some more. "Mulloney," he snorted. "Fellow who bought a mountain. What's he goin' to do with a blamed empty mountain, now tell me? Ain't nothin' up there but buzzards and scrub."

Janice closed her eyes in brief prayer. He'd made it here in time. She hurriedly returned her attention to her informant. "I believe he means to ranch. He has a fondness for horses. Does he get to town much?"

Henry gave her a shrewd look. "Not that I know of. Ain't seen him since he came through here a month or more back. Horses, you say? Seems a mite strange to buy a mountain for horses."

Janice smiled brightly. "My husband is an eccentric man. Did he buy supplies when he came through? I might need to buy floor and sugar and such if he didn't."

That distracted him sufficiently. With a real live customer on his hands, Henry became all business, suggesting more impossible staples than Janice could ever want or need. While the men outside repaired the wagon and unburied her luggage, Janice set about showing the storekeeper that she wasn't entirely a greenhorn. A box of pepper that would last her into eternity and a barrel of pickles that had already grown soft were not high on her list of necessities.

But she was persuaded to buy a bolt of muslin and some dyes. She hadn't been able to bring her sewing machine, but she had the rest of her sewing kit with her. She had expected to be sewing baby clothes, but she could still make Betsy a few things. She also eyed some tanned deer hides and furs in one corner, but her supply of money was running low. She didn't want to be caught out here with no means of leaving. Perhaps if Peter found his gold, they could indulge in some warmer winter clothing.

The sun was already sliding behind the hills when the wagon was finally loaded and ready to go. Henry suggested she and Betsy might want to overnight in the empty barber/physician's office, and the man called Martin agreed. It would be better to start off at first light. Peter's ranch was way up in the hills.

Reluctantly Janice agreed. She spent the night tossing and turning on blankets on a hard wooden floor, worrying about what she might find on the morrow. If Peter had arrived safely and bought his mountain, why hadn't he come down and wired for her by now?

She had sent her message to the Hardings, but she hadn't received any answering one telling her about any message from Peter. And no one in town seemed to have seen him recently. That meant something was wrong. She wouldn't believe that it meant he'd decided he didn't want her out here. She refused to terrify herself with wild fears. Peter had never claimed to love her. He'd wanted a wife and had made a practical choice. She would rely on his practicality faster than she would something so ephemeral as love. He needed her. She knew it.

And she would show him what a good wife she could be by arriving when he needed her. She knew very well how to make herself useful. She had spent a lifetime refining her talents. She couldn't believe anyone would want her for herself, dull old maid that she was, but she knew for a fact that people wanted her for her efficiency and organization. She would make Peter glad to see her.

And maybe he would be a little glad to see her in his bed too. It wasn't one of her talents, but he hadn't complained earlier. She would learn that part of married life soon enough, once given the chance.

Reassuring herself with that notion, Janice finally drifted into sleep, only to be woken by the kicking of a boot on the wooden door at dawn.

Groaning, she dragged herself out of the bedroll, straightened her sadly rumpled attire, pulled on her long mantle to conceal some of the wrinkles, and helped Betsy to dress. Today they would go home.

That thought cheered them as the wagon rocked and tilted up the rocky mountain path in the cool hours of morning. Betsy pointed out jackrabbits and bright birds flashing wings of blue. The stranger pointed out buzzards circling dead prey. Janice admired the cool clean air and the refreshing glimpses of green and gold after years of grays and browns. The stranger muttered ominously of early snow.

The whole town seemed to be made of cynics. Janice refused to fall prey to the same skepticism. The air was invigorating. The thin aspen woods teamed with wildlife. She had lived in towns all her life, but she wasn't immune to the beauty of nature. Having lived inside herself all these years, she wasn't concerned about the lack of neighbors. All she wanted was a roof over her head and food in her stomach. Surely Peter could manage that.

"Have we met before, Mr. Martin?" she asked at one point.

The man jerked his hat brim down. "Don't reckon."

She couldn't place him in Mineral Springs, but she finally traced him to Natchez—the man at the race. But that man had worn a beard. She didn't dare stare directly at him, but she studied him carefully. Both men had worn their hats over their eyes, concealing their faces to a great extent. That didn't mean anything. It was something about the attitude, the way they carried themselves.

She frowned. "Do you have any cause to go to Natchez sometimes?"

"Maybe." He sent the whip cracking over the ox and pointed out a bright woodpecker to Betsy.

She might as well talk to the trees as try to get information out of this old goat. She ought to be grateful that he'd agreed to help her and leave the man alone. She encouraged Betsy to sing a song while she unpacked the lunch Henry's malcontented wife had prepared. She would keep in good cheer until she knew better.

The sun was setting by the time they rolled into the valley Martin said was their destination. Janice didn't think they had traveled fifty miles, and she glanced at him quizzically. "Are you sure?" We couldn't have gone much more than ten miles, could we?"

He shrugged. "About that."

She looked at the cabin, trying to picture Peter in such a remote and empty place. "My husband said he was fifty miles out of town."

"He ain't here," the man pointed out unnecessarily.

"Then where is he? We can't stay in someone else's home."

"He's up the mountain. This here is his." He stopped the wagon outside the narrow log porch.

Janice didn't know why she had assumed Peter would be living in a house instead of on a mountain. How foolish of her to think he would do anything so simple. She glared up at the pile of rocks and trees towering over this place where Peter presumably abided. If it would do any good, she would shake her fist at it—or him. She wasn't sure what or whom she was angriest at. She had come out here to find her husband only to be left admiring his empty house.

There was nothing for it. She had come all this way and she couldn't go back. With stoic resignation, she helped unload their numerous bundles and bags and supplies. At least the roof over their heads would be their own.

The minute Janice walked into the dim interior she had her doubts about this assumption also.

Cast carelessly over the room's one chair lay a woman's heavily embroidered and deeply ruffled petticoat.

# Thirty

B etsy darted past Janice and grabbed up the offending article, holding the petticoat up to her with delight. "Look! Uncle Peter left you a present! Do you think he left anything for me?"

Since Peter knew full well that his wife wore fashionable bustles and shifts and not outdated crinolines, Janice didn't think this surprise had any relation to a gift, but she had no desire to disappoint Betsy. As Martin stepped up behind her with the first load from the wagon, Janice smile and answered, "He's probably waiting for you to tell him what you want. He doesn't know much about girl's clothes, remember."

Betsy nodded happily and danced off to inspect the rest of the cabin. Behind her, Martin grunted and shoved his way past to drop a trunk on the floor. Janice stared at the offending article a little while longer, trying to create some reasonable explanation, but her mind had come to a halt. Silently she returned to the wagon to help with the unloading.

Martin shot some squirrels and skinned them. Janice set about preparing stew in the pot over the fireplace. She couldn't believe she was learning to cook over a fireplace. She had married a man for his wealth and was cooking in a backwoods cabin over a primitive fire. She must have done something terrible to deserve this, but she couldn't think of anything for which she hadn't been punished enough already.

The petticoat still made her temper boil. While Martin unloaded the wagon and the stew simmered, she inspected the bedroom. It contained one large feather bolster on leather-strung tree trunks. A colorful Indian blanket was the only cover. With a grim look, Janice hauled the mattress from the house, strung a rope between two trees, and hung it out to air. The idea of sleeping in the same bed another woman had shared with her husband ate at her insides, but she hadn't been able to bring her own bed, and she didn't intend to sleep on the floor another night.

Later, after they devoured the stew, and Martin announced he would sleep in the barn, Janice dragged the bedding back in and made it up with the sheets she had managed to bring with her. They were good quality sheets with a fine linen weave and hand-embroidered edges. She had worked hard for them. She meant to enjoy what little luxuries she had left.

Betsy slept beside her that night. Despite the pleasant comfort of the bed and the quietness of the mountain night, Janice didn't sleep easily. Somewhere on that mountain out there she had a husband who entertained women who wore crinolines. She wasn't certain whether to kill him or worry that someone or something had already done it for her.

Instead, she made up lists of chores and finally drifted off to sleep.

In the morning Janice found a broom and a mop and began cleaning the cabin from the inside out. Martin took one look at the flurry of activity, lifted his hat in farewell, and promised to come back with some chickens and a goat that needed a good home. Janice barely noticed his parting.

She had a husband up on that mountain and no means of reaching him. But surely he would have to come down once the snow started falling, and from the feel of it, that would be any day now. She would have his home ready when he arrived.

By the end of September she had the cabin spotless, a garden plot hoed ready for spring, a goat and chickens in the barn, but still no husband.

The stranger Martin occasionally arrived bearing fresh game that she cooked and shared with him, but he was as taciturn and uncooperative as ever when she asked him about Peter. She knew the perverse man could find Peter if he wanted, but for some reason, he wouldn't do it. The frustration left her less than gracious about his offerings for her larder.

Nailing the newly dyed curtain to the window one crisp day, remembering the night Peter made curtain rods for her, Janice was too lost in thought to notice the rider coming up the hill. The night of the curtains had been a turning point in her feelings for Peter. She hadn't believed an heir to the Mulloney fortune would actually sit in her humble living room and carve cheap curtain rods. He had suddenly become more human that night. She wondered if it might not have been better if he'd remained a cardboard cutout she could hate.

Betsy sat in the sun, attempting to imitate the brilliant color of the aspens on her canvas. Janice kept one eye on her as she nailed the final curtain panel. Not until then did she notice the rider. He had dismounted and was staring at Betsy.

She couldn't swallow. She stared out the window and tried to keep calm. No more panicking. It couldn't really be him. Anyone could have blond hair. He was smaller than she remembered. She closed her eyes, remembering. Even after all these years, she couldn't forget. He could have lost his hair and gained a hundred pounds, and she would remember. She couldn't fool herself. Stephen had found them.

Hiding her shaking hands in her apron, Janice climbed down from the chair and went to the door. She didn't want to see him. She didn't want to talk to him. She didn't know why in hell he had come all the way out here or how he had even known to come. She didn't want to know. She just wanted him gone.

But he was staring at Betsy, moving closer, and she had to stop him. She had to do anything to keep him from her child. Betsy was her child, not his. Other than that one miserable night's coupling, he had nothing whatsoever to do with that innocent child sitting in the meadow. And now that she knew what lovemaking could really be like, she knew he hadn't even made love to her that night. He'd just taken his pleasure on her body and left her.

She loathed him. But she let none of that show in her face as she deliberately walked into the yard, drawing his attention away from her daughter. Once Stephen saw her, he led his horse toward the house and away from Betsy. The child didn't even seem to notice.

"Good morning, Janice." His eyes were the deceptive gray-blue she remembered. They looked her over with the same appreciation as they had then.

She didn't think her dusty gingham work dress was anything to brag about, but then, he wasn't really looking at her dress. She used to blush when he looked at her like that. Now, she just wanted to smack his face.

"What are you doing here, Stephen?" she forced herself to ask calmly. There was no point in denying him. She knew who he was, even after ten years. He had grown from a handsome boy into a handsome man, but years of hard living appeared in the weathered lines around his eyes. He hadn't found a life of ease since he'd left her.

"I came looking for you," he said carefully. His gaze focused on her face. "You haven't changed much, Janice. You're lovelier than ever."

"Hog spittle. Name your business and go." Janice untied her apron and began folding it over her arm. Past his shoulder, she could see Betsy finally looking up from her absorption with the painting. She prayed the child would have the sense to stay put.

"Janice, I've come a long way to find you. Won't you even hear me out?" Stephen stepped closer.

Janice held her place. She refused to let him back her into the house. "You haven't got anything to say that I want to hear, Stephen. It's far too late for that. I can only figure you're here now to cause trouble. I've got a shotgun back in the house. Don't make me fetch it."

His lips tightened slightly. "Janice, you didn't used to

be this disagreeable." He glanced over his shoulder to the golden-haired child watching them. "She's mine, isn't she? They told me back home that you had her, but some said she was sickly and wouldn't live. She looks fine to me."

"She's not yours, Stephen, so get that notion right out of your head. You never gave me anything but misery. I'm expecting my husband home anytime now. I'd advise you to get out of here before he does." The words didn't sound very brave when she said them, but at least she didn't grovel and plead with him to leave. He was scaring the wits out of her. She couldn't think of any good reason for him to be here.

"You've grown hard, Janice. After I've come all this way, shouldn't you invite me in? We're old friends, after all. I'd like to hear how you're doing."

Once upon a time that silky voice and knowing smile would have turned her into jelly. They were even more effective now that he'd grown a mature man's confidence. He wasn't as tall as Peter, but he was wide-shouldered and well made. She could imagine him seducing girls in every town between here and Ohio. She was no longer one of them.

"We were never friends, Stephen. I was a stupid kid who idolized you and you were a selfish bastard who used me. You haven't got anything I want and vice versa. Now get out of here before I go for the gun."

His smile diminished slightly. "You don't really mean that, Janice. I've never loved another woman but you. I thought I was doing you a favor by staying away rather than dragging you down the holes I fell in. I came looking for you as soon as I got back on my feet."

In another time and place she might have been swayed, but Peter had shown her what a real man was. A real man stayed around even when trouble was neck deep. A real man sought solutions instead of excuses. A real man made commitments instead of promises. They might still have their differences. Peter might have a few explanations to make. But the reason she was here was because he had taught her he could be trusted, that he wouldn't run in the face of adversity. Stephen didn't even come close to measuring up to the yardstick Peter had set.

"Well, you've found me. Now you can turn around and go back. I've got work to do." She started toward the house.

Stephen grabbed her elbow and jerked her back around. Janice saw Betsy jump from her seat, and she shook herself free.

"Don't ever do that again, Stephen Connor," she warned him quietly. Betsy hovered uncertainly in the background. "Now go before you upset my sister. She's likely to tell Peter, and he isn't likely to look at this calmly."

Stephen threw a look over his shoulder to the golden-haired child standing beside the easel. His expression wasn't particularly pleasant when he turned back to Janice. "You can't deny me my child, Janice. She's no more your sister than I am your brother. You can lie to the rest of the world. You can lie to your husband. But you can't lie to me. She's the spitting image of my mother. She's mine."

"Don't delude yourself, Stephen." Janice shook so hard inside that she was surprised her words came out straight. She forced herself to concentrate on the words and not the terror. "There isn't a court in the world that will accept your word over mine. Now tell me what it is that you really want and get out of here."

He reached to touch her hair. This time, she didn't hesitate. She smacked his arm sideways.

"Keep your hands to yourself, Stephen. I will not be publicly mauled. Just name it straight out. What do you want from me?"

She stood straight and unbending, the mountain breeze whipping rebellious tendrils of fine hair about her face and plastering the thin cotton of her dress against her slender body. There wasn't much mistaking the look in Stephen's eyes as they fell to her breasts, but she didn't give an inch. Reluctantly he raised his gaze back to her face.

"I want you back. You're the one reason I kept going all these years. Whenever the going got tough, I'd see your face and know I couldn't quit. I've worked hard and I came to take you back. Look at how he's got you living. This isn't what you were meant for. The parsimonious bastard has a bank full of money and he makes you live like a tramp. You can't stay here. I'll take you and the kid back to civilization where you belong."

Janice wondered how long he'd practiced this speech. She hadn't realized until now that all the pretty words he'd ever said to her had been memorized verses from his book of seduction. Even after all these years she had hoped there really had been something between them, that he really had meant to come back for her. Disillusionment left a sour taste in her mouth, but it was better swallowed now when she had a promising future ahead of her. She wished Peter were here.

"I don't buy horse manure anymore, Stephen. I can shovel it out of the streets. I'm happily married and have no intention of leaving my husband. You're too late. If you'd been half a man, you'd have come back for me after you seduced me. But you abandoned me and I have no intention of ever forgiving you for that. Get that through your head now so you can get out of here."

Betsy was packing up her paints. Janice carefully edged in her direction, meaning to place herself between Stephen and her daughter.

"You're wrong, Janice. I came back for you, but your father told me you were gone. I tried again later, but you'd disappeared. I had nothing to offer you then. I just wanted to see you again. It got worse after that, and I thought you were better off without me. You're a beautiful woman. I knew you could have any man you wanted. I tried to do what was best for you."

"Save it for another fifteen-year-old virgin, Stephen," she answered wearily, keeping her eye on Betsy. "I've been through hell and back since then, and I don't believe anything I can't see with my own eyes. What I'm seeing with my eyes right now is a pile of horse manure." She had never talked like this to anyone in her life, but she didn't seem to get through to him in any other way. She wanted him gone, five minutes ago, preferably.

"Let me prove myself then. I'll stay around and help you out until your husband comes back, if he's coming back. I hear in town he's disappeared. You might need me. Don't send me away yet."

He struck a low blow, hitting all her fears, crumpling all her careful barriers. Pain rang through her, tears formed in her eyes, but still she wouldn't bend. Peter had to be alive. She couldn't believe anything different.

Janice shook her head decisively. "I'll give you to the count of ten before I go for the gun. One." She started walking toward Betsy. "Two." She was practically running by the count of five.

She caught Betsy's hand and started for the house and the gun. Stephen was already swinging back onto his horse.

He smiled down at Betsy. "Hello there, Betsy. You're just as pretty as your mother, you know that? Shall I bring you some rock candy when I come back?"

Janice wished she'd gone for the gun first.

Sending Betsy into the house with a gentle shove, she glared up at Stephen. "Ten."

Then she turned and strode after Betsy.

He rode off before she had to display the shotgun in front of her daughter.

# *Thirty-One*

"We've got enough to pay off the loan, Mulloney. Snow's coming. We're not going to find anything up here in winter. Let's get out while we can. There aren't enough supplies to last a blizzard."

Shouldering his pick, Townsend weighed the pouch of gold in his palm, his eyes shadowed as he watched his partner. Mulloney was sweating like a hog even though the temperature was so cold they could see their breaths. The man was sick. He could barely lift the tool in his hands. But he still swung futilely at the side of the mountain.

"I can't go back as broke as I came in," Mulloney muttered obstinately. He was swaying where he stood.

"Your wife would rather have you alive and broke than dead and rich," Townsend offered carefully. He knew little enough about Mulloney's family and background, but he'd guessed a lot. He wasn't certain he was prepared to like the new Mrs. Mulloney.

"Can't do that to her." Peter swung the pick again, almost falling to his knees as it struck. "Got to strike gold. I promised."

Townsend waited patiently until Peter worked off another burst of fury on the relentless rocks. When his partner finally fell to his knees and couldn't get back up, Townsend pried the pick from his hands and set it aside. "Come on. I'm taking you back to town before we both die out here."

Mulloney was practically a skeleton of himself when Townsend tried to lift him, but Peter still had more than enough strength to shove him backward and grab for the pick. Townsend dodged as Peter swung the pick with all his might and sent it flying into the mountainside.

"Damn a God who feeds thieves and starves innocents!" he screamed at the chilly mountain air as the pick sank into a pocket of dirt and remained there, high above their reach.

Townsend wouldn't have worded it exactly that way, but he reached stoically to help Peter up again when he fell. It was a long trip down the mountain, and those clouds looked like snow.

Janice lay awake staring at the moonlight trickling through the parted curtains. A cold wind had started some time after sundown, and gusts pushed their way into the house through all the cracks and crevices. For the first time she thought seriously of giving up. Peter should have been back by now. She couldn't risk Betsy through a mountain winter with no one to look after them. She couldn't risk Betsy to Stephen. She needed to go somewhere safe.

The sound of horses came to her as if out of a dream. She wished she would hear them, and so she did— phantom hoofbeats haunting her mind, taunting her, making her misery that much worse. She wanted so badly for the sound to be Peter coming home that she could actually hear him. She clenched the heavy comforter tightly and willed the sound to go away.

Instead, it came closer. The horses were right outside her door.

Suddenly frightened, she eased out of bed and reached for the shotgun she now kept permanently at her side. She had learned how to shoot long ago, when she'd first come west. But she'd never had enough ammunition to waste in target practice. She didn't know if she could hit anything. But she knew how to try.

Barefoot, she crossed the cold floor, leaving Betsy asleep soundly in the bed. Cold drafts blew through her thin night shift, but she felt only pure terror as she heard

the "thunk" of boots on the wooden porch. She didn't
know who was out there, but they couldn't mean well arriving in the middle of the night. She lifted the shotgun
and sighted the front door carefully.

A man's voice uttered a curse. The thud of a heavy
weight fell against the door. If she didn't know better, she
would think a drunk was trying to get in.

A stranger's voice called softly through the door. "I
saw the smoke. Is anyone in there? Mrs. Mulloney, that
you? I need some help with your husband."

For a brief moment panic seized Janice's veins and she
froze. She didn't even try to decipher the words or their
meaning. She didn't know how long she stood there before she shook herself free of the stupor and walked to the
window to peer out.

A man as large as her husband stood on the porch attempting to hold up another man whose arm wouldn't
stay around his shoulders. The awkward weight of the unconscious man occupied both the stranger's hands, and he
couldn't manage the door. Janice had only to take one
look at the man in his arms before rushing to open the
door for him.

The stranger practically fell through. Righting himself,
he started carrying his burden to the bedroom, muttering
a soft "Thanks" as he passed by her.

Janice hurried to move Betsy out of the bed. Wrapping
her in a small quilt, she lifted the sleeping child to the
floor. The stranger dropped his burden on the warm bed
and gave a sigh of relief.

"He's a heavy bastard. Excuse me, ma'am." He
straightened and pulled awkwardly at his hat. "I'm
Sherman Townsend, your husband's partner. He took a fever a while back, but I couldn't get him down here until
he passed out."

Janice smoothed her hand over Peter's forehead, finding the heat, hearing the labored breathing. Panic still
laced her veins, but she could handle it now that she
could touch him again. He was here. He was alive. She

could handle anything now. She cried softly as she wiped
the perspiration from his brow.

"Thank you, Mr. Townsend. I'll build up the fire.
Maybe if I can bathe him in a little warm water . . ."

He headed for the door before she could turn around.
"I'll do it, ma'am. I'm near cold as blue blazes anyhow."

Janice was grateful for his departure. She wanted to be
alone with her husband. She didn't want anybody to see
how her hand shook. She didn't want them to see her cry.
She didn't know what was wrong with her. She had Peter
back. She ought to be relieved and happy. But she trembled like an aspen as she fumbled at his shirt. He didn't
even know she was here.

Townsend brought a bowl of warm water a little while
later. Some of the fire's warmth already seeped into this
room. Betsy squirmed on the floor on the other side of the
bed, but she continued sleeping. Janice left her there. She
took the bowl gratefully.

"There's stew keeping in the pot on the porch. Warm
some up for yourself, Mr. Townsend. I'll be out to make
coffee in a minute."

"I can make the coffee. You just look after Peter. I'll go
down after the doctor as soon as it gets light."

He was a big man and awkward around her, but Janice
scarcely noticed. She could love him for saying all the
right things. He would fetch a doctor. Peter needed a doctor. She didn't have the slightest idea what to do for him.

She heard Townsend open the door and look for the
pot, but she didn't listen to the rest of the sounds as he
puttered around her kitchen. She found her robe and slippers and hastily pulled them on. Peter moaned when she
leaned over to cleanse his face with a warm cloth.

His hands were so cold. She laid one against her cheek
to warm it. His fingers moved restlessly, and she had to
let him go. Her insides shivered as if she were the one
nearly frozen. Her teeth were beginning to rattle.

With great effort she stripped off Peter's filthy, frozen
clothing. She had little light to see by, but she could al-

most feel his ribs beneath her fingers. He had worked himself to skin and bones.

But his upper torso was hard and ridged from his efforts. Janice ran the warm cloth over the bulge of Peter's shoulders and upper arms, reassured by their solidness. There hadn't been enough touching in their short married life. She wanted to touch him all over now. But she limited herself to cleansing him with the warm cloth. He was shivering by the time she finished.

She took a towel and rubbed him briskly, needing to keep busy, to keep from thinking. She found an extra quilt to add to the sheets and comforter already on the bed, tucking them around him. His shivering slowed, but he didn't wake.

She heard Townsend settle down for the night. Still shivering, now as much from cold as fear, Janice climbed between the covers to lay beside her silent husband. He was a stranger to her again, this man who had stayed upon a mountain, killing himself for gold. She didn't know why he had done it, and she had no desire to speculate. She just wanted the return of the man who had climbed in her window like Rapunzel's prince.

She curled beside him and dozed off and on until she heard noises in the front room again. Dressing hastily, Janice slipped out to fix some breakfast for the man who had brought Peter home. Townsend had already started the fire and the coffee. Shy at the sight of her, he headed out to see to the horses while she fixed biscuits and eggs.

She left him to his breakfast and returned to the bedroom to check on Peter and to wake Betsy. Peter tossed restlessly, and she hastily adjusted the bedding to cover him. She didn't know if he had any change of clothing. She would have to wash what he had worn last night.

Betsy exclaimed in delight at having Peter home. Janice just let her think he slept, and once she dressed, she ushered Betsy out of the room. Townsend was cleaning his plate and mug in the sink. He looked up sheepishly, murmured his thanks, asked after Peter, and edged to the door, promising to send a doctor as soon as he found one.

As soon as he found one. Janice didn't like the sound of that, but she smiled and waved farewell as Townsend disappeared down the mountain road. As soon as he found one. How soon would that be? Would he have to go all the way to Gage? She wished everyone wasn't so far away. Daniel couldn't help her now.

Knowing Peter needed nourishing liquids, she set the last piece of venison Martin had brought to boiling. Then she put Betsy to mending and returned to the sickroom.

Peter was still feverish, but he opened his eyes when she talked to him and drank the water she gave him. She didn't think he knew her, though. She showed him the chamber pot by the bed, and discreetly left the room. When she came back, he was asleep again.

"Are we rich yet?" Betsy inquired once, peering around the bedroom door as Janice tried to get some of the broth down Peter's throat.

"I don't think so," Janice answered when Peter only opened his mouth for the spoon. He didn't seem at all aware that they existed.

"Well, as soon as I start selling my paintings, we will be," Betsy assured her before returning to her chores.

Janice had to smile at this example of childish confidence. If only everything could be that easy.

She made Betsy's bed up in the front room beside the fire that night. Their firewood would run out if they kept the fire going too many nights in a row, but both Betsy and Peter needed the extra warmth right now. She would just have to learn to chop trees if Martin didn't come back.

Janice put on her nightdress in the silent bedroom and climbed in beside Peter. His body was like a small furnace, but he alternately shivered and perspired. When he was cold, she cuddled close to him. When he was hot, she bathed him with cool water. She simply didn't know what else to do. She had treated Betsy through all her fevers. this way. She didn't know if it worked for grown men.

When Peter seemed particularly restless, she fed him a little whiskey with the water. Townsend had left the bottle as his only medicinal aid. It seemed to work, and she drifted into a light sleep when Peter did.

Janice woke to the raspy sound of Peter calling her name. Before she could entirely orient herself, he leaned over her, and pawed at her breast. Gasping, she tried to move away, but he threw his leg over her hip and bent to kiss her throat. It was more of a suck than a kiss, and she moaned slightly at the sensation.

"Jenny!" he whispered, as if just discovering her existence. "Jenny," he murmured again as he pulled at her gown until the hem was up to her waist.

Janice nearly leapt from her skin as his hot fingers probed between her thighs. She could tell by the way Peter moved restlessly, his voice scarcely coherent as he moved his mouth to her breast, that he was still fevered. But that didn't keep the blood from flowing hot and heavy through her veins as she felt his body over hers, searching for the relief they both needed. She didn't know how he had the strength. His skin felt like a human torch. But she was wet and ready for him when the male part of him surged aimlessly against her. She untangled one thigh from his and opened herself to him, and he found his goal instantly.

This was mindless lust compared to their prior lovemaking, but Janice no longer cared about the difference. She had her husband back, and she would make everything better again. She had to. She held him and let him use her body and cried when he surged deep inside her, releasing his passion but leaving hers unsatisfied. She knew what she was supposed to feel now and missed it, but she had given Peter some peace. He rolled over and slipped into a sound slumber.

She lay there awake awhile longer, feeling his seed seeping from her. It had been foolish of her to allow this. What if the fever took him and she found out later she was pregnant? How would they live if she couldn't work? But her heart had set on the tiny child that might be forming inside her already. She wanted Peter's baby, and she wanted to savor every minute of its growth as she hadn't with Betsy. So she would have to make Peter live, if by sheer strength of will alone.

She rose with the dawn, washed and dressed, and went to see about breakfast. She left the door open behind her in case he woke.

Peter thought the smell of bread baking woke him. Barely conscious, he lay there feeling so hollow he thought it would take a trainload of food to fill him. But oddly enough, he felt satisfied.

As he gradually gathered his senses and realized he was warm and dry and sleeping on a cloud, he also realized he was waking without the painful erection that had brought him out of slumber every morning for months. There had been days when he had almost been tempted to give up and go after Janice rather than suffer this denial one minute longer. It wasn't easy to find water out here, but he'd managed to find a cold stream to drown his lust in. He didn't think a cold stream had made him feel as satiated as he did now.

He felt warm and satisfied, and now that he noticed, the undeniable scent of sex lingered on the linens. Hell, what had he done? Linens. He was sleeping on linen.

Peter pried his eyes open and stared at the log roof overhead. He recognized the peculiar knot in the log to the right side of the bed. He was in his own house. And there were sheets on the bed. And bread baking.

Cat? That couldn't be. He'd heard back in town that Catalina had run away with some salesman some months back. She'd left the petticoat he'd bought for her eons ago as a parting present, he'd discovered on his way up the mountain. He didn't know why she'd left it, if she meant to throw it back in his face and taunt him with it, or if she merely meant to pass it on to the next woman who came here. He never did have much luck at understanding women. Except Janice. Janice never left him guessing.

Janice. Peter winced inwardly and tried to will himself back to sleep. He'd failed her. He'd left her stranded, without a nickel, without any means of support. And now it seemed as if he'd indulged himself with another woman. He'd never be able to explain it to her. He would have to take some of the gold they needed to pay off the loan and go back to her to try to explain.

His head hurt too much for explanations at the moment. Not that he'd been able to think of any over these last months when it became apparent that the gold either wasn't there in any quantity or was inaccessible. He'd just kept chipping away at the mountain, hoping hell would open up and swallow him. He'd gambled their future away. There was no other way to look at it.

His stomach rumbled loudly. He didn't know if he dared get out of bed to see who was in the other room. For all he knew, Catalina had come back. Surely no other woman would crawl into bed with a naked man. The idea of betraying an innocent lady like Janice with a whore repulsed him, but that was scarcely the worst of his sins. He'd have to face up to the rest of them sooner or later.

Peter tried to sit up and keep the covers around him at the same time, but he was weaker than he thought. His head spun dizzily as he looked around for his clothes. The quilt kept slipping downward as he balanced at the edge of the bed, and he shivered.

Lost in concentration, he didn't see the sprite materializing in the doorway until a childish voice called, "Janice, Uncle Peter's awake!"

Half naked and shivering, he nearly fell backward at the sound of that voice. He turned and found Betsy standing in the doorway.

The bread baking had new meaning. He was home.

With surging joy, Peter glanced around and finally noted the curtains on the windows, the clean towels on the washstand, and the rag rug at his feet. He was home.

His wife was here!

# Thirty-Two

Janice appeared in the doorway, and Peter didn't think he'd ever seen a more lovely sight in his life. Her loose braid was on the verge of self-destructing, there were deep shadows under her luminous eyes, and flour covered the stained apron she wore to protect an old gown even he could tell was beyond mending. She looked like an angel.

"I don't think I've earned heaven," were the only words Peter seemed able to push from his tongue. The room began spinning, and he toppled like a tall tree.

Janice caught him before he fell, pushing him gently back to the mattress, pulling the covers up around him.

"I'll warrant you haven't earned heaven, either," she murmured as she tucked the covers in. "And you'll not gain it now if I have anything to say about it. Die on me, and I'll follow you into hell, Peter Mulloney."

The words were more anguished prayer than harsh recrimination. Peter smiled foolishly at the ceiling. Even angry, his wife didn't turn her back on him. She'd be even angrier soon. His smile faded. She'd turn her back when she learned he wasn't going to be wealthy after all. She kept her part of the bargain. He'd failed royally.

"I've got some broth heating. Can you sit up a little?" She tried to tuck pillows behind his back.

Peter contemplated starving himself to death rather than tell her they were still broke. For himself, it didn't matter so much. He could always make a living. But he didn't want to see the disappointment and fear on Janice's face. And he didn't want to be around when she walked out on him. He'd rather die than see her walk out.

He knew he was feverish and not thinking clearly. He looked up to see Janice hovering over him anxiously, her face pale with worry. He couldn't do that to her. He would have to go back up the mountain.

Obligingly he attempted to return to a sitting position. His gaze fell on Betsy, and with a hoarse voice he didn't recognize as his own, he inquired, "Nightshirt?"

Janice threw a glance over her shoulder, shooed Betsy from the room, and bent to kiss his forehead when he sat up. It was then that Peter realized why he'd felt so satisfied upon waking this morning. A brief glimpse of his fevered dreams returned to him, and he reached to stroke the rounded breast not inches from his face.

"I love you," he murmured mindlessly, pulling her down to him.

She stiffened, resisting, then sat down on the side of the bed and rested her head on his shoulder for a minute. Peter clasped his arms around her and held her there, not caring for the hows and whys of her presence, only grateful that it was so.

He must have slipped from consciousness again. In his next moment of awareness, Janice was attempting to pull the nightshirt from his saddlebag over his head. He struggled into it and felt too weak to lift his head when they were done.

Peter didn't remember much of that day. He sipped at heavenly warm broths and demanded hot bread that he could barely swallow. Cool hands bathed him when he grew feverish and covered him when he got cold. He turned away from the water she offered but drank it eagerly when she laced it with liquor. He found the chamber pot and knew life was returning to his body. He knew it even more when darkness fell and he waited with undisguised anticipation for Janice to come to bed.

He fell asleep before she could climb in beside him.

He woke again in the wee hours of dawn. He leaned back against the inviting pillows, feeling his erection making a tent of the heavy covers. Beside him, his wife slept soundly. He couldn't bear to wake her. She looked as if she hadn't slept in weeks. Besides, he had about as much strength as a newborn babe. He would wait for the need to subside.

It didn't. Peter tried to tell himself that they couldn't afford to have babies yet. Janice worried herself sick about having children and not being able to raise them. But his body had this overwhelming urge to procreate, and the woman he wanted to be mother of his child lay just beside him.

Of course, the urge driving him right now had little enough to do with children. If they came along, that was fine. But his goals right now were a little more short term. He wanted the bliss of release inside his wife's body.

He also had this crushing need to know if she wanted him. Janice was an odd duck. She hadn't wanted to be married, hadn't wanted to go to bed with him, hadn't wanted any of those things he desired. But she had responded when coaxed. It would be nice to know that she had learned to desire him as he desired her, that the money wasn't important anymore, but that was asking a lot.

So Peter tried to ease his position and go back to sleep, but his efforts failed. He ached. He ached all over but mostly he ached in the one place that Janice could satisfy. He turned slightly and tried to cup her against him. She squirmed and tried to break away.

And then she woke. He could sense it though she didn't reveal it openly. He touched her breast, stroking it through the flannel gown. She tensed but didn't move away. Peter loosened the ribbon and fed his hand into the opening. The touch of her warm flesh sent a jolt through his loins that practically left him gasping. She arched slightly to give him better access.

The nipple puckered willingly beneath his fingers, and he couldn't be patient. He pressed her down against the mattress and bent to suckle at her breast. She gave a cry of pleasure, and he was lost.

She returned his kisses with increasing fervor. Peter relished their intensity. He lay back and rolled her over so he didn't waste his strength. She kissed him back, then sought his chest to return the pleasures he had given her. He choked back a cry as she bit lightly at his nipple. He had to have her soon or burst from trying.

"Janice." He caught her mouth and kissed her again, then dragged her off the bed and on top of him. "Make love to me," he demanded, or begged, he wasn't certain.

She didn't seem to know what he wanted, but he wasn't slow to show her. He pulled her gown up until he found the soft warmth of her, felt the moisture there, and guided her to where he needed her. He could sense her uncertainty, but Peter couldn't wait any longer. He caught her lips and pressed downward. She gave a cry and sank down on him.

That was all he wanted. He could have easily lived that way, feeling her warm woman's flesh surrounding him. But then she moved slightly, and it wasn't enough. It would never be enough. He surged upward and felt her tighten around him and he didn't want to be anywhere else.

She rocked against him, eager to learn her own pleasure, finding it and sharing it with him at the same time. The double explosion rattled Peter to his bones and left him drained, but he couldn't let her go. He turned over and held himself inside her.

"Don't leave, Jenny," he murmured into her hair. "Don't ever leave."

It was a reference to more than their current physical intimacy, but Janice had no way of knowing that. She curled into the strength of Peter's embrace, relaxed with his legs entwined with hers, and went back to sleep.

When he woke again, it was full day. The bed beside him was empty and cold, but Peter could smell heavenly scents coming from the miserable fireplace that was his kitchen. That's when he knew what he had to do.

He didn't flinch at the thought. There came a time in a man's life when he had to make a choice. He could wander the face of the earth seeking some elusive rainbow, or he could settle down and make himself a home. He was going to do the latter.

His clothes lay folded on a chair beside the bed, all neatly laundered and ready to wear. He used to have a closet full of clothes and a manservant to care for them. He hadn't appreciated what he had then, but he appreciated what he had now. Who he had now. He had a woman who would travel to the ends of the earth to make a home for him. The least he could do was give her the very best home he could provide.

Peter dressed slowly, uncertain how long his strength would last. He no longer burned with fever, but he wasn't exactly himself. Part of him was completely recovered, though. Just thinking of how Janice had made love to him last night made him hard. He had some difficulty buttoning the denims.

The spinning in his head steadied as he sat on the side of the bed. Fastening the last of his shirt buttons, he stood up slowly. When he didn't immediately fall back down, he took a step toward the door. And another.

Peter leaned his shoulder against the doorjamb to admire the sight of Janice bent over the cooking pot, her face flushed with the heat of the fire, golden tendrils of hair clinging to the graceful line of her neck. Even in rags she was a beautiful woman. He might be courting real trouble when he dressed her in evening gowns, but she deserved the best.

He didn't see Betsy in the room. The tightening in his loins returned full force, but he restrained himself. First he had to let Janice know that he wouldn't let her down.

He cleared his throat, and she swung around immediately. The smile she gave him warmed Peter clear through the middle, but the flush flooding her cheeks as their eyes met roasted him to the bone. He had made his imperturbable schoolmarm blush.

"Something smells awful good, Jenny," he managed to

say, lifting his shoulder from the doorjamb and walking toward her.

She looked flustered. "It isn't much. I've not learned to cook well over a fire yet." She gave him a look of concern. "Shouldn't you still be in bed? I can bring you breakfast in there."

He caught her shoulders and pressed a kiss to her cheek. "I'm a new man, madam. And it's all your fault."

She gave him a quick hug, then backed away shyly, as if she had been overly forward. "Well, sit down, and I'll pour you some coffee."

Peter didn't let her escape. He caught her waist and held her, forcing her to look questioningly up at him. "I imagine it's snowing farther up the mountain right now. We're going to have to get out of here before we're snowed in. Did Townsend leave any of that gold here?"

Janice nodded toward some cloth bags in the corner by the fireplace. "He went to find a doctor for you. I don't know when he'll be back."

Peter counted the bags and sighed in relief. Townsend had left all of them. "We'll catch him on the trail or in town. There's enough there to pay our debts, but that's about all. I'll have to borrow some of it to get us back on our feet again."

She looked relieved. When he released her, she pushed him gently toward the plank bench that served as chair for the table. "Gage looked like a fine town. I wonder if they need a schoolteacher?"

Peter sank down in the seat gratefully. He wasn't as strong as he would like to be. He sipped at the coffee she handed him before answering. "They can find one without our help. I mean to take you back to Ohio."

Janice swung around and stared at him in disbelief. "Ohio? Why would we go back there?"

He had thought she would be relieved to know they would be returning to civilization. Maybe she didn't understand. He tried to explain more carefully. "So I can go back to work for my family. And you and Betsy can be with your family again. We might have to live with my parents for a while until I can save enough for a home of our own, but that house is big enough to hide a regiment of soldiers. We'll get along fine."

Janice looked as if she wanted to test his forehead for fever again. She rubbed her hands nervously in her apron, then returned to frying potatoes over the fire. "I thought you could borrow the money and start up a little store here. I could help with the bookkeeping and such, and even Betsy can help with the dusting and keeping the shelves stocked. If I can find a teaching job, we would get by just fine."

Irritated that she didn't seem to comprehend what he was offering her, Peter set his cup down. "I'm not going to become some dried-up little store clerk whose wife has to work to pay the bills. I told you I'd take care of you and Betsy, and that's what I mean to do. We'll go back to Ohio, and you'll not have to work at anything but keeping yourself pretty. You'll have gowns like Georgie's. Betsy can go to a good school and have art lessons."

Janice swung around and glared at him. "I like working! And I don't want to go back to Ohio. Neither do you, if you'll just admit it. Don't be foolish, Peter. We'll make our own way just fine right here."

This time, he slammed the cup down and glared back at her. "We'll make our way just fine, I'm sure, with you working your fingers to the bone and dressing like a rag-picker's wife while Betsy scrubs and dusts. That's not how I mean to take care of you. I made a promise, and I intend to keep it. We're going to Ohio."

Janice stripped off her apron and threw it at his feet. Putting her hands on her hips, she glared up at him when he stood to tower over her. "You can go to Ohio if you like. I'm not going back there to have people point at me and make fun. My sister works in your damned store, Peter! So does her husband. Shall I have them come over and visit us wearing their best store clothes, their cheap cottons and celluloid collars, and introduce them to a company of your friends and relations in their silks and laces and fancy cravats? What will that make me look like? And how will it look to their friends when they hob-nob with the boss's wife? Any promotions they earn will look like favoritism, no matter how hard they work. It won't do, Peter. I never liked it back there. I'm staying out here where people recognize me for the work I do and not who my family is."

Furious now, Peter grabbed her arms and held them pinned to her sides before she could brush him off and escape. "I don't give a damn what people think! It will take years out here to make enough money to keep you properly. What happens when children come along and you can't work? How will we pay a doctor when they get sick? I'm not going to let you lead that kind of life again."

Janice struggled violently against his hold. "Don't I have any say in this? What about what I want?" When she couldn't free herself, she glared up at his obstinate expression. "Is this the kind of husband you mean to be then? It only matters what you want? Am I to have no say in how we live at all? I'm just supposed to bake your bread and dress your children and open my legs when you want it?"

The crudity jarred him, and he released her. They were practically screaming at each other. He'd never screamed at anyone in his life. But he wanted to yell and shake her and make her see sense. "I'm not going to let you starve out here in the wilderness, and that's final," he responded gruffly, not knowing how else to say it.

A distant cry of "Janice!" broke off into a wail of terror, shattering the thick silence between them.

They both ran for the door. Janice slipped through first, arriving just in time to see two men on horses riding headlong down the hill and around the bend, bearing a screaming Betsy with them.

"Stephen!" she cried in outrage. Then she picked up her skirts and ran after them.

# Thirty-Three

"**B**etsy!" Janice's anguished cries rang off the distant hills, echoing in the wind. The first few flakes of snow blew around her head from the thick, scudding clouds overhead.

Peter threw his saddle on his horse and jerked the girth straps around. Realizing she couldn't chase the horses down the hillside, Janice ran back to the house and grabbed Peter's heavy fleece-lined jacket and the pistols and rifle Townsend had carried in with the saddlebags. Peter was already climbing into the saddle when she returned with them.

He shrugged the coat on, leaned over to give her a kiss, and accepted the weapons. "I'll catch up with them. There's only one trail out of here."

He was barely strong enough to sit in the saddle, and he meant to chase down a mountain after two desperate men. Janice wished she knew how to ride so she could be the one to go, but she could see the sense in not arguing the point. Peter had to be the one who rode.

She screamed inside as she watched him leave. She would scream out loud if she didn't fear giving Peter cause to doubt her sanity. She wanted to scream and scream and bring the mountains tumbling and send the clouds whirling. Why was God tormenting her like this? Why did He make her so helpless?

She had to stand here watching her ill husband ride out after a man who wasn't worth the polish for Peter's boot. How could she have been so blind when she was young? Why was she still so helpless? She had spent years teach-

ing herself to handle anything and everything that came
her way with unruffled efficiency. And now here she was
again, left terrified by the same man who had put her in
that position once before. She wanted to scream and grab
the shotgun and ride out after him. This time, she would
kill him.

But she couldn't do any of those things. Trudging back
to the cabin, Janice dug out her warmest clothes and began to dress. If only one trail left here, she could follow
it. She wouldn't sit here and do nothing while Betsy was
being kidnapped. She wondered who the second man
was, but she didn't really want to know. All she wanted
was Betsy and Peter back again.

The old shotgun Martin had given her rested next to the
bags of gold. Gold. Stephen would listen to the sound of
gold. She may not have understood him very well at fifteen, but she was ten years older now and wiser to the
ways of mankind. Stephen would take gold in exchange
for his daughter.

The bags were too heavy for her to carry. Glancing
around, she remembered the loose stones she'd had to
push back into the fireplace. Wiggling the rocks, she
found several more. Gritting her teeth and praying the
whole chimney didn't fall on her head, she pried a hole
behind the dying fire. Stamping out the last embers,
she dragged the bags across the packed earth beneath
the grate and shoved them into the hole. She filled her
pockets with lumps of rock from the last bag, then shoved
it too into the hole. She hadn't realized gold looked like
lumps of rock. She certainly hoped Peter and his partner
knew what they were doing. Feeling the weight loading
her down, she hurriedly replaced the loose stones, scuffed
up the dirt, and replaced the ashes and burned wood. The
fireplace looked the same as it ever had.

She packed every spare bit of food she could find into
a burlap sack. Then wrapping a shawl around her head
and donning her heavy mantle, she picked up the shotgun
and the sack of food and left the cabin. With only one
road down the mountain, she would have to come across

Peter and Betsy sometime. She hoped it would be to find them coming home, but she didn't mean to leave them out there alone.

The snow came down heavier as she trudged along the path the horses had taken. It had snowed often enough in Ohio. She had walked to work every day, even with gray sheets of ice beating against her. She had slogged through filthy mush in thin shoes with holes in the bottom. She hadn't had to suffer that since she moved to Texas and she couldn't say she missed it, but she knew how to do it. And this time, she had good strong leather ankle boots without holes in the soles.

The going was easy at first. She could even catch sight of the trail of hoofs racing down the mountain. She wasn't an expert at tracking so she couldn't tell one set of prints from the other and most of them just looked like smeared mud, but she was reassured that she was going the right way.

But as the snow came down harder, the tracks disappeared beneath a layer of white. Everything disappeared beneath a layer of white. She couldn't even be certain of the road, such as it was. She kept to the widest space between trees and scrub and prayed.

Whenever she left the protection of the trees, the wind howled around her, searching for openings in her layers of clothing. Her toes and fingers turned numb first. Her nose didn't grow numb. It hurt. She wrapped the shawl more firmly around the lower half of her face, but the icy particles flying from the sky stung like a swarm of bees. The snow she knew had never been like this.

She didn't consider turning back. There was nothing back up that road for her. Her life was ahead, down the mountain. She didn't know how she could help, but she meant to be there in case she was needed.

When she thought it might be noon, she stopped beneath the overhanging branches of an evergreen and brought out a piece of cheese and bread and gnawed on them for a while. She couldn't remember how long it had taken to ride this trail from town in a wagon. Surely go-

ing down it on horseback would be faster. Maybe Peter
and Betsy were already holed up in the general store with
Henry and Gladys, cheerfully sitting by the fire and
drinking hot chocolate. She hoped so. Peter was too ill to
be out in this storm for long, and Betsy had never been
healthy enough to stay out in the cold. They needed
warmth and nutrition.

She conserved most of her supplies just in case. Fate
had never been particularly kind to her or her loved ones.
She would hope they were safe, but she would plan for
the worst.

The snow gave no evidence of stopping as Janice
trudged through drifts up to her knees in places. She had
difficulty dragging her soaked skirts and petticoats
through the drifts and tried to work around them, but she
feared stepping into deeper holes if she wandered too far
off the course she hoped was the road.

She tried to calculate in her mind how many miles she
could walk in an hour and how many hours she had been
out here. Hadn't Martin said it was less than ten miles to
town? Surely she could walk that before the light faded
entirely. She threw a doubtful look to the lead sky. It
would be dark early.

She comforted herself with the fact that there wasn't
any sign of Betsy and Peter. Surely Peter had realized
they would have to stay in town until the snow stopped.
He would probably be furious when she showed up. He
had actually shouted at her this morning. He would shout
even louder when she walked into town. But try as she
might, she would never make one of those humble wives
who sat beside the fireside waiting for their husbands to
provide.

Her ears were numb. She could barely move her frozen
feet. The wind seemed to laugh as it whipped down the
mountainside and froze her skirt to her legs. And though
the snow grew less as she came off the highest elevation,
the sky grew gradually darker. She was going to be out
here on the mountain in the dark.

She thought she heard the howl of a wolf. Her fingers

could barely hold the shotgun, but she forced them to move into position on the trigger. She scanned the landscape ahead, seeing only gray shapes that could be anything rising out of the thin layer of white. She waited for a shape to move, and to her surprise, one did. She froze beside the nearest tree trunk and watched until it moved again.

She had little or no protection out here. She had left the mountain and had reached the rolling hillside where scrub and rocks covered the landscape. Did wolves roam the lower terrain?

If that was a wolf, it was an injured one. The gray shape seemed to hump over and try to rise again. Janice felt her mouth go dry and her throat close up. The movement was only too human.

If it was Stephen or his crony out there, she ought to let them die. She wanted them to die. But they could tell her where to find Betsy. She had to know.

She approached cautiously, holding the shotgun the way she'd been taught. The shape almost made it to its feet, staggered, and fell again with a low moan. That was when Janice lowered the shotgun and felt all her hopes dry up and blow away with the wind. That moan had to be Peter's.

She ran as best as she could in wet skirts and shoes, her petticoats catching at her legs and the icy wind searing her lungs. She nearly fell down beside him, sliding and grabbing at his shoulders as he struggled to his feet. They both tumbled to the ground, and Janice wrapped her arms around him and fought the sobs welling up inside her.

"My God, Jenny." Peter caught her close and held her, repeating her name over and over as if she were a dream that the sound made real.

"What happened? Where's your horse? Where's Betsy?" Fighting her fears, Janice struggled to free herself, struggled to get them on their feet. She was wet to the bone, and so was he. They would freeze out here on the mountainside if they didn't get moving.

"They shot at me, winged the horse." Using her shoulders, Peter fought to find his feet. He coughed, a racking cough that came from the lungs. Janice held him, terrified, familiar with that sound. People died from coughs like that. She shuddered and held him as he swayed slightly once he reached his feet.

"The horse reared and I lost my seat. I'm sorry, Jenny. I just couldn't hold on. And I didn't dare shoot back." Keeping his arm around her shoulders, he started moving down the hillside. "We've got to get out of this cold. What in hell are you doing here?"

He didn't have the strength to yell at her. Janice couldn't even smile at this consolation. She was too paralyzed with fear. Out of instinct, she reached for her bag of supplies. With numb fingers, she produced the hunk of cheese and offered it to him.

He didn't seem much interested in the food. She suspected if her fingers could feel, she would find him burning with fever. He had ridden out into a storm like a madman with no thought to himself. She wanted to weep for his foolish bravery. She wanted to weep for her foolishness in allowing him to go. She wanted to weep for a life gone mad.

Instead, she forced him to eat the cheese and tried to act as anchor for his swaying steps. He was heavy and she was exhausted. When she stumbled, he caught her. She liked it better with Peter by her side, however. She wasn't as afraid of the little things, like the shape of that rock ahead or the darkness slowly consuming them. She didn't want to die, but if she had to, she didn't want to be alone.

But she couldn't die and leave Betsy motherless. They had to live. She didn't think she could do it without Peter. His cough kept her preoccupied. His arm around her kept her warm inside. His reassurances that they were on the right road, that they were almost there, kept her going. She surrendered herself entirely to his care, going where he led, hearing only what he said, feeling only the weight of his arm around her. The rest of the world ceased to exist.

"There's a light just ahead, Jenny. We're going to make it." Peter squeezed her shoulders. "I couldn't have done it without you."

She couldn't have done it without him, either, but she hadn't the breath left to tell him. It hurt just to breathe. Her feet felt like lumps of lead. The darkness was so thick around her that she would never have been able to move forward had it not been for Peter's sense of direction. She might have wandered around out here forever. Even now, she couldn't see the light he did. She clung to his waist and let him guide her.

The tilted shape of the nearest shack slowly came into view. There wasn't a light in it, but Janice would have settled for stopping right there, getting in out of the wind, anything but this constant howl of ice and cold. Peter forced her to go on.

"You've got to have a fire, Janice. We've got to get you warm. And they may have news of Betsy. Someone had to see them."

His words were warm against her ear. They seeped down inside her, giving her strength to manage a few more steps. She wanted to rip off her hampering skirts. They weren't of any use to her anymore. They only weighed her down. But she dragged them a little farther, forcing one foot in front of the other.

Peter coughed harder now, but he had the strength to keep her going, to push her forward. He practically carried her by the time they reached the overhang of the general store. Light came from the rear of the store where the living quarters were, but neither of them had the strength to go around. Peter pounded on the door, then reached for the latch. They practically fell through when the door opened.

"Land sakes! What you all doin' out in this?" Henry's laconic voice almost evinced a small amount of excitement as he lifted his lantern to examine the intruders.

"Mulloney," Peter gasped between coughs, staggering to keep his feet. "My wife, Janice. Horse threw me."

That highly expurgated version was sufficient to gain

them entrance. Slamming the door against the wind, Henry led the way through the cluttered shelves of merchandise to the rear door. Janice hadn't realized how much she had been leaning into the wind until it was suddenly taken away from her. She lurched forward, almost coming unbalanced. Her skirts tangled around her, and she tripped. Peter kept a firm grip on her and held her upright.

She wasn't certain how she made it to the back room and the fire. Her mind was as numb as the rest of her. She didn't know how long she drifted in this comatose state before she gradually emerged, becoming aware of the crackling flames as more than a source of warmth, hearing the voices around her, recognizing Peter's hacking cough.

"The stage left at noon," someone was saying. Janice forced her mind to focus on the voice. Gladys. She remembered the fat woman with the bad disposition.

A low rumble followed. She couldn't distinguish the words, but the sound rippled through her. Peter. She closed her eyes and let herself ride on the sound of his voice. Peter. Warmth seeped around the place where her heart should be. Peter would find Betsy. She didn't know how she knew that. It was a foolish thought. He was ill. He had no horse. But she let herself drift on the sound of his voice and didn't attempt to arouse herself again.

She wasn't even aware when Henry and Gladys left the room. She only knew the comforting fingers finding her buttons, stripping back the damp cloth, peeling off the layers that kept her chilled and shivering. A hot mug was shoved into her hands, and she forced it to her lips, sipping slowly until the heat swirled around in her stomach. She tasted whiskey in it. She hated the taste of whiskey. She drank it anyway, because it was warm.

"Stand up and let me pull these skirts off, Jenny," the voice was saying. A blanket had already miraculously appeared around her shoulders.

She couldn't remember the last time someone had taken care of her. Surely her mother must have done it sometime in the distant past, but she couldn't remember. She stood obediently and allowed the filthy, sodden skirts and petticoats to fall to the floor. She shivered as a draft hit her bare legs, but a quilt was hastily pulled around her, a warm quilt, one that had baked by the fire. She sighed in relief.

"Let me see your toes, Jenny."

That sounded vaguely obscene, but obligingly she held out her leather-clad feet. He struggled with the wet laces and finally cut them free. She could scarcely feel her feet when he pulled off her fallen stockings. Still sipping her drink, she looked with curiosity at the blue toes he uncovered.

Strong, capable hands rubbed at them, and she felt a painful tingling. She tried to jerk away, but he wouldn't let go.

"I think they'll be all right. At least you had sense to put on warm stockings. What in hell did you think you were doing walking down that mountain?"

She couldn't tell if he was angry with her or not. It didn't matter. She just wanted to sleep. She pushed her hair out of her eyes and tried to concentrate. Peter still wore his wet clothes.

"Get those off," she murmured, swaying where she sat.

He looked vaguely startled as he glanced up from her toes to see her face. When he saw the direction of her gaze, he grinned feebly. "Yes, ma'am," he agreed, without the teasing reply he might have given upon another occasion.

She gathered her blanket and quilt around her and watched as Peter stripped to the skin and dried off with another blanket. He might have lost weight, but he was still an imposing sight to behold. She gave a small sigh of wonder, closed her eyes, and nearly toppled into the fire before he caught her.

"Our gracious hosts allowed that we could sleep in front of the fire. It isn't much of a bed, but we'll be warm. Come here, Jenny. Let me hold you."

She didn't object but quietly curled up against his nakedness and allowed him to make a bed and covers of the quilt and blankets. It felt right to have his nakedness against hers, his warmth feeding hers. For the first time, she truly felt married, knew what it was to be a part of another person besides herself. It felt good.

As she slipped into unconsciousness, Peter lay awake behind her, trying to keep his cough from waking her.

The stage had left at noon with Betsy and her kidnappers on it. It wouldn't run again until the roads cleared, which could be next week or next spring.

How could he tell Janice that Betsy was gone?

# Thirty-Four

"**W**hat is she doing?" Stephen nodded his head toward the child rummaging around in the cold ashes of the prior night's fire. The hotel was a dismal one, and no one had come around this morning to relight the cold kindling.

"Told her she could look for a charcoal stick if she wanted. It keeps her happy." Bobby Fairweather sipped at his beer and ignored the greasy bacon that was his breakfast.

A few minutes later the child was happily ensconced at a table by the window, drawing on the back of an old wanted poster she'd found nailed to the wall. Somehow, she had managed to comb out the worst of the snarls in her curls, and she looked more like a fairy child than a human perched daintily at the edge of the splintery chair. Stephen frowned and glanced worriedly out the window. He knew Janice couldn't follow him, but he still felt as if lightning would come down out of the sky to strike him dead.

He shoved that idiocy aside and verified the time with the slatternly woman who came to remove the plates. The train would be coming soon. He gathered up his saddlebags and crossed the room to his daughter.

"Come on, kid, it's time to go." He glanced down at the paper. She didn't even look old enough to write, but he assumed she had to be. He didn't need to worry. She was sketching a man's face. At his command, she smiled, signed her name and the date with a flourish, and handed it to the woman who came to take away the milk she hadn't drunk.

"It's not very good, but I thought you might like it," she whispered shyly to the waitress.

The woman grunted, gave the man who hadn't tipped her an evil look, and shoved the paper into her apron pocket. Betsy gave her artwork a sad farewell look, then obediently followed the man who had dragged her away from home and family. He'd said he was her father, but she knew he lied. She also knew Peter would come after her, and this man didn't. She had more confidence in her thoughtful brother-in-law than in this tight-fisted, surly man who ordered her about as if she hadn't a brain in her head.

While they waited for the train to pull into the station, she used her charcoal stick to sketch on a poster advertising the train schedule. Stephen didn't seem to care that she defaced public property. She checked the features of the man who accompanied him and went back to sketching.

"My horse hasn't turned up yet. He may have gone back up the mountain." Peter hoped he'd left enough fodder in the stable. The gelding was a damned good mount. "I'm going to rent the wagon."

Janice began gathering her few possessions around her. "We'll need more food. That trip took almost two days by stage." She took one of the chunks of rock from her pocket. "Will Henry be able to take payment with one of these?"

Peter shook his head in dismay and amazement. His wife was a never-ending source of surprise. "No wonder those skirts fell like a lump of lead last night. I just thought they were frozen. You mean you've been toting those rocks around on you?"

She looked at the lump in her hand and back to Peter. "This is the gold, isn't it? I couldn't carry a lot, but I thought . . ."

He took the rock and hefted it in his hand. "It's not

been processed, but Henry might accept it. Townsend says it's pretty poor quality, but it's better than an IOU." He caught her hand as she reached for her wool mantle. "You're staying here."

She shook herself free and reached for the mantle again. "I am not. You try to leave without me and I'll shoot you myself."

Peter scowled and turned his back on her, heading for the store in the front of the building. He knew he was still feverish. His cough hadn't improved with the cold night on the floor. He felt like hell. He knew he would feel much better having Janice by his side on that lonesome journey out of the hills. She'd saved his life yesterday. Having her with him might improve his odds of surviving again. But they would decrease the odds of her survival by more than he meant to wager. She would staying here, where it was safe.

He bought supplies and some heavy blankets, made arrangements for the wagon and a horse, and went outside to check the weather. Janice was already in the wagon bed, overseeing the loading of his purchases.

Peter glared at her. She wasn't a large woman. He knew when he held her in his arms she was fragile and vulnerable, and he tried to take great care not to hurt her. But she could be a raging Valkyrie right now with thunderbolts and lightning at her fingertips for all he could tell. He knew he would either have to take her or tie her up.

"What do you think you're doing?" he demanded unnecessarily. He damn well knew what she was doing. He just didn't know how to talk her out of it.

"I'm going after Betsy. She's my sister." She didn't raise her voice, but she hadn't wasted her years as a schoolteacher. Her tone had all the authority necessary to carry her point.

"That's something we need to talk about," he said ominously, checking the traces on the animal he'd hired.

Behind him, he felt Janice grow still. He didn't mean to hurt her any more than she had been, but if he was going to find Betsy, he had to have the whole story. Men didn't generally ride to the top of a mountain to kidnap a ten-year-old girl for nothing.

She returned to her tasks in silence. Apparently she had accepted his threat as a trade: information for her accompaniment. Maybe that's what he had meant when he said it. He didn't know. He just knew he didn't mean to argue with her about this. That exterior of hers was so brittle, Peter feared it would break at the slightest touch, and he already knew too well how vulnerable she was beneath that facade. He'd like to remove the brittle shell, but not until he could better care for her.

The horse was ancient, but not yet doddering. It pulled the wagon at a steady pace through the frozen ruts of mud and snow that made up the road out of town. The woman beside him was as frozen as the mud. She scarcely said two words as they waved to Henry and Gladys and set off down the road. He could see her fingers clenched tightly in her lap and knew how close she was to shattering.

"Tell me, Janice. Who was he and why did he take Betsy?"

She jerked nervously. Peter wanted to hold her and tell her everything would be all right, but that was quite probably a lie. He kept his gaze fastened on the rough road and his attention on the reins.

"His name is Stephen Connor. I didn't see who was with him."

"It looked like Bobby Fairweather to me." Peter felt her turn and stare at him with surprise. He dared a quick look. Her face was as pale as the snow, and her eyes wider and grayer than the sky.

"Bobby? Why would Bobby be out here?" She frowned and turned her beautiful eyes to the road, although Peter didn't think she saw it. "Ellen said he'd left town after the baby was born." She gnawed at her bottom lip as she tried to remember what else Ellen had said. "Ellen said Stephen had talked to Bobby quite a bit. Stephen tried to spread nasty rumors about you." Peter felt her look back at him again. "Why would they be working together?"

"You tell me," he answered quietly. "I don't know either of them. Who is Stephen Connor?"

She went still then. He could almost hear the wheels turning in her head. Finally, when he thought he would have to drag it out of her, she answered, "He's Betsy's father."

In that moment Peter discovered suspicion wasn't the same thing as knowledge. She'd carried another man's child. The truth burned through him, making him feel hollow inside. And then he remembered Betsy's age and Janice's circumstances, and he sent her a quick look. "And you're her mother."

Janice nodded, not daring to look at him.

He scowled. "You couldn't have been more than a child yourself."

"I was fifteen."

He thought he might be sick. Fifteen. Five years older than Betsy. Knowing her innocence had been stolen at that age made him want to weep. Knowing she'd carried a child all alone at that age made him want to kill the scoundrel when he got hold of him. "The bastard," he growled, not even realizing he did so aloud.

"You can't blame Stephen entirely. It wasn't all his fault."

Peter smacked the reins to urge the horse to go faster. It didn't satisfy his desire to kill. "You were fifteen! It damned well was his fault. How old was he?"

"Twenty." Janice hugged her arms around herself and stared straight ahead. "But he thought I was older. I . . . I matured early. And I was the oldest, so I . . . I acted older too. I worked at the restaurant at the train station. I lied about my age. They thought I was eighteen."

Peter felt some of the rage seep out of him. He cast her a swift look and realized the truth of her words. He doubted if Janice had ever had a chance to be a child. She was a beautiful woman now. She must have made a stunning adolescent. He could see himself falling all over her if he'd met her back then. He grinned wryly.

"The bastard had good taste. I wish I'd known you then."

She gave him a startled look, then hurriedly turned back to the road. "So you could have done the same thing? Thanks."

He sighed. "Give me a little credit, Jenny. I would have married you, not left you pregnant and alone. What happened?"

She shrugged. "It was only one night. I had to work that night and my parents trusted me to go straight home while they went to visit a friend for a holiday. Instead, I spent it with Stephen. We were in love, or so I thought." She sat silent for a minute. "I didn't like what he did to me. It wasn't the same . . ." She flushed and knit her fingers together.

Peter reached over to grasp them. "Boys don't know a whole lot. He wasn't much more than a boy. They don't even realize a woman should feel something too. Even men can be jerks." He remembered his first time with her. He'd been more than a jerk.

She clasped his gloved hand. "I know a lot more now than I did then. But what he did kept me frightened for years. We fought that night, and he didn't come back for weeks. He came back after your father laid off all the railroad workers and he was out of a job. He just came to tell me he was leaving town to look for work."

"My father?" Peter searched for a ten-year-old memory. He didn't have his father's confidence much at that age. He'd never really had his father's confidence. They had argued continuously over his business practices. He couldn't remember the railroad situation. He shook his head. "All I know about my father's involvement in the railroads was his decision to sell most of his stock some years back."

Janice took a deep breath and nodded. "It's all right. I hated your entire family for a long time. I can see now that was foolish."

"No." Peter watched the sway of the horse's rear end and felt a kinship with that particular portion of the animal's anatomy. He tightened his mouth bitterly. "You had a right to hate us. We lived more than well off the money my father made from people like you. It took twenty-five years before I ever thought to question where it came from."

"You had nothing to do with Stephen leaving. He could have found another job, but he got in with a bunch who wanted to form some kind of union. They got into trouble, and he had to leave town. He could have found a job and sent for me. He didn't. I never heard from him again."

"Until yesterday?" Peter asked incredulously.

She stared at her hands. "Until a few weeks ago. Ellen had told me he'd been asking after me in Mineral Springs, but I just thought it was some kind of coincidence. But I warned Tyler not to tell him where I was. I didn't want him to know about Betsy. Betsy really thinks she's my sister. I couldn't ruin her life by letting her know she's illegitimate and that I'm a fallen woman."

Peter jerked the horse to a halt and turned and grabbed Janice's shoulders. He glared down into her frozen face. "You're not a fallen woman. Don't you ever dare call yourself that again. You're an absolutely remarkable woman, a woman who can fight adversity and win. There's not one woman in twenty who could have done what you have. I'm damned proud of you, and so is Betsy. There isn't anything anyone can say that can change the facts. You were a child, but you raised her better than most grown women could. She knows you love her. That's all that matters."

Janice's teeth were chattering, and he jerked her into his arms, holding her close against his chest. She wrapped her arms around his back, and he felt her dry sobs. She was breaking. Peter could feel her crumbling in his hands, and he didn't know what to do about it. He kissed her ear and pushed her shawl back to kiss her neck. The sobs lessened, and she rested her head against his shoulder, not fighting him but accepting.

"I didn't want you to hate me," she whispered.

He stroked her hair and held her close. He was growing accustomed to this business of fighting the virago and loving the vulnerable woman. He thought he might even love the virago. He smiled against her hair. "Hate is the absolute very last thing on my mind right now," he admitted. "When I first met you, I thought we were of the same age. I wanted you so much I dreamed about you at night. I thought you were experienced. I didn't care if you'd had lovers. I was glad, because that gave me a better chance. After that first night, I knew I was wrong, and the responsibility terrified me. I didn't know if I could teach you how good we could be together. I'm not very good at dealing with women."

She gave a muffled laugh against his coat. "You could have fooled me." She quieted, then reluctantly pulled from his arms. She studied the rugged lines of his face, the hollows and shadows put there by illness and worry, and she touched his unshaven cheek. "You're the best thing that has ever happened to me. Thank you."

Peter gave a halting grin, then turned back to set the horse in motion. He wasn't used to being embarrassed, and he didn't know how to respond. This woman beside him made him feel emotions he hadn't thought himself capable of feeling. They were all stirred together in a cauldron of confusion right now. He tried to stick with the known and leave the unknown to settle itself out.

"Why did Stephen follow you here?"

Accepting this change of topic, Janice wiped her eyes and went back to watching the road for any clue of Betsy. "I don't know. He showed up by himself a few weeks ago. He tried to talk as if he'd seen me yesterday instead of ten years ago. He knew Betsy was his. Everyone in the town where I came from knew it back then. He must have gone home and heard the rumors sometime. I don't know why he chose now to seek me out."

Peter didn't want to think about what she meant by Stephen's talking as if he'd seen her yesterday. He could imagine the sweet words a loving couple might have said to each other. He scowled. "Did he touch you?"

"I wouldn't let him in the house. I told him if he didn't leave, I would shoot him ."

Peter's eyebrows soared. "Shoot him? You had a gun?"

"Mr. Martin left a shotgun. It was in the house, but I could have gotten it if I needed it. I didn't. Stephen finally got the message and left."

"Mr. Martin?"

Janice sent him a curious look. "Mr. Martin. You know, from town? He helped me to find your cabin. He brought us supplies a time or two. He's been real kind to us. I thought he was a friend of yours."

"I don't know any Martin. What does he look like?"

Janice's eyes widened in surprise, then narrowed as she tried to think. "He's tall, maybe even taller than you. He's kind of grizzled and a bit stoop-shouldered though, so I figure he's not young. He always keeps his hat pulled over his face so I can't see much. He wears a holster and has a rifle with him, and he wears a really ratty-looking leather vest. I thought it looked worse than Jason's. As a thought hit her, she turned to stare up at him expectantly. "I asked him once if he'd ever been in Natchez. I could have sworn he was the same man I spoke to in Natchez. He never answered me."

Peter's mouth tightened into a grim line. "And he calls himself Martin?"

Janice thought a minute. "He never called himself anything. One of the men in town called him Martin."

"Damn Daniel to hell and back," Peter muttered, slashing at the reins.

Janice glanced at him in surprise.

When she said nothing, he sent her a grim look. "If it had been anybody else, I would have my doubts, but Daniel has a hole where his brains ought to be. He's sent Pecos Martin to look after us."

Janice stared at him in astonishment. Pecos Martin was the imaginary hero of Daniel's books. Peter must be losing his mind.

# Thirty-Five

J anice didn't have long to reflect on the possibility that her husband was madder than the proverbial hatter. The sound of wagon wheels and horses coming up the road swung her attention back to the immediate.

Peter settled his rifle across his lap and guided the horse to a wide space at the side of the road. Janice closed her hands tightly over her shotgun. There wasn't any question of running. The people riding around the curve were coming at a pace much greater than theirs.

The first horse burst from the cover of the trees and Janice let out a gasp. Manuel! It didn't seem possible. What could he possibly be doing out here?

The next horse to follow explained everything. Daniel Mulloney's lanky figure was unmistakable even after five years of absence.

By the time the wagon rounded the curve, Peter groaned in surrender. Setting the rifle aside, he watched as Tyler whipped a four-horse team up the narrow road and Evie clung to the seat beside him. Peter wouldn't have been in the least surprised if Georgie had been with them. He gave Daniel's wife credit for having the sense to stay home and take care of her new babe. He assumed she'd had the babe by now or Daniel wouldn't be here.

Manuel and Daniel reared their horses to a halt and whooped at sight of the wagon. Daniel leaped from his saddle and pulled Janice from her seat before she could protest. He swung her around and kissed her roundly, then set her down and grinned up at the fury on his younger brother's face.

"I'm damned glad to see that ugly mug of yours, Aloysius." Daniel grinned as Peter's expression soured even further at the sound of his hated middle name. "When I'd got word that you'd gone missing and left your new bride alone, I thought I would have to come find you and strangle you."

Peter turned his sour look from Daniel to Manuel and back to Tyler. The line of communication here was rather obvious. Janice had left Carmen worrying. Carmen had immediately told her brother Manuel, who had told their cousin Evie. Evie of the big mouth had instantly informed both Tyler and Daniel. This wasn't a family that kept secrets from one another.

"As much as I would like to spend time expressing gratitude for your concern, I haven't got time. Did you just come up from Gage?"

Tyler was out of the wagon and standing with the others by now. All three men turned at Peter's tone. Janice climbed back up beside him. Her face was pale and set and not one of joy as they had anticipated.

"We were on the noon train. We spent the night at the stage station," Daniel answered for them. "What's wrong?" His eyes narrowed with concern as he finally noted the shadows of illness on his brother's face.

"Betsy's been kidnapped. I don't know if you remember her. Did you see any little girls at the station?" Janice spoke quickly. Daniel had been her friend when she had most needed one. He'd always been kind to Betsy, but that had been five years ago.

Tyler was already running back to the wagon. Evie held the horses' reins, easing them to the side of the road so they could turn around. Manuel cursed and climbed back into his saddle. Only Daniel remained where he was, hanging on to the wagon wheel and staring up at the worried couple on the seat.

"We'd all know Betsy if we'd seen her. We didn't. I think you'd better tell me the story while we ride." Instead of mounting his horse, Daniel tied it to the back of the wagon. Before Peter could protest, he climbed in the wagon seat, shoving Janice over and taking the reins. "You look like hell. Save your breath for talking. I'll drive."

Janice adjusted her position between the two men and managed to capture one of Peter's hands before he could reappropriate the leather. Daniel was right. Peter's cough had not improved with the ride. He ought to be lying in the back of the wagon instead of driving. She didn't dare push him that far, but she could keep him from arguing foolishly. She leaned against him, and he instinctively wrapped his arm around her. Daniel set the wagon into motion the instant Tyler had his turned around.

The story was a long time in the telling since it had to begin with why Peter had disappeared for so long. Manuel served as messenger between the two wagons, carrying snippets of the story up to Evie and Tyler, then coming back for more.

It was while Manuel was with Tyler that Peter answered one of Daniel's unspoken questions.

"Townsend says what we've found ought to be sufficient to repay Tyler's loan. We own the mountain. One day we can come back and try to excavate deeper. For now, I want to bring Janice and Betsy home."

Janice jerked her hand away from him and sat up straight, but she didn't contradict her husband in public. She just clenched her teeth and kept her eyes on the road. Betsy came before any argument over where they were going or when.

Beside her, Daniel gave them a thoughtful glance, but Manuel was already on his way back. He answered simply, "You know you're always welcome. Mother asks about you constantly. That's one of the reasons I'm here."

Peter lifted a scornful brow. "Didn't your friend Martin tell you where I was?"

Daniel shifted a little uncomfortably on the seat. Janice could almost swear he flushed a little.

"He's not much of a letter writer. He does what he wants. I haven't heard from him in weeks. Have you seen him?"

"No, but Janice has. I didn't even know he was out there. He does his job well, I'd say. How long have you had him following me?"

Daniel shrugged. "I wouldn't exactly say I had him following you. I just asked if he'd keep an eye out for you when I hadn't heard from you in a while." He turned and winked at Janice, who listened to this with astonishment. "The last I heard from Pecos, he said my brother had good taste in women. He must have decided looking after you was more important than looking after Peter. Or more interesting."

Janice ignored the implied compliment. "You aren't really telling me that man was Pecos Martin, are you?"

Daniel grinned. "It's a little like saying I talk to Santa Claus, isn't it? But those dime novels get written about real people often enough. You've heard about Buffalo Bill and Wild Bill Hickok and Annie Oakley. They're all real people. Why shouldn't Pecos be real?"

"I'm not even sure the others are real," she muttered. "Nobody can do the things those dime novels say."

"Well now, that's another story entirely. I make up Martin's exploits for my books. He comments on them occasionally. He didn't like it when I had him wooing women, for instance. He's not much of a skirt chaser. I think he meant to correct me physically at one point, but he's come to enjoy the notoriety some. I doubt if he has any real friends, but he's willing to help out upon occasion."

Peter growled and pulled Janice closer to him and away from his brother. "I don't fancy some outlaw gunslinger hanging around my wife. I'd suggest you call him off."

"I'll drop a note to his box, but I can't promise when he'll pick it up. I'm surprised that he didn't go up the mountain after you, or take off after these men who took Betsy. That's more his style than flirting with the ladies." Daniel sent Janice a look of concern. "Why would anyone kidnap Betsy? Do they know about the gold?"

Peter hadn't mentioned her relationship to the kidnappers. Janice glanced down at her hands, letting him explain as he thought best.

"I think one of them is a cowpoke I tangled with back in Mineral Springs. His name is Bobby Fairweather. Remember those fires I told you about?" Peter addressed this to Daniel over Janice's head.

Daniel nodded. "You thought they were set, but you were the one who got blamed for them."

"I'm almost certain the first one was set. I did some nosing around, and Bobby's name came up a time or two too often." Peter ignored Janice's look of surprise. "He's the spiteful kind who lines to get revenge for every sort of imagined slight or wrong. He talked against Janice in the presence of some of his cronies a couple of times." He gave Janice a wicked grin. "You weren't very nice to the boy, you know."

"He's a malicious drunk and a lazy no-account," Janice replied serenely.

Daniel chuckled. "And no doubt you told him so to his face."

"I don't believe in talking behind people's backs." She squeezed her hands together. It had never occurred to her that Bobby would be so small-minded as to try to get even with her for words said in argument.

"That's mighty high-minded of you, but Bobby took offense. And then there are always those who thought a woman shouldn't be teaching their young ones and so on and so forth, so he probably convinced himself he was doing a good deed. Besides, he was drunk most of the time and probably liked showing off at fires."

Manuel intervened. "I caught him setting a prairie fire once. The boy is sick. I told Jason to keep an eye on him, but Bobby's always been good at playing possum."

Peter nodded. "I haven't got any proof on either fire. No one saw him either time except afterward, when he was helping to put them out. But he's been known to have words with the bootlegger who died in that shack. He was there gambling that night. I know that much. But I asked a few too many questions after that first fire. Bobby heard about it and we had words. He could have set the second fire just to get even with me, knowing who the sheriff would go after."

"And now he's here with Stephen. What does that mean?" Janice clenched her hands in fury as much as anguish. She'd never liked Bobby Fairweather, but she was ready to murder him now.

"Probably just that birds of a feather stick together. Stephen asked after us. Bobby repeated some malicious gossip. Their minds started working in the same direction. They could have come here with just this plan in mind."

"Why?" Janice cried.

Peter looked at Daniel, then looked at the road ahead. "I suspect Stephen knows who I am," was the only reply he made.

He didn't need to say more. Daniel sent him an instant look of understanding. "He's from Ohio?"

Janice nodded. "But not from Cutlerville."

"It doesn't matter. Mulloney Enterprises is known beyond Cutlerville." Daniel grimaced. "And I'm probably the one who told him about your marriage. I had it announced in all the papers."

The final piece fell into the puzzle. Stephen hadn't come looking for her until after he'd heard about her marriage to a wealthy man. Janice closed her eyes and tried not to think about it. She'd married Peter for his money. It served her right to have it thrown back in her face this way. She should never, ever have done it.

Peter caught her hands and kept her from clenching them into little balls that would have been painful if she hadn't worn gloves. "We'll find him, Jenny. He can't get away from all of us."

She kept telling herself that over and over as the wagons rolled down the hills and back toward Gage. She even tried to believe that Stephen had just wanted his daughter, that he hadn't known where to find her until he saw the marriage notice. She wanted to believe that everything would be all right, that no one would hurt a little girl, but she had seen too much of the world to believe her own lies. Even if Stephen didn't hurt Betsy deliberately, he didn't' know how to take care of a child with Betsy's delicate constitution. Anything could happen to her before they caught up with him.

"What in hell is she doing now?" Stephen asked irritably as the train bumped and jerked into the next station.

Bobby had grown tired of watching the kid and was half asleep in his seat. He opened one eye and watched as Betsy handed the conductor a folded sheet of paper. Stephen grabbed it before the man could look at it, and Bobby shrugged and closed his eyes again, wondering why his companion had bothered asking.

The conductor frowned and eyed Stephen suspiciously as he opened the paper, but Stephen ignored him. He should have known the paper would just contain another one of her interminable sketches, but he couldn't take any chances. If she could sign her name, she could write messages asking for help. He folded the scribbling back up again and handed it to the conductor, shrugging and saying, "Kids. You never know what they're up to."

The man still didn't look too happy, but he smiled at the sketch when he opened it. "She said she'd draw me a picture if I gave her my pencil. It's a fair exchange." He patted Betsy on the head and wandered off.

The child looked completely angelic sitting there, her hands folded in her lap and her smile innocent. Stephen didn't remember much about Janice when she was young, but he remembered himself well enough. The little brat was up to something.

The train chugged to a halt. Grabbing Betsy's hand, Stephen jerked her from the seat and headed for the door. His plans didn't count on anybody finding them until he had what he wanted. The Mulloneys owed him, and he meant for them to pay.

It took Bobby a moment before he realized they were getting off. He staggered to his feet and followed, protesting, "I thought we were going to San Antonio. What in hell are you doing?"

"Losing anybody who tries to follow," Stephen replied curtly, half dragging the child by the hand across the station platform to the street.

"I thought you said nobody would follow." Bobby took a hasty swig from his flask. He liked things to be easy. He didn't like the thought of Peter Mulloney coming after him with a gun. "I thought you said there wasn't anybody there but the woman, and she can't ride."

"She got up there somehow. She'll find some way to get down. We're not taking any chances." Stephen reached the porch of the dilapidated hotel across the street. He halted and shook Betsy's arm until she looked up at him with that wide-eyed innocent gaze he was coming to despise. "Not a word out of you. If I hear you talking to another soul, I'll slap you until your ears ring. Do you understand me?"

Betsy had never been slapped in her life. She continued staring at him as if he were an alien from another planet. He gave her a disgruntled look and pulled her into the hotel lobby.

Once the three of them were upstairs and behind closed doors, Stephen pulled out the meager contents of his pocket and handed a bill to Bobby. "Go buy some boy's clothes that look like her size," he commanded. "And don't you dare spend any of that on whiskey or I'll break the bottle over your head. If you want your share of the proceeds, you're going to have to start holding up your end of this deal."

Bobby looked at the bill, then at Betsy. Even half-drunk Bobby could tell there was nothing boyish about the kid. He had serious doubts about this whole affair. He was ready to go back home. Ellen might be a pain sometimes, but she didn't nag and complain like this bastard did, and she provided certain comforts he wasn't likely to find on the trail. And if this idiot thought he would hide the kid by putting boys' clothes on her, he was a little cracked in the brainpan.

"She don't look like no boy," he tried to offer.

Stephen reached in his pocket and opened the folding knife he kept there. "She will when I get done with her."

Before either of his companions knew what he would do, he grabbed a handful of Betsy's newly grown curls and hacked them off.

# Thirty-Six

B y the time the wagons reached Gage the next day, Peter's fever had returned full strength. Janice sat beside him in the wagon bed and tried to get water down him, but he shoved her hands away more often than not.

Evie tried to offer help, but Janice couldn't relax her silent vigil. Her daughter had been stolen by a madman and now fever tried to steal her husband. She was all but helpless in both cases, but she didn't intend to give up. Setting her lips grimly, she lifted Peter's head and brought the canteen of water back to his mouth.

Daniel ran from the town's biggest hotel and climbed into the wagon bed. "I've got you a room. Let's get him out of here."

Tyler and Manuel joined him, and between the three of them, they half carried, half hauled Peter through the hotel and up the stairs, Janice following close behind.

A cry from the lobby below caused her to look around.

"Mrs. Mulloney!" Sherman Townsend stood in the front door, staring up at her.

Evie caught her elbow and whispered, "Do you know that man?"

"He's Peter's partner. He came looking for a physician." Picking up her skirts, Janice hastened back down the stairs. "Did you find a doctor?" she asked before she was halfway across the room.

Townsend shook his head. "I've asked all over creation. I rode to Silver City first, but that one's gone to San Francisco. I took a chance and came here instead of over to Lordsburg, but the man here got shot in a brawl just last week. I was thinking about going on over to Lordsburg. That'd be easier than El Paso. I tried telegraphing you. Didn't you get the message?"

Janice shook her head. "The telegraph operator left to visit his mama a few days ago, Henry told us." With fear clutching her heart, she looked up at the rough man who had stood beside Peter all these months. "I'll look after Peter myself, but my little girl has been stolen. You haven't seen any little girls around here who look like her, have you?" She didn't even notice the admission she had made. Neither did the man in front of her. Beside her, Evie blinked but said nothing.

Townsend crumpled his hat and stared down at her, shocked. "Stolen? Who in hell would steal a kid?" Then a look of bitter knowledge crossed his face. "Someone heard about the gold?"

Janice shook her head. "No, I don't think so. It's personal." Then realizing they had left everything this man had worked for these last months in an unprotected shack, she motioned for him to bend over. When he did so, she whispered in his ear. "The sacks are behind the rocks in the fireplace." When he nodded and straightened, she added honestly, "I had to borrow some to get down here."

He looked more worried than relieved. "Tell me what I can do to help find your little girl."

Evie apparently decided it was time for her to step in. She caught the big man's arm and led him toward the stairs. "Come upstairs with us. We're going to have a council of war. The more heads, the better."

Janice tagged after them, sick to her stomach. She didn't see how anybody could miss seeing Betsy if she'd been here. It wasn't exactly as if a town like this teemed with children. What if Stephen hadn't come this way? Where else would he go?

She listened and tended to Peter while the others talked. Manuel ran to fetch the sheriff at one point. Daniel went out to talk to the local telegraph operator. Evie sketched Betsy's likeness on dozens of sheets of paper as the men argued. Peter woke long enough to take some broth and insist that wires be sent to every station along the Southern Pacific line, both east and west. The expense would be enormous, but even Townsend didn't object when Peter ordered Janice to hand over what gold she still carried.

Tyler and Daniel had fits, but they couldn't argue for long with an unconscious man. Peter slipped back into delirium not long after, and Evie chased them out of the room. Daniel prepared to catch the evening train going east to post Evie's sketches at those stations. Townsend offered to catch the next westbound train. Not trusting the sheriff to do a thorough job. Tyler set out to question everyone in town, leaving Manuel to look after the women.

They spent an uneasy night. Janice refused Evie's help and stayed beside Peter, feeding him when he woke, sleeping beside him when she could. She heard Tyler wander in sometime after midnight. She figured if he had good news, he would stop to tell her, but he didn't stop. Manuel took a blanket and slept outside their door, taking his position as guard and messenger seriously. Janice encouraged him to find a bed, but he refused, and if she would admit it, his presence reassured her. This wasn't exactly a quiet town on a Saturday night.

She wasn't sleeping very soundly at dawn when Peter woke. She felt the heat of his skin as he pulled her closer, and she stiffened, but he did no more than hold her.

"Is there any news?" were the first words he spoke.

"None," she muttered worriedly. It was good to have Peter's arms around her, but she couldn't relax while a man with no pride or morals hauled Betsy around the countryside.

Peter was silent for a while. Finally, he said, "I let you down, didn't I? I meant to take care of you so you would never have to worry again."

"You couldn't have foreseen this." It might be easier if she could blame somebody, but she couldn't. She had learned long ago that life took strange twists and turns and one couldn't predict them. She could only build fortresses against those things she knew about. She'd thought marrying Peter for money would give her added protection. Maybe it would in some ways, but not the ways that counted.

"I could have forgotten the damned mountain and taken you back to Ohio. I could have been with you."

She'd had those thoughts, but they were empty ones. She shook her head. "And made it easier for Stephen to find us?"

He kissed her nape. His lips were dry and hot, but she shivered at the touch.

"A man could learn to love a woman like you real easily," he murmured.

"A woman who marries for money?" she asked scornfully.

"A woman who marries for love. You married for Betsy, didn't you?" His hand stroked her breast lightly through the nightgown.

She nodded at the truth of that. Everything she had ever done for ten years had been for Betsy. Tears welled in her eyes, but she wouldn't give in to them.

"We'll find her."

He climbed out of bed before she could protest. Janice sat up and stared as Peter reached for his clothes. His clean clothes had gone with the horse and his saddlebags. He could only put on the ones he'd been wearing for nearly a week. They were stained and crumpled and beyond repair, but he didn't even seem to notice. She could remember a time when he dressed in silk shirts and frock coats. She shook her head. That wasn't the same man.

The man standing there now was unshaven. His unruly dark curls hung around his shirt collar. She could see the dark hairs on his chest above the open top button of his shirt, something she would never have seen back in Ohio. She didn't think the fever had completely left him, but instead of being pale, his face was dark and weathered from overexposure to the sun and wind. This man would never fit in a fancy department store back East.

That's when Janice knew she loved him. Her heart ached as she watched Peter pull on the holster he had been wearing when he fell from the horse. She loved him beyond all sense and reason, and he was going to kill himself looking for her daughter. He did this for her, despite the fact that he couldn't really love her, that she had married him for money, that she had lied to him, that she'd had a child that wasn't his.

She opened her mouth to tell him, but a knock pounded on the door.

"Janice, are you awake? I've brought breakfast."

Evie. Sighing, Janice threw her legs over the side of the bed and reached for her dress. Peter threw open the door and gestured for her to come in. Evie eyed him doubtfully for a minute, then brushed by him to deposit the tray on a table.

"You look like hell, Peter Mulloney. If you're going to take after Daniel and play at being a hero, I'm going to help Janice strap you to the bed."

Peter didn't waste time in answering. He bent over and kissed Janice on the forehead and walked out. She didn't have the strength to throw the pillow after him .

Evie looked at Janice with concern. "Where does he think he's going?"

Janice ran her hand through her hair and found it as tangled as she had feared. "After Betsy," she replied absently. She was too dizzy with new knowledge and lack of sleep to seek any other explanation.

Peter came back within a few hours, half dragging a terrified woman in his wake. Looking almost as haggard as Peter but wearing clean clothes, Tyler was already there to report his latest failure. They all looked up as Peter barged in.

"Show them the sketch," he ordered the trembling woman as he released her.

She looked frantic as she saw the circle of anxious faces, but she pulled a piece of crumpled paper from her pocket. "She gave it to me," she whispered. "I didn't do nothin'."

Janice took the paper with shaking fingers. Carefully she unfolded the creases and smoothed it out on the table. The face on the paper was unmistakable. The signature beneath it was certain proof. She gave a sigh of relief and murmured, "Stephen."

Tyler grabbed the paper, studied it, then passed it to Evie. "That's him, all right. That's the one who came nosing around sometime back." He turned a sharp eye to the waitress. "How long ago did they come through?"

Somewhat reassured now that she was surrounded by seemingly sensible people instead of being mauled by a madman, the woman shrugged. "Came in Friday night, I reckon. She gave me that yestiday mornin'."

Janice looked up at her anxiously. "How did she look? Was she all right? Were they treating her right? Did she say anything at all?"

The woman's face softened. "She your'n? She's a real pretty gal. Kinda quiet. The bastard with her didn't give me no tip, but she gave me the picture. I thought it was right fine work."

Evie caught Janice's hand and hushed her while the men continued the questioning. Other than the fact that Stephen apparently meant to catch the morning train, they couldn't get anything else of use from her.

Tyler gave the woman some coins and sent her on her way while Peter searched through the stack of papers accumulating on the table. "Where's that train schedule?" he demanded, scattering papers left and right.

Evie pulled it out from the bottom of the stack and handed it to him, then sat down to begin copying Betsy's sketch.

"Saturday morning. That's the El Paso train. Saturday's the only day it comes through twice. Daniel is fifteen hours behind him. There's no train out today." Peter cursed, flung the schedule back to the table, and started for the door.

Tyler grabbed his arm and jerked him up against the wall. "Where the hell do you think you're going?"

"After Betsy." Peter wrenched his arm free, shoved past Tyler, and started for the door again.

Janice had already placed herself in front of it. "How are you going to do that?" she demanded. "You just said there's no train out today."

"I'll buy a damned horse. You don't think I'm going to sit here and wait for the villain to send us love notes, do you?"

"Daniel's right behind him. They've got to get off somewhere. He'll wire us when they do." Tyler didn't get between husband and wife but stood behind Peter, waiting to grab him if he made another move toward the door.

"He could miss them. He could get off at the wrong stop and have to wait who knows how long for the next train. Anything could happen. I've got to do it myself."

Janice sighed and crossed her arms across her chest. "That's what we've been doing all our lives, Peter. We've been doing everything ourselves. It's hard. Can't we ask for a little help just this once?" She wanted to touch his cheek, feel his forehead, but she didn't dare call attention to his weakness in front of their friends. "Please?" was all she dared say. The thought of losing Peter terrified her as much as the thought of losing Betsy.

Peter stared into her frightened face. She wasn't one to beg easily. He shook his head in doubt. "I can't sit here, Janice. I've got to go after her."

From behind him, Tyler replied, "I'll go, but somebody's got to stay here and look after Evie. She's likely to decide to take a helium balloon or some other nonsense otherwise. And someone's got to take the wires. The telegraph operator means to intercept any going to Butte as well as those from Daniel and Townsend. Somebody's got to be here to get them. Daniel should be checking in before long."

Peter hesitated, and Janice held out a hand to him. "Please, Peter. You've got to get your strength back. Let Tyler and Daniel do the running around. You can keep them going in the right direction. I'll need you with me when they find her. We can go together."

Another knock pounded at the door. Before Janice could move, Manuel shoved it open. Excitement danced on his face as he saw everyone was present.

"She took the El Paso train yesterday morning!" He waved another copy of the train schedule. "She drew a picture of Fairweather on the board and circled the time. I've ordered my horse brought around."

Young and brimming with energy, he filled the room with his eagerness and impatience. Peter gave Janice a wry look.

"There isn't much point in all of us going, is there?" he admitted painfully.

Janice caught his arm in relief. "Not yet. Not until we know where they are. Then we can go get them. I need you here, Peter. What would I do if Daniel wires he's lost them?"

Peter studied her eyes with wonder. No one had ever needed him before, but he could see the very real need in her eyes right now. Her fingers clung to his arm, afraid to let him go. His courageous schoolmarm was terrified and doing her best not to show it. Only he could guess how close she was to hysteria. It was there behind her eyes, the empty terror she must have suffered through a thousand nights. She needed him to help her get through these next few days.

Peter turned and gave Tyler a curt nod, sending the older man to follow Manuel. Men like Tyler were meant to act without thinking. Brought up in the civilized East, Peter had learned to think first, act later. It was time for him to do what he did best.

By the time Tyler and Manuel were prepared for their journey, Peter had Evie's copy of Betsy's sketch, a train schedule, and a list of checkpoints and check-in times ready. If they missed any one of the times, he would be on the next train out. And if they didn't find word waiting for them when they arrived, they could assume he'd heard from Stephen and was on his way.

It was a crude plan, but it would have to work. Once Stephen reached El Paso, he could take either of two trains, and their work would double. Time was already against them.

# Thirty-Seven

Peter came in carrying the third telegram of the morning. He handed it wearily to the women waiting for him. "It's from Daniel. There's a conductor who remembers seeing them get off at El Paso. Nobody remembers seeing them after that."

"Shouldn't we be hearing from the kidnapper by now? Shouldn't he be asking for ransom?" Evie set aside her constant sketching to ask what Janice was too worried to think of.

"He'll want to hole up somewhere where he figures we won't be able to find him first." Peter stared glumly out the hotel window. "It would be stupid of him to choose El Paso. He's better off taking one of the lines out of there and losing himself somewhere in Texas. It's going to take us days to figure out which train he took as it is. By the time we know if he headed for San Antonio or Fort Worth, he could have hidden himself anywhere."

Evie began gathering up her sketches. "Well, Tyler and Manuel are there now to help Daniel, and Townsend says he's coming in on the evening train. I say we leave him here to forward messages. You're going to need as many hands as you can get in El Paso."

Janice was off the bed and reaching for her bags before the final words left Evie's mouth. Peter turned and watched, but made no attempt to halt them. He had every intention of going to El Paso himself. It probably wasn't wise to leave the women behind.

They met Townsend at the station, informed him of his

new position as message coordinator, and took the same train heading east.

They showed Evie's sketches of Betsy and the two kidnappers to everyone they met. A salesman remembered seeing them somewhere but couldn't remember where. One of the boys selling newspapers remembered Betsy distinctly, but the "uncle" traveling with her hadn't let her talk to him. A conductor frowned and thought he'd seen one of the men take the Fort Worth train, but he didn't remember a little girl.

By the time they reached El Paso, they were exhausted and still didn't have any reliable information on which to proceed. A telegram waited for them from Townsend informing them that Daniel had taken the Fort Worth train on the basis of a sighting of Fairweather. They already knew Tyler and Manuel had arrived and had rooms at the hotel. Peter hired a porter to help with their baggage and they set out to join the others at the hotel.

By the time Evie had gone off to join Tyler, and Peter had found them a room, Janice was too depressed to do more than remove her mantle and lie down on the bed. The ceiling above her was cracked and chips of paint or plaster threatened to fall on the bed. The roof probably leaked when it rained.

Peter dropped their bags and came to sit down on the bed beside her. He stroked her brow and brushed away straying strands of fine hair. "We'll find her, Jenny, I promise. He just doesn't know yet that he hasn't got a chance."

There was such reassurance in his voice that Janice closed her eyes and let it seep down inside her. She wanted to believe. She needed to believe. Surely Stephen didn't mean to keep Betsy. He couldn't. She just had to be patient and place her confidence in Peter and his family.

She opened her eyes slowly to gaze upon her husband. Lines of exhaustion creased Peter's brow and made dents beside his mouth. He hadn't been given a chance to regain any of the weight he'd lost in the mountains. She

feared fever still lingered in the glitter of his eyes, but determination flared there too. Despite his illness, he was a
strong man. She could see it in the set of his shoulders
and the jut of his jaw. He wasn't bent with defeat. He
grew stronger to meet the challenge.

She smiled faintly and stroked his jaw. "I know you'll
find her, Peter. It's just so hard to worry every minute."

He bent and kissed her lips lightly. "I know I can't
keep you from worrying, but let me share the burden. The
load is lighter if we share."

She held out her arms to him, and he lay down beside
her. The chemistry between them was muted, buried beneath exhaustion and worry. What they had to offer each
other now was different—the comfort of understanding
and sharing and a common goal. They fell asleep that
way, fully clothed and in each other's arms.

When they woke with the first light of dawn, Peter
brushed a kiss across Jancie's cheek and swung out of
bed as if he'd never slept. "I'm going to scour the train
station. Betsy's been pretty good about leaving clues.
There has to be something there the others have over-
looked."

"I don't want to stay behind doing nothing. What can
I do?" Janice climbed from the bed and opened her bag to
find the brush Peter had bought for her in Gage.

"Talk to the women who work around the station.
There's a Harvey's restaurant and hotel. I don't think
Stephen would have taken her there, but they might have
seen her coming or going. Tyler and Manuel need to take
the posters over to some of the cheaper hotels. I'll go
over and check to see where they've already looked."

Peter had purchased a clean set of clothes for himself
in Gage, but he'd been wearing them for days. The blue
denims were holding up fairly well, but his black cotton
was wrinkled and covered with lint from the bed. He
didn't even seem to notice. His mind was making lists
and organizing actions and setting priorities. Janice could
practically see the wheels turning. This was the man who
had managed one of the largest enterprises in Ohio. She

had known it intellectually; she could see it for herself now.

"I'll be ready in a minute. Come back and get me after you've talked to Tyler."

Peter gave her a nod and walked out without a kiss or a word of comfort. Janice didn't mind in the least. She knew where his mind was, and she had no objection to taking second place to the search for Betsy. He would probably always have his mind elsewhere, except when they were in bed. She would reap the benefits from all that concentration then.

She was coming to know Peter much better than she had ever expected, and she liked what she was discovering. She couldn't remember ever truly liking a man before. She'd had a passion for Stephen, but she'd never known him well enough to like him. She'd worked with Jason, had even understood him and considered marrying him, but she couldn't say she particularly liked him. He was a man's man and had paid her little heed, like most men she knew. Peter was different.

It was good to know that she could like the man she loved. Love was an unreasonable emotion that she was having difficulty dealing with. She'd struggled with her love for Betsy for years until she had finally come to accept it as the gift it was. She couldn't be so certain that loving Peter would be a gift. For the moment, it kept her in constant turmoil.

But she understood action and took orders well. Under Peter's direction, they fanned out to cover different territories. He had calculated the most likely time of Betsy's arrival in El Paso and the next trains leaving. They concentrated on finding people who had worked around the train station during those hours and at the hotels between those hours. El Paso wasn't so large that they couldn't find all of them sooner or later.

Peter first recognized the significance of the sketch of a little boy tacked to a dark corner inside the ticket office. Since Daniel and Tyler had already thoroughly questioned the ticket clerk, he was growing a little testy. Peter desperately tried to think of some new angle from which to approach him when his wandering gaze fell on the piece of paper blowing idly in the breeze.

He pointed at the partially concealed drawing. "Is that artwork?"

The clerk looked baffled and followed his finger. He shrugged and pulled the paper off the wall, handing it to Peter. "Kid stuff, looks to me. Other fella who works here must of stuck it here. Mean something to you?"

Peter smoothed the paper flat and gave a prayer of thanks. The angelic eyes of Betsy smiled back at him from beneath the disreputable brim of an overlarge felt hat. The girl had talent. He'd see that she had the best art teachers money could buy. He practically kissed the paper, but the clerk was already looking at him oddly.

"Tell me how to find the other man who works here," he demanded, passing a folded bill to the suspicious clerk.

"He's off visiting in Las Cruces. He'll be back in tomorrow." The clerk slipped the money into his pocket and went back to work.

Peter clenched his teeth in frustration and stalked down the street to the restaurant where he'd left Janice. The other ticket clerk had to have seen Betsy. He'd know what train they took. It would take as much time to get to Las Cruces and back as it would to wait for him to come back here. They were losing too much time.

Janice was engaged in conversation with an attractive waitress, but she looked up the moment Peter approached. She had the sketches of Betsy and her kidnappers spread out on the table in front of her, but the waitress was shaking her head. Peter threw down the new sketch.

Janice studied it and shook her head. "Poor Betsy. She was just getting her curls back. He must have cut them all off again. Did he really think he could disguise her as a boy?"

The waitress picked the sketch up and studied it. "She's pretty even under that awful hat." She frowned at her own words and called over her shoulder, "Leilah!

Come here and look at this. Didn't you tell me you'd seen the prettiest little boy in here the other day?"

A second waitress sauntered up, giving Peter an experienced look before turning her attention to the sketch. She raked her fingers through her long red hair and nodded. "Cute kid. He drew me a cartoon while they were eating." She glanced speculatively up at Peter. "He yours?"

"She's ours." Peter placed a calming hand on Janice's shoulder and reached for the other sketches. "Were these the men with her?"

The redhead shrugged. "The one could be. There was just the two of them. He wasn't bad-looking, but he had a surly temper."

Janice wrapped her fingers around Peter's. "The cartoon? Do you still have it?"

The woman grinned. "Yeah. It was real cute. I hung it up back in the kitchen. I'll go get it."

A train pulled into the station and the restaurant manager began to look a little nervous as his waitresses gathered around the one table while ignoring the others. They passed the sketches back and forth, trying to remember the day the cute little boy had been in. Peter placed both hands on Janice's shoulders and rubbed while listening to every word said for any clue that might be helpful.

The redhead returned with a sketch drawn on the blank side of a paper menu. Janice spread it out on the table and Peter studied it from over her shoulder. It showed a bull sitting at a table across from a little heifer in a restaurant similar to the one they were in. A cattle train was pulling into the station that could be seen through the window beside them.

Peter didn't see the point of the cartoon until the waitress leaned over and showed him the pieces of paper sticking out from under the rumps of the strange patrons.

"See? Those are our menus they're sitting on. She said it shows we've got beef on the menu. Isn't that the greatest thing you ever saw?"

Beef on the menu. Surely the child wasn't developing

a warped sense of humor at this late date. Every sketch she'd left had been a clue. Stephen obviously kept an eye on her so she didn't dare write anything. What was she trying to say? Peter picked the paper up to study it closer.

Cattle train. Beef. Idly, he flipped the menu over. The word "beef" was circled under "roast beef sandwich." Peter's stomach clenched. He scanned the menu. Various numbers were circled as if randomly. If they meant what he thought they meant, the damned kid was as clever as her mother.

He peeled another bill off the roll Daniel had given him. "I think Betsy may have meant this as a message to us. I'll have her send you a new one as soon as we find her, but we'd like to keep this if you don't mind."

He didn't give her a chance to argue, not that she meant to argue after pocketing the cash. Peter caught Janice's elbow and helped her to her feet, well aware that she watched him with renewed hope. She stayed silent until they reached the street.

"What does it mean? That they took a cattle train?" She hurried to keep up with his long strides.

"Maybe. I want to get back and compare these numbers to the train schedules. There's not too much cattle being shipped through here. I can't imagine them taking a cattle car."

Seeing Tyler heading down the street, Peter flagged him to hurry. He waved and veered away to fetch Evie. Within minutes, they were all in the hotel room studying the sketch and the menu. Manuel ran in to join them not long after.

"We need to be looking for people carrying pencils. Betsy seems to be improving the kind she's using at each stop," Evie commented wryly as she passed the sketch back to Peter.

"I'll sew one in all her petticoats as soon as we get her back," Janice promised vehemently.

Peter squeezed her hand and began copying the circled numbers from the menu onto another sheet of paper. He ran his finger up and down the train schedules looking for corresponding sequences. He stabbed at a train number and circled it, then drew a line beneath the times and destinations listed after it.

Looking over his shoulder, Janice breathed softly, "Train number 242, arrives Langtry at 2:35."

"Langtry! Hell," Manuel exclaimed in disgust. "There isn't anything out there but dust and desperadoes."

Tyler gave him a look that should have killed. "Shut up, Rodriguez. You're not helping any."

Manuel reddened beneath his deep bronze and gave Janice an apologetic look. "Sorry, Jenny. I was just surprised, that's all. They've got law of a sorts out there now. Shouldn't be hard at all finding a pretty little thing like Betsy there."

A knock at the door intruded, and Tyler answered it, handing the messenger a sizable tip for the telegram he carried. Everyone sat silently waiting as he read it.

He passed it to Peter. "Daniel found a conductor who remembers Bobby Fairweather getting off at Fort Worth. He didn't see Betsy or Stephen."

Peter glanced over the telegram, then back to Manuel. "You know Fairweather better than Daniel. If he knows where Stephen's headed, we're going to have to shake it out of him. You can get the Hardings to help out, can't you?"

Manuel took the telegram, folded it, and put it in his pocket. "I'll take the next train to Fort Worth. Wire ahead to tell Jason I'm coming. He can be looking out for Fairweather and hold him for me if he shows up."

"Thanks." Peter handed over enough cash to cover the ticket and expenses. He would be in debt to Daniel for a thousand years, but he didn't care any longer. The money was pointless while Janice clung to a cliff of fears. He knew they'd find Betsy one way or another, but he wouldn't leave Betsy or her mother hanging on that cliff for long if pieces of green paper could get them off faster.

"I'll send a wire to Townsend telling him where we're going." Tyler spun on his heel and walked out. Evie didn't have to be given instructions; she followed close behind, heading for their room to pack their bags.

Peter stood up and took Janice in his arms, hugging her close. The only way he would ever be able to pay his debts would be to return to Ohio when this was all over, but he didn't tell her that. He already knew how she felt about Ohio.

He didn't think he could bear to part with her, but he couldn't ask her to go back where she would be unhappy. He loved her too much for that.

If he had to leave her to make her happy, he would.

Peter covered Janice's mouth with his and drank deeply of the nourishment he needed to live. Going to Ohio without her would be like dying and going to hell, but he could do it. He'd promised to take care of her, and he was a man of his word if he was nothing else.

# Thirty-Eight

The train wailed through the desert night. Janice clung to the hand holding hers. She knew Peter was as awake as she was, but they sat silently, pretending to sleep.

"Please, God, stay with her," she prayed, her lips barely moving. As if he had intercepted the prayer, Peter squeezed her hand. It would be all right. It had to be.

"They must have dozens of cattle ranches out there," she murmured, continuing an earlier argument as if it had never ended.

"The porter told us the train Stephen took had a bull on it destined for the Crooked R. We'll start there," Peter recited patiently. "That could be why Betsy drew bulls in the cartoon."

Starting wasn't enough. She wanted to talk about ending. Janice bit her lip. Everyone was more than kind and doing everything within their power. She couldn't fault them for anything. But she'd been walking around with her stomach tied in knots for nearly a week now, and she was having difficulty being patient.

Langtry was just a little cow town. Surely somebody had seen Betsy—if they'd read the clue right. If Stephen had taken the train he told Betsy he was taking. If he didn't change his mind.

She could think of a dozen more "ifs," but she tried not to. Betsy was there and they were going to find her.

Laughter erupted among the traveling performers at the front of the car. They'd been sharing a bottle of whiskey and playing cards since leaving El Paso, and the noise wasn't conducive to sleep. Tyler and Evie had joined them briefly earlier, but they'd gone off to find some rest. That left Peter and Janice to be distracted by their antics. At the moment a man in a red clown wig and no face paint was honking his rubber nose and declaiming Shakespeare. Janice smiled slightly at the sight and curled up against Peter's shoulder to rest.

A telegram awaited them when they reached the nearly deserted train station at Langtry. Amid the clamor of the performers being forcibly evicted from the train, Peter leaned against the board wall and tore the message open, scanned it, and handed it wordlessly to Janice.

The wire from Stephen had finally arrived. Townsend forwarded the message in its entirety. Stephen wanted ten thousand dollars delivered to a post office box in San Antonio. He'd leave Betsy at an unspecified location after he received it—if he wasn't followed. If anyone followed him, they'd never see Betsy again.

Janice handed the paper to Tyler and curled into Peter's arms. Ten thousand dollars. Stephen had to be insane.

Tyler cursed softly and handed the telegram back. "What do you want us to do, Mulloney? Daniel and I can scrape together the cash by this time next week, I reckon."

"We're not giving him a dime," Peter answered firmly. "Let's find a place to stay first. Evie needs to make some more sketches so we can hand out new posters. Then the two of you might go to San Antonio and see what you can find out from that end. We'll discuss it in the morning."

The raucous argument behind them escalated when the circus car was unhitched from the rest of the train and left abandoned on a side rail. Never having seen a circus before, Janice glanced over her shoulder to get one last glimpse of the performers. There were women as well as men, and most of them seemed quite drunk. Losing interest, she quietly followed the others to the nearest hotel.

If she'd thought the hotel in El Paso shabby, this one could be called little more than a shack. They dipped pitchers of water from a barrel to take to their rooms for washing and discovered the mattresses too bug-infested to sleep on. Janice tried to imagine what horrendous place Betsy could be sleeping in now, but she couldn't picture anything worse than this.

Peter spread Janice's mantle on the floor for a bed and used his carpetbag for a pillow. When they were curled together in the folds of cloth, he whispered, "I'm sorry, Jenny. I meant for you to have the best of everything. I wish I could go back to last spring and undo it all."

Janice lay quietly in his arms, listening to his heart thump against her breast. "I don't," she whispered, and she knew that it was true. She may have been through several kinds of hell these last months, but she'd seen the pinnacles of heaven too. For the first time in years, she felt fully alive.

Peter's arms closed tighter around her, and she smiled. He would find Betsy, she knew. Her husband was a much smarter man than Stephen.

Evie spent the better part of the next day producing more sketches of Betsy in boy's gear. If Betsy was nearby, it didn't seem wise to announce their presence to Stephen by circulating the posters around town, but Peter wanted them available if needed.

He and Tyler separated and circumspectly made the rounds of saloons and stores, listening to gossip and asking general questions that would not directly implicate their interest in the Crooked R. Left to her own devices in a less-than-respectable town, Janice donned her schoolmarm disguise and took up tatting on the lone wooden chair in the hotel lobby. Even dressed as an old maid, she attracted interest.

That was how she came to meet the circus people.

She had watched their comings and goings from the hotel window just as she kept a careful eye on everyone else who passed her perch. It was easy to identify the circus folk, and she watched them only out of curiosity. The men who inspected her, ejecting tobacco juice into a nearby spittoon before walking on by, she watched for a different reason. Any one of them could know where Betsy was hidden. She thought if she studied them long enough, she could read their guilt in their faces.

Several of them stopped and tried to engage her interest, but Janice had long ago learned the tactic of ignoring men. Most of them wandered on, but one didn't. He leaned over and removed her spectacles instead. Janice gave a screech of outrage and grabbed for her glasses, but the bully held them out of reach.

"Give me a kiss, missy, and I'll give them back."

"I'd sooner kiss a jackass. If you don't return my glasses, I'll call my husband." Recovering from her surprise, Janice retreated behind her facade of propriety. Returning her tatting to her bag, she gathered up her skirts and prepared to leave. The bully stood too close to get around him.

"I believe the lady has expressed her disinterest, sir. I'd suggest you return her property and remove yourself from her path." A gold-knobbed cane tapped insistently on the cowboy's shoulder.

Snarling, the man swung around, his arm raising a clenched fist. With a cry of fury, Janice grabbed his upraised arm while the intruder brought his ebony cane down over the wrist clenching the spectacles. Attacked on both sides, the man howled in anger. He dropped the glasses but attempted to swing his fist with Janice still clinging to it.

Her caped rescuer laughed and stabbed the head of his cane at a particularly sensitive portion of his assailants anatomy. The man bent over immediately with a howl more of anguish than anger this time. Janice released his arm and grabbed her spectacles from the floor, retreating quickly from the injured man's vicinity.

"Thank you, sir," she managed to murmur as she backed toward the hotel door. The man holding his privates and howling looked ready for murder, and she wished to be out of his reach when he recovered.

"It was my pleasure, madam," the courtly old man responded. "If I may, I'd like to suggest that we find some other place to exchange pleasantries. I dislike having to break my last walking stick over the head of one unappreciative of my sacrifice." He held out an arm garbed in a frock coat with elbows polished from wear.

Janice accepted and they fled the lobby.

"If your esteemed husband is within walking distance, might I suggest we locate him?" the stranger offered gallantly.

"My sentiments exactly. Might I have the honor of knowing to whom I speak so I may introduce you properly?" Janice answered him in the same exaggerated formality he used.

He laughed in appreciation. "Very good, my dear. You are a natural mimic. You may introduce me as Theodophilus Charlemagne, proprietor of The Great Hammond's Traveling Circus and Magic Show."

"Very well. I am Janice Mulloney. It's a pleasure meeting you, Mr. Charlemagne." Her eyes twinkled at the ridiculous name but she refrained on commenting upon its history.

Several doors down, Peter slammed through the swinging doors of a saloon and came running in their direction. Beside him a small boy in short pants tried to keep up. When Peter saw Janice, he slowed his pace to better observe her companion.

"I heard there was trouble," he said cautiously, holding out his hand to his wife and eyeing the stranger in his incongruous black cape and straggling gray hair.

Theodophilus shook his shaggy head at the small boy jumping up and down with energy and excitement. "The lad is a trifle impetuous, I fear, although he puts two and two together very well. He not only thought to save my frail neck, but to obtain a quarter or two for his efforts. Clever, Milo, but no cigar. Get on back to your mother, now."

Almost managing a grin, Peter flipped the child a coin before he ran off, then turned his attention back to Janice, who was now clinging to his elbow. "Are you all right?"

"Very well, thank you, thanks to Mr. Charlemagne. I think I should like to own one of those very handy walking sticks."

Theodophilus lifted the cane to his head in salute. "You were quite fierce on your own, madam. I could never have performed so well without your aid."

By the time Tyler caught up with them, the episode had been thoroughly reviewed, reenacted, and rehashed, and had to be repeated for his benefit. The tale became much funnier with each retelling, until even Janice was learning to smile at the older man's theatrics.

"Ahh, she does smile!" he exclaimed upon noting the curve of her lip. "I feared the sun had gone into permanent eclipse."

Tyler laughed and clapped the old man on the back as he introduced him to Evie, but the main topic on their minds quickly replaced their momentary mirth. As Tyler and Peter exchanged notes, the circus proprietor audaciously eavesdropped. When Peter concluded that Tyler and Evie would have to go to San Antonio to cover all possibilities, Theodophilus frowned in thought.

"Perhaps I may be of some assistance," he offered during a lull in the conversation. At the instant interest of his companions, he coughed lightly. "I happen to be . . . ahem . . . a trifle financially strapped after a poor season among the heathens. If I put the multitude of talents of my many performers at your assistance, perhaps we might come to a mutually beneficial arrangement."

Evie and Tyler grinned at the old fraud's blatant appeal, but Peter's brow drew down in thought. As Janice listened in astonishment, Peter arranged for half the circus performers to follow Tyler and Evie into San Antonio for the price of their train fare. In exchange, they were to canvas the town with posters of Betsy. Within minutes, with the help of the circus proprietor, Peter had arranged a search they could never have accomplished on their own.

Another day was lost by the time the train to San Antonio pulled into the station. Janice watched with worry as Tyler and Evie entered the train with the throng of crazily appareled performers. The atmosphere of the travelers was that suitable for a circus. They laughed and sang and every so often one of them would come up and hug Janice to reassure her all would be well. Betsy's story had spread among them with rapidity, and they were buoyed with hope for their gallant mission. Janice only wished she could have their confidence.

Theodophilus remained behind with the rest of his merry band. They surrounded Peter and Janice as the train pulled from the station, waving and shouting encouragement and promises to see each other soon. When the train rattled out of sight, the old man banged his cane against the wooden platform and stared at his new employer.

"Well, Mr. Mulloney, it's time you and your charming wife joined the circus."

# Thirty-Nine

"Word is the Crooked R just received a bull and some visitors. They're not a social lot out there, so no one knows exactly who the newcomers are." Theodophilus sent Janice a concerned look and managed to indicate to Peter that he had more to say but he didn't wish to say it in front of Janice.

Peter glanced to his wife who was ostensibly mending one of his shirts. "Janice, do you think they've got any more of that coffee downstairs?"

She didn't look up from what she was doing. "You didn't drink the first cup. And if I don't hear what Mr. Charlemagne has to say now, I'll just pry it out of one of you later. You might as well save yourself the trouble of repeating it."

Peter grimaced but leaned his chair back so he could touch Janice's hand. She gave him a quick, untranslatable look, but the understanding flowed between them. He nodded his head at Theodophilus. "Go ahead. She'll only imagine worse if we don't tell her."

Theodophilus noted the current between the two handsome young people and nodded sagely. "It is good that you both have strength so one does not need to carry the other at times like this. I don't have much else to impart but the fact that the Crooked R was apparently named for more than the brand it uses on cattle. Rumor has it that the owners are cattle rustlers or worse. The men they have working for them are particularly loathed in these parts."

Janice held her back stiff and straight as she jabbed her

needle into the shirt while looking out the window that she faced. "In other words, Stephen would fit right in."

The circus proprietor bowed his head in acknowledgment.

Peter's lips tightened as he contemplated this latest piece of news. A delicate girl like Betsy shouldn't be subjected to the crudities of a household of thieves and kidnappers, providing that was where Stephen had taken her. So far, no other clues had been located. Wherever Betsy was, she hadn't been able to leave a trace behind her.

"I want to go out there." Peter stood up and paced the room restlessly, trying to imagine the best way to obtain his objective.

"You can't just ride in," Janice protested reasonably. "If Stephen was ever in Cutlerville, he could very possibly recognize you."

Peter nodded and fingered the cleft jaw he had just shaved. "I should have let my beard grow out."

Theodophilus eyed Peter's height with doubt. "You would need more disguise than that. If he knows what you look like, he will be watching for you in the face of every stranger." He grinned unexpectedly. "You will need to be someone he recognizes."

Both Janice and Peter turned to stare at him. He chortled at their disbelief.

"Everyone knows the circus is in town. As I said before, it is time you joined the circus. Forgive me if I have guessed wrongly, but this Stephen will not except Peter Mulloney to arrive as, say, a circus clown?"

Peter blinked. Janice gasped. They turned to each other, and their lips began to twitch. "A clown?" they both managed to say at the same time. The clash of words erupted into laughter.

The suggestion had been made easily, but the actuality took a great deal more work. Janice refused to allow Peter to go unless she went with him. The real clowns were called in for their expertise and stayed to create the perfect disguise. More of the performers circulated in and out of the room with ideas and suggestions until Janice felt as if she really were a part of a three-ring circus.

Jugglers practiced while critiquing the makeup as it was applied. Acrobats did handstands to work off kinks from sitting still while sewing together the new costumes. The animal trainers came in stinking of their charges to lend their opinions to the choice of animals to be used for this next performance. And Theodophilus choreographed the entire scene with manic gestures and booming voice until half the town expected the tent to be erected in the hotel lobby.

By the time all the roles had been assigned and two new characters added to the circus, the town never thought of Peter and Janice as anything else but part of the group. They had arrived on the same train and been seen with the proprietor from the first day. None could say any different.

Janice wasn't certain that gave her any more confidence when they finally set out along the dusty road to the Crooked R. Posters announcing the arrival of Hammond's Traveling Circus and Magic Show appeared overnight all over town. The mangy tiger, aging horses, and half-blind elephant kept in the circus car were paraded through the center of town as a prelude to the performers. Without half·the cast, the parade was rather short and uninspired, but out here where the only entertainment was a barroom brawl, no one noticed.

While a bedraggled tent was erected on the outskirts of town, the elephant led a smaller parade into the countryside. Atop the elephant rode a female in the silk finery of a harem dancer. Close inspection might reveal the heavy makeup that darkened light eyebrows and reddened pale lips, but the black shoulder-length wig was undiscernible. From a distance, the image was quite exotic.

Beside the elephant walked a clown in orange wig and white makeup. A bulbous red nose and painted down-turned lips effectively disguised the square jaw and striking profile of the man beneath. A baggy suit and ruffled collar distracted the eye from the clown's height and broad shoulders. The presence of the rambling, wrinkled, and malodorous elephant effectively distracted from any particular notice of anyone anywhere near it.

From her uncertain seat on the rickety platform atop the elephant, Janice scanned the horizon for their destination. Barbed wire to one side of the road indicated the ranch's boundaries. A weathered fence post bearing a tottering plank with the insignia of the Crooked R was the only sign that they were near. The cow path past the sign didn't seem to lead to anywhere.

But at Peter's signal, the animal trainer maneuvered the elephant up the meandering trail. Janice would have felt better if the clowns and acrobats ambling alongside were armed lawmen, but they did the best they could with what they had. They didn't know of a certainty that Betsy was even here.

She knew Theodophilus had a derringer. Peter had his revolvers under his clown suit, accessible through the baggy pockets but certainly not with any great speed. The animal trainer carried a whip and a small pistol. She had a rifle attached to her seat, but she barely knew how to use a shotgun. She was as likely to shoot the good folks as the bad.

She prayed they could do this without violence. Surely Stephen wouldn't harm his own child. He might be desperate, but she couldn't believe he was that desperate. Of course, all this relied on the possibility that he might be here. He could already be in San Antonio for all she knew.

An assortment of weathered shacks and crumbling adobe appeared on the horizon. A corral containing a few idle mares gave proof that someone lived there. As the strange parade gradually wended its way through the sagebrush, a few figures appeared near the corral fence.

Janice scanned each and every one for the small form of her daughter, but she saw no sign of her. Frantically she searched the main house and the outbuildings for any signal that Betsy might be there. They were still too distant to tell.

A scruffy cowboy in leather chaps and unshaven jaw mounted one of the horses and rode out to meet them. Peter signaled for the trainer to keep the elephant moving even when Theodophilus was forced to stop and talk with the man. The cowboy sent them a dirty look, but stopping an elephant wasn't as easy as shooting a coyote. Since the animal sensed water, even the trainer would have been hard-pressed to halt those heavy strides.

Janice could hear Theodophilus expounding on the greatness of his shabby little circus, calling it the opportunity of a lifetime. The cowboy seemed less than impressed, but he wasn't making any dangerous motions. Although Peter had objected, Janice knew her part. She waved a bare arm adorned with tinkling bells and watched in amusement as the man's jaw dropped open.

She had never thought of herself as an object for a man's attentions, but she had learned a little more confidence since Peter had entered her life. He made her feel feminine and beautiful, and she could almost believe that she might distract the rough men in this place while the others searched for Betsy. She certainly seemed to have distracted that one.

Smiling at this first success, she put particular effort into swaying with the elephant's stride. The men still standing around the corral followed her movement with rapt attention. She could hear Peter mutter a pithy curse under his breath, but she was on top of an elephant. There wasn't any way those men could get near her.

The clown persona Peter had donned was a mute one. He scuffed his over large shoes in the dust, creating a cloud that caused the real clown to go into the routine they had worked out. In his bright yellow wig and polka-dot suit, this much smaller clown began a high-pitched jabbering, dancing around Peter with his arms upraised in boxing stance. As expected, the men watching roared at the incongruity of the match. Ignoring his attacker, Peter ambled like a village idiot toward the cluster of buildings ahead.

The elephant plodded straight toward the water trough.

The juggler found branding irons on the porch of one house and began tossing them up in the air and catching them with yells of triumph and much self-congratulation. Gradually the little party spread out throughout the court-yard, and amused at this unexpected entertainment, no one came forward to object.

Janice was the first to see a small white face appear in the unglazed high windows of one of the deteriorating adobe buildings. In a prearranged signal, she used a whis-tle and precariously raised herself on the platform to dance. One of the acrobats lifted a flute to his lips, and Janice waved her hands and arms in time to the music as another of the performers had taught her. She didn't feel particularly graceful as the platform rocked unsteadily be-neath her feet, but the performance attracted plenty of at-tention.

Even the cowboy who had come out to greet them joined the circle of men surrounding the elephant. Below her, the yellow-haired clown turned somersaults and whooped. The red-haired clown slipped off in the direc-tion Janice indicated with the arm dangling tinkling bells.

She had never dreamed of being the center of attrac-tion. She felt conspicuous and awkward as she swayed her hips and tossed her hair. But she felt a surge of tri-umph as Peter disappeared behind the house where she had seen that small face. She had accomplished her part of their appointed task.

The hard part was yet to come. That point was effec-tively brought home when a shout and gunfire erupted somewhere beyond her view. Even the racket made by the flute and her jangling bracelet and the clown's antics couldn't drown the sound of gunfire. Janice felt the grip of panic but continued dancing as if she were stone deaf.

Fascinated, some of the men refused to move. A few of the more cautious ones eased away from the crowd to search the area. At the quiet urging of Theodophilus, the animal trainer had the elephant slurp up more of the water in the trough. Janice began to wiggle in what she hoped was a seductive manner.

To no avail. Furious shouts echoed from the row of buildings, and a comical figure came dancing and prancing from the crumbling adobe shack. Everyone whirled to watch as the mute clown leapt up and down and pointed an indignant finger at a man racing after him. The second clown raced to his rescue, tooting his horn and making a raucous clamor.

Shivering, Janice recognized Stephen. The gun in his hand swung helplessly from the prancing clown to his equally ridiculous accomplices. The acrobat did handstands and feinted at boxing jabs. The juggler threateningly pitched ropes and branding irons and pitchforks through the air. Amid the confusion, a small figure darted from the shadows of the house to the barn near the water trough.

Elation whipped through Janice as she fell to her knees and tugged the elephant's reins as she had been taught. The elephant raised obediently to his hind feet, let out an earsplitting bellow, and promptly sprayed the entire populace with the contents of the water trough.

Screams of both terror and fury roared through the drenched crowd, but thoroughly distracted, none noted as the small figure darted from the barn to the now quiet elephant. Theodophilus moved quickly to lend a hand, the elephant made an elegant bow on bended knee, and Janice reached down to grab small, familiar fingers. In seconds she had Betsy lying facedown beneath the garish carpet covering the platform.

She wanted to cry and whoop and run for safety, but Peter was still fending off an irate crowd. The performers had managed to stay out of the way of the elephant's spray, so his disguise was intact, but Stephen still protested and raised a ruckus. Janice signaled the trainer and the elephant began backing out of the scene.

The red-haired clown hopped up and down as if fearful his ride would depart without him. He danced all around Stephen, jabbing his fists, mimicking a fistfight. Their audience, uncertain of what was performance and what was not, watched with grins and chuckles and stayed out of the way while keeping a wide berth between themselves and the elephant. Several still wrung water out of their hats.

The yellow-haired clown raised a clamor and indicated the departing elephant and troop of performers. The red-haired clown swung as if to race after them. In so doing, the object in his fist connected soundly with the back of Stephen's head. Stephen crumpled silently to the ground.

Leaping up and down and making "Ooo-ooo" noises, the red-haired clown flapped his silly shoes in an awkward escape, running after the rest of the circus. The yellow-haired clown chased him, shouting nonsense curses and shaking his fist. Their audience laughed and poked each other and waited for Stephen to stand up and join them.

By the time Stephen rose with great pain and much fury, the circus was racing down the road. From her lofty perch, Janice could see the figures huddling in the courtyard, but she couldn't help the feeling of triumph welling up inside her. She could hear the sound of Betsy's giggles from where she watched beneath the carpet, and the sound was as welcome as an angelic choir. Sitting beside the slender lump in the rug, she rested her hand possessively on Betsy's back and let joy ring through her.

As they passed around the curve and behind concealing piñon trees, Peter stripped off his red wig and costume and ran to fetch a horse he'd left tied to a tree trunk. When he returned with the horse, the animal trainer made the elephant kneel, and Peter reached to help Betsy down from the platform. Then he climbed up beside Janice, hugged her, and clambered down again.

He and Betsy were on his horse and galloping out of sight within seconds. By the time the irate party from the ranch rode up in a cloud of dust, the dancing girl was idly scattering bits of yarn from the rug tassels to the ground and the rest of the performers were passing around a bottle of whiskey.

A thorough search of the elephant and the platform revealed nothing. One of the acrobats had donned the clown suit and wig, and he protested wildly at being accused of knocking a man unconscious. He even attempted to punch one of the cowboys and fell over backward when the man shoved him away.

The man in charge of the Crooked R finally gave Stephen's wild ravings a look of disgust and mounted his horse.

"If the brat got away from you, Connor, it's your own damned fault for not tying her up. She's likely hiding in a haystack somewhere. Unless you want us to gun down the clowns or kidnap the dancing girl, there ain't a thing else we can do here."

Several of the men looked expectantly to the half-dressed figure in silks atop the elephant. Lying sprawled across the carpeted platform, Janice propped her chin in the palm of her hand and pouted an overred lip in Stephen's direction. She winked one heavily kohled eye, and the juggler began to spout curses at her as if she were his possession. When the outraged juggler reached for the nearest rifle, she shrugged laconically, sat up cross-legged, and stared over the elephant's head, dismissing her audience.

In her head, Janice laughed madly as Stephen cursed heathen foreigners and mounted his horse to ride back to the ranch. He had never known her, as he had not known her now. She was free of him at last.

# Forty

"Let me see you honk your nose again, Peter, puleeze." Betsy bounced on the vermin-laden bed, no doubt frightening the fleas into permanent hiding.

Peter graciously donned the bulbous rubber nose and honked it loudly. Betsy bent double with laughter, and watching her, Janice trembled with joy.

Theodophilus expounded upon his own part in the rescue while half a dozen other excited conversations went on at the same time. The tiny hotel room had somehow expanded to include a major part of the circus population, all of them bursting with the triumph of their escapade.

Janice still wore her harem girl clothes. With a room full of people, she could scarcely change into anything else. She had abandoned the hot wig, and her makeup was melting, but nothing could wipe the smile off her face. She wanted to bounce right beside Betsy on the bed.

Her gaze kept straying to Peter. Although he seemed to be relaxed and smiling and enjoying Betsy's attention, a shadow lingered behind his smile. When he looked up and caught her gaze, he sent her a look that melted her insides more hopelessly than her makeup. She wanted the room cleared of occupants so she could thank him properly, in the way of love that he had taught her.

It didn't seem likely that anyone would leave soon. The flute player took up his instrument, and Janice was forced to repeat her performance for those who had missed it. Attracted by the party atmosphere, complete strangers entered the fringe of the crowd and clapped as loudly as the rest of the audience.

It was into this chaos that Daniel arrived, trailing Evie and Tyler. The three of them stared in disbelief as the staidly proper schoolmarm performed a harem dance in gossamer silks, while the stiff, arrogant Easterner honked a rubber nose and shuffled around in overlarge shoes to the amusement of everyone watching. At the sight of Betsy throwing herself into Peter's arms and hugging him, all became clear.

Her hair once again cropped to silver curls, Betsy was the first to notice the new arrivals. With a cry of complete joy, she launched herself in their direction.

"Uncle Daniel! Uncle Daniel!" Even though it had been five years since she had seen him last, she leapt into his arms as if it had been yesterday. With a pleased grin, Daniel scooped her up and swung her around.

Over her head, he grinned at the red-nosed clown and the harem dancer. "We thought we were arriving to lend reinforcements. I take it we've arrived for the triumphant celebration instead."

"Peter rescued me!" Betsy informed him. "And Janice came as a dancing girl so the bad men wouldn't see what Peter was doing. And I left clues so they could find me. Did you see my clues?"

Tyler slipped in the door and pulled Betsy from Daniel's arms, throwing her up in the air and catching her as if to reassure himself that she was real. "We found your clues, little Miss Clever. Your Aunt Evie copied your sketches and they're posted all over the West by now."

"Really?" Thoroughly thrilled, Betsy looked to Evie for confirmation.

"Those sketches were so good, people recognized them instantly," Evie assured her. "I'm going to send some back to my father so he can see them. He'll be proud of you."

Betsy beamed. Behind her, Tyler and Daniel gestured for Peter to join them. Reluctant to let either of the women in his life out of his sight, Peter hesitated, but he was well aware other matters needed tending. With a glance to Janice, he indicated his direction. She seemed to understand immediately and nodded. Just the knowledge that they could communicate with each other this easily warmed his insides. He'd thought never to have that kind of understanding with a woman. He was blessed to have her as his wife.

He edged around the crowd and followed the other two men out the door. He sent a questioning look to Daniel.

Daniel interpreted the look easily. "I found Bobby Fairweather with Manuel's help. After a little persuasion, he told me about the Crooked R. I don't think he'll be leaving Mineral Springs anytime soon. Harding's told him there'd be a warrant out for his arrest for kidnapping the instant he left his wife and babe." Daniel gave his brother a curious look. "I thought to wait until I got back here before telling you where to find Betsy so I could lend a hand. Looks like you got the jump on me."

Peter had removed the wig and nose. He bounced them in his hands now, impatient to return to his family. "Betsy's clues gave us the direction. We just didn't know if we were reading them right."

"So you sent a circus to find out? And here I thought Daniel was the eccentric in the family," Tyler commented wryly. "I don't suppose you gave any thought to what Stephen is doing right now, or have you got him tied up and in the tiger's cage?"

Peter shrugged. "Our first thought was to get the hell out of there. But I've talked to a friend of Daniel's since then." He sent Daniel an enigmatic look. "Pecos says if you put this adventure into a book, he'll scalp you alive."

Daniel grinned and crossed his arms over his chest. "Did he now? And what did the old boy do with the dastardly villain?"

Peter scratched the back of his head where his hair stood on end from the wig. "Well, I was for turning the bastard in to the law, but Pecos said the law around here is rather peculiar. For some reason, he didn't think Connor ought to be turned over to a hanging judge." He raised an eyebrow at Daniel. "He seemed to think you might know about this Judge Roy Bean? Said you'd understand."

Daniel's grin disappeared. "Yeah, I've read about him. Still, I'm not certain Connor shouldn't be hung, and that's what the judge would do to him, all right."

Peter didn't offer his theory on why the gunslinger wouldn't have Stephen Connor hung. He couldn't imagine Janice telling Pecos Martin who Connor really was, but somehow the man seemed to know things he shouldn't. Peter knew Janice wouldn't want to see the father of her child hung, and somehow the gunslinger knew it too. He didn't mention that to Daniel and Tyler.

"Anyway, Pecos is taking Connor back to Fort Worth for a proper trial. That ought to keep him out of our hair for a while." Peter turned to go back into the room.

Daniel's voice caught him. "What are you going to do now? I understand the snow in the mountains will keep you from exploring your mine until spring."

Peter stared blankly at the door facing him. "I'll be going back to Ohio, I guess, providing you can make room for me in the business somewhere."

"You know you have a better head for management than I do. Of course you'll be welcome." Daniel watched with concern as his brother disappeared through the door into the room where Janice waited. He turned a questioning look to Tyler.

The older man shrugged his broad shoulders and stared at the closed door. "He thinks he owes you. You're not ever going to convince him otherwise."

Daniel's long, lean face set in a grim expression. "Want to bet on that?"

Through Daniel's generosity, the remainder of the circus took the next train to San Antonio. The rest of the weary travelers had to wait for the Fort Worth train.

While they wandered up and down the station platform at the scheduled time, Janice sat on her satchel and watched her husband. She was relieved to note that Peter was coughing less now, but the strain of these last days had left its toll in the lines upon his face. He paced rest-lessly, with renewed energy, but she didn't like the shad-owed look of his eyes. The brilliant green that once danced with excitement now had a muddy look of resig-nation. She didn't like that look one little bit.

Her gaze caught on a tall, stoop-shouldered man in a disreputable leather vest standing near one corner of the station. He hadn't been there earlier, she was certain. He seemed to blend in with the shadows, but this time she knew who he was. She got up from her makeshift seat and approached him directly.

She thought for a moment he would bolt, but he squared his shoulders and stayed where he was. The oth-ers were at the far end of the train platform, listening to the wail of the whistle as the train approached. Janice stopped in front of the aging cowboy.

"I want to thank you, Mr. Martin, for everything you have done. It's a pity there aren't more men like you and fewer like Stephen."

"It's only human to take the easy route, ma'am. I'll see the law takes care of him. He won't be bothering you no more." He shifted nervously from one foot to the other, glancing in the direction of the station where he kept his prisoner tied.

"It takes a true man to take the difficult route. You were always there, keeping an eye on us, weren't you? But you let us do it our way. I don't know if I ought to thank you for that, but I thank you for being there."

Pecos shrugged. "That man of yours wouldn't of appre-ciated it if I'd done anythin' else. He never did need me anyways. I just kept an eye open to make that brother of his happy. I don't reckon you'll be needin' my help any-time soon."

"Not your help, maybe, but your friendship. Keep in touch, Mr. Martin." Daringly Janice stood on her toes and planted a gentle kiss on the cowboy's rugged cheek.

He colored beneath his tan and backed away. Janice smiled at the way the tough hero of Daniel's novels melted like wax around a woman. Distracted by the sound of the train pulling into the station, she turned briefly. When she looked back, he was gone.

But he was there somewhere. Smiling and whispering farewell, she hastened to join the others as they gathered up the assorted oddments they had accumulated over these last days. Janice hugged Betsy for good measure, then grabbed Peter's arm and clung to it with pride and joy as the train clattered to a halt. For a brief moment he smiled at her with the genuine happiness she had once known, but then he turned to the business at hand with the brusqueness she was beginning to learn.

Her patience with her husband's managerial attitude lasted into Fort Worth. Peter and Daniel spent the better part of the trip talking business, and Janice had already promised herself to understand this part of her husband's nature. But when he sent her on to the hotel with Daniel and the Monteignes while he remained behind to see to various matters, she began to lose a little bit of her forbearance.

She pulled Daniel aside as he arranged for their accommodations for the night. The clerk at the hotel desk smoothed his dark mustache and waited impatiently as Daniel bent to listen to the dowdy female who had accosted him. Janice could sense the nattily dressed clerk's opinion of her travel-worn attire, knew she looked out of place in this exorbitantly expensive hotel, but she no longer cared about appearances.

"Daniel, could you arrange for Betsy to have a room in Evie's suite? Peter and I need some time alone." She ought to be thoroughly embarrassed at making such a request, but once her mind was set, she disregarded all else. Besides, Daniel was an old friend. She counted on him to understand.

He didn't even grin. He nodded in comprehension. "If anyone can straighten his thinking, you can, Miss Janice. I've never had much patience with human sacrifices. For some reason, he seems to think that's what's required to make you happy." Daniel gave her a quizzical look.

Janice's lips set in a grim line. "The man doesn't understand women very well, does he?"

Daniel grinned at that. "You got that right. He's never had one ounce of sense when it came to women. A schoolteacher like you ought to be able to teach him a lesson, though. I'm counting on it."

He turned back to the desk clerk to make the arrangements requested.

By the time he reached the hotel, Betsy was happily settled in a suite with the Monteignes, Daniel had disappeared elsewhere, and Peter found Janice all alone, luxuriating in her very first bubble bath.

He closed the door carefully behind him, using it as a support as his gaze took in the sight of fluttery bubbles drifting over rounded curves, occasionally parting to reveal glimpses of pink. He had always known Janice was a beautiful woman, but the sight of her now with her golden tresses stacked high and loose on her head, revealing satin neck and shoulders flushed to an enticing pink from the heat made him realize he'd never known how truly beautiful she could be. She lifted her arms to soap them, and her breasts bobbed temptingly above the bubbles.

The seductive smile she bestowed upon him when she saw him standing there sent Peter's fingers flying to his shirt buttons. He didn't know where Betsy was and didn't care. Getting out of his clothes as quickly as humanly possible crowded out all other thoughts.

He had been weary when he entered the room, but now he felt horny as hell. It struck him as highly efficient to have a woman available when he needed one, but it was that same damned female who had created the ache in the first place. Women were a mixed blessing at best, but he meant to enjoy this part of his wife's nature. He had his boots off and his shirt stripped by the time she soaped her feet. The sight of her curved calf propped on the edge of the tub put a new edge on his impatience as he tugged off his pants with some difficulty.

She eyed him dubiously as Peter approached the tub

completely naked, but she only gave a breathless squeal
when he swept her up and settled himself in the water,
bringing her down on top and facing him. Water sloshed
over the sides, but he didn't even notice, much less care.

"Peter . . ."

He didn't know what she meant to say. He stopped her
words with a kiss that seared his insides, scalding him as
if he bathed in boiling water. The water ought to be boiling the way he felt now.

There were simply too many words to be said so he
didn't say any of them. He kissed her, soaped his hands
with the bubbles on her breasts until she gasped, then slid
his hands over and beneath the generous curves of her
hips, lifting her to where he needed her.

She gave a cry of ecstasy that almost caused Peter to
lose it right then and there. Forcing himself to go slowly,
he tried to take her gently, but she was beyond that already. With his own groan of joy, he followed her lead,
driving himself deep inside over and over until the water
churned with their frenzy.

By the time they achieved satisfaction, there was more
water on the floor than in the tub and someone was bang-
ing on the door in protest. Peter grinned and pressed a
kiss to his wife's reddened cheeks before climbing out of
the tub and wrapping a towel around himself to chase
away the intruder.

By the time he placated the hotel manager, Janice had
toweled herself dry and was wriggling into a long nightgown. Peter grabbed the cloth from her hands and jerked
it back over her head, flinging the gown to the far corner
of the room.

"I've got to make up for lost time," he murmured when
she attempted to protest. Lifting her from her feet, he
carried her to the bed.

Janice grabbed the covers and rolled up in them, glaring at him as if he had suddenly turned into the devil himself. "Not until we talk," she informed him coldly.

Peter didn't bother drying off. He dropped to the bed,
rolled over until he had her legs trapped beneath his, then

methodically began removing the covers from her grasp. "We can talk anytime. We don't often have this much privacy to do what I want."

"At least tell me where you're taking me. I have a right to know where we'll be living." She grabbed the sheet away from him and pulled it back over her breasts.

"I'm taking you back to Mineral Springs where you have friends. You said you didn't want to go back to Ohio. I'll build you a house there and buy you a new bicycle." Peter peeled the sheet back again and filled his hands with her deliciously scented flesh. He couldn't resist tasting, and he felt a surge of satisfaction when she wriggled and moaned with pleasure beneath him.

But Janice wouldn't be put off. She grabbed a handful of his hair and jerked until he had to look at her. "And how do you mean to earn the money for all these wonderful things?"

"The same way I always have, by hard work. Despite what you've seen, I am capable of keeping a wife." Peter turned to nibble at her ear while his hands sought the pleasures of soft curves.

Janice caught his biceps and tried to shove him away. "I don't doubt your abilities in the least. Just tell me how and where you mean to do this work."

Growing a trifle angry at this continued resistance, Peter pushed himself up and glared down at her. "What difference is that to you so long as I provide for you as I promised?"

She tried to scramble out from under him but his legs and the tangle of sheets and blankets held her trapped. She pushed herself up by her elbows and glared back at him. "I'm your wife, you stone-headed idiot! You can't just pretend I'm one of your employees not deserving of managerial secrets."

Her hair had fallen from its knot and now tumbled in glorious disarray across her breasts and shoulders. He had loved that hair from the first instant he'd seen it. Peter filled his hands with it now as he sat back on his haunches and forced himself to say what he would have given a fortune to postpone.

"I'll be going back to Ohio to help Daniel run the business. He can use the help. The pay is good. I'll have us out of debt in no time."

With a cry of rage, Janice slammed both hands against his chest and shoved him off the bed.

For the second time in as many weeks, he fell with the loud crash of a tree toppling.

# Forty-One

"Who in the damn hell do you think you are?" Janice raged above him, kneeling naked on the edge of the bed, her waist-length hair rippling down her back and over her shoulders like some Viking Valkyrie.

Peter lay on his back, looking up from the floor in more astonishment than anger. This was his mild-mannered schoolmarm?

"This is a marriage, not a business!" She grabbed a pillow and flung it at him.

He threw up an arm and shielded himself from the bombardment, knocking the pillow aside. He was rather too aware that he was naked and relatively defenseless, but his astonishment melted into the anger that had only been simmering before. "I keep my promises, dammit!" he yelled back. "I promised to make you happy and to take care of you, and I damned well mean to do just that. I don't own a ranch. I can't keep you here without making money somehow. So I'm doing it the only way I know how."

He jumped up and grabbed the next pillow she meant to fling at him.

"By leaving me here! Damn you, Peter Mulloney, what do you think I am? A liar? I told you I love you. Didn't that sink into your thick head?"

The noise they created had someone pounding on the door again, but they both ignored the intrusion.

"Love hasn't got anything to do with money! Hell, for all I know, it won't even last longer than it takes to say it. It sure as hell won't last if you're shivering in some log cabin watching the babies we make starve. I told you I'm not going to do that to you, and I mean it!"

The pounding at the door was now accompanied by shouts to open it. Janice grabbed the pillow from the floor and slammed it against Peter's head.

"I . . . love . . . you . . . lunkhead," she screamed, beating him with the pillow in time to her words. Peter ducked his head, dodged, and scrambled for the second pillow. Janice continued bringing her pillow down upon his back and shoulders. "I'm your wife! Where you go, I go. If you're too ashamed to take me back to Ohio, just say so. Don't give me this other nonsense."

Peter gave up on his weapon and grabbed hers instead. The struggle tore open a seam, sending feathers flying in a snowy blizzard. The pounding at the door escalated.

"Ashamed! Hell, Janice, I don't know what you use that brain of yours for, but it sure ain't for thinking. I didn't marry you out of shame! I married you because you were the best damned woman I would ever find. I'd be proud to show you off. You're the blamed fool who won't go back with me. A man wants the woman he loves by his side, but I don't mean to keep you where you won't be happy."

Janice was so startled by his admission that she let her side of the pillow go. Peter found himself grasping just the pillow cover as the casing flew out of his hands, scattering the remaining chicken feathers high in the air. They both stared in distraction as feathers settled everywhere, covering the bed, their hair and shoulders, the floor, lighting on the dresser and washbasin, blowing in the draft from the door.

The door. Peter grabbed Janice in his arms and held her against him as someone's shoulder bounced against the solid wood. Tyler's curses followed, and Janice turned a wide-eyed look up to Peter's taut jaw. As someone else slammed against the panel, Peter began to grin.

"I think we're being rescued, my love. Who do you think will be embarrassed most if they succeed?"

Janice looked down at their nakedness, at the feathers

coating their arms and torsos, not to mention the room, and her shoulders began to shake.

"You're not going to cry, are you?" Peter asked anxiously, catching her arms and staring worriedly down at her bent head.

Janice whipped her hair back and forth and tried not to let the laughter erupt, but it was more than she could control. Everything was more than she could control. Her whole life was totally out of hand, and she was laughing so hard that she couldn't keep from shaking. The sound of her merriment pealed above the shouts and curses outside the door.

Peter's laughter began as a grin at the absurdity of their situation. It grew with the infectiousness of Janice's mirth. Aside from the fact that they were both quite certifiably insane, he had never felt better in his life. The joy ripped out of him with guffaws that welled from deep inside of him. He wanted to roll on the floor with happiness, but he retained sufficient sense to grab a sheet to wrap around Janice. He wanted to shout his love to all the world, but he wasn't about to share her with anyone. He hadn't changed that much.

But they had changed. As the hotel manager unlocked the door and Tyler and Daniel came stumbling in, that much was obvious to all concerned. The stoic pair who seldom smiled, who always planned ahead, who never had a moment for nonsense, were standing in a snow cloud of feathers, stark naked, and laughing. When they saw the faces of their would-be rescuers, the couple erupted in renewed peals of hilarity.

The manager broke into Spanish curses and threats at the destruction around them, but Tyler and Daniel merely exchanged glances, grinned, and shoved the man out of the room. The only rescuing needed here was their sanity, and that was probably dispensable.

# *Epilogue*

"Just because my mother gave you those damned things doesn't mean you have to wear them." Whipping the oxen to a faster pace, Peter glanced down at the offending article showing in a tantalizing ruffle beneath Janice's skirt.

"They keep me warm. Besides, I'm wearing a skirt over them. It's not as if I'm wearing them as pants. And besides that, you don't need to look at my legs. You've already got what you want." Janice rested her hand on the high curve of her stomach, just beneath her breasts. She lifted her ankle slightly to admire the ribbon threaded through the ruffled anklet of her stylish bloomers. They would look very nice when she was allowed to ride a bicycle again, but she wouldn't tell Peter that.

Peter gave a smug grin as he noted where her hand rested. "I'll admit that the thought of you carrying my baby tickles me no end, but that isn't all I want. I've made inquiries, and we have plenty of time for what I want."

A hint of color stained Janice's cheeks as she turned her attention to the rough road ahead of them. "I won't ask to whom you made your inquiries. You come from a family of real rapscallions, you realize. I don't know how your sainted mother has endured it all these years."

Peter snorted. "My 'sainted mother' has become a true harridan in her later years. If I didn't know him so well, I'd pity my father."

Janice smiled and watched Betsy ride her pony up the trail ahead of them. "He's only getting what he deserves for keeping her under his thumb all this time. And your brothers are learning to follow Daniel's example and let her tirades go right around them. In a few years, they'll be able to run Mulloney Enterprises without any help at all."

Peter gave her smile a suspicious look. "Just because I made a little profit on that stock sale doesn't mean we have enough to live on for very long. We might be back there by winter again."

The mountain they were riding up didn't seem to have changed much from the inclement weather of winter. The coming of spring had brought a renewed green that she didn't remember from the prior autumn, but the smell of the pines was the same. Janice drank it in happily and leaned back against the wagon seat to give the child inside her more room to move.

"If that's what you want, I don't mind. We'll just have to wait until the baby is old enough to travel," she answered serenely, not taking up the challenge in his voice.

"I'll never get rich this way," he warned. "I can't keep going back and forth between this damned mountain and Ohio and ever get ahead. If we don't strike gold this time, we might be better off going back East and staying."

"If that's really what you want to do." She knew it wasn't. She knew he wanted to be out here in the vast open spaces where men were judged by what they did and not who they were. He wanted to show he could make it on his own. He didn't want to be counted a failure out here. But she knew he wouldn't be. Peter had the ability to do whatever he set his mind to. All she had to do was keep his formidable mind diverted from worrying about her and the child.

Knowing when he was being placated, Peter gave a grunt and concentrated on getting the oxen up the hill to the cabin. He'd set out this time with enough money to provide some of the niceties for their home, and the iron stove they hauled made progress slow.

"Do you think the gold we left behind will still be there?" Janice asked casually. She really didn't care about the gold now that the child inside her consumed all her concentration, but Peter's thoughts needed diverting. Pillow fights worked very well in the bedroom, but in public she had to be a little more diplomatic. "It was good of Tyler to let you wait until now to pay him back."

Peter grinned. "He was feeling generous after he made all that money on that stock I told him to buy. He had enough to buy that crazy horse of his back and then some." He shrugged as he got back to her question. "I don't see any reason why the gold shouldn't be there. It's just dangerous to take it down to be assayed until we have the operation going and more protection up here."

A shout from Betsy had Peter grabbing for his rifle and halting the oxen. He had the horse he'd left behind tied to the rear of the wagon, thanks to Townsend and the town storekeeper. If he could get to it . . .

Betsy and her mount burst around the curve of the trail, followed more sedately by Townsend on his rugged pony. Betsy slid to a halt beside the wagon, and Townsend lifted his hat back and grinned through a winter's worth of beard.

"Glad to see you back, partner. Thought maybe you'd grown soft and decided to desert me."

"Leave you with a mountain full of gold? Do you take me for a fool?" Peter grumbled, but the jest was in his eyes.

"Silver," Townsend replied, "mountain full of silver."

Janice's eyes widened but she remained silent as Peter stared at his partner. Betsy bounced up and down and showed a rock in her hand, but Janice continued to hold her breath while she waited for Peter to say something. Peter knew this man. He would know whether this was a joke or not.

Townsend nodded to the rock Betsy held out. "That came from the lode you struck when you pitched that fit and threw your pick into the mountain. It's a mite hard to get at, but once I made my way up there, I found plenty more. Gold's still there, too, but I figure we can use the silver for start-up money until we can get the excavation going."

Peter took the rock and held it up to the light. As he looked from the rock to Townsend, he slowly began to grin. "I'm the money manager around here, remember. I'll figure what we go after first."

Townsend tugged his hat down to disguise the laughter in his eyes. "Yassuh, massuh, suh." He glanced at Janice's newly rounded figure. "But it looks to me like you found other business to tend to and now you're going to be short one bookkeeper. That don't look to me like any way to run a business."

Peter gave a long whistle and turned to Janice. "When the hired help starts getting uppity like that, it means there's money in his pockets. We might be building that mansion on the hill yet."

Janice smiled serenely and gave Betsy a hug as she climbed on the wagon seat to join them. "Just so it has a bedroom with a door that closes and lots of pillows, that's all I ask."

Peter smiled happily and set the team into motion. "I want a bathtub with lots of bubbles." He sent Janice a sideways glance. "I made sure that harem outfit got packed."

Janice pursed her lips and tried to look disapproving, but a smile kept tugging at the corners of her mouth. "I'm sure I can find the clown costume," she replied evenly.

Betsy gave a hoot and patted Janice's stomach. "I think the clown suit will fit better on Mama Janice." She gave a sly look through her lashes at the tall man beside her. "So I guess Papa Peter will have to wear the pretty silks."

Townsend roared with laughter, and the others soon joined him, but Peter and Janice managed an exchange of looks over Betsy's head. Whatever Betsy guessed about her parentage she seemed to have accepted with the blithe innocence of security. They were well on their way to being more than the parents of an infant. They were going to be the proud parents of an exceptionally talented and devious ten-year-old.

Janice hugged her daughter and Peter whistled a happy tune as they pulled into the cabin clearing. He hadn't even known he could whistle, he realized as they stopped before the home they could call their own.

It wasn't much, but it was theirs.

Betsy clambered out of the wagon with a ten-year-old's disgust as Peter leaned over to kiss his wife. It would be years before Betsy would understand that it was love that made them wealthy. For now, she was more interested in finding the paints she'd left behind.

Peter tipped Janice's chin upward with his knuckle so he could look into her eyes. "I love you," he murmured so only she could hear.

"I know, and for that, I'll forgive you anything." She met his lips with her own.

"Anything?" he murmured wickedly against her mouth.

"Almost anything," she answered severely, pulling his head down closer.

And because he knew he was an impossible man, he knew he would put that promise to the test more often than he cared to think. He also knew that she would never fail him.

He closed his eyes and deepened the kiss. He might covet gold, but he'd already found his treasure.

Turn the page
for a preview of
Patricia Rice's
next wild romance
*Denim and Lace*
coming from Topaz
in the summer of 1996. . . .

# *Chapter 1*

*Sierra Mountains*
*October 1868*

"I may have to kill him."

The words were horrifying even though said in the most thoughtful tones that could be produced by a soft, feminine Tennessee accent.

The wagon lurched over a rock, and the speaker hauled on the reins while her companion grabbed her bonnet and held on to the rough wooden seat.

The October air was pleasantly mild for this high in the Sierras, but the occupants of the wagon weren't aware of that. Too tired to admire the occasional flutter of a golden leaf as it blew by on the breeze, they had their eyes set on the swirl of gray smoke coming from just over the next hill. Two thousand miles they had come, and the end was near.

"You can't kill him, Samantha. They'd put you in jail and hang you and then we would all starve. What would that solve?"

Sam grinned a trifle grimly. Leave it to Harriet to see things in a practical perspective. Her younger sister had the bright blue eyes and golden curls of a china doll, but she had the brain of a first-class merchant. If anything, Harriet's looks were her downfall. Had she been as homely as Samantha, she could have started her own mercantile store and no one would have thought twice about it. As it was, men only laughed at her when she tried to persuade them she was more than qualified to run a store.

On the other hand, Sam was just as plain as they came, but she didn't have a penchant for sitting in a musty old store counting pennies. She wanted to work the land, and she watched the plant life around her with more than just a casual interest. Her father had promised that the valley he had found would be temperate enough for good crops despite its location. He'd said the soil was rich and the water plentiful, a veritable treasure trove better than any gold or silver a man could want. Sam knew her father well enough to have her doubts, and they grew by leaps and bounds at the sight of rocky soil and towering evergreens, but it was much too late to go back now.

"What am I supposed to do when I meet the man?" Sam returned to the subject, casting aside her doubts about the future for the worries of the present. "Ask him politely what he did to our father? Smile and tell him we haven't heard from him since he threw him out of town? Demand he find Daddy or we'll call the law? From what I understand, this character is the law here."

Harriet gave Sam's drawn face a worried look. Two thousand miles had taken their toll on her sister. As the eldest, Sam had always been their father's favorite, the son he'd never had. She'd imitated everything her father had done since she was little more than a toddler, and she resembled him in more ways than anyone else in the family. She had always adopted a boy's attire and preferred the occupations of males to those of females, but after two thousand miles of acting as man of the family, Sam was actually beginning to look like a man. Her hands were callused from days hauling on the reins of recalcitrant oxen. Her always slender figure had slimmed to wiriness from riding her horse in search of game. No hat brim could keep the pounding sun from setting freckles running rampant across her nose and cheeks. And she'd cropped her hair short for ease of care. The red curls were growing out now, but they were the only real evidence that she might be other than a half-grown boy. That, and her voice. Samantha's sultry tones could be a trifle disconcerting coming from a redheaded tomboy wearing pants.

"Maybe someone has shot him already," Harriet said decisively. "A man like that is bound to be shot sooner or later. Then we can just find Daddy and tell him to come back."

Samantha sighed. She loved her father dearly, but she knew better than anyone that her father wouldn't be content to settle in a valley and raise crops and chickens. He had a wandering mind that kept him flitting from one project to another, always forsaking them as soon as the challenge was solved rather than carrying it through to riches. He might come back to visit if they settled here, but he would never stay. At least now they would be close enough for him to visit.

"There it is! There it is!" Twelve-year-old Jack galloped his pony ahead of the two wagons, sending up swirls of dust in his wake.

The dust worried Sam, too, but she tried not to think about this evidence of lack of rain as she gazed eagerly at the scattering of buildings in the road ahead. She sighed with relief that they were more than the shacks and tents she had seen in the mining towns. Good solid adobe had been used in the construction of these buildings, a certain sign of permanence. Her father hadn't been dreaming when he had chosen this town.

Jack galloped away, and Sam bit her lip in displeasure. Her Uncle William was supposed to have acted as head of the family when they joined the wagon train. A widower with a young son to raise, he had thought it a good idea to join his brother in California rather than suffer the aftermath of a war he'd never believed in. But William had died of the cholera long before the wagons had reached the plains, and Jack had run wild ever since.

Conscious of Harriet's excitement and the eagerness of the women in the wagon behind them, Sam urged the weary beasts to a faster pace. As if sensing the end to this journey, they plodded obediently onward.

They had left the rest of the wagon train behind some days ago, following the directions from Emmanuel Neely's letter. This had to be their new home. If nothing else, their father gave excellent directions. He'd said the old Spanish mission town would be easy to find. He'd bought the deed to their house from the Spanish grandee who owned the original land grant after the church left. The description of their new home would have been sufficient to draw them out here without all the other factors that had induced their move.

The sun settled low on the horizon as they rattled down the hill. The wagons threw up clouds of dust, but the little town appeared serene and golden in the dying light. The hotel and trading post looked just as Emmanuel had described it: the lower half of adobe and shaded by a gallery on the wooden second floor. As Emmanuel had said, the town still looked like an old mission plaza. The hotel formed one side of the square. Stables, a blacksmith shop, and a harness-maker formed most of another side. Instead of a church, however, the third side held a lovely old home with sprawling porches and glass windows and trees forcing their way through the desolate dust of the front yard. That would be their home.

Nearly faint with relief that her father had actually found them decent accommodations, Sam took her time examining the rest of the town. She couldn't tell if the rest of the buildings on the plaza contained shops or residences, but most of them seemed solidly built with tile roofs and adobe foundations. A few wooden shacks were scattered in the streets off the plaza, but this was definitely not a mining town. She had seen enough of them as they had come over the mountains. Her father had written colorful letters describing some of the activities of the miners. Her gently-bred mother had nearly expired at the words. She would have never survived in those crude surroundings.

As it was, Sam's father had been ominously silent on the subject of their new neighbors, except for that last letter mentioning his confrontation with Sloan Talbott. The man had to be a menace, even if her father's description hadn't confirmed it. Greedy, stingy, mean-tempered, and violent—Sloan Talbott didn't sound like the kind of acquaintance one looked forward to making. But that was the only inhabitant of the town they knew anything about. He was the man Sam thought she might have to kill.

As the wagons rode slowly into the deserted plaza in a curtain of dust, a few people came forward to examine the novelty. After a sharp whistle or two, more came out to observe the sight.

Sam itched uneasily, watching the watchers from the corner of her eye. Every last filthy one of them was male.

Hideously conscious of the fact that they were four women and a boy, Sam donned her most menacing expression and shifted her gunbelt forward where it could be seen. Pulling her hat over her face, she prayed that they thought she was a man. Seeing her in a loose checkered shirt and a leather vest, they shouldn't be able to tell much else. For the moment. She found the rifle at her foot and eased it closer.

Sam clenched her teeth at the sound of whistles and shouts. Bernadette must have her bonnet off. She cast a quick glance at Harriet, but as usual, the practical twin was examining their new home with an experienced eye and wasn't in the least aware of the attention they were attracting. It must be nice to be so accustomed to attention that one could ignore it. Scowling, Sam looked for Jack as she halted the oxen in the shade of the town's only trees.

He was nowhere to be seen, but his pony was tied to the porch post. Men were already sauntering across the plaza before the second wagon could come to a halt. Grabbing her rifle, Sam jumped down and started back to her mother's wagon. If Harriet would step to it, she could be off the far side of the wagon and into the house before the men reached her. Sam's goal was to reach her mother and Bernadette before every man jack in town had them surrounded.

Alice Neely was cautious enough to see the danger and was already pulling her long skirts around her as she climbed from the wagon. Bernadette, however—despite her mother's warning—was dreamily admiring the shaded porch of their new home, as completely unaware of her swarming admirers as her twin.

"I'll get her in the house, Sam," Alice said, hurrying toward the lead oxen. "But there isn't any way we can keep them out. We're going to need their help to unload the wagons. Distract them with hard work and offers of payment and I'll see what I can do."

Sam wasn't certain if the crowd of approaching men was the equivalent of being attacked by man-eating Zulus, but her protective instincts were the same. At least back in Tennessee she had known the scores of admirers that had haunted their front room in hopes of some sight of the twins, and she had known their weaknesses well enough to keep them off balance. Ever since the Neelys had set out for California, however, it had been a constant battle. There had been women with the wagon train, but none of them quite like the twins. And once they reached California, there seemed to be a dearth of females in every town they passed. Miners waved bags of gold at them in hopes of drawing the twins' attention. Less scrupulous men had crept up at night and tried to carry them off. She had every right to be wary of this crowd coming at them now.

Sam glared at the crowd and held her rifle crossed in front of her. They stared back with all the interest of curious puppies. What appeared to be the town drunk still had his whiskey bottle in hand as he politely ran his palm over his vest to clean it off before offering it for a handshake. He was short and wiry and had a hank of sandy hair hanging over his face—and a gun belt slung dangerously over his narrow hips.

Sam ignored him and turned her glare and her rifle to the next man who dared get too close. He towered over her with a grim expression to match her own, but there was an odd gleam of satisfaction in his eyes as he stared back.

"Sloan ain't going to like this one bit," he announced without preamble, before adding, "Welcome to Talbott." He might have added more, but a swift inspection of the red-haired creature confronting him left him doubting the proper form of address.

Before Sam could reply, another man staggered forward, this one elderly, stooped, and squat, but with the distinctive long tresses of an Indian. A face weathered to the brown wrinkles of a walnut shell stared back at her, and Sam found herself eye to eye with the wisdom and pain of the ages. He grunted something noncommittal before heading toward her cattle.

Sam didn't like Indians around her cattle. She had gained enough experience on this trip to know that Indians and cattle had a tendency to depart in the same direction, and that direction wasn't her own.

She turned to call a halt, when an ominous rumble began at

the rear of the house and migrated forward until the entire town was shaking with the impact of an explosion that sent a spiral of smoke and dirt straight up into the air.

"Jefferson Neely!" Samantha screamed, before sprinting in the direction of the house and the billowing smoke.

# Chapter 2

The tall man who had greeted them grabbed a shovel and ran after Samantha. The others scattered in search of equivalent tools as the first flash of fire shot into the air. Sam nearly fell in the dust as she slid around the back corner of the house but righted herself in time to see bits of flaming paper fly upward, threatening the wooden porch of their new home.

"Jefferson Neely!" she screamed again as she discovered her cousin just where she expected him to be—right at the center of trouble.

A blackened ring of smoke circled his face around his spectacles, but he didn't look the least deterred by the chaos around him. Not until Samantha grabbed his ear lobe and jerked him backward out of danger did he look in the least repentant.

The tall man shoveled a mound of dust on the already dying flames. Other men ran to join him waving pickaxes and shovels of every degree of repair. The noticeable absence of water to douse the flames made Sam's heart plunge a little further. What had they got themselves into now?

Refusing to give in to her fears, Sam jerked her cousin around to face her. "What in blue blazes did you think you were doing?"

"Owww! Sam, let go of me! I didn't do nothing." Jack wiped at his chubby face with the back of his dirty sleeve. "I just wanted to celebrate with fireworks like Dad did last Fourth of July."

Samantha tried to harden her heart as she grabbed his shirt collar and shook him, but she heard the cry behind the defensiveness and she couldn't give him the punishment he deserved. He had probably been saving that gunpowder all across the country to use as a celebration when they finally arrived. That would be just like something his father would have done. And not knowing how to do it properly but experimenting anyway would be just like his uncle. The Neelys were known for their curiosity but never for their caution.

"He needs a man to tan his hide," the tall man offered as he wiped the sweat from his brow and came forward. "Dr. Cal Ramsey, at your service, ma'am." He held out his hand in introduction.

Samantha sighed. Her disguise had worked for as long as it had taken for her to open her mouth. Praying this was a man she could trust, she took the offered hand and shook it. "Samantha Neely, sir, and this is my cousin, Jack."

The others were already crowding around, offering names, making welcoming noises, and looking her over like she was a prized heifer. When men even took to looking at her, she knew they were desperate. She tried not to glance at the house where her mother had kept the twins hidden despite the excitement. She had the uneasy feeling that this town wasn't going to have a lot of women to call on for help.

"We didn't mean to stir up such excitement upon arrival, gentlemen." Sam leapt into a lull in the conversation. At the sound of her voice, they all fell silent. Unnerved by this rapt attention, she tried to politely send them away. "We thank you, but it's getting late and we need to unpack. If there's any of you who could lend a hand unloading some of our things, we'd be happy to pay."

She had scarcely got all the words out of her mouth before several of the younger men were peeling off from the crowd and loping toward the wagons. A voice from the remaining crowd cried out, "Do you cook, ma'am?"

Flustered by their continued stares, Samantha resorted to a spurt of temper. "Of course I cook. Do I look helpless?"

Ramsey stepped in to smooth ruffled feathers. "He means we don't really need to be paid to help, but there isn't a one of us who wouldn't appreciate a home-cooked meal."

Oh, Lord. Sam's heart fell to her stomach as she glanced nervously toward the house. They all meant to help. Her mother would die of exhaustion just trying to keep the twins away from them. Drawing a deep breath, she tried again. "Well, we'd be mighty glad to oblige, but our supplies are a little low. . . ."

That statement wasn't even out of her mouth before men were yelling, "I've got chickens!" "There's flour at the trading post!" "I've been saving those tinned peaches!" And before she could even comment, they were off and running.

It looked like the payment for unloading two wagons was to feed the entire town.

"I don't think you ought to go out there just yet, Samantha," Alice Neely protested as she made biscuits from some of the supplies left over from the prior night's meal. "They all seem friendly enough, but you don't know what will happen if you go out there alone."

Sam knew her mother's real worries without her saying them aloud. Emmanuel Neely's enthusiastic letters had come to a grinding halt the day he left this place. Chances were very good that he never left here alive. If he had been killed by someone in this town, would that someone hold the same grudge against the entire Neely family?

It didn't seem likely, but death came so easily out here that it seemed safest to hide from it. Samantha felt the ache of her father's absence, but he had been gone from as much of her life as he had been in it, so she could hide the ache well. She wasn't the dreamer that her father was. She was a provider, and she meant to provide.

"I'll take a gunbelt and a rifle. It isn't likely anyone will bother me. And I suspect it's too early yet for any of them to be up and about. I'll be back before they have time to besiege the house, I promise."

Alice smiled faintly. "Dr. Ramsey seemed like a gentleman. He seemed quite smitten with you."

"Doctor?" Uneasy with the thought that someone had been watching her when she hadn't known it, Sam shifted from foot to foot, waiting to make her escape. "He doesn't look like any doctor I've ever met."

"Men are different out here. We'll get used to it, I'm sure."

Men were the same everywhere, and she would never get used to it, but Samantha nodded obediently and made her escape. Men and thoughts of men made her uncomfortable, but she would feel fine once she was in the saddle with a rifle in her hand. She didn't have to think about men and their sly looks and knowing touches when she was wandering the woods in the early dawn. She could pretend the only living things on God's earth were the birds singing in the trees and the rabbits she meant to have for supper.

The sun took a long time rising over the mountains, but Sam was content to weave her mount through needle-strewn paths and smell the air. This was her idea of heaven, and she hesitated to disturb it with an explosion of gunfire. Maybe she could meet some Indians who would teach her to use bows and arrows. Somehow, that seemed a much more civilized manner of hunting in these pristine woods.

So lost in her thoughts was she that she almost didn't see the shadow darting from tree to tree near the clearing ahead. When she did take notice, she narrowed her eyes. No animal she knew moved with such furtive clumsiness. It had to be a man.

Gripping her rifle carefully, Sam eased her horse off the path and closer to the clearing. Whatever the man was watching was in that direction. Perhaps there was a pond and ducks. She hadn't had roast duck in a long while. Mouth watering at the thought, she climbed down and tied the horse to a tree, then hid behind a massive evergreen at the clearing's edge.

Disappointment at not finding a pond almost distracted her from the scene unfolding before her. She knew the other hunter was poised and ready to strike just beyond that other stand of trees. But the only animal to be seen was a horse with a saddle on its back taking water from a meager stream. There was too much game in these mountains for any sane man to want to eat horse.

She was a second too late in realizing another man stood on the far side of that horse. Screaming a warning, Sam aimed her rifle in the direction of the furtive shadow, but her target fired first.

The horse whinnied in terror, raising up on its hind legs and crashing down again. Sam sent a bullet winging toward the hidden assailant before he could fire again. The man at the stream got off one shot before he staggered backward, but his attacker had quietly disappeared. To Sam's horror, she could see the man at the stream drop to his knees and lose his grip on his gun while his horse reared and kicked over him.

Without thinking, she flew into the open clearing. The horse was wild-eyed and prancing too near to the place where the man had gone down. Snorting through red-edged nostrils, it towered over her, tossing its tangled mane. A bigger, meaner looking stallion she'd never encountered, and it didn't appear to be half-broke. A horse like that could trample a man and never know the difference.

Catching the horse's reins, Sam stood back, murmuring the soothing words she had learned at her father's knee. She was no stranger to horses. Her father had raised some of the best horses in the country before he decided he'd done his job and needed something new to do. The stallion jerked in fear, trying to free itself, but she gentled it with words and touches until it stood shivering but still.

Then she looked for the wounded man.

He was on his knees and struggling to rise, but blood seeped through his fingers from the wound in his shoulder. He was the biggest man she'd ever had the misfortune to come across, or perhaps it was just the idea of being this close and needing to help him exaggerated his size. Whatever it was, it made her heart squeeze into her throat and block her breathing as she crouched down beside him.

"Put your arm around me. We've got to get you into the saddle."

Icy gray eyes muddied with pain turned to study her with contempt. Her eyes were almost on a level with his when she kneeled beside him, giving some indication of her height. But she was slender, no bigger than a gangly youth, and his expression conveyed his opinion of her offer. "I'll manage. Just go back to where you came from."

Shocked at his rudeness, Sam thought she really ought to do just that. Perhaps she ought to shove him over and make him work a little harder just for the meanness of it. But it wasn't in her nature to ignore the injured or hurt the helpless. Smiling unpleasantly, she grabbed the handkerchief he was pulling from his pocket and applied it firmly to the wound.

"I can see why they took a shot at you. Hold that tight so it doesn't bleed so much." Without asking, she grabbed his good arm and hauled it around her shoulders to help him stand.

He was heavy. There was no getting around that. She staggered as his weight shifted to her shoulders when they stood up. She thought he might be deliberately giving her all his weight until she glanced up to see his eyes closed against the pain. He couldn't bend his wounded arm to hold the cloth to it, and blood poured down the sleeve of his dark shirt.

The amount of blood made her waver, but the cynical flicker of his eyelids as she hesitated straightened Sam's spine. "I can't get you into that saddle. Is there any place close I can take you until I can get help?"

He gave her a wary look. Even wearing her usual checkered shirt and vest, it was evident up close that she wasn't a boy. Sam waited as he took in this fact and nodded slowly. She breathed a sigh of relief that he no longer rejected her help.

"Cabin up the path. I can make it."

Sure, and hell had tulips, but Sam didn't mouth that sentiment out loud. Wishing she'd had the sense to bind the wound before she'd lifted him, she moved her feet in the direction indicated. Tending the wounded had always been her mother's job. She didn't have much experience at it.

Concentrating on the task ahead, neither of them spoke as they staggered up the dusty path into the pine woods. If the gunman was still around, they would make splendid targets, but he had obviously run at the first sign of a witness. That was one thing in her favor, Sam counted as she shuffled along with the stranger's heavy weight across her shoulders. She couldn't think of any others to count right off hand. Not crumpling to the ground might make number two.

Muttering to herself in this manner she managed to distance herself enough from the task to reach the cabin. It wasn't more than a collection of split logs, but it offered shelter of sorts. It hadn't seemed quite humane to leave the man lying on the ground while she went for help.

He collapsed on a low-lying pallet strung to the walls. His eyes were closed again, and the dark shock of curls falling across his forehead made his skin seem pale. Nervously, Sam pulled the handkerchief from his dangling hand and tried to apply it to the gaping hole in his shoulder, but blood had matted the shirt and his skin and she couldn't be certain what she was doing.

"I've got to get help. I don't know what to do." She didn't even have a petticoat to rip up and use for bandages. What did men use when caught unprepared? Their shirts. Flushing at that thought, she glanced around helplessly for likely clothes.

"Get my shirt off. Use the clean side to wrap it." His words were more a moan than an order, but the effect was the same.

Setting her teeth, Sam ripped at the buttons of his shirt, surprised at the expensive black cambric beneath her fingers but distracted by the amount of man revealed when the buttons popped open.

Her father was the only man she'd ever seen partially undressed, and this man looked nothing like her father. Dark hair curled on a broad chest that appeared to be made of steel for all that it was tanned a burnished brown. A ripple of pain moved through the muscles beneath her hand as she pulled at the shirt, and she nearly jerked her hand away in fear.

This would work a whole lot better if she could close her eyes. Taking a deep breath, she peeled the shirt off his good arm. If she could only tear it off his back, it might be easy, but this was good cloth and not easily torn.

"You're going to have to sit up. I can't get this off you otherwise."

He didn't waste breath on words but used his good arm to prop himself up, allowing her to pull the shirt around him. When it reached the matted blood on his shoulder, he cursed, and Sam halted.

Dropping back to the pallet, he opened his eyes and gave her a look of disgust, then grabbed the shirt from her hands. With a single rip he tore the shirt from the wound and off his other arm.

"There's a knife in my boot. Cut the shirt in half and wrap it tight around my shoulder. That should stop the bleeding."

If it wasn't obvious that he was fighting unconsciousness, Sam would have told him what he could do with his knife. She didn't take orders easily, and she certainly didn't take them from men who looked at her as if she were little more than a mindless lump of lead. But he apparently knew what he was doing and she didn't, so she took his words and applied them to action.

He grunted with pain when she had to move him to get the shirt around his shoulder, but he clenched his teeth and kept silent as she tied the shirt and pulled it as tightly as she could manage around the padding of his handkerchief.

"That'll do. Ride back and get Injun Joe. Give him a pot of coffee before he comes up here. He'll take care of the rest."

Sam looked doubtful. It was obvious the stranger was about to pass out from pain and loss of blood. What he needed was a doctor and not an Indian medicine man. "Injun Joe? The old Indian? He doesn't look like he can ride. Why don't I get Doctor Ramsey?"

The man grimaced. "Ramsey won't come. You're talking about Chief Coyote." He pronounced the word Ki-oat. "Coyote can tell you where to find Joe."

Sam wasn't going to argue with a man who was in the process of bleeding to death. Without a word, she ran out of the cabin and toward the horses waiting in the clearing below.

Her patient lay breathing heavily into the silence the patter of her departing feet left behind. He didn't know who the hell she was or what kind of woman wore pants, but he would remember that anxious look in stunning blue eyes for the rest of his days. It had been a long time since anyone had looked at him with anything resembling concern, and he knew full well that those eyes would never look the same at him again once she reached town.

As the pain came to claim him, he savored the picture of riotous red curls and young breasts pressed against thin gingham. Maybe they were making women different these days. He'd have to live to find out.

Be sure to catch the other titles
in Patricia Rice's *Paper* trilogy.

# *Paper Tiger*

## *THE BROTHERS' BRIDE*

Beautiful young heiress Georgina Hanover's future
seemed set. After a taste of European sophistication,
she was returning to her home in Ohio, to the perfect
marriage. Handsome, hard-driving Peter Mulloney was
all she could want in a husband—and everything her
father wanted as a business partner.

Then she met the man who called himself Daniel
Mulloney and claimed to be Peter's brother. With his
crusading journalist's pen, this man of mystery
attacked Peter's wealth and power. With his stirring
words, he made Georgina question what she as a
woman could and should do in a world run by men.
And with his searing passion, he awoke her desire as
Peter never had. Georgina had to decide which
brother's bride she should be ... the one who offered
the ideal marriage, or the one who led her to ecstasy
beyond her dreams. ...

# Paper Roses

## LOVE OUT OF REACH

Evie needed a skilled gunslinger to escort her safely to Texas. Her dime novel said Pecos Martin was the best. Unfortunately the golden-haired gambler she mistakenly approached at the Green Door Saloon was a hellraising womanizer named Tyler Monteigne. Evie had grown up in a genteel St. Louis home as a "boarder." In reality, she was an abandoned love child with no one to love her—until a letter from Texas told her where to find her true identity.

Tyler could shoot straight enough, but he was also an expert con, and he knew this pretty gal was wrestling with inner demons—just like him. Sure he'd take her across the river to Texas. Yet he didn't foresee the dark passions rising to sweep them away, making Evie all he wanted—and making him exactly what she most feared.